AUTHO

Dear Reader,

Welcome to *Rosie's Dilemma*!

As it is set in the Second World War, I have included a note at the end telling of my own memories. I was only a small child, born in 1941, but there are some things I remember with extraordinary clarity. I hope these memories have helped me paint a picture of what English people suffered, and I hope you enjoy the results.

Once again, the setting is my fictional mining town, Hillsbridge, as well as occupied France – here I can't claim any personal knowledge, but I hope my research has made this setting come to life too.

My next venture is to be a series telling the stories of orphan children back on familiar ground for me: the early years of the 20th century. I hope you will look out for them, and enjoy them as much as my mining novels.

Thank you so much for buying my books and getting in touch with me. I love to receive letters and messages. If I'm sometimes a bit tardy in replying, it's because I am absorbed in my writing!

With love
Jennie xx

Praise for Jennie Felton's captivating sagas:

'Believable characters, a vivid sense of time and place,
thoroughly enjoyable' Rosie Goodwin

'Fans of Katie Flynn will love this' *Peterborough Evening Telegraph*

'Enthralling . . . Jennie Felton . . . writes her stories straight
from the heart . . . evokes time and place with compelling authenticity,
and conjures up a feisty heroine and a cast of engaging characters'
Lancashire Evening Post

'Sweeps us back to a time of struggle and hardship in a story packed
with high emotion, dramatic landscapes and the harsh realities of
living and working in a mining community' *Blackpool Gazette*

'Has everything a family saga should have – happiness, extreme sadness,
love, death, births, etc. but above all it was a real page turner . . .
Thank you, Jennie, for writing such a wonderful book' *Boon's Bookcase*

'If you like the style of Catherine Cookson, Josephine Cox
or Katie Flynn then you'll enjoy this'
Books With Wine And Chocolate

By Jennie Felton

Rosie's Dilemma

JENNIE FELTON

HEADLINE

First published in 2024 by
HEADLINE PUBLISHING GROUP LIMITED

First published in paperback in 2025 by
HEADLINE PUBLISHING GROUP LIMITED

1

Cataloguing in Publication Data is available from the British Library

ISBN 978 1 4722 9679 5

Typeset in 10.75/14pt Calisto MT Pro by Jouve (UK), Milton Keynes

Printed and bound in Great Britain by Clays Ltd, Elcograf S.p.A.

Headline's policy is to use papers that are natural, renewable and recyclable
products and made from wood grown in well-managed forests and other
controlled sources. The logging and manufacturing processes are expected
to conform to the environmental regulations of the country of origin.

HEADLINE PUBLISHING GROUP LIMITED
An Hachette UK Company
Carmelite House
50 Victoria Embankment
London EC4Y 0DZ

The authorised representative in the EEA is Hachette Ireland, 8 Castlecourt
Centre, Dublin 15, D15 XTP3, Ireland (email: info@hbgi.ie)

www.headline.co.uk
www.hachette.co.uk

For my granddaughter, Amelia Rose Carr, with much love.
Wishing you every success as you begin your BA Degree Course.
You'll smash it!

Chapter One

3 September 1939

That morning, the despair that had kept Winnie Mitchell awake most of the night still hung over her so heavily that she felt it would suffocate her.

It was beginning to look as if another war was inevitable. Her memories of the last one were still fresh in her mind. The terrible death toll – boys who'd marched off singing and believing they could defeat the enemy by Christmas but had never come home. The tales of those who did make it back – shivering with fear in the muddy trenches, the constant bombardment, the advances across open ground and the forays into no-man's-land to bring wounded survivors back behind British lines. The grief of families who had lost loved ones. The girls who lost sweethearts and never married. 'The war to end all wars', they'd called it. But they'd been wrong.

Winnie had known many of those who had given their lives or come back forever scarred by their experience, but fortunately had not lost anyone close to her. This time it could be very different. Her son, Don, had joined the army as a regular as soon as he was old enough. Who knew where he'd be sent? What he'd have to endure? Who knew if he'd survive, or die a horrible death? And her daughter, Rosie, was living in London, which would almost certainly be a target for the enemy . . .

Winnie sighed and gave herself a shake. The war hadn't even begun yet, and if she went on like this she'd be a nervous wreck long before it was over. She'd try to forget about it for the moment and think of happier times. Times when they'd all been together – Ern, her husband, lost to a heart attack three years ago, Don and Rosie. Today was a Sunday, and in the past she'd loved Sundays. Lazy days when she didn't have to go to work at Bramley Court, where she cleaned, did the washing and ironing and helped out in the kitchen if help were needed. No shops open. No distractions – even a game of cards was frowned upon. A whole day when she could do whatever she liked in the little cottage in the grounds of Bramley Court where Ern had been the gardener.

She'd enjoyed spending the morning preparing a roast dinner – a shoulder of lamb, perhaps, with vegetables from their own vegetable patch, fresh mint sauce in summer and onions in white sauce in winter, and a fruit pie and thick sweet custard to follow. They'd eat it, the four of them, sitting around the kitchen table and listening to the wireless. Afterwards, when it had been cleared away, the children might go out to meet their friends, and she and Ern would sit down with the papers – the *Sunday Pictorial* for her, the *News of the World* for him, though he often fell asleep over it.

She didn't cook roasts any more. It didn't seem worth it just for herself. But she shouldn't complain, Winnie knew. It was only right that children should be free to live their lives. She'd said as much to Rosie when she'd realised the girl was hesitating about going to London because she was reluctant to leave her mother alone.

'Don't you worry about me,' she'd said. 'I'll be all right. You'll love being with Freda – after all, you've been friends all your lives. As long as you're happy, that's all that matters to me.'

She'd been putting a brave face on it, of course. She really didn't want Rosie to go. But she'd known how important it was to the girl to get away. Her heart had been broken by Julian Edgell, son of the well-to-do family of brewers at Pridcombe House, whose grounds adjoined those of Bramley Court, home of Sir James Hastings. She'd been obsessed by Julian ever since she was a little girl, when she used to play with Anne Hastings, daughter of Sir James. Anne's brother Philip had been great friends with Julian, and while Philip hated the girls following them around, Julian had encouraged them, earning Rosie's seemingly undying devotion.

Winnie hadn't been happy when, in her mid teens, Rosie had begun meeting Julian secretly. She'd known it wouldn't end well. Someone like him would never settle for a gardener's daughter. He'd want someone of his own class, like Anne Hastings, and Rosie would end up with a broken heart. Julian was at medical school, for goodness' sake, going to be a doctor, while Rosie worked at Dick Bendle's garage in town. Winnie had tried to reason with her daughter, but she couldn't make her see sense. As far as Rosie was concerned, the sun rose and set with Julian Edgell and that was that.

Inevitably something had gone wrong, just as Winnie had always known it would, but she suspected there was more to it than just a broken heart. The way Rosie clammed up when Winnie asked her what had happened, it was almost as if she was ashamed of something. Winnie had sincerely hoped she hadn't done something she'd regret that could have . . . consequences. Surely Rosie would have more sense than that! But where Julian Edgell was concerned, Winnie couldn't be sure. Oh well, she wouldn't be the first and she wouldn't be the last,

Winnie had told herself philosophically. But to her knowledge at least, that hadn't happened.

Since Rosie had gone to London just over two years ago Winnie had missed her badly, but she'd never regretted encouraging her to go. From her letters and visits home, it seemed she was enjoying herself there. Dances, the pictures, even the theatre sometimes; her life seemed to be a whirl of social distractions. She'd even mentioned a few boys she'd met, and Winnie hoped she was beginning to forget all about Julian Edgell.

Winnie's thoughts returned to the threat of the impending war. It had been brewing for a long time, of course, but she hadn't really understood what was going on. Austria, Czechoslovakia – they might have been on the moon for all she knew. And when she'd heard the prime minister, Mr Chamberlain, on the wireless, saying he believed it was 'peace in our time', she'd thought all the trouble was over.

Then that spring it had all started up again, and it seemed that a war with Germany was coming down the line like the Pines Express. The air force had taken delivery of 400 new planes and were calling for nearly 6,000 extra pilots. The strength of the Territorial Army was to be doubled and drill halls built. Deep air raid shelters were to be sunk. Plans for the evacuation of children from vulnerable cities were drawn up. And conscription was being introduced.

But it was when Germany invaded Poland just two days ago that the dark shadow truly fell over the whole of Europe, and it was that which had kept her awake half the night. Dread of what was to come, and most of all fear for her children.

With an effort she tried to pull herself together. 'What will be will be. You can't do nothing about it.' That was what Ern would have said if he was here. But he wasn't.

Winnie had a sudden thought. She'd go to chapel.

She wasn't a regular. She'd been a few times after Ern died, thinking it might help her come to terms with her grief – they'd been married for close on forty years, after all, with rarely a cross word. Ern had been a peacemaker who liked a quiet life; it had been almost impossible to get into an argument with him, let alone a full-blown fight. And he'd been her rock in good times and in bad. But she'd found no real solace in prayer, and had come to expect none. She'd just got on with her life, telling herself she was lucky Sir James had let her stay on in the gardener's cottage as long as she continued with her domestic duties.

Today, however, she thought it couldn't hurt to go to chapel and say a prayer for Don and Rosie. And if there was a God, perhaps he'd hear her.

She washed her face, pulled a comb through her curly hair, which seemed to have more grey in it every day, and had some breakfast, still in her dressing gown. Just a pot of tea and a bowl of Kellogg's All Bran – she swore by Kellogg's to keep her regular. Much healthier than the fried bread, bacon and eggs they used to have. She washed up her bowl and cup and saucer, tidied them away, and got dressed in her best frock – home-made on her Singer sewing machine. Some of the women in the congregation would be wearing hats, she knew, but she didn't like wearing one. They never sat right on her curly mop, and usually gave her a headache. To cover her arms, she put on the jacket of the costume she'd worn for Ern's funeral. She might be too hot in it – it was only the beginning of September, after all – but it would do the job. Then she slipped into her best shoes, fetched her handbag and made sure she had some change for the collection, and set out on the long walk into town.

As she reached the spot where the lane met the main road, a motor car engine shattered the quiet that had only been broken by the church bells ringing in the valley. It came closer, and to her surprise pulled up alongside her. A big grey Humber she recognised at once. The window rolled down and Sir James himself leaned across his wife, who was in the passenger seat, and called to her.

'Going into town, Mrs Mitchell?' Flustered, she nodded. 'Hop in then. We'll give you a lift. We're on our way to church.'

Winnie knew that the couple often went to church, but she was surprised Lady Frances could spare the time today. When the Women's Voluntary Service had been launched last year, she'd been put in charge of the district, and on Friday when Winnie had been working at Bramley Court, her ladyship had been busy making arrangements for the evacuee children she was expecting to arrive in the not-too-distant future. Winnie had heard on the wireless that the first wave had already been sent away from London and the northern cities to the countryside.

Lady Hastings was wearing her WVS uniform now, a tweed jacket and skirt and a smart felt hat, and Winnie thought it suited her. With her vitality, endless enthusiasm and commanding presence, she was cut out to be an officer of one sort or another.

'How nice to see you out and about, Mrs Mitchell,' she said, swivelling in her seat and smiling at Winnie. 'We work you far too hard, I'm sure.'

'Not at all, milady,' Winnie said dutifully.

'Nevertheless, there is a great deal to be done at the moment, given the situation we face,' Lady Hastings went on, 'and I'm wondering if I might be able to persuade you to join our band of volunteers. The WVS is going to need all the help it can get, and your contribution would be invaluable.'

'Oh my goodness!' Winnie was horrified at the suggestion. Working for the gentry was one thing; having to mingle with a lot of local toffs was quite another. 'I don't know that I'd be any use. Housework is all I know about.'

'There would be plenty of things you could do!' Lady Hastings enthused. 'Practical things. We need volunteers from all walks of life. And you've not to worry about buying a uniform just yet. As long as you wear an armband to identify you as one of us, you can wear your own clothes.'

'Don't let her bully you, Mrs Mitchell,' Sir James said over his shoulder.

He was such a nice man, Winnie thought. A real gentleman, and kind with it, letting her stay in the cottage. Plenty of lords of the manor would have turned her out. He'd always been good to Rosie, too, when she was a little girl and went to play with Anne.

'When have I ever bullied anyone, pray?' Lady Hastings demanded, but there was a playful undertone in her voice, and the glance she gave her husband was almost flirtatious.

'When you want something, my dear, woe betide anyone who crosses you,' Sir James teased her in return.

When they reached town, he negotiated the two sets of level crossings that bisected the main road, then took a left turn and came to a halt outside the lias-stone building that was the Methodist chapel.

'Thank you so much, sir.' Winnie fumbled with the door handle.

'My pleasure. It's a long walk. If we see you on the way home, we'll stop and pick you up,' he replied.

'And please, Mrs Mitchell, do think about what I've said,' her ladyship added as Winnie climbed out onto the pavement. 'It would be good for you, I'm sure.'

Oh my word! thought Winnie as she started up the path to the chapel door. Joining the WVS was not something she wanted to do at all, but she didn't want to upset her ladyship either.

Not having had to walk, she was early now for the service.

Only a few people had arrived so far. A little clique Winnie knew by sight were setting out teacups at the hatch that led to the kitchen of the adjoining meeting room; Mr Watts, the blind pianist who played for the hymns, was tinkling a few notes; and a man she didn't recognise was arranging a thick sheaf of papers on the lectern – a visiting preacher, she assumed.

The minister, Reverend Colville, appeared, his eyes lighting on Winnie, who had slipped rather self-consciously into one of the back pews. He stopped to speak to Mr Watts, then made his way down the aisle.

'Mrs Mitchell! It's not often we see you here.'

Winnie managed an apologetic smile. 'No, I'm sorry. I should come more often, I know. But . . .' She tailed off, no good excuse presenting itself.

'But you're here now.' The minister patted her arm. 'We all need to come together at a time like this.'

Winnie could only nod, and when the minister had returned to his preparations for the service, she clasped her hands and began to pray.

The chapel filled, slowly at first, then all of a rush, and just as the service began, a few stragglers crept in, doing their best to be unobtrusive. Winnie joined in with the Lord's Prayer and the responses and sang along with the hymns, smiling to herself as Mrs Dury, the dentist's wife, held the last note of each verse longer than anyone else – very loudly – just as she always did. As Winnie had feared, the visiting preacher droned on at some length, and she thought she was going to miss the chance of a lift home with Sir James.

The final hymn – a rousing 'I Vow to Thee, My Country' – was under way when Edgar Collier, the newsagent whose shop was almost next door to the chapel, entered through the main door and went straight up the aisle to the minister. He seemed agitated, Winnie thought. Perhaps there'd been an accident in the street outside the chapel.

But as the last note died away, the minister raised a hand for silence, his expression grave.

'I am afraid Mr Collier has just given me some news which, though not totally unexpected, is the last thing any of us would want to hear, and something that will impact on every one of us. At eleven fifteen this morning, our prime minister, Mr Chamberlain, broadcast to the nation. I regret to say we have declared war on Germany.'

Winnie's stomach clenched. Her worst fears had been realised, her prayers gone unanswered.

The minister, however, was not about to give up so easily.

'Before we leave, will you all join me in prayer?'

The shocked congregation fell to their knees, and Winnie knelt too. But the words rang hollow in her ears. Much good will it do you, she thought bitterly. And wondered what would become of all of them before this was over.

'I shall have to go home.'

Rosie Mitchell and Freda Dobbs, who had been friends through school and beyond, were sitting in stripy canvas deckchairs on the tiny patch of lawn behind Freda's Bermondsey house. Freda had moved in to care for her grandmother when she had become too infirm to look after herself, and Granny Dobbs had left the house to her in her will. Since Rosie had come to London to join her, it was what they liked to do on sunny summer Sundays when Rosie wasn't on a shift at the Lyons teashop where she worked as a waitress.

Today, however, the conversation was quite different from their usual topics: the latest film, the latest fashions, and young men.

War had been declared on Germany.

They'd heard it on the news. Rosie had been in the little kitchen making the pastry for a treacle tart when Freda had called to her from the living room.

'Rosie! Come here – quick!'

The urgency in her voice and a man's solemn tones that she could just hear coming from the wireless was enough to make Rosie leave the mixture of flour and butter she was rubbing in in the earthenware pastry bowl. She'd hurried through, wiping her hands on her apron as she went and scattering some of the little globules onto the floor, just in time to recognise the voice of Mr Chamberlain himself.

'I am speaking to you from the cabinet room at 10 Downing Street. This morning the British ambassador in Berlin handed the German government a final note stating that unless we heard from them by eleven o'clock that they were prepared at once to withdraw their troops from Poland, a state of war would exist between us. I have to tell you now that no such undertaking has been received and consequently this country is at war with Germany.'

Rosie froze, more floury blobs falling onto the worn carpet as her hands tightened to fists in the folds of her apron, while Freda sat forward in her chair, one hand pressed to her mouth, listening intently. But to Rosie, much of Mr Chamberlain's speech was a blur, though certain phrases penetrated the thick fog that came from realising her worst fears had become reality.

'. . . no chance of expecting that this man will ever give up his practice of using force to gain his will. He can only be stopped by force . . . now that we have resolved to finish it, I know that you will all play your part with calmness and courage.'

For a long moment after the prime minister had ended his address, neither girl moved or spoke as they took in the enormity of what they had just heard. Then Freda looked up.

'That's it, then. The balloon's gone up.' Still Rosie was silent, and she went on, 'Well, we knew it was serious really, didn't we, when those air raid shelters turned up on the doorstep back in the spring. They were getting ready even then.'

'Yes,' Rosie said in a whisper. 'I suppose we did. But . . .'

They'd tried to laugh it off when sections of tunnel-shaped shelters made of steel had been delivered to every house in the road, blocking the pavement in both directions. With them had come instructions for erecting the shelters in case of emergency and advising that they should be partly sunk in the ground. It should be a simple job for two people, according to the leaflet.

'They haven't seen our back garden,' Freda had said, pulling a rueful face. 'We'd be lucky to get a spade into it even if we had one.'

Granny Dobbs had been paying a neighbour a few shillings every month or so to keep the garden tidy, but when she died, he'd stopped coming. He must have been using his own tools, because there were no spades or forks in the shed, just a trowel, a pair of rusty secateurs and a reel of green twine. There was also a small lawnmower, which Freda hauled out and ran across the grass when it got long. She'd intended to get some other tools so as to clear and plant up the little square vegetable patch, but somehow it had never happened. Although Rosie paid her way, by the time Freda had bought the essentials, there was never much money left over from her wage as a shorthand typist in the office of the nearby brewery, nor hours in the day by the time she'd cooked, washed, and kept the house clean and tidy. Now the ground – stony at the best of times – was baked hard from the summer sun. The very idea that they could dig a hole big enough to accommodate the shelter was laughable.

'Putting it up would be way beyond me in any case,' Freda had said. 'I haven't even got the patience to do a jigsaw.'

'I expect I could work out how to do it,' Rosie had offered. But in the end they'd simply carried the steel sheets through the house and stacked them against the fence at the end of the garden, where they had remained.

Now, however, nothing about this was a laughing matter.

'Perhaps we ought to try to put that thing up,' Freda said.

Rosie didn't reply, her mind clearly elsewhere, and Freda went on, 'On second thoughts, let's not bother. Under the stairs is good enough for me. Agreed?'

'Whatever,' Rosie said off-handedly. 'I've got pastry to make.'

She returned to the kitchen, thrust her hands into the bowl of flour and butter and rubbed it between her fingers and thumbs, still thinking about the decision she'd made as the situation had worsened. She didn't think Freda would be very happy about it, and she was putting off the moment when she'd have to tell her.

Neither of the girls had much appetite for their dinner of pork chops cooked under the grill followed by Rosie's treacle tart, which she had managed to burn around the rim. They pushed their food around their plates in gloomy silence. A few times Freda attempted to start a conversation, but Rosie was uncharacteristically uncommunicative.

It was only when they'd cleared away, washed up, and settled into the deckchairs on the patch of lawn that Rosie broached the subject that had been on her mind ever since Mr Chamberlain's broadcast.

'I shall have to go home.'

'Are you sure?' Freda, who was well aware of the reason Rosie had come to London to join her, swivelled her deckchair so that she was directly facing her friend.

Rosie nodded. 'I don't think I have any choice. If there's going to be a war, I don't want Mum to be on her own.'

'She's not entirely on her own,' Freda pointed out; she really didn't want Rosie to go. 'She's got the Hastings family nearby, and she's up at the house most days.'

'But what about at night? That's when the planes are most likely to come. She'd be frightened to death.'

'Sir James has got an Anderson shelter, hasn't he?' Freda argued. 'Your mum wrote to you about it – a great green hump in the middle of the garden, she said. They'd let her go in with them if there was an air raid, surely?'

A great green hump. They'd laughed, imagining it when Rosie had read the letter out to Freda. All very well for the Hastings family. They had plenty of money and men they could call on to dig it in and even cover it with earth and turf so that it was less of an eyesore.

'I'm sure they would, but it's not the same as having me there,' said Rosie, miserable yet stubborn. 'You know how guilty I felt leaving her in the first place. She's not a young woman, Freda. She was in her forties when she had me. And she'll be worried about our Don too. You know the army's been put on standby, and goodness knows where they'll send him. No, I'm sorry, but my mind's made up.'

'What about your job?' Freda asked, clutching at straws. 'You can't just walk out without giving notice.'

'Why not? It's different for you. You're a valued member of staff. I'm just a glorified skivvy.'

'What will you do for money?'

'With any luck Mr Bendle will take me on at the garage again. If not, I'll find something else.' Rosie chewed on a fingernail, feeling guilty at abandoning Freda. 'Why don't you come with me?' she asked after a moment. 'I'm sure your mum and dad would be glad to have you home. And London's bound to be bad. If they bomb anywhere, it will be here. That's why they've started sending the children away to safety.'

Yesterday they'd seen the youngsters leaving their homes with their little suitcases, frightened and clutching their mothers' hands. Some were in tears, and it looked as if the mothers were a bit tearful too. But they were also resigned. The children's safety was the most important thing.

But Freda shook her head. 'I don't want to leave Granny's house. There'll be all sorts of scoundrels breaking in if they know there's no one here. Her stuff means a lot to me. The pottery honey pot in the shape of a country cottage, for a start. It was always on the table at teatime when I was little. I loved it. And what about her wedding and engagement rings? And the clock they gave Grampy when he retired . . .'

'I shouldn't think burglars would want a cottage-shaped honey pot,' Rosie said. 'And if a bomb dropped on the house it would all be gone anyway – and you with it.'

'Well, I'm not leaving,' Freda insisted. 'I don't want you to go, and I don't think you want to either. But if you must, you must, I suppose.'

She reached for her glass of ginger beer. 'Do you want to take a couple of bottles with you?'

Freda laughed. 'I don't think so. I wouldn't have room, and if it got shaken up . . . well, you know what the result might be. Panic! Everyone on the train would think a bomb had gone off.'

Freda laughed too at the memory.

Making the ginger beer had been a project they'd enjoyed. They'd saved their empty lemonade bottles instead of returning them to the shop as they usually did to get some money back, bought the ingredients they needed and followed the recipe to the letter. What they'd forgotten was that the baker who'd sold them the yeast had warned them to loosen the bottle tops every day or so to let out the gas that would accumulate during fermentation. One of the bottles had exploded, spewing the contents all over the ceiling and walls of the cupboard where they'd stored it, and covering the floor with shards of broken glass.

Rosie became serious again. 'I think I'll go tomorrow, so I really should make a start on my packing,' she said.

She got up from the deckchair, and Freda's eyes followed her all the way to the back door.

In a hotel room in central London, a tall, muscular man was also packing his clothes and belongings into a large suitcase and a rucksack. Most of his worldly goods, and for the job he had to do and with a war looming, he probably wouldn't need half of them.

As Clarke Sutherland fetched his toiletries from the bathroom, he caught sight of his reflection in the mirror over the sink. Dark hair, cropped close to his head. Startlingly blue eyes. A nose that had been broken more than once, a scar that had faded with time but which he could still see clearly, and a rugged but slightly crooked jaw. It just about told the story of his life, he thought. And wondered what the future would hold.

Too late to worry about that now, though. A whole new chapter was beginning, and he was ready for it.

Chapter Two

When Rosie had finished her packing, she went back downstairs to find Freda in the kitchen making a pot of tea.

'Have you got any change for the telephone? I don't think I've got enough, and I ought to ring Bramley Court and ask if someone could let Mum know I'll be home tomorrow.'

'Why not ask the operator to reverse the charges?' Freda sounded uncharacteristically impatient. 'The Hastings family can afford it.'

'Oh, I couldn't do that!' Rosie protested.

'Trunk calls cost an arm and a leg,' Freda warned her. 'You shouldn't be wasting money like that. And in any case, I still think you're making a big mistake. You're dreading seeing Julian Edgell after what happened, you know you are. And after London you'll be bored stiff in Hillsbridge. Two pubs, a working men's club, a few things going on at the town hall – though there probably won't be now the war's started – and the market. Oh, and the coal mines. Let's not forget the coal mines.'

Rosie was a little shocked to hear Freda refer so sarcastically to the mines that peppered the district. A stranger might think them a blot on the landscape – the clusters of dust-blackened buildings in the pit yard, the head gear and pit wheel rising behind them, not to mention the mountains of spoil that were known locally as

16

'batches'. But to both girls they had been part of the landscape of growing up, and should evoke happy memories of home. Some of the older ones now sprouted trees and undergrowth on their upper reaches. But lower down, the steep bare slopes made wonderful sled runs for local children, Rosie and Freda included, who slid down them on tin trays and dustbin lids, whooping as they gathered speed and not caring they would be 'for it' when they returned as black with coal dust as any miner.

'There aren't that many decent jobs, either,' Freda went on. 'Well, you should know that.'

Rosie flinched. Freda, who had gone from school to the technical college to learn shorthand and typing, had always been a bit sniffy about Rosie working in the local garage. But Rosie had loved it. She didn't mind wearing shapeless overalls, or the grease she could never quite get out from under her nails. She enjoyed being around motor cars too much. Manning the petrol pump, checking oil and water pressure, even learning how to change a battery or spark plugs, and later progressing to helping with engine repairs. Motors fascinated her, always had, ever since Julian had let her have a go at driving the car his father had bought him when he was due to start medical school. Just around the grounds of Bramley Court, of course, but she smiled wistfully at the memory.

Philip Hastings had been outraged – after all, Julian was his friend, not hers.

'You haven't even let *me* have a go yet,' he'd said, peeved. 'She's not old enough, anyway. She's only thirteen.'

'Fourteen!' Rosie had corrected him indignantly.

'Well, that's still not old enough.'

'This is private property, isn't it?' Julian pointed out mildly enough, though Rosie thought there was an underlying edge to his tone, and opened the driver's door for her to get in.

And how magical it had been!

The purr of the engine. The smooth, warm feel of the leather seat beneath her bare legs. A whiff of Julian's Brylcreem mingling with the faint smell of petrol. The sun glinting on the tiny blond hairs on his tanned forearm. The patience in his voice as he told her, 'Don't worry. Everyone does it at first,' when the car jolted and kangaroo-hopped as she tried to move off. The touch of his hand on hers as he caught the steering wheel to correct their direction when she veered towards the shrubs that lined the drive . . .

No! Don't think about it! Sweet as the memory was, it was too painful. And not just because those days had gone for ever, but because within a few years her friendship with Anne had drifted. At fifteen, Rosie had left school to work in the garage, and once Anne had gone to finishing school in Switzerland, their paths had rarely crossed. If they'd remained close, Rosie would never have become involved with Julian. Knowing that Anne was as infatuated with him as she was, she'd have shied away from betraying her friend. But distance had been more than mere miles. They no longer really had anything in common, and if she'd sometimes felt a twinge of guilt, Rosie had ignored it, blundering blindly on towards the humiliation and heart-break that had made her flee Hillsbridge.

'Why are you being so horrible?' she asked Freda now.

Freda shrugged. 'Just trying to make you see sense. Not that you ever had much where Julian Edgell was concerned.'

'Well, it won't work,' Rosie said shortly. 'I've made my decision, and that's an end of it. You just don't want me to go, Freda. Admit it.'

Freda deflated. 'You're right. I don't. But I don't think you want to go either. And I don't want you to be miserable.'

'I'd be miserable here, thinking of Mum on her own. I'll come back, I promise, when this is all over.'

'It might be too late,' Freda said lightly. 'Ron might ask me to marry him if he gets conscripted into the army. And Jim mightn't be waiting for you either.'

It was the last straw. 'You know I don't give two hoots about Jim!' Rosie flared. 'None of the boys I've been out with mean a thing to me. And if you marry Ron, you'll live to regret it. The only one he cares about is himself! I'm going for a walk.'

As the front door closed after her, both girls burst into tears.

This was no time to fall out with your best friend, Rosie said to herself as she walked down the tree-lined road. Perhaps it was what war did to you. Put you on the edge of your nerves.

By bedtime, Freda had apologised for the things she'd said and Rosie had promised her that she'd come back to London as soon as the war was over. Having made up their differences, and exhausted by all the emotional upsets of the day and anxiety over what lay ahead, Rosie had fallen asleep almost as soon as her head touched the pillow. But before long she was awake again, and remembering the days of her youth. Happy days when the family had all been together – Mum, Dad, her older brother Don and herself. When she and Anne had been inseparable. Halcyon days when the future had stretched ahead of her as full of promise as the long sunny days of the seemingly endless summer.

Though they could scarcely have been more different, in many ways the two girls complemented one another. Where Anne was quiet and reserved, Rosie was a chatterbox. Anne was risk-averse, Rosie adventurous, encouraging her friend to overcome her caution, while Anne was able to dissuade Rosie from some of her wilder – and more dangerous – ideas of fun. When Rosie fell from a tree she was climbing, winding herself, it was Anne who helped her regain her breath; Rosie taught Anne to swing upside-down over a gate, steadying her until she was confident enough to do it unaided. Anne blossomed while Rosie learned some restraint.

But there was one thing they had in common. They both adored Philip Hastings' best friend, Julian Edgell. He was, they agreed, the most handsome boy imaginable, with fair hair that shone like burnished gold, blue eyes, and the sort of classical features that made him look like one of the Knights of the Round Table in a history book. What was more, he seemed to enjoy making a fuss of the two little girls.

When Rosie was just five years old, Julian, a grown-up ten, had helped her learn to ride Anne's Fairy bicycle. He ran behind her holding onto the seat as she wobbled across the lawn, picked her up and dusted her down if she toppled over when he let go, and then did it all again.

It had caused one of Rosie and Anne's rare disagreements. 'I'm going to marry him when I grow up,' Anne had said, and Rosie had shot back, 'No you're not! I am!' But the altercation had soon been forgotten.

As the years passed, they'd seen less of Julian – he and Philip were both away at boarding school. But Rosie had thought of him constantly, dreaming her dreams and longing for the day when he'd be home again. And when he was, the magic was still there, and as she entered her teens she began to experience a quiver deep inside her that was new and exciting. A quiver that had only grown more intense with time. A desire that could still make her tremble, in spite of what had happened . . .

She shook herself out of her trance. She didn't want to think about that evening, two and a bit years ago, when her dreams had been shattered. Winnie had warned her that her dalliance with Julian would end in tears, but Rosie had taken no notice. She'd been too happy.

What an idiot I was, she thought, and the shame was back, making her face burn even though she was alone.

She'd never get back to sleep now, she knew. She threw aside the patchwork coverlet and got out of bed, then padded downstairs in her bare feet.

Her suitcase propped up against the wall by the front door was another stark reminder that tomorrow, for the moment anyway, she had to go back to everything she'd run from, and would almost certainly come face to face with Julian. She'd heard from Winnie that he was qualified now, and had bought into a practice in Bath – or at least his father had bought it for him.

Rosie flinched inwardly. It would be so embarrassing! And painful, too. In spite of everything, she still felt the same way about him as she always had. Still loved him, and couldn't imagine ever meeting a man who could usurp him in her affections.

But it was done now. She'd made her decision, and she knew that however difficult it would be for her, it was the right one. She wouldn't have been able to live with herself if she wasn't there to support and comfort her mother through whatever the future held.

She went into the kitchenette, poured some milk into a pan and set it on the gas ring. When it was hot, she stirred in a spoonful of honey and a little drop of the brandy Freda kept for setting light to the pudding at Christmas. She took it upstairs, got back into bed and sipped it. Mercifully it did the trick. When she put the empty cup down on the bedside table and lay back, it wasn't long before sleep claimed her.

Winnie had gone to the kitchen in search of Maud Hawkins, the cook at Bramley Court, and found her making rissoles from the remains of yesterday's roast beef, which she'd already run through the mincer fastened to the edge of the kitchen table.

For all that they could well have afforded fresh meat every day, Sir James was insistent that nothing edible should go to waste. Winnie couldn't imagine that any of the other local gentry would request such a thing as rissoles, but the Hastings family seemed to enjoy them.

'Morning,' she greeted the cook.

'Morning. 'Aven't you got any work to do?' Maud had begun cutting the onions she'd peeled earlier into chunks that would fit into the bowl of the mincer, and her eyes were beginning to water.

Winnie ignored the barb. She was used to Maud's abrupt manner. 'I was just wondering – has her ladyship said anything to you about joining the WVS?' she said.

Maud put down the knife, reached into her pocket for a big white handkerchief that belonged to Walt, her husband, and mopped at her eyes, which were now streaming tears down her plump, rosy cheeks.

'Bloomin' onions!' she grumbled, then nodded. 'Yes. Has she asked you too?'

'Yesterday. And I don't know what to think about it. Are you going to join?'

Maud sniffed and blew her nose. 'I suppose we shall have to. Just as long as we don't have to buy uniforms. I'm not going to do that. And Walt would have something to say about it if I did, I can tell you.'

'She said we wouldn't need to,' Winnie said.

' "For the time being" is what she said to me,' Maud responded tartly. 'Well, my mind's made up. If it comes to that, I shall give in me notice.'

'You wouldn't leave your job!' Winnie exclaimed, shocked.

'Course not! No, her WVS. An' I'll do the same if I don't care for whatever she tries to foist on us. I'm not being anyone's skivvy unless I get paid for it. What about you?'

Winnie considered. It would look bad if Maud joined up and she didn't. But equally, if Maud pulled out, she couldn't be blamed for doing the same.

'All right then,' she said. 'We can go together, can't we? I didn't fancy being the odd one out among her cronies.'

'Oh, you wouldn't be. She'll be rustling up working-class women from the town, you can be sure of that. She'll want to have members to do the jobs none of her fancy friends would stoop to. And she'll be a tartar, if I'm not mistaken.'

Maud picked up a handful of onion chunks and dropped them into the mincer bowl. 'I've got to get on, Winnie, or these rissoles won't be cooked.'

'I must too,' Winnie said. 'But to tell you the truth, I can't think straight this morning. I'm worried to death about our Don – and Rosie too.'

'Still in London, is she?' Maud broke an egg and added it to the meat mixture. 'Won't she come home?'

'I don't think so.'

Maud didn't know why Rosie had gone to London, and Winnie had never enlightened her. Nor anyone else, for that matter. She didn't want Rosie talked about, and laughed at, too, for being so presumptuous as to imagine she'd be good enough for Julian Edgell. 'She's settled there with her friend, and I think she's got a young man.'

'Well, he'll be called up for sure – unless there's something wrong with him, of course.' Maud chuckled scathingly. 'He hasn't got a wooden leg or a false eye, has he?'

'Not as far as I know.' Winnie was annoyed that Maud could make light of all this. But then that was Maud all over. She didn't have children whose lives could well be in danger.

23

But Lady Hastings did, she remembered. Philip was a pilot in the RAF – that was as bad if not worse than being in the military like Don. And Anne was in Bristol, working in an art gallery, and Bristol was just as likely as London to be bombed. Perhaps that was the reason she was throwing herself whole-heartedly into the WVS – to give her something to take her mind off her worries.

Winnie thought of telling Maud she shouldn't be so hard on her ladyship, but decided against it. It wouldn't change her mind and Winnie didn't want to get into an argument.

'I'll leave you to it then,' she said shortly. 'I only came in for some furniture polish.'

She headed for the storeroom, foreboding for what was to come hanging over her like a dark cloud.

Rosie and Freda stood on the doorstep of Freda's house in Lynton Road.

'Promise me you'll come home if things get too bad here,' Rosie said.

'I'll be fine,' Freda assured her. 'They'll be putting in proper air raid shelters soon. And if they don't, I can always go up to the Underground at the Elephant.'

'All the way up the Old Kent Road? You'd be out in the open for far too long,' Rosie pointed out.

'Mm.' Freda changed tack, not wanting Rosie to start trying to persuade her to leave London again. 'Are you sure you don't want me to come with you that far at least? We could take turns at carrying your suitcase.'

Earlier she had suggested going with Rosie all the way to Paddington, but Rosie had refused.

'I don't want to say goodbye on a busy station platform, Freda. We'd both be in tears, and it would be so embarrassing,' she'd said.

'I don't suppose we'd be the only ones,' Freda had argued. 'There are sure to be others saying their goodbyes.'

But Rosie wouldn't be swayed, and Freda hadn't been altogether surprised. Rosie didn't like anyone to see her cry. Freda had often heard her sobbing quietly in her room when she'd first come to London, but she almost always managed to hold back her tears when they were together.

'Well, I want *you* to promise *me* something then,' she said, resigned. 'You'll stay away from Julian Edgell.'

Rosie smiled thinly. 'Don't worry, I will.'

'And try to forget about him.'

'You know I can't promise you that.'

Freda sighed. 'I know. But I wish you would, Rosie, for your own sake. It's not healthy, nursing these dreams. And it won't make you happy.'

'Do you think I don't know that?' Rosie asked bitterly. 'Do you think I enjoy it?'

'Maybe.'

Rosie swallowed hard. Sometimes she wondered herself why it was she couldn't get Julian out of her head – or her heart. It wasn't for the want of trying and there had been times when she'd thought she was getting there. The good times she'd shared with Freda. The river boat trips, the days out to the seaside, trying food she'd never tasted before – whelks and jellied eels to name but two – that they bought from kerbside booths. The shared meals and chats at the end of the day. She *had* enjoyed them. It was the dances and the bars where she met young men that were difficult. She'd forced herself to accept offers of dates; she really felt she should, if only to please Freda. But all the while the shadow of Julian was there. No one she'd met could match up to him.

It hadn't been so bad when they went out as a foursome with

Freda and Ron. But when she was alone with her date and he tried to kiss her – or worse – she felt nothing but revulsion, and she could only think how different it had been with Julian. How much she wanted his arms around her, his lips on hers. The smell of his Brylcreem. The way the sun on the fair hairs on his forearms made them shimmer like molten gold. And the way her stomach had flipped and her heart beat faster . . . Then the pain would come rushing in. The humiliation. The sense of loss . . .

She gave herself a small shake. 'I really should get going,' she said. 'There's a train at eleven o'clock, and I'm not sure when the next one is if I miss it.'

'Come here.' Freda opened her arms and they hugged, tears stinging their eyes just as Rosie had predicted.

'Take care.'

'You too.'

'I'll miss you so much!'

'I'll be back, I promise.'

Rosie slung the canvas bag containing her gas mask over her shoulder, picked up her suitcase and walked down the front path. At the gate, she turned to see Freda still in the doorway, her hand pressed over her mouth. Rosie lifted her free hand and waved half-heartedly, and Freda waved back.

The hot tears coursed down her cheeks now as she walked away, and she didn't look back until she reached the end of Lynton Road. Freda was still there on the doorstep watching her.

One last wave and she turned the corner, heading for the Old Kent Road, which was just the beginning of the trek to the Elephant and Castle and the journey across London.

At more or less the same time as Rosie was rattling along in a crowded Tube train on the last leg of her journey to Paddington,

Clarke Sutherland, the dark-haired man with the startling blue eyes and the crooked jaw, was hailing a black cab in the street outside his hotel in central London.

He was impatient now to be on his way. At last, a chance to make use of his expertise in a positive way and perhaps banish the dark shadow that haunted him still. He'd seen death many times since, but none had affected him as that one had. He'd been young and green and he'd never been able to exorcise the guilt he'd felt then. The guilt that he had survived while his friend – his hero – had died. Stupid, perhaps. Yet it had influenced his whole life from that day on. This, he hoped, would help him to put the past behind him, where it belonged. He'd lived under that shadow for far too long.

Chapter Three

By the time she reached Paddington, Rosie was exhausted and thirsty. The long trek up the Old Kent Road had been followed by the need to check which line she needed, and when the train finally arrived, her legs as well as her arms were aching and she considered herself lucky to find a seat. Then at Paddington she had to haul her suitcase up the escalator to the main-line station and wait in a long queue at the ticket office. Her ticket bought, she went back onto the concourse and checked the departure board. Her train would apparently leave from Platform 1, and she had about half an hour to spare until it did.

She'd get a cup of coffee, she decided, but yet another long queue snaked out of the café and along the concourse and she just couldn't face it. With any luck there would be a restaurant car on the train. She made her way to the platform, buying a *Daily Mirror* from a news-stand en route, found a seat on a slatted wooden bench and sank onto it with a sigh of relief.

When she'd got her breath back, she spread the newspaper out on her lap. The front cover was almost completely filled with a huge picture of Mr Chamberlain addressing the nation, and inevitably page after page inside was devoted to information concerning the war. There were also photographs of lines of children with their suitcases and Mickey Mouse gas masks waiting to board trains that would take them away from the city to the relative safety of the countryside. A lump rose in her throat to see little ones, perhaps no more than four or five, being shepherded by a brother or sister scarcely older themselves, and a couple of women with babies in their arms.

A shadow fell over the page, and Rosie looked up with a start to find herself surrounded by three young men she didn't like the look of at all.

'Well hello, beautiful.' The one standing directly in front of her was leering at her. He was short and stocky, with greasy hair falling untidily over his face and big ears that stuck out at right angles to his head. He was wearing a faux-leather jacket, black, over a none-too-clean shirt and equally grubby gabardine trousers. His friends were just as scruffy. The face of one was covered with angry-looking pimples, while the other, tall and bony, had a mean, pinched look about him.

Rosie glared at them, then looked down again at her newspaper. If she ignored them, they'd go away, she hoped. No such luck.

'Come on, Miss Hoity-Toity,' Big Ears said. 'Don't be like that. Give us a kiss!'

'Go away.' Rosie hoped she sounded confident and unafraid, although actually they were unnerving her, crowding her as they were.

'Yeah, give us a kiss.' The bony youth's voice was reedy, his tone a high-pitched whine. 'We're gonna be off soon, fighting fer the likes o' you.'

'Show a bit o' gratitude,' Spotty Face added.

'Just a kiss!' Bony whined again. 'That's not too much to ask, is it, when we're off to war?'

Throughout this exchange Big Ears was silent, a crafty – and satisfied – look on his piggy face, as if he was letting his henchmen do all the groundwork for him. Now he leaned towards her, bringing with him a strong smell of beer.

'A kiss?' he sneered. 'Nah – a feel would be more like it.'

To Rosie's horror, his hand shot out and grabbed her breast. She squealed, hitting out at him, but he only squeezed more tightly, and the other two louts closed in, jeering and jockeying for position. Big Ears began tugging at the neckline of her dress, and she squealed again, 'Get off me!' But the top button was coming away from the floral cotton, and as the two sides of the bodice parted, the lout's hand slid inside, sticky and sweaty, grasping and squeezing.

One of the others whooped. 'My turn next!'

'No – mine!'

Throughout it all passengers passed by, staring with either disgust or curiosity but making no attempt to intervene. Until . . .

'Hoi! You! Stop that!'

Rosie didn't have a clear view of the man who spoke; he was half hidden by the yobs clustered around her. But the pressure of that greedy hand eased as Big Ears turned towards him, a sneer that was also a threat curling his lip.

'Oh yeah? You gonna make me?'

'If you don't get away from that lady this instant, then yes.'

'Ha!' Big Ears sneered. 'You an' whose army?' He turned back to Rosie, his hand tightening on her breast once more, his face so close to hers that the stink of his rancid breath made bile rise in her throat.

And then, quite suddenly, he was jerked away from her and she realised the man had dragged him upright by his collar. Instantly Big Ears swung round, fists raised, thumbs over fingers in the classic manner of a boxer. Oh Lord! He was going to hit the man who was trying to help her. And from the look of him he was no stranger to a fight . . .

Exactly what happened next Rosie was never quite sure. She only knew that before Big Ears had the chance to land a single punch, he was arcing through the air and landing flat on his back on the platform.

His pals were no longer laughing and jeering but gaping in shocked disbelief, so startled they might have been turned into gargoyles. The man was casually dusting off his hands as he faced them.

'So – which one of you's going to be next?'

'Bloody bastard,' Big Ears gasped. He sounded breathless and was struggling to sit up, wiping a stream of snot from his face with the back of his hand but still half-heartedly defiant.

The man ignored him, speaking instead to Rosie. 'Are you all right?'

She nodded, holding her bodice together with both hands and shaking too much to be able to find her voice.

The man turned back to Big Ears. 'Let that be a lesson to you, smart-arse. Now scarper, the lot of you.'

Bony and Spotty Face came slowly back to life and helped their friend to his feet, all the while watching the man warily as if they expected the same treatment to be handed out to them at any moment.

'I'll get you back, you sod, see if I don't,' Big Ears muttered defiantly as his two friends led him away, but he was slumped between them, all the stuffing knocked out of him along with most of his breath.

'Yeah, he will right enough!' Spotty Face threw over his shoulder as they went.

During all the confusion a train had pulled in and come to a halt, disgorging passengers, and a porter, who had no doubt witnessed the disturbance and chosen to keep well out of it, approached the man.

''Avin' trouble, sir?'

'Just a little, but it's over now,' the man replied nonchalantly, and turned to Rosie. 'Is this your train?'

'I don't know.' Rosie's head was still all over the place.

'Where are you going?'

'Bath.'

'Then yes. This one is yours. Let's get you safely on board once all the arrivals have cleared the decks.'

He picked up his own suitcase with one hand and hers with the other. 'First class or third?'

'Oh, third . . .' The likes of her didn't travel first class. Sometimes Rosie wondered why there was no second class.

As soon as the last passengers had left the train, heading for the barrier, where a ticket collector stood waiting, punch in hand, the man nodded towards the nearest coach.

'This one's third if I'm not mistaken.'

The door was standing open; Rosie climbed the step and the man followed. Yes, this was definitely third class. The seats were slightly grubby and covered in a heavy chenille-like fabric, brown patterned with yellow; there were posters depicting seaside scenes and families enjoying the sunshine aligned under the luggage racks; and the carriage reeked of cigarette smoke. The man hoisted Rosie's suitcase onto the rack, which sagged under its weight.

'Would you like me to stay with you? Just in case those louts are on this train and decide to try their luck again.'

A flicker of alarm crossed Rosie's face. 'They've gone, haven't they?'

'Perhaps. But what were they doing on this platform if not waiting for a train? They could easily have boarded further down and we wouldn't know. Then they could wander up the corridor looking for you once we're on the move.'

Rosie shuddered. It didn't bear thinking about.

'So?' The man threw her a questioning glance, one eyebrow raised. He had startlingly blue eyes, she noticed.

'I'd be grateful if you would,' she said.

She took a window seat at the far side of the carriage. He hoisted his own suitcase onto the rack beside hers and sat down opposite her.

Now that she was no longer in a blind panic, she saw that the startlingly blue eyes belonged to a face that was essentially masculine. His nose was ever so slightly crooked, his mouth generous, his jaw firm and angular. His dark hair was cut short. And there was a hint of a wicked twinkle in those very blue eyes.

Quite suddenly she was overcome with a rush of self-consciousness that he'd witnessed what the louts had been doing to her, and with it a feeling of shame, as if she had somehow invited it.

'I'm sorry,' she said. 'I haven't thanked you properly for coming to my rescue.'

He shrugged. 'No problem.'

'How did you do . . . whatever it was you did . . . to that thug?' she heard herself asking.

His smile broadened, creating dimples in his cheeks. Not pretty little girlie dimples, but long and deep.

'Practice,' he said.

Rosie had no idea what he meant by that, but she wasn't going to ask. He was, after all, a stranger. A stranger who had stopped to help her while others passed by on the other side, but a stranger nevertheless.

All along the train doors slammed. People were still moving past in the corridor, deciding where they would sit, but to her relief she didn't see the gang of thugs among them. Only one other passenger had come into their carriage, a wizened old man with nothing but a battered attaché case, and he had taken the seat in the far corner.

Rosie was surprised the train wasn't packed. She had imagined it would be crowded with people anxious to get away from the capital. But that was Londoners for you. Nothing if not gritty and stubborn, and as reluctant to leave their homes as Freda was.

The guard blew his whistle and clouds of steam billowed past the window and up to the vaulted glass roof as, with a jerk, the train began to move.

As they passed sidings and workshops, the old man settled back in his seat, resting his head in the corner where it met the window, and even before they left behind the suburbs and the rows of tightly packed terraced houses, he was asleep and snoring gently.

Perhaps the air raid siren last evening had alarmed him so much he hadn't been able to sleep, Rosie thought. Certainly it had given her and Freda a scare for a moment when it had begun its mournful whoop. But almost immediately afterwards the all-clear had sounded. It was just a test, the two girls had realised. Well, of course it was! Did they really think the German bombers would come so soon after the declaration of war?

'Do you live in Bath?' Her rescuer's voice, with just the hint of an Irish accent, she noticed now, brought Rosie out of her reverie.

'No, actually I live in London now. But my home is in Hillsbridge. That's eight or nine miles south of Bath.'

'So you're evacuating?'

'Not exactly. Well . . . I suppose I am. But I wouldn't be if it weren't for the fact my mother is widowed and my brother is away in the army. I don't want to leave her all alone now we're at war.'

'That's kind.'

'She *is* my mother,' Rosie said defensively. She didn't think of what she was doing as kind. 'Isn't it what any daughter would do?'

'Plenty wouldn't.'

'Then shame on them.'

'Good for you!' he said. 'I can see you're a woman of principle.'

'I just try to do what's right.'

After a moment's silence, he asked, 'How are you getting from Bath to Hillsbridge?'

'By bus. They run every half-hour or so,' Rosie said, and added ruefully, 'I only hope I won't just miss one. All I want now is to get home and have a nice cup of tea.'

'Well . . . in that case perhaps I can offer you a lift,' he said. 'I'm getting off the train at Bath too, and I think I shall be passing right through Hillsbridge on my way to where I'm going. It's certainly south of Bath. A car will be waiting for me at the station.'

Rosie was taken completely by surprise. A car waiting for him – that must mean, surely, that he was someone of importance. 'I couldn't possibly impose,' she said, a little primly.

The wicked twinkle was back in his eyes. 'Don't you trust me? Not surprising considering what happened to you at Paddington, though.'

'It's not that at all!' Rosie protested. 'Of course I trust you. But . . .'

'Perhaps you'd feel more comfortable if I told you my name?' He raised an eyebrow at her and then went on, 'I'm Clarke Sutherland, and before you ask, it's Clarke with an "e", not Clark as in Clark Gable. My mother was one of the Clarkes of Dublin, don't you know, and she had some idea she'd like me to carry the family name.'

The Irish accent was more pronounced now and the very blue eyes and dark hair made sense to Rosie. He was of Gaelic origin, and for some reason she liked that.

'Rosie Mitchell,' she said. 'Well, Rosemary actually, but no one calls me that except my mother – and then only when she's angry with me.'

'So you'll accept my offer of a lift?' There was a wicked twinkle in those very blue eyes, but Rosie didn't feel in the least threatened.

'I'd be an idiot not to, wouldn't I? Thank you. You're very kind.'

'Happy to be of service,' he said.

Back in London, Freda was struggling to tack an old piece of linoleum over the living room window to create a blackout as everyone was supposed to do. But success was eluding her. The linoleum was thick and stiff, she was having problems getting the pins through it, and it kept falling down and curling back into a loose roll. Each time it happened she had to climb down from the kitchen chair she was standing on to reach the top of the window and start all over again. This time, however, she'd had enough.

'Oh blow it!' she exclaimed, frustrated and ready to give up. If the air raid warden came knocking on her door, she'd jolly well ask him to come in and help her. And tomorrow she'd try to get hold of something more manageable. Or use her charms on Ron to get him to come round with a hammer and nails.

She was missing Rosie already. If she was here, they'd have had a good laugh about it. But she wasn't here, and wouldn't be for the foreseeable future. Oh, Freda hadn't wanted her friend to go, but she hadn't realised just how empty the house would seem without her. Making tea only for herself had seemed like a mountain to climb; in the end she'd decided not to bother. Instead she made toast and heated a tin of baked beans on the gas ring, and ate flicking through the *Evening Standard*, which, bizarrely, was on the news-stands by early afternoon.

But her mind was on Rosie, and not just because she was wishing she was here. The truth was she was worried about her. How in the world would she cope with being in such close proximity to Julian Edgell? Rosie was an otherwise sane, sensible and down-to-earth girl, and her obsession with him was incomprehensible to Freda.

Julian was almost a religion for Rosie, she thought. She worshipped him – always had. It was the first secret she had shared with Freda when they'd met at junior school and become friends. Freda had been fascinated by the way Rosie had come to life just talking about him, sparkling almost, but she was also puzzled. Boys weren't anything to get excited about. Most of them were disgusting, scruffy and often dirty, like her brothers.

They chewed gum and blew bubbles that exploded in their faces, and when they'd finished with it they'd roll it into a blob and stick it under the school desk, or wherever was handy. They picked their noses and sometimes ate it. They got into fights, rolling around the playground and trying to grab one another's private parts. And sometimes they used words that would certainly earn a clip round the ear from her mother if she heard them. No, Freda couldn't imagine why Rosie would feel this way about a *boy*.

Later, when they were at secondary school, Freda sometimes cycled over to Rosie's at weekends and on light summer evenings. It was on one of these occasions that she first set eyes on Julian Edgell, and she'd realised then just what it was that Rosie saw in him.

To begin with, he was older than the boys she knew, and if

he'd ever had any of their disgusting habits – which was hard to imagine – he'd long since outgrown them. And secondly he was very handsome. It really was the only way to describe him. 'Good-looking' simply didn't do him justice. But – for goodness' sake! – he was way out of Rosie's league. She was whistling in the wind if she thought she stood a chance with him.

So it had come as a great surprise, years later, when Rosie had confided in one of her letters that they were meeting in secret. Just how much she was exaggerating Freda was never sure, and she suspected that at least some of what Rosie told her was wishful thinking. Whatever. It had ended in tears, just as Freda had always thought it would. And in the end it had been up to her to pick up the pieces.

When crunch time came, Freda was no longer living in Hillsbridge but in the house her granny had left her in Bermondsey. Although the two girls corresponded regularly, it had been some time since Rosie had mentioned Julian, and Freda had assumed it had all blown over. So it had come as a complete shock to receive a letter from her friend asking if she could come and stay with her.

She'd agreed, of course. The bond between them was still strong, and she couldn't deny she had been delighted that Rosie would be here, sharing Granny's house with her. But when Rosie had told her the whole story, her heart had bled for her, devastated that the dreams she'd cherished since childhood had turned to ashes.

She'd done her best to help Rosie get over her shame and heartbreak, and she'd been optimistic that she was succeeding. But now, going back to Hillsbridge was going to be very painful for her. She'd put a brave face on it, of course she would, but since Julian was now a qualified doctor with a practice in Bath, Freda thought it was inevitable she would bump into him from time to time, even if he was no longer living at home.

It was possible, of course, that he was engaged or even married now, and Freda felt mean for rather hoping this was the case. Rosie would be upset, yes, but at least she'd have to accept once and for all that there was no hope for her and get on with her life. But Freda couldn't forget what Rosie had said when they were arguing yesterday. *None of the boys I've been out with mean a thing to me.* All this time, and although she'd pretended to be enjoying life it was still Julian on her mind – and in her heart.

Freda shook her head sadly. Unless things changed dramatically, Rosie was never going to find happiness, and there was nothing more she could do to help her. Except . . . An idea occurred to her, and there and then she decided to act on it.

As the train pulled into the platform at Bath Spa, Clarke retrieved their suitcases from the rack and took them out into the corridor, Rosie following. It had been a long journey with numerous stops. She was tired and hungry, and she thanked her lucky stars that she wasn't going to have to drag her suitcase all the way from the station to the Old Bridge, which was used as a terminus for the buses heading south out of the city.

Clarke slid down the window in the carriage door so he'd be able to unlatch it from outside, and fresh air streamed into the corridor. The railway line here was open to the elements. Only the platforms were covered, so the smoke and steam didn't collect here as it did in Paddington. As the train came to a halt, Clarke opened the door and climbed out, set down the suitcases and offered Rosie his hand to help her negotiate the step and the little gap between platform and train.

'How well do you know the station?' he asked.

'Not very. But we have to go down there . . .' She indicated a flight of stone steps a little way to their left.

'So you wouldn't know where I'd find the station master's office?'

'Sorry, no.' But she was puzzled. 'Why?'

'I have to collect the keys for my car.'

'I thought someone was meeting you,' Rosie pointed out.

'No, I said a car would be waiting for me. Oh well, I expect the ticket office is in the main foyer. I'll enquire there.'

Rosie was totally bemused now. Why on earth would anyone leave a car here for Clarke when he didn't have the keys for it?

They joined the other passengers streaming down the stairs. At the bottom a ticket collector was waiting, and Rosie found her ticket in her purse. Unfazed, Clarke set down one of the suitcases and fished his own ticket out of his pocket, nodding towards the rear of the concourse.

'That looks like the ticket office.'

'It is,' she confirmed.

He deposited the two suitcases in a corner. 'Will you mind these while I go and ask?'

'Of course.'

She stood guard in front of the suitcases, watching him weave his way through the departing passengers and hoping he wouldn't be too long. Her shoes had begun to pinch now, to add to her discomfort.

Clarke had almost reached the front of the queue at one of the cubbyholes, and Rosie let her gaze wander to the main entrance. She could see a stall just outside that looked as if it was selling tea, coffee and soft drinks. She wondered if she could buy one to take with her. They'd do paper cups, surely?

Everything had quietened down. Most of the passengers had left, and only a scattering of people were entering the station when one caught her eye. She did a double-take. Goodness, that man looked just like Julian! Tall, fair, wearing a cream linen jacket – not that she'd ever seen him wearing a linen jacket . . .

He was looking around, and at that very second his eyes lit upon her and he raised his hand, a look of relief crossing his handsome face as he started towards her.

Oh dear Lord! Rosie froze, shocked and dismayed. It *was* Julian! What on earth was he doing here? What could she say to him? She wasn't ready, in no way prepared to face him for the first time since . . .

Yet for all that, her racing pulse warned her that for her nothing had changed.

'Rosie!' he greeted her. 'I've been waiting outside. I was beginning to think you must have missed the train.'

'Julian!' She couldn't think of a single other thing to say.

He indicated the suitcases at her feet. 'Two! You must be worn out managing both of them! Oh well, let's get them out to the car.'

'The car?'

'Oh, I don't suppose you know.' Julian smiled, that smile that had always beguiled her. 'Your friend – Freda, is it? – telephoned Bramley Court, said you'd be arriving on this train and could somebody meet you. So here I am!'

Chapter Four

Before she could stop him, Julian was reaching for the closer of the two suitcases.

'Whew! This is heavy.'

'No! That's not mine!' Flustered, Rosie laid a hand on his arm and a puzzled frown creased Julian's brow. 'That one belongs to a man I met at Paddington. He—'

'A man you met at Paddington?' Julian repeated.

'Yes. His name's Clarke . . .' She stopped short, unable to recall what he had said his surname was.

'Clarke who?' Julian had noticed her hesitation and the look of panic in her eyes.

'I don't know,' Rosie admitted. 'But he was very kind. He—'

'Kind? In what way?' he pressed her, his tone heavy with suspicion.

'Oh, it's a long story, but he offered to give me a lift to Hillsbridge to save me having to wait for the bus, and—'

Julian set the suitcase down with a thud and looked directly at her.

'Don't tell me you were going to get in a car with a strange man whose name you don't even know! How could you be so foolish? Where is he now?'

'He's gone to collect his car keys. Julian, please, you don't understand . . .'

But Julian wasn't listening. 'Thank God I came in and found you when I did! Goodness knows what could have happened to you.'

'No. You've got it all wrong . . .'

'Having trouble again?'

Rosie hadn't noticed Clarke making his way across the concourse, and although his tone was light, almost jokey, there was something that spoke of danger in his stance, as if he were a coiled spring. Remembering the way he had dealt with the young thug at Paddington, she intervened quickly, a cautionary hand raised between the two men.

'No. This is Julian Edgell, an old friend of mine. I wasn't expecting him, but he's come to meet me off the train. Julian, this is Clarke, who I was just telling you about.'

'Really.' Julian's tone was arch. 'I understand you kindly offered Rosemary a ride home, but obviously that's not now necessary.'

'No, I realise that. I'm just happy to see that someone is going to take care of her,' Clarke said easily, but beneath it that edge was still there. He turned to Rosie. 'I've enjoyed your company, and I'm glad I was there to help you out of your predicament.'

'I can never thank you enough,' Rosie said, meaning every word. 'But as you can see, I'm fine now.'

'Good.' Abruptly Clarke reached for his suitcase. 'I'm pleased to have met you, Mr Edgell.'

'Doctor, actually,' Julian corrected him.

'My apologies, *Doctor.*'

The sarcasm wasn't lost on Rosie, who was already squirming inwardly. Why was Julian being so pompous? What on earth had got into him? She touched Clarke's arm.

'Thank you. Really. For everything.'

'My pleasure.' For a brief moment his eyes held hers, then he turned and walked away in the direction of the exit.

'We should get going too.' Julian picked up Rosie's suitcase. 'Your mother will be expecting you. She's very much looking forward to seeing you, I imagine. It's been a long time.'

Rosie's stomach lurched uncomfortably. Had he guessed the reason behind her flight to London? Probably. Was he going to bring up the subject of what had happened the last time they'd been in one another's company?

And did he regret it as much as she did? No! she scolded herself. That was just wishful thinking.

'Thank you for this,' she said as he loaded her suitcase into the boot of his car – a Ford Prefect, she noticed.

'No problem.' Now that Clarke was no longer on the scene, Julian had relaxed into the man she remembered.

There was a brief silence as he opened the passenger door for Rosie to get in, settled himself in the driving seat and started the engine. Then he went on as if there had been no interruption.

'I was in Bath anyway – my surgery is here. When your friend called Bramley Court to let us know you were on your way, I was obviously the first person Frances thought of to meet you and drive you home.'

Frances, is it? Rosie thought.

'I do have an apartment in town,' Julian went on, 'but since I'll be in Hillsbridge I'll stay at Pridcombe tonight and drive back to Bath in the morning.'

'Mum mentioned in one of her letters that you'd qualified and were practising in Bath,' Rosie said, glad of the opportunity to talk about something – anything! – that was in no way connected to their last awkward encounter. 'You were lucky to find a position so close to home.'

Julian laughed. 'Debatable. There are pros and cons to being no more than a half-hour away. But we won't go into those. Papa's mind was made up. My partners are old friends of his, and he provided the necessary to buy me into the practice, for which, of course, I'm most grateful.'

'That's amazing,' Rosie said. 'You've done so well, Julian.'

'I'm quite pleased with myself, since the only things I was interested in at school were rugby and cricket. But I'd certainly have been in the dog house if I hadn't made good after all the money Papa spent on my education.'

He pulled out of the station forecourt and onto the road.

'But enough about me. How have you been?'

'Oh, fine,' Rosie said as lightly as she could manage. 'There's so much to see and do in London.'

'I'm sure there is.' His tone was slightly sarcastic, and Rosie felt a flush creeping up her cheeks. Of course Julian would have been to London. Many times, probably. He halted at a junction, then turned left towards the Old Bridge. 'Tell me, though, I'm curious. What predicament did your new friend rescue you from?'

'Oh – it was embarrassing really. There was a gang of thugs at Paddington who decided I was fair game. Clarke was the only person who stopped to help me. He saw them off, and then stayed with me on the train in case there was any more trouble.'

'I see.'

Rosie could see too – what it might look like. Julian thought Clarke was an opportunist. And perhaps he was. But whatever, she wasn't going to debate it.

'What about this war then?' she asked, changing the subject. 'What is going to happen, do you think?'

'It's going to be bad,' he said bluntly. 'Hitler is a madman. He's not going to stop until he's got what he wants. A Germany that governs half the Western world, if not all of it. It's a good thing you've come home, Rosie. London is no place to be when it all gets going.'

He changed gear as they reached the top of the hill leading out of Bath, then went on, 'Neither is Bristol if it comes to that. The docks, the aeroplane factory – they're sure to be targeted. I wish Anne would do the sensible thing as you have and come home, and I know Frances is hoping for that too. But at the moment I think she's up to her eyes getting all the precious artefacts into storage somewhere safe.'

'Of course! The art gallery! She still works there then?'

Julian chuckled wryly. 'Just try prising her away! She loves it. I can't see the attraction myself, but you know Anne. Set her loose among oil paintings and priceless pieces of china or glass and she's in seventh heaven.'

From what he said, it seemed Julian was still in close contact with Anne, and Rosie experienced a sharp little jab of what felt very much like jealousy. She couldn't forget what her mother had said when she'd warned her of pinning her hopes and dreams on Julian. That when push came to shove he'd end up with someone of his own class. Someone like Anne Hastings. She'd been hurt by Winnie's bluntness and even felt a bit resentful of the girl who had been her childhood playmate. Anne had had everything handed to her on a plate; it seemed unfair that she could have Julian too if she wanted him. And she had certainly wanted him, when they were young anyway. Perhaps she would marry him after all, just as she'd said.

But jealous or not, Rosie didn't like to think of Anne caught up in enemy air raids. She was so gentle. So vulnerable really . . .

Almost echoing her thoughts, Julian went on, 'If she does come home, I've no doubt Frances will rope her into some kind of war work. You know, don't you, that Frances is the local organiser for the WVS? She's in her element, as you can imagine. But I can't see Anne as a nurse or an ambulance attendant, or even a fire watcher come to that. Can you?'

'I wouldn't really know,' Rosie said. 'I haven't seen her for ages.'

They had left Bath behind now and were driving through open countryside.

'Anyway, leaving Anne aside, Frances will certainly find something for you to do that will keep you out of mischief. So be prepared,' he warned her.

Still wondering just how much he saw of Anne, Rosie managed a dry little laugh.

'Believe me, Julian, these days I'm prepared for anything.'

Winnie was at the cottage window, watching and waiting. She couldn't settle, hadn't been able to since Lady Hastings had sought her out while she'd been at work at Bramley Court earlier to tell her the news that Rosie's friend had called from London – reversed charges – to say that Rosie was on her way home.

Winnie had gasped. 'Oh my goodness! What – today?'

'Yes, today. Now, you're not to worry about a thing. I've been in touch with Julian Edgell and he will meet her at the station and drive her home. So when you've finished the work that won't wait, I suggest you take the rest of the day off and get ready for her.'

'Oh my goodness!' Winnie repeated, overwhelmed. 'But you shouldn't have gone to so much trouble! And Dr Julian, too . . . he's such a busy man these days.'

'It's the least we can do,' Lady Hastings said. 'You're pleased, I imagine. You must have been very worried about Rosemary with the situation as it now is. And it's a long time since she's been home, isn't it?'

'Oh yes! Of course I'm pleased, but . . .' Another thought struck her. 'Her friend reversed the charges for the phone call, you said? You must take it out of my wages.'

'Don't be foolish, Mrs Mitchell,' Lady Hastings admonished her. 'I shall do no such thing. Please, say no more about it.'

'Well, that's kind, milady. Thank you.' Winnie still felt a little uncomfortable. She didn't like to be beholden to anybody. But all the same . . .

'I can go, though, can I when I've finished my duties?' she asked. 'I'll make the time up, don't worry. But I've got all sorts to do if Rosie's coming home.'

'So I imagine.' A shadow fell across Lady Hastings' face. 'I only wish Anne would do the same.'

'Oh, she will, milady, don't you worry.' More than anything Winnie wanted to share her good fortune, and for all that her ladyship was in a totally different class to her, she was a mother too, when all was said and done.

'Yes. Well.' Lady Hastings became her brisk, no-nonsense self once more. 'Just one last thing. I'm calling a meeting for my WVS volunteers early next week. I'm hoping to see you there.'

'Oh, of course, milady!' Winnie replied hastily. In the wake of her employer's kindness, how could she refuse?

She hurried to the kitchen to tell Maud the good news, and then rushed through her chores, only slowing down when she almost knocked over a priceless Ming vase as she dusted the cabinet it sat on.

Back in her cottage, her mind had continued still racing in frantic circles. There was so much to do! Making up Rosie's bed with fresh sheets and pillowcases. Cleaning and tidying everywhere – she didn't want her coming home to dust and muddles. Deciding what to make for tea tonight and preparing it . . .

Once again excitement had made her do stupid things she

normally never would. She burned her thumb on the hot flat iron as she pressed the creases out of the sheets for Rosie's bed. She overturned the dustpan just when it was full of fluff and dried mud that had traipsed in from the garden and had to sweep the floor all over again. And silliest of all she forgot to add the butter to the white sauce she was making to complete the dish of leeks and sliced ham that was one of Rosie's favourite meals. Cross with herself, she had put the sauce back in the pan, added the butter and a drop more milk and brought it back to a simmer, hoping it would be all right.

'Take your time, m'dear!' She could almost hear Ern saying it. And it seemed to work. But now everything was ready, she was back and forth to the window like a terrier, watching for Julian's car on the drive though she didn't think it was time yet.

Despite her elation, a little concern was nibbling at her. It was good of Julian to drive all the way out of Bath and back again in order to make sure Rosie got home safely, of course, but would it resurrect all her silly hopes and dreams? It was high time she found a good steady chap, settled down, and gave Winnie the grandchildren she longed for. But unless she came to her senses and forgot about Julian Edgell, that wasn't going to happen.

Winnie sighed. With a determined effort she left the window to go and put the kettle on for a nice cup of tea.

So this was Hillsbridge.

Clarke Sutherland had slowed the shiny black Austin as he approached a long, sharp bend, and now, as the road straightened out, the town came into view in the valley below. From here it was possible only to see a cluster of buildings and a church tower rising into the skyline, but as he reached the bottom of the hill, he was confronted by level-crossing gates, which were closed. He drew up behind a charabanc and looked around. To his right was a two-storey building with a short flight of steps leading up to the door; the painted sign above it read 'The Miners' Arms'. Facing it from the other side of the road was another inn – the George – and beyond an open square in front of it stood what looked like a market hall. From here he could see little more than what appeared to be a river bridge and a curious little shop at a junction jutting out over what he imagined must be a river.

Just then a goods train steamed over the crossing, the gates were opened by a man in railway worker's uniform and Clarke followed the charabanc through what must be the town centre, judging by the number of shops lining the road on one side, and up a steep curving hill. He was through the rest of the town in what seemed like a flash, seeing nothing but houses, some large and set back, some small and terraced, then, confusingly, passed a road sign that suggested he had moved seamlessly into another town. High something – he hadn't had time to read it properly before he had passed it.

So that's the place you call home, Miss Rosie Mitchell, he thought, and was a little annoyed with himself for being so interested. It wasn't like him to keep thinking about a girl he was never likely to see again, even if he had been very taken by her long brown hair and hazel eyes and the way she'd recovered herself after her frightening experience so that she seemed vulnerable and resilient both at the same time. It was the task that lay ahead of him he should be concentrating on. A task that would require him to call on every bit of the experience and expertise he'd acquired during his years as a bomb disposal expert with the British army.

His destination – a mansion in the heart of the Somerset countryside – had been requisitioned by the government to serve as an operational base for Section D (D for Destruction) of the

Secret Intelligence Service, to which he was now attached. That was what he should be thinking of, not Miss Rosie Mitchell – who in any case, it seemed, was spoken for by that pompous stuffed shirt who'd come to meet her at the station. Clarke had been sorely tempted to plant a fist in the middle of his oh-so-handsome face.

At a road junction he passed what appeared to be a school playing field – boys in football kit on the pitch closest to the road, girls in gym skirts with hockey sticks chasing around further away. Some more houses, and then before long he was in open countryside, heading out towards the Mendip Hills. Yes, it was time to forget all about Rosie Mitchell.

The declaration of war had delivered him a new challenge. And he would give it his all.

'Do you mind if I have an early night, Mum?' Rosie hung the tea towel she'd used to dry the dishes on its rack.

'Course I don't mind, love. You're tired out after the day you've had, I shouldn't wonder,' Winnie said.

'I am really. But it's so nice to be home. And your ham and leek pie was really delicious.'

'I know it's one of your favourites. And you couldn't tell I had to do the sauce twice, could you?'

'Not at all.'

Winnie smiled, satisfied. Truth to tell, she hadn't stopped smiling since Julian Edgell's car had finally rolled up the drive and Rosie had climbed out and run up the path to hug her. Never in all her life had she been happier to see her daughter.

Dr Edgell had carried her suitcase up to the front door, and for all the misgivings she had about him, Winnie had felt obliged to invite him to share the meal she had ready and waiting for Rosie. Thankfully he'd declined, saying his parents were expecting him, so she and Rosie had been able to enjoy the time together, just the two of them.

Rosie had insisted on helping Winnie clear away and wash up, but there was no doubt in Winnie's mind that it was her bed the girl needed most now.

'You go on up, love,' she said. 'It's all nice and clean for you.'

'Thanks, Mum. You're the best.'

They hugged again, and Winnie dropped a kiss on Rosie's head.

'It's so good to have you home,' she said. 'And there's another day tomorrow.'

As she watched her beloved daughter climb the stairs, her eyes were full of tears. But they were tears of joy and gratitude.

Perhaps her prayers hadn't been in vain. Perhaps the God she wasn't sure she believed in had heard them after all.

Rosie lay in her own familiar bed enjoying the crisp feel and fresh soap-flake smell of the sheet that she had pulled up to her chin. Both the sheets and the pillowcases were sparkling white, she'd noticed. Mum must have given the rinsing water a swirl of the blue bag, if Rosie wasn't mistaken.

She closed her eyes, wondering what Freda was doing. Perhaps she'd gone out for a drink and something to eat with Ron. Rosie didn't much like him, but it was good Freda wouldn't be alone. Then, inevitably, it was Julian she was thinking of. He'd put himself out to come and meet her. And the way he'd reacted to Clarke . . . He really hadn't liked that she'd travelled from London with another man, who had also been going to give her a lift home. Was it possible – was it just possible – that there might be hope for her yet? If she meant nothing to him, why would he care?

Her eyelids were growing heavy. She let them droop, turned her face into the soft feather pillow and began to drift. She was happy. And not just to be home. She was beginning to think Julian must have missed her. Perhaps been sorry for the things he'd said. Regretting them . . .

In a sweet haze, Rosie fell asleep.

Chapter Five

It was time for Winnie to go to work at Bramley Court. Rosie had not yet surfaced, and when Winnie went upstairs, she found the door to her bedroom still closed.

She hesitated, wondering what she should do. She was reluctant to disturb her if she was still asleep. Poor lamb must have been exhausted. But neither did she want to leave without letting her know. Making up her mind, she turned the door knob as quietly as possible and cautiously peeked round the door.

'Rosie?' she said softly.

No response. Rosie was still dead to the world, her rich brown hair fanned out across the pillow, her face flushed with sleep, long lashes brushing her cheeks. Winnie crept towards the bed, her heart filling with love as she looked down at her sleeping daughter.

She was lying the way she always had, on her left side, arms wrapped loosely around herself, one leg drawn up, one straight. A lump rose in Winnie's throat. It was almost as if the years had melted away. This Rosie might still be the little girl she used to sing to sleep. In her memory she could hear herself crooning in a low voice, 'Now the day is over, night is drawing nigh; shadows of the evening steal across the sky.' Except that the day wasn't over, of course. Sunlight was creeping in through the gap in the curtains where Rosie hadn't quite closed them when she'd gone to bed last night.

She'd had a favourite verse, too, one she'd asked Winnie to sing over and over again. 'Guard the sailors tossing on the deep blue sea . . .'

Winnie had never quite understood why as a child those lines had fascinated her so. It wasn't as if they lived on the coast, and she'd only ever got to paddle in the rippling breakers on the rare occasions when they'd gone on a charabanc outing to Weston-super-Mare or Weymouth. Perhaps in her imagination sailors and the dangers they faced were in some way romantic.

Nostalgic tears pricked Winnie's eyes. Where had the years gone? She longed to plant a kiss on her daughter's cheek, stroke her soft hair – how lucky that she hadn't inherited Winnie's coarse curls! – but she wouldn't. Let her sleep. She must need it.

She crept out of the room and closed the door quietly after her. Downstairs she scribbled a note to Rosie and propped it up against the milk jug on the breakfast table. Then she collected her bag and left for work.

As Rosie slowly surfaced from her deep sleep, a faint smell of frying bacon tickled her nostrils. Mum's cooked breakfast. Bliss. She opened her eyes – daylight! She must have slept for hours. She turned her head slightly on the pillow so as to look at the small white-cased clock on the bedside table, and a twinge of guilt marred the aura of peace. Half past eight! Unbelievable. Even on days when she didn't have to work, she liked to be up with the lark.

She lay for a few more minutes luxuriating in the comfort of her old bed and revisiting the things that had surrounded her since childhood. In those days she'd occupied a tiny room in the attic, but her parents had furnished it with a bed, a tallboy and a small dressing table, all of which she'd taken with her when Don had joined the army and the pecking order had changed. The three green pottery rabbits that used to sit on the tallboy were now lined up on the windowsill – Daddy, Mummy and Baby, Rosie had always thought. The picture that had once dangled from a beam now hung on the wall – a little girl in pinafores in a setting meant to represent the nursery rhyme 'Hickory Dickory Dock'. When she'd moved into Don's room, she'd thought about replacing it, but somehow she had never been able to bring herself to get rid of it, despite the fact that the blue binding that held the glass in place was grubby and worn, though she had also hung a seascape. And her books, which had been piled up against the tallboy, were now lined up on a shelf. *The Secret Garden*, *Anne of Green Gables*, *Black Beauty*. She'd read them all from cover to cover more times than she cared to remember. There was even an old Playbox Annual that she'd found in the pillowcase that served as a stocking one long-ago Christmas.

This, she thought, was where she belonged. It was a good feeling. She'd been afraid to come back because she hadn't felt able to face Julian, but she need not have worried. He'd behaved as if he'd forgotten all about what had happened on that last night, and perhaps he had. It wouldn't have been such a big deal to him as it had been to her. The tension between them that she had so dreaded hadn't materialised. In fact . . .

Last night she'd fallen asleep thinking about Julian and feeling ridiculously happy that he'd cared enough to fetch her from the station. Been protective of her when he'd thought a strange man might be trying to take advantage of her. But in the light of day the rose-tinted glasses had dimmed somewhat. It seemed he still saw quite a bit of Anne. Perhaps they were in a relationship. It was possible. But he hadn't said they were actually dating, so perhaps there was hope for Rosie . . .

She caught herself. Don't go there. She couldn't risk being hurt and humiliated all over again.

She must get up. She pushed aside the patchwork quilt she'd helped her mother to make, got out of bed and opened the curtains. Sunshine dappled the parkland beyond the little kitchen garden beneath her window, but she saw that the trees were beginning to change colour for autumn, little splashes of red and gold amid the green.

She pulled on her old dressing gown, still hanging on the peg behind the door where she had left it when she'd gone to London, and went downstairs.

The smell of bacon was stronger now, but the house was very quiet. Her mother wasn't there. She must have gone to work. But there was a note propped up on the breakfast table. Rosie picked it up and unfolded it.

Sorry, love, but I can't wait any longer. There's bacon in the oven – hope it's not too dried up. I'll be back at dinner time.

She turned on the gas ring and set the kettle to boil. Her place had already been set at the table, though Winnie had cleared away whatever she'd had herself. Rosie checked the oven; the bacon was crispy, but Winnie had left the temperature low enough to keep it warm without spoiling. She picked out one small rasher and nibbled it while she cut a slice of bread and put it under the grill to make toast.

Oh yes, however much she had dreaded it, it certainly was good to be home.

While she was eating, Rosie thought about how she would spend the morning – what was left of it! – and decided she would go into town, have a look around the shops and, most importantly, pop into the garage to see Mr Bendle and find out if she could get her old job back. It was a bit of a nerve to imagine she could just walk in and continue as if she hadn't been gone for almost two years, but she did so want to be working with cars again. Then, when she'd finished eating, she switched on the wireless to see if she could catch the news.

She'd resisted tuning in earlier, afraid of what she might hear. She hadn't wanted to spoil her breakfast with bad news about the war. Supposing she heard London had been bombed? She'd be worried to death about Freda.

In the event, there was nothing shocking or sensational. Just more of the same – talk of precautions and evacuations and advice about blackout curtains and sandbags and being sure to take your gas mask with you if you were going out. Rosie huffed contemptuously at that. She hated the rubbery smell of her gas mask and felt as if she was being suffocated, and she couldn't imagine needing it in town today. The only gas she was likely to smell would come from the gasworks, whose chimney rose more or less directly behind the garage forecourt.

She washed at the kitchen sink, got dressed in a clean blouse and dirndl skirt and applied a little lipstick. Then she set out for town.

She didn't see a soul as she walked along the main road, and no traffic passed her, but when she reached the first houses, large detached and semi-detached stone-built dwellings on one side of the road and long terraces on the other, there were a few more signs of life. She passed a young woman with a basket of shopping and a toddler wearing reins, and an elderly man who she guessed was a retired miner, from the rattle of his laborious breathing as he struggled up the shallow incline. There was a Co-operative bakery cart drawn up to the kerb, the horse standing patiently in the shafts as the roundsman delivered bread from the basket over his arm to a woman in a floral wraparound overall who waited in her doorway. Otherwise all was quiet.

Then, as she rounded a bend and started down the last steep slope, past a row of cottages, a woman who was scrubbing her front step looked up and saw her.

'Well, Rosie! I thought you were in London!'

'I only got home yesterday,' Rosie said, not stopping. Mrs Bennett – Gert – was a known busybody, and she really didn't want to encourage her.

'Mother all right, is she?' the woman called after her.

'She's fine,' Rosie replied over her shoulder, and kept on walking.

At the bottom of the hill she crossed the main road onto the forecourt of the Miners' Arms, which she was surprised to see had sandbags piled up beside the steps leading to the main entrance, and tape of some kind criss-crossed over the windows. It was to stop them being blown in in the event of a bomb blast, she realised. She'd seen protection of that sort on buildings in London, but it was something of a shock to find it here, in sleepy Hillsbridge. But at least the landlord was showing some defiance. A Union Jack fluttered bravely from the flagpole, and red, white and blue bunting was draped around the taped-up windows.

There was just one car in the yard that fronted the garage workshop, a white Ford Anglia that was none too clean. Rosie glanced fondly at the petrol pump, then made her way towards the workshop, the doors of which stood wide open.

There was another car inside – one that was shinier, grander and much better cared for than the white Anglia. The rear wheels had been jacked up, and Mr Bendle's legs stuck out from beneath the body. Of Jack, his son, who worked with him, there was no sign.

Rosie hesitated. She didn't want to startle the garage owner. If she made him jump, he might well crack his head on the undercarriage. But at that moment he slid out, very agilely for a man well past his prime, and raised himself on his elbows, still holding a spanner in one greasy hand.

'Rosie! Wot are you doin' 'ere?'

'Come to see you, of course. But if you're busy . . .'

'Always got time fer you, me cocker. This'll 'ave t' wait.' He rolled himself over onto his knees and pulled himself up by way of the rear passenger door. ''Twon't do Harvey Moon no harm to know not everybody jumps to attention when 'e gives the order.'

Harvey Moon was the general manager of the glove factory, and one of the most universally disliked men in Hillsbridge. But all the same . . .

'You shouldn't upset your customers, Mr Bendle,' Rosie chided him.

'Don't say no more about it, Rosie, or you and I be gonna fall out.' He reached for a rag that looked to be every bit as oily as his hands. 'Come on, I'm ready for a cup of tea if you bain't. Our Brenda's not 'ere today, but it's a bad job if I can't put the kettle on an' do it meself.'

Rosie was sorry she'd miss Brenda Bendle. They'd always got on well. But it was Mr Bendle she'd come to see, not his wife. 'You're just waiting for me to offer, admit it,' she said with a smile.

'Well . . . if you like, m'dear. I wouldn't say no.'

The café where Rosie had helped out when she first started work at the garage was housed in an outbuilding to one side of the workshop. Six tables covered with red and white checked cloths were set out in a small room, and beyond it was an even smaller kitchen. Rosie had sometimes wondered just how Brenda Bendle managed to cook the meals she served to office and factory workers in such a cramped space – stews and hotpots with extra vegetables on the side in winter, stuffed marrow in season, and a pudding – spotted dick and custard or jam roly-poly perhaps – to follow. But she did, and it was no wonder her customers were regulars. A good feed at dinner time and all for a very reasonable price.

Rosie went into the kitchen and set the kettle to boil. When the tea was ready, she poured it and took the two mugs back into the café area, where Dick Bendle had sat himself down at one of the tables.

'Well done, girl,' he said after taking a hefty slurp of hot sweet tea. 'You haven't lost yer touch. An' you remembered just how I like it, too.'

'How could I forget?' Rosie asked. 'Very fussy, you can be, Mr Bendle.'

'Ah well . . . I taught you well, didn't I?' He cradled the cup between both hands. 'So are you just here for a few days, or back for good?'

'I've come to be with Mum while this war is going on,' Rosie said. 'I couldn't bear to think of her on her own. So I shall be here for the foreseeable future. That's one of the reasons I've come to see you. I was wondering if there was any chance of having my old job back.'

Mr Bendle frowned and took another slurp of tea before replying.

'I don't know about that, Rosie. You'd'a know I'd 'ave you back like a shot if things were normal, but they bain't. I don't think there's gonna be much work goin'. The powers-that-be are requisitioning any motors they can use to turn into ambulances and the like, an' there's talk that petrol is gonna be rationed. Unless they decide to use me t' look after the vehicles wot'll be on official business, I can't see how I'm gonna make enough to pay you.'

Rosie's heart sank, but she did understand his position, especially since his son was as much a fixture in the garage as Mr Bendle himself.

'And you've still got Jack to help you,' she said.

Dick Bendle twisted the cup between his hands, looking more wretched than ever.

'I 'aven't, as it happens. You know 'ow he loved his TA? The weekly meetings and the summer camps?'

'Oh.' Yes, Rosie remembered how Jack had been a keen member of the Territorial Army, and remembered too how proud he had looked in his khaki uniform. She had a feeling she knew exactly what was coming next.

'Got called up straight away, didn't 'e, when they thought there was trouble brewing. Several months ago now. An' I took on a young lad wot left school in the summer four days a week. He's not our Jack, o' course, but I'm trainin' him up an' he's keen as mustard. I wouldn't like to let 'im down now he's got his hopes up.'

'No, of course you mustn't do that,' Rosie said swiftly. 'And really I didn't expect . . .'

''Twas nice you thought o' me, though.' But anxiety was etched on Mr Bendle's leathery face, and Rosie knew it was more than regret at having to turn down her request.

'You must be worried about Jack,' she said.

'Well, to tell the truth, I am – an' so's our Brenda. But 'twas only to be expected really. And from the sounds of it, he'd be called up now anyway. Eighteen to forty-one, they're sayin'. Single men first.'

He pulled an oil-stained handkerchief out of the pocket of his overalls and blew his nose. 'That's enough o' that. Tell me wot you've bin up to, Rosie. An' wot it's like in Lunnon. Never bin there meself, y'know.'

They chatted for another ten minutes or so, then Mr Bendle got to his feet.

'It's bin good t' see you, m'dear, but I'd best get on. Or else I'll 'ave 'Arvey bloody Moon on me tail.'

'Good to see you too, Mr Bendle. And I didn't just come to ask about getting my old job back, honestly.'

'So call in again. Whenever you feel like it.'

'I will.'

As Rosie washed up the tea things, she thought sadly just how much this war had changed everything already. And it had only just begun. What havoc would it have wreaked in all their lives before it was over?

The manor house that had been Clarke Sutherland's destination lay some twelve miles south of Hillsbridge. Most recently it had been the home of a racehorse trainer, and from the window of his room on the first floor, Clarke could see the stable block, now empty, and an expanse of open grassland that had been used for gallops. When war had become almost inevitable, the trainer had moved his business lock, stock and barrel to a remote corner of Exmoor. Though it was unlikely enemy bombers would target the area in which Withy Manor was located, he wasn't willing to take any chances with the elite bloodstock in his care.

It was then that the government had stepped in. They were requisitioning country houses and estates as regional centres for the three sections that made up the Secret Intelligence Service: guerilla warfare, inexplicably known as GS, a propaganda section known by the initials EH after its base, Electra House, and his own section, D, which dealt with destruction and sabotage.

Once the war had become inevitable, Clarke had fully expected that he would be working on the front line, wherever that might be. He had been surprised to learn that his job would be to instruct the prospective special operations recruits in the use of explosives. He would also train them in weaponry – mostly guns that were light to carry and easy to use – and prepare them, as far as humanly possible, for the dangers they would face. It would be down to him too to weed out those he believed were unsuited to the dangerous task of undermining the enemy in countries where they had taken control. There would almost certainly be some who made the grade who would face capture, torture and death. Perhaps he'd also have the opportunity to teach some classes in self-defence – another of his skills – but he wasn't sure how much opportunity the recruits would have to use the techniques against German soldiers. The guns they'd be issued with would be their best defence. But in the last resort they might still have to take the suicide pill they would be given before being dropped into occupied territory, for death would be the only escape from what they would be subjected to during interrogation.

Headquarters had given Clarke sheafs of regulations to study, as well as precise instructions as to what he should cover during the training sessions, and he supposed he should make a start on wading through it. Somewhat reluctantly he turned away from the window, extracted a file from his suitcase and sat down on the bed to study it. But try as he might to concentrate, Miss Rosie Mitchell was still invading his thoughts, and he found himself wishing he could see her again. Not that there was much hope of that. Yes, he had a car and could drive to Hillsbridge when he was off-duty. But he had no idea how he would find her, or how she would react if he did. She'd been shaken up and grateful to him for rescuing her, but when she'd got over her experience, it could be a very different story.

And what the hell did she see in that jumped-up young toff? Clarke wondered, not for the first time. A meal ticket to a bright future perhaps? After all, he didn't really know her; didn't know what made her tick. If it had been a straight contest, he reckoned he could see the blighter off. But he couldn't compete with class and wealth, if that was what she was after.

Forget all about her, he told himself. You have enough on your plate without worrying about a girl you'll probably never see again.

With an effort of will, he spread the official paperwork out on the bed beside him, selected a page and began to read.

Anne Hastings was kneeling beside a packing case in an anteroom of the gallery in Bristol where she worked as a curator. She was in the process of wrapping yet another artefact in sheets of newspaper to protect it while it was being transported to the crypt of one of the city's churches, where it would remain until there was no more threat from the enemy.

She paused for a moment, looking at the little figurine. Once it had been regarded as a talisman, a bringer of good luck to those who held it in their hands. An ancient superstition, of course, but Anne couldn't help wondering if there might be something in it, if only the effect it had on the mind of the believer.

She half closed her eyes, imagining she could feel a power of some sort passing from the sheer crystal into the palms of her hands, and feeling them tingle a little. Then she snapped herself out of the semi-trance she had willed herself into, shaking her head and smiling at her own stupidity.

Her hands were tingling because she'd been holding the crystal artefact too tightly. That was all. But at least it had provided a few minutes' respite from the tedium of this endless packing.

What was she going to do, she wondered, when it was all done and the gallery was an empty shell? Her mother wanted her to come home, but Anne was reluctant. Yes, she'd be safer there than here in Bristol. Yes, she was sure Frances would find plenty of things to keep her busy. Her mother was relishing her position as the local organiser for the WVS and had already come up with a suggestion as to what Anne – who had long ago learned to drive – could do. Frances knew it was highly likely her precious car would be requisitioned by the government, but if by some miracle she managed to argue successfully that she needed it for her war work, she intended to have it converted into an ambulance for use by the WVS. If Anne took first-aid classes, she could be the designated driver.

Anne had stalled, saying she didn't have time for anything at the moment except getting the gallery's precious artefacts into safe storage. But the truth was she didn't want to do anything that would mean she was back under her mother's control. Since leaving home, she had come to value her independence too much.

Until she'd cut loose, she'd been cosseted, spoiled almost. She had wanted for nothing; had everything done for her. But with hindsight, she could see that it hadn't been good for her. She'd been stifled by the sheer force of Frances's personality. All her decisions had been made for her, and because she loved her mother, wanted to please her and had actually come to believe Frances knew best, she had fallen into the trap of toeing the line without question.

Taking the job at the Bristol gallery had been the first and only time she had stuck stubbornly to her guns. It was her dream job. She'd always been fascinated by the past, drawn in by the historic portraits, furniture and effects that remained in Bramley Court to this day. After spending a year at finishing school in Switzerland – at Frances's insistence – she'd taken a course in the conservation of historical remains, and this had led to an offer of a position with the gallery. Frances had objected – she didn't want Anne to be so far away from home; a ridiculous argument really, since Bristol was only some fifteen miles from Hillsbridge. But for once Anne had been determined not to go along with her mother's wishes, and eventually Frances had been forced to concede defeat. Privately Anne had always thought that was due in part to her father's intervention. Sir James was the only person who could influence Frances and talk her round to his way of thinking.

Living and working away from home had made Anne a different person to the rather timid girl she had once been, and she had no wish to return to having her life ordered for her, however comfortable that might be. But it wasn't easy to escape the chains of duty. Little as she wanted it, she could feel the ties drawing her back, and she honestly didn't know how to resist.

Besides all this, there was Julian. She'd always been so sure that they would end up together, and things had certainly seemed to be heading that way. Until she'd discovered that he'd been cheating on her with Rosie. Whoever he'd taken up with she'd have been hurt, she knew. But that it had been her childhood friend had made it a thousand times worse. She'd been angry with her as well as with Julian and would have liked to have it out with her, but by the time she'd found out, Rosie had hightailed it to London, and they hadn't met since.

Julian had been contrite. Begged her to forgive him. Told her that it had been nothing but a silly fling. Against her better judgement, she'd decided to give him another chance, but how could she ever trust him again? Things had gone well for a time, but recently she'd begun to suspect he was cheating on her again. If that was the case, she made up her mind she must forget him, even though she still had feelings for him. If she went home, she wouldn't be able to avoid him. He was a doctor in Bath; if she was driving an ambulance, their paths would be bound to cross.

Anne didn't want to be in a position where she had to choose between her heart and her head. It was just too hard. But resisting her mother would be a battle.

When she'd broken free to come to Bristol, she'd had the excuse that she was fulfilling her dream. Now, apart from feelings that she would never be able to bring herself to explain, there was no good reason for her not to go home.

She cupped the little crystal artefact between her hands again, wishing with her whole heart and soul that it would show her the way out of this dilemma, and once again imagining the tingling in her palms and fingers. Then, after a few moments, she reluctantly released it, wrapped it in a sheet of newspaper and laid it in the packing case along with the other treasures, still nursing a faint hope.

Who knew? Perhaps the ancients had known something that had been forgotten through the ages. She could only hope that perhaps they had been right.

Chapter Six

'Can you tell me wot good we'm doin' 'ere? Maud Hawkins grumbled to Winnie. 'I'll be blowed if I want to spend me evenings on a hard chair in the church hall.'

'Well at least we got to ride in a motor car,' Winnie said. 'And there's a good few like us here too. I thought it would be all her ladyship's friends, and I didn't fancy that at all.'

'True. They'm 'avin' their meetings in private, I wouldn't be surprised, where they'll be nabbin' all the best jobs.'

'Shh!' Winnie cautioned, and they fell silent as Lady Hastings entered the room. She strode to a small table that had been placed at the front so that it faced the rows of chairs where Winnie and Maud sat with the other volunteers her ladyship had been able to muster.

'Good evening, ladies, and welcome!' Her ladyship's booming voice echoed around the plasterboard walls and ceiling of the church hall. She set an impressive-looking folder on the table and surveyed her audience for a moment before continuing.

'It is gratifying indeed to see so many of you in attendance, and I hope this is a meeting place that will prove convenient for you. As I'm sure you realise, I would have welcomed you to Bramley Court, but it is a long way out of town and I could hardly expect you to have to walk so far.'

She paused, waiting for the expected murmurings of appreciation, and then went on. 'As you may have noticed, I have brought two of my own staff with me this evening, and since most of you almost certainly know one another, I hope you will make them welcome. May I introduce Mrs Hawkins, my cook, and Mrs Mitchell, whose late husband was our gardener.'

She waved a hand in the direction of Winnie and Maud and indicated that they should stand up. 'Do please make yourselves known, ladies.'

The two women exchanged horrified glances, then got awkwardly to their feet. The rest of the assembly seemed at a loss to know what they were expected to do, then someone began clapping and the others followed suit.

As the applause died down, Lady Hastings once more took control of the meeting.

'Now, the reason I have called you all together is so that we can decide how best to utilise our talents and capabilities to do our bit for the war effort, and I know you will all be unstinting in your enthusiasm and determination to do just that. There will be mobile canteens to cater for any troops based in the area, and emergency rest centres for anyone unfortunate enough to lose their home to enemy bombing, and these will need to be staffed. When the evacuation of children from the cities begins again, we shall need teams of volunteers to marshal the operation, and, of course, families with whom they can be placed. I have begun to compile a list of those who will be willing to take one – or in the case of siblings who need to be accommodated together, two or more – and if any of you feel able to add your names to that list, please see me after this meeting.' She let her gaze roam around the attendees, smiling encouragingly.

'It may not always be easy,' she went on after a moment. 'These children are likely to be homesick and frightened. They will need love and understanding – and sometimes, perhaps, a firm but kindly hand. But I can guarantee it will be a most rewarding experience, and I feel sure many of you will be willing to offer your assistance.'

'Fat chance!' Maud whispered to Winnie. ''Tis bad enough with that lot next door, always screamin' and shoutin'.'

A woman sitting in front of them looked round accusingly, and, embarrassed, Winnie put a finger to her lips and shook her head warningly at her friend.

Lady Hastings, however, gave no sign of having heard what Maud had said.

'I also intend to organise some fundraising events, which I hope you will support by selling tickets and helping out with preparations – anything that needs to be done. That, of course, is for the future. But what can we be doing now?

'Well, I am sure all of you are proficient with both your knitting needles and sewing machines. Winter is coming, and it may well be that our brave soldiers and sailors will be in need of woollen scarves, socks and jumpers. If we begin now, we should have a good stock ready for when they are needed. And those of you who are more ambitious may care to make soft toys that can be given to the evacuee children. To that end I am suggesting we meet once or twice a week, here in the church hall when it is free, or perhaps in one another's homes, for what I will call a "needlecraft bee". Working together will be satisfying and inspirational.'

Maud huffed under her breath but to Winnie's relief said nothing.

'I have already booked this hall for next Wednesday evening, from seven until ten, and Friday morning from ten till one. I hope to see a good many of you here, with whatever you will need – and if any of you have leftover wool at home, perhaps you could bring it with you and we can pool our resources.' Lady Hastings nodded at a woman in the front row. 'Could you organise that, please, Mrs Maggs?'

'Oh yes. Yes, of course!' the woman said, pleased no doubt to have been singled out, and the person who had begun the clapping to welcome Winnie and Maud put her hands together once again.

'Wot a load of tommyrot!' Maud whispered under cover of the applause.

'I think it's a nice idea,' Winnie said, beginning to despair of her friend's negative attitude.

'And it would be good to have some refreshment to reward our efforts.' Lady Hastings addressed another woman, also in the front row. 'Can I leave that in your capable hands, Mrs Bendle? Catering is your forte, I believe. I'll give you a float to cover the purchase of tea, milk, sugar and biscuits if you see me after the meeting.'

'Well!' Maud exploded, her nose put out of joint, Winnie guessed, since she was a professional cook while Mrs Bendle was just the wife of the garage owner. Winnie would enlighten her later, if she didn't already know, that Mrs Bendle ran a very popular café.

Yet another round of applause drowned out Maud's disgust, but Winnie was beginning to hope that Maud was going to tell Lady Hastings the WVS wasn't for her. Really, she was nothing but an embarrassment, and Winnie was beginning to think she herself was rather going to enjoy these meetings. She already knew several of the volunteers to speak to, and they certainly looked to be a friendly bunch. It would be quite a treat to meet up socially once or twice a week, and Lady Hastings could hardly complain about her not being at work on a Friday morning if she was doing things for the WVS.

'Ah! Just one last thing!' her ladyship said now. 'The Red Cross are running classes in first aid and nursing. If any of you are interested in going down that route, I have the details you will need. Now, perhaps we can discuss who would like to do what. Mrs Maggs, will you find someone to help you take down names and ideas?'

'Well, seeing as how what I do best is already spoken for, I won't be putting my name down for anything,' Maud declared, though this time quietly enough that Lady Hastings wouldn't hear.

After an hour or so, her ladyship clapped her hands to call the gathering to attention. 'I think we have covered quite enough for our first meeting, and I look forward to the next. Thank you all for coming along, and I hope to see you again soon.' She closed her file and sat down.

'Well, I'm not waitin' for her,' Maud said truculently as a general hubbub broke out. 'Look at that queue wot's wanting to speak to her. I'll go on and walk it.'

Winnie nodded. She wasn't surprised, given Maud's mood, and in any case, it wasn't that far for her – she lived in one of the terraced houses on the road between Bramley Court and town. She wouldn't tell Maud she already knew about the first-aid classes – Lady Hastings had suggested to Rosie that she should attend them, and Rosie had actually gone to one this evening. It might well put her nose even further out of joint if she thought Rosie was one of the elite who were getting special treatment.

'See you tomorrow then,' she said, and settled back in her chair to wait, wondering how her daughter was getting on. She'd do well hopefully. She permitted herself a little smile of pride. Both her children were a credit to her and Ern. They mightn't have achieved much to boast about in their own lives, but at least they'd got that right.

* * *

Rosie had cycled to the first-aid course Lady Hastings had suggested she should attend. A nursing qualification would mean there would be a number of different options for her contribution to the war effort, from working as a hospital auxiliary to being an ambulance attendant, and the latter particularly appealed to her. The course was being run by the Red Cross at the TA hall in High Compton, Hillsbridge's twin town. They were linked by two quite different roads – the main A367 along which Clarke drove on his way to south Somerset, the other, Rosie's route, followed the river valley through open countryside. Lady Hastings had offered to give her a lift into Hillsbridge along with her mother, but she would still have to walk the rest of the way to High Compton, and she had decided she would rather go under her own steam.

Her red Hercules bicycle was still in the garden shed, where she'd left it when she'd gone to London. She had got it out, hoping it hadn't gone rusty since she had last used it, but to her relief it looked as good as ever, and apart from having to brush away a few cobwebs and pump up the tyres, there was nothing she needed to do before riding it again.

Now, as she pushed it up the steepest part of the hill out of town, she was feeling pleased with herself. She'd enjoyed the ride, and enjoyed the class even more. This evening they'd been learning about dressings, bandages and tourniquets, and they'd practised covering an open wound with gauze and lint and making a triangular bandage into a sling for a broken arm. It had all come quite easily to Rosie. While some of the other students had struggled, she was among the first to complete the tasks, and earned praise from the instructor for the neat results she had achieved.

'How did you *do* it?' the young woman next to her had wailed as she struggled to get a safety pin through several layers of bandage without piercing the rubber model they were practising on.

'I don't know,' Rosie had replied, genuinely bewildered that anyone should be having such problems with something she had found so effortlessly easy.

'I can see you haven't got any children,' a woman with rather pinched features chimed in, sneering at the unfortunate girl who had made such a hash of the exercise. 'If you 'ave, I pity 'em when you're changing their nappy.'

Rosie had thought that was unnecessarily unkind, and felt a little guilty that she, a newcomer, had without meaning to shown the poor girl up.

'Don't worry, you'll get there,' she had said encouragingly, and been rewarded by a grateful, if rather subdued, 'Thanks.'

She heard a car coming up the hill behind her and tucked in close to the wall, angling her bicycle in front of her. To her surprise she saw it was Lady Hastings' car, with her mother in the passenger seat.

The window rolled down. 'Rosie,' Winnie said, 'her ladyship wants to talk to you.'

Lady Hastings, holding the car on the clutch, leaned across Winnie, and Rosie saw her mother sit up a little straighter. She looked awkward somehow, as if she had breached an unspoken code of etiquette.

'Could you pop up and see me, Rosemary?'

'Tomorrow?' Rosie asked, wondering what Lady Hastings wanted with her.

'No. This evening. If you're not too tired, of course.' She glanced at her watch. 'It's not yet nine thirty.'

'Yes, of course,' Rosie said. 'I shall be home in another ten minutes or so.'

'Capital. I'll see you then.'

Lady Hastings let out the clutch and released the handbrake, and the car pulled away, leaving a puzzled Rosie to push her bicycle up the hill until the road flattened out sufficiently for her to be able to ride the rest of the way.

Freda had decided that this war wasn't going to be much fun, especially now that Rosie had gone home. The house felt silent and empty without her, the living room was depressingly dark now that she'd managed to get the blackout blinds up, and she'd fallen out with Ron. She'd met him last night as arranged and they'd gone for a drink in the Lord Nelson on the Old Kent Road as they often did. But this evening a whole bunch of his pals were there, drinking, and Ron had more or less abandoned her for a game of darts with them. That had been bad enough; Freda had felt very conspicuous sitting alone at the little table where the ring marks suggested no one ever bothered to use the beer mats, the ashtray was overflowing, and she seemed to be the only woman in the room.

When Ron had deigned to come over to see if she wanted another drink, she'd asked him if they couldn't go now, as she wanted him to help her with the blackout blinds. She couldn't put a light on until they were up for fear that the jumped-up man who called himself an air raid warden would come knocking on her door and threaten to report her, but she didn't want to have to have her bedtime cocoa and biscuit in the dark.

'Oh give it a rest, Freda,' Ron had replied, not best pleased. 'I 'aven't seen Cocky Sparrow for months. 'E's been at sea, and 'e's off again tomorrow.'

Cocky was in the merchant navy, Freda knew. But she also knew that when Ron spent an evening with him, he was likely to end up the worse for wear. Cocky could drink anyone under the table.

'Can't you help me with my blinds and then come back again?' she had asked. 'He'll be here until closing time.'

But Ron's pals were calling to him across the crowded bar.

'Come on, mate! It's yer go!'

'Ah, leave 'im. 'E's under the thumb already, more fool 'im.'

'D'you want another drink or not?' Ron asked bad-temperedly, and Freda had had enough.

'Not if you'd rather be with that lot than with me, no. I'll see you when I see you.' She'd got up, grabbed her bag and walked out, and a peal of raucous laughter had followed her. Some joke at her expense, no doubt.

She'd gone home fuming. But at least today she'd managed to get hold of some proper blackout material that was left over from covering the brewery office windows. She'd gone next door to borrow a hammer and nails, and Mrs Pruitt's son, who had been fixing hers, had come round and done the same for Freda.

'Sod you, Ron Freak,' she'd thought, but still hoped he'd turn up at her door this evening. He hadn't, and Freda had realised just how alone she was. They'd been a foursome, her and Ron and Rosie and Jim. Winter, with its long dark nights, was just around the corner, and goodness only knew what was going to happen with the war.

She heard the click of the letter box and went into the little hallway to find a leaflet had been pushed through. She took it into the kitchen, where the gas mantle was giving a reasonable light, and looked at it, surprised to see it was an official pamphlet. *For a happy, healthy job, Join the Women's Land Army!* it proclaimed across a picture of a smiling girl in what looked like jodhpurs and boots holding a pitchfork. The background showed a field of hay, and for some reason Freda was overcome with bittersweet nostalgia. She could almost smell the sweet new-mown grass and picture clearly all the details that were missing from the illustration. The thresher, the tractor, the wagon loaded high with bales, the lumbering carthorses . . . Fascinated, she read on.

The Women's Land Army had been formed back in June, she discovered, to replace the male farm workers who would be called up to fight. Volunteers would be provided with a uniform and would live on the farm where they were employed.

A bubble of excitement was forming in her throat. Oh my goodness, she'd love to do that! Until that moment she hadn't truly realised just how much she missed the countryside. It would be wonderful to be woken in the mornings by the crowing of cockerels instead of the cooing of pigeons, to hear cows lowing rather than motor engines and honking horns, and to have her meals prepared for her from fresh produce in a big homely farm-house kitchen. She might find herself working with other girls who would become her friends. Suddenly it seemed like her idea of dying and going to heaven.

There and then Freda made up her mind. It was serendipity that the leaflet had fallen through her letter box just when she'd been feeling fed up with everything here. This was an opportunity to leave the sandbags and the blackouts and the threat of bombs behind, make new friends and do something useful that she would really enjoy.

Her reluctance to leave her grandmother's house unoccupied forgotten, Freda made up her mind. She was going to volunteer for the Land Army and go wherever it took her!

'Ah, Rosemary, my dear.'

Lady Hastings rose from her favourite leather chesterfield chair, which Rosie thought must be almost as old as the house.

From her frequent visits when she had been a child playing with Anne, Rosie knew that much of the furniture at Bramley Court had indeed been handed down through generations of the

Hastings family. She had marvelled at the spindle-legged Georgian sideboard that Anne had told her had once been used for serving buffets, the oak corner cabinet with a bowed front, and the exquisitely carved oak chests. But it was the family portraits that hung on the walls that she liked looking at most. Men, some in powdered wigs, some with hair that fell in waves to their shoulders, almost all wearing stern expressions. Ladies dressed in fine satin gowns, and one old dowager in a mob cap who somehow still managed to look regal. Anne had been able to tell her who they all were, her ancestors from the Hastings line.

The portraits that fascinated her most, however, were a pair that sat side by side on one wall with a lamp angled above them.

Both seemed to depict family groups, father, mother and children, but although it was clearly the same gentleman in both pictures – tall, broad-shouldered and handsome – the ladies were quite different. One was fair and fragile, her arm around a blond-headed toddler, the other blessed with glorious chestnut hair. The stout little boy in the first picture was recognisable as a young man in the second, and there was another boy of about the same age, but of the little fair-haired child there was no sign.

'Who are they?' Rosie had asked Anne.

'That's my father's great-great – oh, I can't remember how many greats! – grandfather,' Anne had said. 'Sir Hugh. He was the one who opened the first of our mines. And that,' she pointed to the fair, fragile lady, 'is his first wife, Imogen.'

'And the other lady?' Rosie had asked.

'Abigail, his second.'

'So are all the children his?' Rosie had asked.

'Freddie, the well-built boy, is, but not the other one of about the same age. His name was Jimmy, I think, and he was adopted. But there's a terribly sad story about the little blond lad with Imogen. He drowned in the lake.'

'That's terrible!' Rosie said, shocked.

'Yes. Daddy says Imogen was never the same afterwards. And when she died, he married Abigail, who had been his son Freddie's governess.'

There was so much history within these walls, Rosie had thought. But now it was why Lady Hastings wanted to see her that she was wondering about.

'Do sit down.' Her ladyship indicated a chair that faced her own.

'So,' she went on when they were both seated, 'how did you find the first-aid class?'

'I really enjoyed it,' Rosie said. 'And I think I did quite well.'

'I'm sure you did. You're a very practical young lady, which is why I suggested that nursing, in some shape or form, might well be your forte. Have you thought any more about which direction you'd like to take?'

'I have to say I like the idea of being an ambulance attendant,' Rosie admitted.

Lady Hastings nodded sagely. 'I think that would suit you very well. Although before that you would have to work on a hospital ward for a couple of weeks at least to finish your training. That's likely to be at St Mark's in Bath. A new wing is being built there to provide extra space to cater for what will undoubtedly be an increase in casualties, and I would imagine the ambulance station will be based there too.' She paused, then went on. 'Taking all that into account, I have a further suggestion to make. Julian Edgell was teaching you to drive at one time, I believe?'

Instantly colour rose hot in Rosie's face. 'He was, yes, but—'

'There we are then.' If Lady Hastings had noticed Rosie's blush, she gave no sign of it. 'If he would be willing to resume the lessons, he'll have you up to scratch in no time, I'm sure. I'll speak to him, ask him to teach you on my car. I'm very afraid it is going to be requisitioned – so many already have been. They are to be converted into ambulances. And while I find the thought of that very distressing, it occurred to me that if you were able to drive it . . . Do you see where I'm going with this?'

Rosie was stunned.

'That . . . I'd be able to drive an ambulance . . .'

'Precisely! You will be more than an attendant, my dear. You will be the driver!'

All this was really too much for Rosie to take in. An ambulance driver! It was something she would never have dared dream of. And she was at a loss to understand why Lady Hastings was doing this for her. She'd always been kind, of course. But to go this far . . . Yet much as the idea excited her, there was one enormous fly in the ointment.

'I don't think Julian would want to give me lessons again,' she said miserably.

'Nonsense! I'm sure he will find the time when I ask him.' As always, Lady Hastings would let nothing interfere with her plans. 'Goodness, he was only too willing to fetch you from the railway station and bring you home. He's fond of you, I'm sure. So leave it to me, and let's hear no more of it. Now – can I offer you something to drink?'

Rosie shook her head. 'Thank you, but no. I should be getting home.'

'Very well.' Lady Hastings rose. 'I'll be in touch as soon as I have made arrangements. And in the meantime . . .' She reached for a pile of books that lay on the occasional table. 'Some bed-time reading for you. I'm sure you will find these interesting, and most informative. And they will supplement what you are learning in your first-aid classes.'

'Thank you.' Rosie took the books, her hands shaking so much she was afraid she might drop them. But somehow she managed to tuck them under her arm, holding them tightly with her other hand, and left without mishap.

Her head was spinning. What was she going to do? It had been bad enough having to face Julian when he had met her at the station, and she was only grateful that he had made an effort to behave as if nothing had ever happened between them. But if Lady Hastings asked him to resume the driving lessons . . .

She cringed inwardly. It was as if her worst nightmare and her fondest dreams were on a collision course, and she couldn't imagine how she could bear to put herself in the firing line for more humiliation. But there was one thing that was in no doubt whatsoever.

When Lady Hastings' mind was made up, there was no stopping her. She'd get her way in the end, just as she always did. And Rosie had no idea how to put an end to this, short of fleeing again, which would upset her mother dreadfully.

She really was caught between the devil and the deep blue sea, with no way out.

Frances, Lady Hastings, sat back in her chesterfield chair, resting her head against the soft leather and relaxing for a rare moment to relish her successes of this evening. Everything was coming together very nicely. And dreadful though war was, it had provided her with a purpose that had been lacking in her life. Being the wife of the lord of the manor was all very well, but her chief role was to support her husband and raise their children. James, however, required little in the way of support – he was universally liked by employees and tenants alike, and too comfortable in his own skin to need either comfort or advice. And the children were both grown now, making their own way in the world, and no longer needed her.

Frances's boundless energy had needed an outlet, and the

war was providing it. Yes, she was concerned for Philip. As a pilot officer in the Royal Air Force, he was bound to be far more involved in action than she would have liked. But there really was nothing she could do about that, and Frances tended not to dwell on matters that were out of her control. Whereas Anne . . .

She and Rosie had always been such good friends, and knowing that Rosie was home from London might be just the carrot that would bring her home. Back into the fold. Back to Julian Edgell's orbit.

Frances had long harboured ambitions of a union between the two families. And Anne and Julian were the perfect couple. There had been trouble between them for a while – she'd never been entirely sure what it was all about, though she'd suspected another woman had been involved. A man as handsome as Julian was bound to attract women like wasps to a honey jar. He and Anne seemed to have put that behind them, it was true, and were once again seeing one another. But Frances couldn't help worrying that now he was a fully qualified doctor with a practice in Bath, the distance between him and Anne, who was still in Bristol, might leave him open to temptation. There must be more than one attractive and eligible woman among his new circle of friends, she thought – debutantes even – and she was very afraid he might be tempted to stray again.

If Anne was at home, much closer to Bath, she felt sure that danger would be minimised. Besides, it would give her the opportunity to move things along. Frances was confident in her own ability to settle matters to her satisfaction. Which in this case meant ensuring that Anne and Julian wed.

Her reverie was interrupted by a voice from the doorway. Sir James.

'So what are you up to now, my dear?'

She smiled enigmatically. 'Why, nothing, James! What on earth can you mean?'

'Just that I know you very well, Frances. But actually I think on this occasion I would prefer to be kept in the dark. Rosemary is a very nice young lady, and I wouldn't like to think you were using her in any way,' he warned.

'Your imagination, James!' Frances teased. 'But now I'm going to have a good stiff whisky and retire to bed. Pour me one, would you, dear?'

He'd do as she asked, she knew. For all that they were so different, he was still in love with her.

Chapter Seven

The more Freda thought about joining the Women's Land Army, the more she liked the idea. But she was a little unsure about how she should set about volunteering. The leaflet had given an address for the headquarters in Chesham Street, London SW1, but did that mean writing a letter, completing a form or simply dropping in? Undecided, she decided she might as well take the bull by the horns and seek advice from Tom Challis, the officer manager at the brewery. She'd have to tell him what she planned if her application was successful, so it might as well be now.

Tom was a big man whose ruddy complexion and gut bulging over the waistband of his trousers bore witness to the fact that he was overly fond of sampling his company's ales. But the brewery owners turned a blind eye to that since they considered he more than earned all he could drink. Besides managing the office, he kept the books meticulously, ran a sales team of three reps and dealt with any staffing problems that arose. He'd worked for the brewery for more than forty years, and the owners wondered how they would manage when he reached retirement age. But at least he wouldn't be called up for military service as so many of their employees had been, so it was a problem that could be put on the back burner for the time being.

It had been mid morning when Freda was called to his office – a tiny room scarcely larger than a cupboard – to take dictation. As a rule she did this easily enough; she'd achieved a speed of a hundred words per minute in the exam she'd taken at the end of her secretarial course and had devised her own short-cuts for the work-related words that cropped up frequently. Today, however, she was struggling to concentrate and was forced to ask Mr Challis to repeat himself several times.

'Got a hangover, Miss Dobbs?' he asked mock-chidingly as he laid the last sheet of notes in the basket on his desk. 'Too many gin and oranges and a night on the tiles?'

'No.' Freda hesitated. 'Actually, there's something I wanted to talk to you about, Mr Challis.'

He leaned back in his chair. 'Oh? And what's that? Not Larry Adams pinching your behind again, I hope.'

A faint flush rose in Freda's cheeks. Larry, one of the reps, was fond of trying it on with the girls who worked in the office, but she hadn't realised Mr Challis knew about it.

'Not today,' she said, trying to disguise her discomfort. 'And in any case, I know how to deal with him when he does.'

'I'm sure you do, Miss Dobbs,' he said with a smile. Then, becoming serious, he went on, 'So, what was it you wanted to talk to me about?'

Freda had been over it a dozen times, working out exactly how to approach what would amount to her handing in her notice, but now Mr Challis's banter had driven the words right out of her head.

'I want to volunteer for the Women's Land Army,' she blurted.

'Good Lord!' He was taken completely by surprise.

'I know, and I'm really sorry if it means I'll be leaving you in the lurch, but I should think it's only a matter of time before they start calling women up too, and I'd rather chose what I have to do than be press-ganged into something I don't fancy.' Now that the worst was over, her words were flowing freely again.

'Well, good for you.' Mr Challis was also recovering himself. 'We'll be sorry to lose you, it's true. But volunteering – it's to your credit. The Land Army, though! I'd have thought you'd want to do something a bit more glamorous than milking cows and mucking out pigsties.'

Freda had to admit those jobs didn't sound quite as enticing as helping to bring in the harvest. But she was undaunted. 'I'm a country girl, born and bred,' she said. 'I know what I'm letting myself in for. But I was hoping you could help me with applying. I don't really know how to go about it, and I thought perhaps you could give me a reference too.'

'Did you now.' The twinkle was back in Tom Challis's eye. 'Of course I'll give you a reference, and a bloody good one, when it gets that far. But I must admit, it's a new one on me. I'll have to see what I can find out.'

Freda fished in her pocket and produced the leaflet that had started all this, folded neatly into quarters.

'It says here where to apply, but it's the other side of the river, in Westminster, and I wasn't sure how I'm supposed to go about it.'

'So you thought you'd get me to do it for you.' But he sounded more amused than annoyed. 'All right, Freda. Leave it with me and I'll see what I can do.'

'Oh thank you, Mr Challis,' Freda said gratefully. 'Do you want this?' She held out the leaflet, but he waved it away. 'You keep that, m'dear. I shall be dealing with the organ grinder, not the monkey.'

Freda had no idea what he meant by that, but she knew better than to ask.

'Right. Get those letters typed up for me, there's a good girl.

I'd like to get them off tonight in case they're delayed. God knows how long it'll take if half the postmen have had to go and join the army.'

'I'll bring them in for you to sign as soon as I've done them,' she promised, and walked back to her own office with a spring in her step.

Lady Hastings' hand hovered over the telephone on her desk. She had been about to call Julian Edgell to ask him if he would be willing to give Rosie some driving lessons before her car was requisitioned, but now she was having second thoughts. Anxious as she was to proceed with her plan, she thought it might be a little too soon to ask another favour of him. He hadn't hesitated when she'd asked him to meet Rosie's train, but she didn't want to appear too demanding. It might be preferable to wait until she saw him face to face, which she almost certainly would when he came home to visit his parents, rather than approach him out of the blue by telephone.

Since speaking to Rosie, it had occurred to her to wonder if perhaps he'd had his reasons for agreeing so readily to her request to drive her out from Bath. She was, after all, a very pretty girl. But Frances couldn't imagine for a moment that he could be seriously interested in someone so far beneath his own class that she'd worked as a garage mechanic, especially now that he was a fully qualified doctor and a partner in a practice. No, if he was going to stray, it would be with a socially acceptable girl who crossed his path. And dangling the possibility of Anne and Rosie working together would hopefully be enough to bring her daughter home and strengthen the relationship between her and Julian. She felt sure that whatever they'd fallen out over would be forgotten by now.

She'd speak to her this evening, she decided. Since Anne had

had a telephone installed in her flat, it would be better to call her there rather than try to reach her at work. Lady Hastings pushed her own telephone to the back of her desk and returned her attention to the list of people who were prepared to take in evacuees if the exodus began again, as it most certainly would before long.

It was midway through the afternoon when Freda looked up to see Tom Challis heading across the office, some paperwork in his hand. She'd left the letters he'd dictated on his desk ready for him to sign, and she hoped he wasn't coming to tell her she'd made a mistake in one of them, though quite honestly she wouldn't be surprised if he was. Her mind had been full of her plans to join the Women's Land Army.

But the paperwork he put down on her desk wasn't the letters. It was a printed form.

'Right, Miss Dobbs,' he said briskly. 'This is what you need. Fill it in and post it to the Ministry of Agriculture and Fisheries. And don't forget to include this.' He pulled a foolscap envelope out from beneath the form and tapped it. 'That's the reference I've written for you.'

'Oh, Mr Challis! Thank you! I never expected . . .'

He smiled ruefully. 'That I'd be so anxious to get rid of you? To tell the truth, I'm bloody well not. But if it's for the war effort, I don't suppose I've got much choice.'

The other typists had stopped work and were listening surreptitiously to this intriguing conversation. But they couldn't fool Tom Challis.

'Not you two as well!' he groaned. 'God knows how this country's going to manage if the menfolk can't get their beer.' He turned back to Freda. 'Just make sure you read the form properly and understand what it is they want to know before you start filling it in. It won't look good if it's full of mistakes and crossings-out. And I would say do it in your own time, but if you get it done now, it can go with the day's post.'

'You mean . . . I can use an office stamp on it?' Freda was anxious not to seem to be taking advantage. Usually all the stamps had to be accounted for to ensure the girls weren't taking liberties with them.

'Soft bugger, aren't I?' He smiled again. 'Get on with it now.' And with that he left the office.

'What was all that about?' Julie, one of the other typists, asked.

Freda told her, and both girls gazed at her in amazement and admiration. Neither of them would fancy leaving London to work on a farm, it seemed.

Freda read the form through as Mr Challis had advised, but it seemed pretty straightforward. Just her full name and whether she was Mrs or Miss, her address and her age. She didn't see how she could make silly mistakes with any of that. She hesitated, though, over a space that had been left for her to mention any training or experience she might have. She had none really, but she didn't want to leave the box blank, so she wrote in it that she had helped out with the harvest at a farm near her Somerset home. It wasn't strictly true, but she'd watched often enough, and helped the farmer's wife take lemonade along with bread, cheese and pickles to the farm workers. The next question asked whether she wanted to work in the local area only or whether she was prepared to be mobile. That made her smile. 'Local' wasn't an option here, so she put 'mobile' and followed it with a request that if possible she would like to be located in her home area, Somerset.

She reread the form while she was waiting for the ink to dry, then carefully folded it in half and slipped it into a quarto-sized manilla envelope. She hesitated again over the envelope that contained Mr Challis's reference, wondering what he had written about her and wondering if she dared take it home with her and steam it open to have a look. But if she did that, she might be too late to catch the last collection from the pillar box at the end of her road, and in any case, when she'd tried once to steam a stamp that hadn't been cancelled on a letter she'd received, she'd made a dreadful mess of it. No. She'd just have to hope that Mr Challis had said only nice things about her. Though if he really didn't want to lose her, who knew?

She slipped the reference into the manilla envelope along with the completed form, and sealed it down. All she could do now was wait – and hope that a favourable response wouldn't be long in coming. Now that she'd got this far, she could hardly wait.

She couldn't wait either to see Ron's face when she told him. Well, it served him right. She wasn't going to cry a single tear over him. He should have treated her better. Even Rosie had seen through him. And in any case, he'd probably get his call-up papers soon. Really, this war was changing everything!

At about the same time that Tom Challis was giving Freda the form he'd collected from the Land Army HQ on the other side of the river, Clarke Sutherland and the two other officers who had been sent to help set up the manor house in readiness for training prospective agents were enjoying tea and hot buttered scones in a sheltered spot in the gardens, and making the most of what might prove to be the last of an Indian summer before autumn set in.

'I wish my Alice could make scones as good as these!' Colin Stewart, whose speciality was communications, spoke through a half-chewed mouthful. Buttery crumbs fell onto his uniform jacket, but he seemed blissfully unaware of it.

'We're spoiled, for sure,' Clarke said. 'I don't suppose we'll be so lucky when things get going here. Mrs Freeman mightn't be willing to cater for so many.'

Mrs Freeman had been cook to the racehorse owner and his family in the days before he had relocated to the wilds of Exmoor, and she had agreed to continue in the post for the time being at least. At present there were just five of them rattling round in the big old house – Clarke, Stewart and Dave Thompson, an unarmed-combat instructor whom Clarke would assist as necessary, Major Firkins, who was the officer in charge, and a prim middle-aged secretary whom they knew only as Miss Mansell, who had been sent here from her usual job at the Ministry of Defence. Short, stout and sensible, she had been selected not only for her secretarial skills and general efficiency, but because it was highly unlikely that she would be subjected to the unwelcome advances that the younger and prettier secretaries would almost certainly attract from the male staff and the agents who would come here for their training.

'Look out!' Thompson warned. Clarke turned slightly in his deckchair and saw that Major Firkins was heading across the lawn in their direction.

Thompson and Stewart got to their feet, but Clarke remained where he was. He was of equal rank to the major, but even if he hadn't been, he didn't think he would have stood and saluted. The man was a pompous idiot, and Clarke thought privately that he was only here because his commanding officer had seized the opportunity to get rid of him.

'Sir.'

Thompson and Stewart spoke as one.

With a brief nod of acknowledgement, Firkins turned to Clarke.

'I'd like to see you in my office, Sutherland.'

The other two men exchanged glances, but Clarke was unfazed. 'Sure. Just as soon as I've finished my tea.' He thickened his Irish brogue as he always did when he addressed Firkins, principally because he knew it annoyed him.

'Yes. Well. Don't take too long about it.' The major turned on his heel and stalked back across the lawn.

Clarke helped himself to another scone. Firkins could jolly well wait.

Typically, Firkins had chosen what had previously been the library for his office. He had moved a leather-tooled desk and captain's chair into the alcove in front of the bay window looking out over the drive, and sat there now, Parker pen in hand, paperwork in front of him, with the intention of giving the impression of importance, Clarke thought.

'You wanted to see me,' he said casually, and pulled up a chair to face the major, raising an eyebrow quizzically.

'Yes.' Firkins put down his pen and pushed the paperwork to one side, replacing it with a notepad covered with handwriting. 'You are to leave us. Temporarily, at least.'

Clarke frowned. 'Why?'

'Patience, Sutherland.' But Firkins didn't look as happy as Clarke would have expected, given that he considered Clarke to be insolent and disrespectful. If anything, he looked almost peeved. 'Instructions from the Ministry. You are to transfer immediately to Buckinghamshire.'

'For what purpose?' Clarke asked coolly.

Firkins' lips tightened. 'It would seem your experience with explosive devices is required there. I regret to say I have not been entrusted with any further details.' He tore off the top page of his notebook and passed it across the desk to Clarke. 'This is the address. They will be expecting you tomorrow. You have been authorised to use the vehicle you were issued with when you arrived here. As to anything further, no doubt your questions will be answered when you get there.'

Totally bemused, Clarke went to his room and repacked his suitcase. He wasn't sorry to be leaving here – at present there was nowhere near enough action for his liking, and he rather relished the secrecy surrounding his summons to Buckinghamshire. Just one thing he found himself regretting. He was leaving Somerset without having had the opportunity to renew his acquaintance with Miss Rosie Mitchell. But that, he supposed, was one of the sacrifices that had to be made in time of war. He'd taken the king's shilling, and now he must earn it.

'What's the matter, my love?'

Winnie eyed her daughter anxiously across the dinner table. She'd finished her own plate of the toad-in-the-hole she'd made specially because she knew it was one of Rosie's favourites, but Rosie had only picked at it, pushing the batter to one side and taking a long time over the sausages as if she had no appetite at all. It had been the same at breakfast. Rosie had turned down her offer of scrambled eggs and opted for a bowl of cornflakes instead, saying she didn't feel like toast.

'Nothing. I'm fine.' Rosie cut off another bit of sausage, but chewed it as if doing so was an effort.

'Don't give me that. Something's up. You've been in a funny mood ever since you got back from seeing Lady Hastings last night.' Winnie pushed her plate to one side and leaned her elbows on the yellow and white checked tablecloth, looking directly at her daughter. 'Did she say something to upset you?'

'No. Just leave it, Mum, can't you?'

'Is it the first-aid class, then?'

'No! I told you, I enjoyed it.'

'Well, there's summat. And I'm not leaving this table till I know what it is.'

Rosie sighed, put down her knife and fork and pushed her own plate aside. 'I don't want to talk about it.'

'Oh love, come on. You know what they say. A trouble shared is a trouble halved. I'm your mother. And if something's upsetting you, I want to know what it is so I can see if there's anything I can do about it.'

'You can't. No one can.'

Winnie shook her head sadly, guessing where the trouble lay. There were only two things that Rosie really cared about in this world – her work at the garage, and the boy she'd been obsessed with all her life. Well, she wasn't being like this because of the garage. Yes, she'd been disappointed that Mr Bendle hadn't offered her her old job back, but she'd accepted that there just wasn't enough work to warrant taking her on. So that left Julian Edgell. Lady Hastings was the one most likely to know the ins and outs of what was going on with him, and it was since Rosie had come back from talking to her that she'd gone right into herself.

'Has Julian Edgell got engaged?' she asked bluntly. 'Is that what her ladyship wanted to talk to you about?'

'No!' Rosie said forcefully, and then added softly and sadly, 'Not that I know, anyway. It was what I'm going to do once I'm trained up in first aid she wanted to talk about. I'll finish the course in a couple of weeks' time, and she thinks I should go on to do some basic training at one of the hospitals.'

'Well, that's good, isn't it?' Winnie said, but she had the feeling it wasn't just that on her daughter's mind, and a moment later she was proved right.

'That's not all, though,' Rosie said a little awkwardly.

She was twiddling a spoon between her fingers as if reluctant to begin, and Winnie could see unshed tears sparkling in her eyes.

'She knows Julian was teaching me to drive before I went to London, and she wants him to give me some more lessons now.'

'Whatever for?' Winnie asked before she could stop herself.

'She's got some idea that I could become an ambulance driver.'

Winnie was completely taken by surprise. It seemed to her to be a lofty ambition for a girl like Rosie, but given her interest in anything with four wheels and an engine, she'd have thought she would be excited by the prospect, not worried and close to tears.

'Is that what you want?' she asked.

Rosie nodded. 'Course it is. But . . .' She hesitated, and then went on. 'I couldn't face Julian being the one to teach me. Not after what happened last time.'

'Ah.' Winnie debated whether she should ask Rosie what *had* happened, and decided to hedge. She didn't want her to clam up again.

'Well, I don't know what that was, Rosie, and I'm not sure I want to. But if you really think you'd like to drive an ambulance, I don't think you should dismiss what her ladyship has suggested out of hand. Julian seems to have put it behind him anyway. Was he funny with you when he brought you home from Bath?'

'Not really,' Rosie admitted. 'It wasn't nearly as awkward as I'd thought it would be.'

'Well there you are then. You need to put it behind you too. Don't go cutting off your nose to spite your face, my love.'

Rosie laughed, a short, mirthless sound. 'To be honest, I don't think Lady Hastings would give me the chance. You know what she's like.'

Winnie laughed too. 'I certainly do. She railroaded me and Maud into joining her WVS, and not even Maud could get out of it, though I think she's going to have another go. But I have to say, I'm really pleased I went. I haven't been out anywhere much since your dad died, and I really enjoyed the company, as well as feeling that with all this going on I can do my bit. You might find it's the same with you. Just get over the first hurdle and you'll be really glad you made the effort.'

'Perhaps you're right,' Rosie said, although she sounded less than convinced.

'Now,' Winnie got up, 'there's a rhubarb crumble keeping warm in the oven, and a jug of custard. D'you think you could manage some of that?'

'I'll try. I do love your crumble and custard.'

'Course you do.'

Rosie was still not quite back to her usual cheery self, but the cloud that had been hanging over her did seem to have lightened a bit.

She'd say no more on the subject tonight, Winnie decided, and with any luck it would all blow over and whatever it was that had driven Rosie away would be settled once and for all. Give her that boy she'd always been dotty about and an ambulance to drive and she'd be like a pig in clover. Forget all about going back to London when the war was over. Smiling to herself, she reached for a cloth and got her rhubarb crumble out of the oven.

Lady Hastings had finally managed to get hold of her daughter.

'Where on earth have you been?' she demanded when eventually Anne picked up the telephone. 'I've been trying to reach you all evening.' It wasn't an auspicious start to a conversation she'd intended to be convivial, but she was unable to contain her impatience.

'I'm sorry, Mother, but I do have a life of my own,' Anne returned tartly. 'I can't sit here waiting for a telephone call I'm not even expecting.'

Frances took a deep breath and softened her tone. 'I was worried about you. At times like this . . .'

'Nothing's happened yet, Mother.'

'No, but it will. And in any case, there are all kinds of dangers in a city at night. You're not in Hillsbridge now. You shouldn't be out on the streets alone after dark.'

'I'm not a child any more. So shall we just leave it, and you tell me the reason you have been trying to get hold of me.' Anne still sounded annoyed, and Frances thought how much her daughter had changed since she left home.

'I just wanted to hear your voice,' she said, doing her best to appeal to Anne's better nature. 'I'm sorry if I've upset you. That's the last thing I want to do. When you're a mother yourself, you'll understand.'

'I'm sure there's more to it than that,' Anne said, but the edge had gone out of her tone. 'Come on, Mother. Tell me the real reason you were so anxious to speak to me.'

Frances sighed inwardly. Anne knew her too well.

'Very well. I was ringing to tell you that Rosemary has come home from London.' She wanted to add that some young women, at least, felt a sense of duty to their mothers, but she bit her tongue. 'She's attending first-aid classes and is hoping to become an ambulance attendant,' she said instead.

'Oh, that's nice,' Anne said non-committally.

'Yes, isn't it? She wants to do her bit for the war effort. Have you thought about what you might do, dear?'

'I haven't really had time. I'm still busy packing up at the gallery.'

'But when that's all done . . .' Frances paused before going on tentatively. 'It just occurred to me, dear, that perhaps you could become an ambulance driver. You and Rosemary were always such good friends, and it would be wonderful if you and she could be a team.'

'It's a nice idea, Mother. I'll think about it. Now, if there's nothing else, I'm absolutely dead on my feet. I'm going to have a hot drink and go to bed.'

'Yes, you do that, dear. I think I shall do the same.'

'I'll give you a ring when I'm not so tired,' Anne said, offering an olive branch.

'Goodnight, Anne. Sleep tight.'

Frances put the phone down, knowing that to press her daughter further would be counter-productive. She hadn't got the response she'd been hoping for, but at least Anne hadn't hung up on her. And she'd planted the seed now. She could only hope it would grow and bear fruit. For the moment, it would have to do.

Chapter Eight

October 1939

Autumn had set in with a vengeance. There was a chill in the air along with the smell of bonfires, and the nights were drawing in at a relentless pace. A gusty wind was blowing the leaves off the trees so that they lay scattered over the lawns and in ankle-deep heaps in the woods that led down to the lake where poor little Robbie had drowned a century and a half ago.

Frances was frustrated that she had heard nothing from Anne as to whether she would come home when there was nothing more for her to do at the gallery, and to add to her bad mood a very rude man had come and taken away her precious Ford Coupe to be converted into an ambulance. Although she'd been expecting it to happen sooner or later, it had still come as a shock, and she was determined not to let the car go without a fight.

'I fail to see how a vehicle such as this can be of any use as an ambulance,' she said with hauteur.

'Well, you don't know everything, do you?' the man returned cheekily.

'Surely it doesn't have to be now?' she argued. 'I realise it may be needed eventually, but I was intending to give a nurse some instruction in it so that she would be able to drive it if necessary.'

The man stood his ground belligerently. 'I'm not gonna argue with you, missus. I've got me orders, and I'm just doin' me job.'

Frances realised she was wasting her breath.

'I trust it will be in good condition when it is returned to me,' she said, and the ill-mannered oaf had laughed scornfully.

'You'll be lucky. They'll have to take that padded roof off for a start. They'll be fitting a canvas cover that'll roll up. An' I reckon they're gonna have to cut off that tapered tail – 'tis the wrong shape – and the rumble seat'll 'ave to go to make room for a stretcher an' somewhere for a nurse to sit beside the poor bugger wot's on it.'

'Then I trust I'll be compensated for the damage,' Frances snapped.

'Well, you can apply for it, but it don't look to me as if you need it.' The man hawked loudly and spat on the doorstep.

Disgusted and infuriated, Frances had tossed him the keys, turned on her heel and gone back into the house, calling for Dimsie Trotter, her very aptly named housemaid, to come and clean the step.

Fifteen minutes or so later, she was still mourning the loss of her beloved car when the doorbell rang. Soon afterwards, Dimsie, armed with a scrubbing brush, tapped on the parlour door and poked her pinched little face round it.

''Tis Mr Edgell to see you, milady.'

'Well, show him in then,' Frances said impatiently. She wished she could get rid of Dimsie, who annoyed her intensely, but she supposed there would be next to no chance of replacing her now that girls were likely to be called up as well as the menfolk.

'In 'ere, milady?'

'If you please.' Frances simply couldn't be bothered with a sarcastic remark. It would only be lost on Dimsie anyway.

From what the maid had said, Frances had assumed her visitor was Giles Edgell. But to her surprise, it was Julian who came into the room.

'Good afternoon, Frances,' he said affably.

'Julian! When my half-witted maid said "Mr Edgell", I assumed she was announcing your father.'

'I haven't disappointed you, I hope.'

'Not at all! It's always a pleasure to see you, Julian!' It was the truth. Frances thought Giles Edgell something of a bore, and totally obsessed with his factory, while she had always had a soft spot for his son. Besides which, hadn't she been waiting for an opportunity to speak to him without actively approaching him?

'Actually, I do have a reason for being here,' he said. 'Has your car been requisitioned?'

'Unfortunately, yes. Such a nuisance.' Frances had no intention of revealing just how upset she was at the fate of her beloved coupe.

'I thought so. I'm visiting Mother and happened to see it being towed away. You'll be lost without it, I imagine, especially since you have so much war work to attend to.'

'I certainly will. I'll have to see if I can get hold of a small one. There must be some for sale since petrol rationing came in.'

'Mother and I have talked, and she asked me to enquire if you would like to borrow hers until you find something to replace your own. She rarely drives these days.'

'That is most kind of her,' Frances said graciously, though inwardly she winced at the thought of being seen in the driving seat of Jean Edgell's poky old runaround. 'Now, can I offer you something to drink? Tea, perhaps? It's a little early for a whisky, I imagine, with the sun not yet over the yardarm, as they say.'

Julian smiled. 'Thank you, Frances, that's kind, but I'm afraid I must be getting back to Bath. This was just a flying visit between surgeries and house calls to see how Mother is holding up. Goodness knows, her nerves are not good at the best of times, and with this war . . .'

Frances saw her opportunity to raise the subject of Rosie's driving lessons in a roundabout way and grasped it.

'As you know, I'm the local coordinator for the WVS,' she began. 'I have a team of ladies who are all anxious to do their bit, and I was wondering if perhaps you could spare an hour or so one evening to give them a talk on how the medical profession is preparing for what lies ahead.'

Julian frowned. 'I would, of course. But just at the moment I'm stretched to my limits. One of my partners is a reservist and has been called up, so Dr Reed and I are having to take on his patients until we're able to find a replacement. We're looking for a retired GP, perhaps, who would be willing to return to work given the current difficulties. Besides that, I'm advising on the new wing that's being built at St Mark's. You know about that, I imagine?'

'I do, yes. I believe some of our members will be volunteering as orderlies when it's ready.'

'I'm glad to hear it. We shall need all the extra hands we can get. But with all that going on, I'm afraid I simply don't have any spare time at the moment. Perhaps after Christmas? Things should have quietened down by then. Although if there is a sudden influx of patients . . .' He broke off, unwilling to verbalise what he was thinking – that if the expected bombing started, those patients might well be casualties with very serious injuries.

'I quite understand,' Frances said swiftly. 'But if you do find yourself a little less stretched, you will remember us, I hope.' She paused for a moment, giving him time to reply, and when he did not, she went on. 'There was another favour I was going to ask of you that you could perhaps bear in mind when you do see a chink of daylight in your busy schedule. Rosemary Mitchell is doing her practical nursing training – at St Mark's, as it happens. She is hoping eventually to work with the ambulance service, and it would be such a help to her if she could drive. You were giving her lessons at one time, I believe, and I wondered if you'd be willing to do so again.'

She looked at him, eyebrows raised quizzically. An expression she couldn't read flickered across his face and was gone.

'Of course, when I have the time I'll be happy to help in any way I can,' he said smoothly, 'but I'm afraid the same goes for driving lessons as for talks to the WVS. Ask me again in the new year if I forget to get back to you. And now, I'm sorry, Frances, but I really must get going, or face a waiting room full of very *im*patient patients.'

When he had left, Frances smiled to herself. She would have liked to be able to treat her WVS members to an interesting talk, but the fact that Julian had said he couldn't consider taking on anything extra until after Christmas suited her very well as far as Rosemary was concerned. It would give her extra time to lay the groundwork with Anne.

The letter must have come in the second post – it hadn't been lying on the doormat when Winnie had popped home at dinner time.

'Yes!' she exclaimed aloud as she turned it over and recognised her son's writing. Capital letters, all running into one another. Why did he always write in capitals? Hadn't they taught him joined-up writing at school? But never mind. She'd been expecting to hear from him for several weeks, and now here at last was a letter.

She took it into the kitchen, sat down at the table without even stopping to remove her coat, and tore the envelope open eagerly. But her pleasure was short-lived.

Dear Mum,

Sorry not to have written before, but it's been all go here.

I might not have the chance to write again for a bit. We're being sent to France tomorrow. They think Hitler is going to invade France like he did Austria, and we're going to back up the French army.

Don't worry, Mum. We'll soon send him packing if he's daft enough to try. I'll be back in Blighty before you know it, and if I get some leave I'll come home to see you and our Rosie.

Your loving son,
Don

She took a few deep breaths, trying to steady herself. She'd been preparing for something like this, but still it had come as a shock. She wished Rosie was here, but it would be hours yet before she got home. Since she'd been working at the hospital in Bath, Winnie never knew how late she'd be.

Should she go back up to the big house and talk it over with Maud? But Maud didn't like interruptions when she was in the middle of cooking dinner. And what could she say anyway? 'He'll be all right, Winnie,' and there wasn't much comfort in that. She couldn't know that it was true. Nobody could. Some of the lads would come back and some wouldn't. And even those that did might not be the same as when they went. Not only wounds you could see, either. You only had to look at Fred Thomas, the butcher, who couldn't speak a sentence without stammering, and whose hands shook so much that it frightened the life out of Winnie when he was cutting up the meat with a big sharp knife or a chopper. She remembered him as something of a Jack-the-lad before he'd gone off to fight in the trenches in the Great War. He'd been quite chipper about it, she remembered, and said much the same as Don was saying now. 'We'll soon show 'em! They won't know wot's 'it 'em, mark my words.' And look at him now.

Winnie went to the sideboard and got out the quarter-bottle of brandy she kept for medical emergencies. She didn't often drink, but oh my goodness, she needed one now.

There wasn't much left – she'd used some to set fire to the pudding last Christmas – but it would have to do. As the amber liquid burned her throat and ran fire into her veins, she calmed down somewhat. But it couldn't dispel the dark cloud that was hovering over, lower than it had been before. Nothing could, until this bloomin' war was over and she knew her children were safe and sound. Until then, she'd just have to weather the storm somehow.

For Rosie it was the end of a long, tiring and rather disappointing day at the hospital – so far her secondment had not lived up to expectations.

Yes, she'd known that the work she would be doing would be menial, but she'd thought that at least she would be on the wards, gaining experience of nursing alongside emptying bedpans, giving blanket baths and cleaning up spills. But as things had turned out, she'd spent little time doing any of these things. Instead she had found herself helping to prepare the prefabricated building that would provide extra wards to cater for the casualties of the expected air raids.

Although the work on the building itself was almost

completed, workmen were still trudging in and out in their dirty boots to fix up the electrics and telephone lines, paint walls and woodwork and erect curtain rails, so that cleaning up was a never-ending and seemingly pointless job. In the midst of all this there were beds and lockers to be pushed into the wards that were more or less finished and blackout blinds to be tacked over the windows, as well as endless boxes of equipment and medical supplies that had to be ticked off on an inventory. Small wonder that Rosie felt she was more of a builders' labourer and charlady than a trainee nurse.

Today had been even more arduous than usual. The blackout blinds had kept falling down, and because it had been raining, the workmen who came in and out had tracked thick mud over her freshly scrubbed floor, so that she had to do it again or risk a roasting from Matron when she did her tour of inspection. By the time Rosie reached the bus stop out on the main road, she had just missed one of the half-hourly services, and though she'd sheltered as best she could under the trees that overhung the pavement, by the time the next bus arrived she was wet through and very fed up. The rain had eased off by the time the bus pulled up in front of Hillsbridge's town hall, but it was too late for her. Her hair hung lankly across her face and the hem of her uniform skirt flapped wetly against her legs as she walked out of town heading for home.

Then, even before she'd had time to change into dry clothes, a worried Winnie had told her about the letter that had arrived from Don.

'Well, there's nothing you can do about that, Mum,' she'd said wearily. Anything else would be just weasel words, she thought, but when she saw Winnie's stricken expression, she'd used them anyway. 'He'll be all right. You know our Don. And he's got plenty of experience behind him, which is more than you can say for most of those poor lads who're getting called up.'

She'd just sat down to the evening meal Winnie had warmed up for her over a saucepan of boiling water when there was a loud knocking at the cottage door. Before Winnie could answer it, the knock came again, alarming in its urgency, and the door was opened from outside. It was Maud Hawkins.

'Oh Rosie, thank goodness you'm here!' she burst out, totally ignoring Winnie. 'Dimsie Trotter's bin an' knocked the onion soup off the stove, and scalded herself real bad. But you'll know wot to do, won't you?'

Rosie dropped the forkful of cottage pie that had been half-way to her mouth back onto her plate and got to her feet.

'All right. Don't worry, I'll come,' she said. She was trying to sound calm, but a wash of doubt was rushing through her veins. This would be the first time she'd had to put any of the first aid she'd learned into practice. Scalding and burns. Yes, they'd covered that, but could she remember what she'd been taught? 'Have you called an ambulance?' she asked.

'I don't know!' Maud wailed. 'Her ladyship fell down too – slipped on the wet floor – and can't get up. An' Sir James won't be 'ome till late.'

This was getting worse by the minute.

'D'you want me to come too?' Winnie asked.

'No . . . Yes.' Rosie was thinking quickly. She'd do what she could to alleviate the situation there and then, but if she was badly scalded, Dimsie would need proper medical attention. And if Lady Hastings really couldn't get to the telephone, Rosie was fairly sure Maud wouldn't know how to make a call. But Winnie would, leaving Rosie free to tend to Dimsie.

She hurried out. Winnie grabbed an umbrella from the hall stand beside the door in case the rain began again and followed, a somewhat reluctant Maud lagging behind.

As she approached the back door of the big house, Rosie

heard agonised moans coming from the kitchen, and for a moment, panic threatened. She swallowed it down and hurried in to be greeted by just the scene she'd dreaded.

On the flagstone floor beside the Aga, a large saucepan lay upturned amidst a flood of still steaming soup with diced onion floating in it. At least it hadn't been thickened with cornflour, which would have stuck to Dimsie's skin like glue. That was one mercy at least. But she still had two patients to attend to, and both were badly hurt from the look of them.

Lady Hastings was on her knees, grasping the overhang of the stout kitchen table with her left hand, obviously trying to pull herself up, but her face was contorted with pain and her right arm hung at an awkward angle.

'Oh, milady!' Winnie hurried to help her rise and supported her to take a seat on one of the sturdy kitchen chairs. 'Whatever 'ave you done?'

'It's broken, I think,' Lady Hastings said through gritted teeth.

'Don't worry, I'm going to ring for an ambulance an' we'll have you in hospital before you know it.' Winnie knew exactly where to find the telephone – didn't she dust it every day? – and she scurried off to make the call.

Meanwhile Rosie had hurried to Dimsie, who was perched on the very edge of another kitchen chair, shaking and rocking so violently that Rosie was afraid she would slip off at any moment. Her cries had died now to sobs and gasps, as if she had no breath or energy left, and her eyes were wild with something close to hysteria. As Rosie steadied her, she saw that both the bodice of Dimsie's blouse and its wrist-length sleeve were soaking wet and still hot to the touch.

No need to ask where the girl had been scalded. This could be very bad indeed.

'Mrs Hawkins, quickly! Get me some lukewarm water, and then fetch some towels and a blanket. Oh – and I shall need gauze and a pair of scissors.' Rosie's training had kicked in now, and her nervousness was forgotten.

'There's some gauze in that drawer,' Maud said with a nod towards the dresser as she hurried over to the sink.

Rosie found both and returned to Dimsie. 'Sorry about this,' she said, and began carefully cutting through the soaked fabric. Just as she had feared, Dimsie's upper arm was scarlet and already swollen, but even more worrying so was a large area of flesh that took in one side of her right breast and stretched down to her waist. She was going to need hospital treatment, not a doubt about it.

Maud Hawkins had filled a tin bowl with water that was neither too hot nor too cold, then gone off in search of the other things Rosie had asked for. Rosie grabbed a couple of clean tea towels from a drawer and soaked them in the water. Then she draped one across Dimsie's breast and wrapped the other around her arm.

Within minutes, Maud was back with an armful of towels and a blanket. Rosie was working almost automatically now, doing what she could to cool the scalded areas and draping the blanket around Dimsie's left shoulder to keep her warm. But a moment later, the panic threatened again when Winnie came back with the alarming news that both local ambulances had been called out on emergencies and the operator she had spoken to couldn't tell her how long it would be before they were able to get to Bramley Court.

'But Dimsie needs proper treatment urgently!' Rosie said, her tone sharp with desperation.

It was Lady Hastings who had the solution.

'Then we take her ourselves. My car has been requisitioned,

but Mrs Edgell has kindly loaned me hers. It's not up to much, but it should get us to Bath.'

'But . . . your arm . . . You won't be able to drive.'

'So, Rosemary. You'll have to.' Lady Hastings' tone was dry, mocking almost.

Rosie stared at her in disbelief. 'I can't!'

'You've had some lessons from Julian, haven't you? Now you're going to have one from me. I'll be in the front with you. It's a pretty straight road, there won't be much traffic about at this time of night, and St Mark's is this side of town. So let's not waste any more time. Put my arm in a sling and we'll be on our way.'

Rosie's head was spinning. She wasn't at all sure she could do this. It was almost two years since she'd been behind the wheel of a car, and she didn't know how much she would remember of what Julian had taught her.

She folded one of the towels into a triangle, placed it beneath her ladyship's arm and fastened it behind her neck with a safety pin, then wadded a hand towel, positioned it between the makeshift sling and her breastbone and instructed her to support her injured arm beneath the elbow in a position that was just above horizontal.

As they left, a concerned Winnie warned her to 'Be careful, my love!' and then she was in the driver's seat of the little Ford with Lady Hastings beside her and Dimsie, who was sobbing again, in the rear. The car gave one of those jolts that Julian had called kangaroo hops, and then they were moving, down the drive beneath the trees.

'Lights!' Lady Hastings barked.

'Where . . .?' But somehow, miraculously, her hand found the switch, and when the drive was a silver ribbon stretching out before her, Rosie was aware of a heady surge of exhilaration that seemed to coexist alongside the calm confidence that had over-taken her nervousness when she had been treating Dimsie. And then she was so busy concentrating on driving, she was unaware of anything else.

Along the lane, onto the main road, through the next village, after which she was negotiating the curving downhill stretch past the Three Feathers pub. There was a sharp double bend at the bottom, she knew, and she hardly needed Lady Hastings' sharp warning to 'Slow down!' Then, as the road rose again on the other side of the valley, she was yelling instructions again: 'Change gear! Second! Second!' Rosie managed it, though she wasn't proud of the crunching noise that accompanied it, but when she topped the hill and saw the road stretching out flat and empty before her, she changed up again almost effortlessly.

'Turn right here,' Lady Hastings instructed.

'I know!' Rosie didn't need to be told where St Mark's was. She'd been coming here every day since her first-aid classes had ended. She crossed the main road, turned into the narrower one towards the main entrance to the hospital, swung left. And then disaster struck.

This was the turning she took when walking to the hospital from the bus stop, but the gateway wasn't wide enough for a car. With a crunch far worse than the one when she'd first changed gear, one wing struck a stone post and the car came to an abrupt halt. Shaking, she managed to find reverse and put her foot down hard on the accelerator, but nothing happened. To her horror and embarrassment, she realised she was stuck fast on the pillar.

'Oh for heaven's sake!' Lady Hastings exclaimed. 'What on earth are you doing?'

Humiliated, close to tears of shock and shame, Rosie could speak only two words. 'I'm sorry . . .'

She attempted to get out of the car, only to find her door would open no more than a couple of inches. 'Oh no!'

'Stay where you are,' Lady Hastings ordered impatiently. 'I'll take Dimsie into the hospital to be attended to and see if I can find someone to come and help you move the car.'

Without waiting for Rosie's reply, she opened her door using her left hand and did the same with the rear door. Rosie began scrambling over the passenger seat, intending to get out and help her, but Lady Hastings was her usual decisive and competent self. By the time Rosie had climbed over the gearstick, she had Dimsie out of the car and was supporting her with her good arm.

'Stay here, I said!' she ordered, and Rosie didn't feel equal to arguing. All the stress of the last hour or so hit her at once, and as her trembling knees gave way beneath her, she sank back down onto the passenger seat, fighting back tears and wondering what in the world she was going to do. If she tried to move the car again, she would only cause more damage than she had already, but she couldn't leave it where it was, and how would she and Lady Hastings get back to Hillsbridge without it? The bus service was much reduced at this time of day, which could mean a long wait, but that wasn't the worst of it. The very thought of her ladyship travelling on the rattly bus with its worn and grubby seats that stank of stale cigarette smoke was a dreadful one. Rosie buried her face in her hands. Think! Think! But for the moment her brain seemed not to be working.

'Well, this is a pretty pickle.'

Her eyes flew open. Standing right beside her, hands thrust into the pockets of a white medical coat, was Julian. Rosie wished the ground would open up and swallow her.

'What are you doing here?' The words were out before she could stop them. She hadn't once seen him at the hospital since she'd been working here.

'Checking on a patient who's taken a turn for the worse. And a good thing I was, it seems. Frances says you've got Mother's car jammed against the pillar.'

'Are they being seen?' Rosie asked anxiously. 'Dimsie's really badly scalded. We had to get her to hospital, but Lady Hastings has a broken arm. She couldn't drive, so I had to.'

'So she tells me,' he said drily.

Rosie shuddered, imagining the tirade Lady Hastings would have unleashed.

'Let me get in then and I'll see what I can do.'

Rosie scrambled out, allowing him to slide into the driver's seat in the same way as she had got out, but doing it with a great deal more ease than she had done. She didn't dare get in beside him, but stood back, leaning against the pillar on the other side of the pathway, as he got the Ford going again and began manoeuvring it gently. Even with Julian behind the wheel she could hear small scraping sounds, but not nearly as bad as the one when she'd hit the pillar, and after a few minutes, to her intense relief, he had eased the car back onto the road.

'Thank goodness you were here!' she gasped. 'Have I done a lot of damage?'

He shrugged. 'I'm not even going to look. It's an old rust bucket anyway.'

'Honestly, I don't know where my head was. This is the way I come in every day . . . I'm training here now. I should know very well this gateway is just for pedestrians and pedal cycles.'

'At least you got Frances and Dimsie here in one piece,' Julian said. 'And as for where your head was . . . Frances says you did an amazing job administering first aid to her and poor Dimsie. It sounds as if you're going to be a very good nurse, Rosie.'

'Oh, well, I did my best . . .' Rosie said, flushing. So Lady Hastings hadn't castigated her. She'd actually praised her!

'She said you had the makings of a good driver, too – at least until you hit the pillar.'

'I didn't think I could do it,' Rosie admitted.

'Well, there you are. Life's full of surprises.' He got out of the car. 'It's all yours then. I'll bring Frances home when her arm's been attended to.'

Rosie swallowed hard. She wasn't keen on the idea of driving again just now.

Julian must have seen the anxiety that crossed her face. 'If you want to wait, you can come with us. And I'll sort out what needs to be done to this heap of junk tomorrow.'

Rosie didn't hesitate. 'Oh yes, I'll do that. Thanks, Julian.'

He took the key out of the ignition, put it in his pocket and smiled at her.

'It might be an idea if I gave you some more driving lessons. We can't have you wrecking what's left of Mother's car. And I dread to think what you'd do to an ambulance if you ever get to drive one.'

Taken completely by surprise, Rosie didn't know what to say, and didn't know what to think either. Was he really willing to repeat the scenario that had left her mortified? And if he was, did it mean things would be different this time?

'Right. I've got work to do. You'll be all right now, won't you?'

Without waiting for her reply, he strode away, heading for the hospital, leaving a stunned Rosie to follow.

Chapter Nine

November 1939

Until he had arrived at the address he'd been given by Major Firkins, Clarke couldn't imagine why he was being sent to rural Buckinghamshire. Over the course of the last year he had travelled the length and breadth of the country in his role as a bomb disposal expert, but it seemed to him that the village of Whitchurch was not a place the IRA terrorists who were waging a bombing campaign against Britain would be likely to strike. They chose places where they could inflict the most damage on ordinary people going about their business – shopping centres, railway stations and the Underground, and always in cities such as London, Manchester, Liverpool and Bristol. There had been incendiary bombs in hotels, magnesium and tear gas bombs in cinemas, letter bombs in postboxes. Ports were likely targets, as were power stations, gasworks and telephone exchanges – anything that would cause maximum disruption – and way back in January, when the campaign had begun in earnest, a bomb had exploded at an electricity pylon in Great Barr, Birmingham, cutting off the supply to the surrounding area. Clarke had been called on to defuse all manner of devices before they could cause untold damage, as well as safely disposing of hauls of explosives that had been discovered, though all too often in the beginning the first anyone knew of a ticking bomb was when it went off.

Somehow, though, he couldn't see them attacking a sleepy village in the Chilterns – it made no sense. When he arrived at the Firs, however, he had been surprised to learn that his being here had nothing whatever to do with the IRA bombings. The gabled manor house set in gated grounds had been requisitioned as a headquarters for the research and development of weapons that could be used in the fight against Hitler. And Clarke was just one of the explosives experts brought together here for a specific task.

He had scarcely had time to unpack his suitcase before he had been summoned to the modest ground-floor study that had been chosen as an office by the major who was responsible for running operations at the Firs.

The study door stood ajar, but Clarke knocked anyway, and when a gruff voice bid him enter, he was confronted by a fug of cigarette smoke. Through it he could see a man, uniformed, but with his collar unbuttoned and shirtsleeves rolled up to the elbow, and a cigarette jammed in his mouth, sitting behind a cluttered desk. He looked to be in his late thirties or early forties..

'Jefferis,' the man barked by way of introduction. Clarke looked at him with new respect. Despite appearances, he knew Major Jefferis was held in regard by those in high places – Winston Churchill, the Minister of Defence, no less.

'Right. Let's not waste time.' Jefferis waved a beefy hand, indicating that Clarke should take a seat. He pulled out the chair on his side of the desk and sat, feeling his eyes sting as the major exhaled a cloud of fresh smoke in his direction.

'I don't need to tell you this is all top secret, but I'll mention it anyway, and then we can get down to business.' Major Jefferis was clearly a man of few words, but to Clarke's relief he stubbed his cigarette out in an outsize but already overflowing ashtray. 'Now, you are no doubt aware that the Germans get most of the iron ore they need from Sweden, and we're doing everything we can to stop them getting it. There will be blockades eventually, but that's not our pigeon. What we have to do is develop a mine that can be used on their waterways. There's a bridge on the Danube – if we can destroy that, it will be another barrier to them getting the iron ore they need to make good-quality steel. And I need all the expertise I can muster to come up with the goods.'

'I'm not sure how much help I can be. I've never worked with underwater devices,' Clarke said, but the major waved his objection away.

'You know how to put a bomb together, don't you? And you'd only be kicking your heels at that place in Somerset. I don't suppose you've trained a single agent yet, have you?'

'Just the one,' Clarke said with a wry smile.

'And I don't suppose you are at liberty to disclose any details. So report to the lab first thing tomorrow morning. Seven thirty sharp.' Jefferis reached for his packet of Senior Service, extracted another cigarette and lit it. 'That's it. I'll see you then.'

The interview over, Clarke nodded, rose, and left the room not that much wiser than when he had entered it. But he had to say he rather liked the major. He couldn't have been more different to the detestable Firkins, who, like too many officers he'd known, was full of himself, puffed up with importance and a darned sight too fond of the sound of his own voice. Jefferis could be crusty, no doubt, and would waste no time in letting you know if you failed to come up to his expectations. But Clarke could live with that. And he liked the sound of the work that was being done here too. It could prove vital if the war against Hitler was to be won.

He liked, too, that Jefferis had guessed that the identity of the single agent he had trained was top secret and hadn't pressed him.

He'd been given the task while he had been in London, and his pupil hadn't been a British recruit, but a Frenchman who was organising resistance fighters in anticipation of the German occupation. Paul Clermont was more or less his own age, but had been born into an aristocratic family and would inherit his father's title along with the estate, the vineyard and the sought-after cognac they produced. Fortunately he was fluent in English. His chief reason for coming to England was to learn all he could about explosives in order to cause as many problems as possible for the Germans, and also to learn about the ways to communicate with contacts in Britain.

He'd already taken instruction in the latter and been issued with a radio by the time he was introduced to Clarke. The explosives training had mostly taken place in a dark vault far beneath the streets of the capital, and during the time they'd spent together there, and in pubs and cafés, the two men had become firm friends.

Clarke often thought of Paul, and wondered if he'd been able to teach him enough to fulfil his objectives. He wondered too how the organisation of his cell was progressing – and even if he would survive or be captured and executed. Something he really didn't care to dwell on.

No, this was a good diversion, and hopefully he could be of some use here in Buckinghamshire.

The weeks that followed had reinforced Clarke's opinion of both Jefferis and the work he was overseeing here at the Firs. And not only overseeing, but contributing to. Jefferis worked the same long hours in the lab as the other experts who had been recruited to research and develop weapons for a war that would most likely be fought on many different fronts, a white lab coat thrown on over his uniform. He was clever, too, the sort of man who was full of innovative ideas. The destruction of bridges was his speciality, but he was also something of an expert in guerilla warfare and the ways explosives could be used in that field.

A few members of the team were engineers, clever, serious-minded men, in some ways almost other-worldly. But there were also three other bomb disposal experts who were men after Clarke's own heart. After a hard day's work they liked nothing better than to relax and let their hair down over a few pints of good local ale and the inevitable whisky chasers. The village of Whitchurch – where historic timber-framed buildings abounded – was within easy walking distance, and the White Swan at the end of the high street was a pleasant hostelry that suited them admirably.

Like Clarke, none of them was in a permanent relationship – the work they did was not conducive to normal family life. Two, Ian Crombie and Stan Beck, had been married, but both marriages had ended in divorce. The strain of frequent separations and the constant fear of a knock on the door by a senior officer to break the very worst news had proved too much for their former wives. Steve Green, the third of the trio, was of the same opinion as Clarke. By far the best way to handle the dangerous path they had chosen was to remain free and single. No responsibilities. No dependants to worry about. The risks they took would affect no one but themselves. And they were going to enjoy every moment that was left to them before one day they were too slow in finding and disabling the mechanism that would set the bomb off. When something would go wrong and they would be blown to pieces.

Clarke had seen at first hand just how devastating such an occurrence could be. A bomb he and his partner had been working on had been booby-trapped. Richard Oldfield had taught Clarke everything he knew, but all that knowledge and experience hadn't saved him. He'd sent Clarke to their vehicle for a piece of specialised equipment, and Clarke had just been making his way back when the bomb had gone off. He had been thrown to the ground, deafened, cut by flying glass and sharp fragments of metal, but he had lived to tell the tale. Not so Richard, who had taken the full force of the blast and was no longer recognisable as the husband, father of two, and seasoned soldier he had been.

The loss of his friend had haunted Clarke ever since, along with the feeling of guilt that he was still alive while Richard was dead. Stupid, he knew. He'd been following Richard's instructions when the bomb had exploded. But somehow it didn't help, and he felt a compulsion to justify his lucky escape.

He'd also made up his mind that he wouldn't tie himself into a close relationship while he was still working with explosives. He didn't want to have to worry that he might leave loved ones in a similar situation.

This wasn't an entirely new decision. He'd been badly hurt once by a girl he'd been deeply in love with, and ever since then he'd avoided making himself so vulnerable again. It had been no hardship. For some reason he couldn't quite understand, the opposite sex seemed to find him attractive, and he was never short of young ladies to keep him company when he wanted it. He never made promises or led them to believe theirs was anything but a casual arrangement. And he never had second thoughts or regrets when they went their separate ways.

Which was why he was puzzled and frustrated that he couldn't get Rosie Mitchell out of his head. Even though they'd only met on that one occasion. Even though he had plenty of other things to think about.

But there was no point worrying about it. He had to make the most of his time here in Buckinghamshire before the first would-be agents arrived at the Manor in Somerset and he was sent back to teach them enough to give them some protection against the dangers they would face in occupied territory.

Winnie had taken a break from her duties and gone to the kitchen to make herself a cup of tea and have a chat with Maud, who was making bread rolls to go with the rabbit stew at lunchtime. But it wasn't long before she was wishing she hadn't. She'd barely taken a sip before Maud had started on a tirade about the war.

'Have you heard the latest? They're going to start rationing sugar and butter after Christmas. How am I supposed to cook without sugar and butter? I wouldn't care if anything were 'appening, but it's not. All a lot of fuss about nothing if you ask me.'

'Well, let's hope so,' Winnie said shortly. She didn't want to get into an argument with her friend, but if all Maud had to worry about was not being able to bake her renowned Victoria sponge cake, she was the lucky one. Just because the bombing raids they'd been expecting hadn't materialised didn't mean it had all blown over. True, the fighting seemed to be largely around Norway and Sweden, and mostly involved the navy, but the government must think Hitler was going to invade France or they wouldn't have sent thousands of troops there. Her Don among them.

She knew Maud wasn't the only one who was getting fed up with all the restrictions that were being placed on them in the name of Victory. Leaflets urged them to carry a luggage label with their name and address on it everywhere they went, as well as the identity cards they'd been issued with. Posters screamed at them from every hoarding telling them to save, dig, buy War Bonds, waste nothing, paint their window frames black – as if the hated blackout blinds weren't bad enough, and the bossy aid raid wardens all too quick to chastise them if so much as a chink of light showed.

Then there were the unlit buses and the dangers posed by the restrictions on headlamps on all motor vehicles. Only one was allowed, and that had to be half covered with cardboard. Nobody had been killed yet in Hillsbridge as far as Winnie knew, though she was sure it would only be a matter of time. She hated walking along the stretch of main road where the pavement ended, and always squeezed into the hedge as tightly as she could if she heard a car coming. The nights were drawing in fast now; before long it would be dark by four in the afternoon, and she was thinking hard about whether she would continue going to the WVS craft meetings when they fell on an evening.

But the car Lady Hastings had promised had never materialised, and there was nothing she could do about Rosie having to walk along the same stretch when the bus bringing her home from a shift at the hospital dropped her off at the stop up on the main road. She knew she would be wasting her breath asking her to give it up until spring and the lighter nights, even though as yet there was none of the influx of extra patients they had prepared for. And each night she worried herself stiff until she heard Rosie's 'It's me, Mum! I'm home!'

No, all in all she thought Maud didn't know how lucky she was. The rationing wasn't even due to start until the new year – Maud would still be able to make a Christmas cake and mince pies as she always did.

'They say it'll be meat and cheese next. An' goodness knows

what else! We'm more likely to starve to death than get killed by a German bomb.' Maud slapped a lump of dough that had been set aside to rise onto her pastry board and kneaded it vigorously. 'But they've got money to waste on stirrup pumps. Everybody I know 'as 'ad one delivered. What's all that about?'

'So we can deal with incendiary bombs if our houses get hit and catch fire,' Winnie said.

As if to take out her frustration on the dough, Maud pounded it far more roughly than was strictly necessary.

'Well, I can't see that pootling little thing being much use if me house was going up in flames,' she declared. 'An' usin' it would give anybody a heart attack. Bloomin' ridiculous if you ask me.'

'I know some of it's a bit irritating, Maud, but you might be glad you're prepared if the worst happens.'

Maud snorted. 'Hmm! There was more killed in that pit explosion than by bombs, incendiary or any other bloomin' sort.'

Winnie knew she was referring to a mine disaster somewhere in Scotland a few weeks ago that had killed twenty-eight men. It was a terrible thing, of course. Living in an area where coal was mined, it was easy to empathise with those involved, and their loved ones. But twenty-eight lives lost would be just a drop in the ocean of tears when Hitler really got the bit between his teeth.

'I think you're in for a shock, Maud,' she said. 'Look at what happened in the last war. You've only got to read the names on our war memorial – and the others in every town and village all over the country – to know how many men and boys died before it was over. I hope and pray it won't be as bad as that, but I'm darned sure of one thing – it'll be a whole lot more than twenty-eight.'

Maud huffed. 'I'm surprised at you, Winnie Mitchell. I never 'ad you down for a doom monger.'

'I'm going, Maud, before I say something I regret.' Winnie drank the last of her tea, took her cup to the sink and swilled it out under the cold tap. Then, without another word, she headed for the door, leaving a startled Maud to stare after her in shocked astonishment.

Rosie had scarcely set eyes on Julian since the night of Dimsie's accident. Just occasionally she caught a glimpse of him on one of the wards or hurrying along a corridor, and if he saw her too he would smile and wave or say hello. But that was the extent of it. She didn't think he'd been home either, or if he had, she hadn't seen him, and she hoped he wasn't staying away to avoid her.

She'd gone over and over what he'd said that evening when he'd dislodged his mother's car from the pillar outside the hospital, cringing with shame that she could have been so stupid as to try and drive through the narrow pedestrian entrance, but also feeling a warm glow of hope that from the way he'd talked to her, that dreadful last encounter before she'd left to go to London might never have been. He might have been the old Julian, teasing her gently but warm and concerned.

It might be an idea if I gave you some more driving lessons, he'd said. Could it be that he was prepared to give her another chance? Perhaps regretting the things he'd said to her that awful evening when she'd made an utter fool of herself? Was it possible he wished he'd reacted differently when she'd revealed the way she felt about him? She was beginning to wonder if she'd misread him entirely. Somehow she couldn't give up all hope.

The new wards were finished now and ready for the expected influx of patients, so there was less work for Rosie there – nothing but a bit of dusting and sweeping and polishing the floor once a week or so. The rest of the time she spent in the main hospital. But she was still dissatisfied with the role she seemed to have been assigned, which amounted mainly to that of general dogsbody. She took bedpans to patients who were not well enough to get to the toilet at the end of the ward, then emptied and washed them in the sluice. She accompanied those who could make it but needed assistance, which was often just as bad since she was expected to ensure that the toilets were left sparkling clean. She mopped up vomit and scrubbed bedside tables and gave grumbling geriatrics bed baths – the nearest she came to any proper nursing. Sometimes she wondered why she'd had to attend the first-aid classes, and worried that by the time she was actually called on to use what she'd learned, she'd have forgotten it all.

She'd confided her concerns to Petra Jenkins, a first-year probationer who was one of the few proper nurses who didn't treat her like an imbecilic skivvy. Petra had loaned her some of her nursing manuals, and Rosie studied them whenever she had a spare minute, determined that when her chance eventually came, she'd be up to the challenge.

Her only comfort was that she'd done all the right things when Dimsie had scalded herself and Lady Hastings had broken her arm. She made up her mind to concentrate on doing all the unpleasant tasks well, so that at some point, hopefully, Sister would decide to let her move on to doing some actual nursing.

Then, quite unexpectedly, everything changed.

It had been one of those dark, depressing November days when it never seemed to get properly light. Rain fell intermittently from a leaden sky and a thick mist hung over the bowl in the hills where Bath sat, so that from the higher ground around the hospital the city was lost in a murky grey soup. As evening approached, it closed in even more and the traffic, cars, buses and the occasional lorry, moved through the fug like spectres, indistinct shapes that only became fully formed at a distance of a few feet when their headlights, half obscured by the obligatory cardboard shutters, pierced the gloom.

Almost inevitably there were accidents, minor shunts and buckled fenders, but there weren't many pedestrians. Sensible people had stayed indoors or, if they had ventured out, gone home early when darkness fell. But clearly not the woman who was brought in to St Mark's following an accident not far from the hospital.

Apparently she had been trying to cross the road to get to her house when she'd been hit by a bicycle. The fog had not only made for poor visibility, it muffled sound too, and neither she nor the cyclist had realised the other was there until it was too late. The cyclist, it seemed, was more or less unhurt. He'd picked himself up and ridden off nursing nothing more than a few bruises and a nasty graze or two. But the poor woman was in quite a lot of pain from what seemed to be cracked ribs and a shoulder that might be dislocated.

Rosie had nothing to do with her care, of course. The accident and emergency doctor and nurses were tending to her injuries. But she'd had her two children with her, a boy of three or four and a toddler in a pushchair. Neither of them had been hit by the bicycle, but both were clearly distressed, and needed to be looked after. But a problem had arisen. Their father, it transpired, was a bus conductor and was working today on one of the country routes, which should be an hour-long round trip but in this weather was likely to be longer. It would be a while before he was back in Bath, and there was no way he could be contacted until then.

As usual when it came to jobs that didn't require trained staff, it was Rosie who was detailed to look after the children until their father, or some other relative, turned up. Even when their mother been treated, it had been deemed that she would be unfit to leave the hospital alone, and certainly not with two small children.

For once, Rosie didn't mind in the least. She collected some toys, crayons and colouring books from the children's ward, and took the pair into a vacant office. When she'd calmed him down, the older boy couldn't wait to get started on colouring in some of the pictures in the book, and Rosie sat down on the floor with the toddler and a cart of bright wooden bricks. The little mite was still crying and looking around for his mother, but when she began building a tower with the bricks, he started to take an interest, knocking them down and waiting for her to build them up again. Eventually she was able to persuade him to stand up, wobbling precariously as he hung onto the handle of the little cart. She reloaded the bricks and supported him as he took one tentative step and then another. Before long he was venturing boldly around the room, falling over when the cart collided with a piece of furniture, but pulling himself up and starting off again with a comically determined expression on his face.

'This is fun, isn't it?' she said, hoping he wouldn't tire of the game too soon.

The older boy had finished colouring in a picture of a little girl carrying a large stripy umbrella. He slid down from his chair and brought it over to show Rosie, who was still sitting on the floor.

'Amazing!' she told him. 'Do you know the colours you've used?'

'Course I do! That's easy.'

'Go on then – tell me. What colour is the girl's coat?'

'Red.'

'And her hair?'

'Yellow.'

Perhaps jealous of the attention his big brother was getting, the toddler suddenly made a rush for Rosie. The brick cart collided with her haunch and toppled over, the toddler lost his balance and landed in her lap, and the older boy took a sharp step away, holding his precious artwork out of harm's way, and tumbled over too.

'My picture!' he wailed.

'It's fine. No harm done. Let your brother see what you've done.' Rosie put an arm round the older boy's waist, pulling him close enough for the toddler to see. And at that very moment a voice from the doorway made her start.

'What's going on here then?'

It was Julian.

Hot colour rushed to Rosie's face and she hastily straightened her skirt, which had rumpled up above her knees. All this time she'd scarcely seen Julian, and he had to choose this very moment when she must look an utter wreck to put in an appearance.

The toddler was wriggling free, backing away and gazing in alarm at the strange man who had invaded his safe space.

'It's all right, I don't bite,' Julian said reassuringly, and to Rosie: 'I heard you were looking after these two rascals. But I think their father is here now, so you won't have to put up with their mischief for much longer.'

'Oh, I don't mind,' Rosie said. 'I've quite enjoyed it. And they've been no trouble really.'

'I'm glad to hear it.'

'Daddy's here?' the older boy asked, his eyes bright with hope.

'Yes. And you'll be able to see your mother soon, too. But no throwing yourselves into her arms. We don't want you hurting her shoulder again.'

'It was dislocated?' Rosie asked, fairly confident that the children were far too young to understand what that meant.

Julian nodded. 'It took two of us to get it back in. It's lucky I came over to check on one of my patients. Ah . . . here's your father now,' he said to the boys, who instantly ran to him.

The man, still in his bus conductor's uniform, scooped up both children, clearly relieved to see they were unharmed and no longer unduly upset by what had happened.

'D'you want to come and see your ma, then?' he asked them, and both nodded vigorously.

'Well,' Julian said when they had gone, 'it looks as if you missed your calling, Rosie. You should be a nanny, not a nurse.'

'I haven't had much chance to do any nursing,' Rosie said ruefully. 'Matron seems to think I'm good for nothing but cleaning up after the qualified staff.'

'Hmm.' Julian frowned. 'Have you applied yet to become an ambulance attendant?'

Rosie shook her head. 'I didn't think I had enough experience for that.'

'That's going to change if I have anything to do with it,' he said firmly. 'You're just the sort of young woman we shall need very badly. We don't want you deciding to leave us. That would be a terrible waste.'

'That's kind of you,' Rosie said.

'Not kind. Just taking the sensible view. You came here as a trainee nurse, not a skivvy. Matron can be a tartar, I know. Very old-school and stuck in her ways. I shall have a word with her myself.'

'Thank you,' Rosie said, only hoping that Julian's intervention wouldn't make things worse for her. But even Matron would have respect for a doctor, surely?

Julian looked at his watch. 'Your shift finished long ago, didn't it?'

'I suppose. But there was no one else to take care of the two boys. I'll go now that I know they're in good hands.'

'I've finished for the day too – unless some other emergency crops up. I'll run you home.'

Rosie's heart flipped and a wave of panic washed over her.

'Oh, I couldn't put you out again . . .'

'Don't be silly. You'll have to wait goodness knows how long for a bus, and it's a filthy night. It's not very safe either, as witness what happened to the mother of those boys, and it's pitch dark now as well as foggy. Frances tells me your mother is already nervous about you walking along the lane where there's no pavement late at night.' He smiled. 'No driving lesson in this weather, though. But it shouldn't be long before we can begin. I think I've persuaded Dr Hamilton to come back and help me out – he's the doctor who retired when I bought into the practice. Not that he took much persuading. I think he's bored to tears now the golf course is too soggy to get a decent game, and he's driving his poor wife to distraction.'

Rosie's stomach gave another flip, though whether from excitement or nerves she couldn't be certain.

'Are you sure? I wouldn't like to think Lady Hastings has bullied you into it,' she said.

He shook his head, smiling. 'Not this time. I've missed you, Rosie.'

This time there was no mistaking it. The flip in her tummy was excitement. Pure, heart-lifting joy. But Julian gave her no time to savour it.

'How is Frances, by the way? Her arm is still in plaster, I imagine.'

'Yes, but it doesn't seem to be bothering her too much. From what Mum says, she's still managing to run her WVS as efficiently as ever.'

Julian smiled. 'Yes, I can't imagine she would let a little thing like a broken arm stop her. What about the maid?'

'She's still off work. She's been in a lot of pain. And she's probably going to be left with some scarring. She's pretty depressed, I think.'

'I'm sure she is. It's not a nice prospect for a young girl. But it could have been a lot worse if you hadn't done all the right things straight away.'

'Well, I hope I did,' Rosie said, flushing at the praise.

'Come on now, get your coat. You'll certainly need it.' Julian was all business now, but warmth was still flooding through Rosie's veins. Perhaps there was hope for her after all.

Chapter Ten

Christmas was quite unlike any other Rosie had known. As usual, they were invited along with all the other staff to the big house on Christmas Eve for mince pies and a glass of sherry, but this year it was a quiet affair. The two gardener's boys had both been called up for military service, and Dimsie, who had not yet returned to work, was not well enough to attend. Maud Hawkins was buttonholing Eric Nash, the gardener who had taken Ern's place, while Walt, her husband, did his best to merge into the background. Rosie felt sorry for him; she could see he wanted to be anywhere but here. And she guessed Maud had bullied him into wearing what was probably the suit he was married in twenty or more years ago – the high buttoned jacket strained across his chest, and she'd spotted what looked suspiciously like a moth hole or two.

Polly, the housemaid, had brought along her sister for support; Sir James's agent and his wife, and his secretary and her fiancé were the only other guests.

Sir James was dispensing the sherry in between rewinding the gramophone and changing the records. Lady Hastings herself was handing round the mince pies, balancing the plate on the cast on her arm, but the mood was awkward and sombre and the absence of the younger generation left a gaping hole that not even the rich, gravelly tones of Louis Armstrong could lift. In years gone by, 'Zat You, Santa Claus?' had got them jiving, but now simply tapping her toe to the compelling beat made Rosie feel sad.

It was inevitable, of course, that Philip Hastings would be missing. With the threat of invasion hanging over them, there would be no leave for the pilots of the RAF. But she'd thought Anne would have been here, and maybe Julian too.

She took her glass of sherry to the padded window seat and sipped it, memories of the old days flooding back, when the whole house had been ablaze with light – from the windows to welcome the guests, from the giant Christmas tree in the hall, shimmering with tiny red wax candles in their silvery holders on every branch, from the chandeliers, and from the roaring fire that sent flames of red and orange up the drawing room chimney. As a child, Rosie had hoped the fire would be out before Father Christmas made his descent with a bulging sack of presents. The mantelpiece had been garlanded with ivy and pure white Christmas roses, sprigs of holly had been tucked into every picture and bunches of mistletoe hung over the doorways.

There had been dishes of bonbons – sugar-coated almonds, soft chocolate truffles and dates stuffed with almond paste – for the children, and boxes of exotic cigarettes for the adults – Sobranie Black Russians with their gold filter tips, and the slender Sobranie Cocktails in shades of pink, mauve, green and yellow. Postcards were always scattered around the room, each bearing a clue for the traditional treasure hunt that would send the children scampering all over the house in search of the hidden prize, and there were party games too, Pass the Parcel and Pin the Tail on the Donkey.

Later on, a favourite game had been Sardines. Well, it had been Rosie's favourite, because sometimes she was lucky enough to find herself squashed into a hiding place with Julian. And later still, the dancing. The furniture would be pushed aside to clear a space where the older folk could waltz sedately while the younger generation jitterbugged and jived. Once, much to her embarrassment, her mum and dad had performed the dance of their youth – the Charleston – and everyone else had stopped dancing to watch and applaud.

But the war had put a stop to all that. How long would it go on? she wondered. And how would their lives be changed before it was over? For a horrible moment the most awful feeling of foreboding overcame her, and she tried to push it aside by reminding herself of the one bright spot – because of the war, she was connecting with Julian again. But she was afraid even to dwell on that. She mustn't read too much into it. That way lay the very real possibility of yet more heartache and disappointment.

'More sherry?' She hadn't noticed Sir James was doing the rounds again with his tray of drinks.

'Oh . . . I don't know if I should,' Rosie demurred.

'Of course you should! It's Christmas!' His lordship took her empty glass and handed her a fresh one.

With an effort Rosie snapped out of her doleful reverie. He was doing his best to make the party go well, even if it was an uphill task. She forced a smile and raised the glass in a toast.

'Merry Christmas!'

Sir James helped himself to the last remaining glass on his tray and touched the rim to hers. 'And to you, my dear. If anyone deserves it, you do.'

Freda had decided to spend Christmas in London with her friends rather than going home. Since she was soon going to be a land girl, hopefully back in the West Country, this might be the last time they could celebrate together. Now, however, she was feeling much as Rosie was. Dark streets, strangely silent. Few motor vehicles, and many fewer revellers since so many young men had been called up. Shuttered windows and blackout blinds instead of well-lit Christmassy displays. Barrage balloons obscuring the moon instead of sky rockets soaring and exploding in bright clusters of stars. Pubs and bars with sandbags piled up beside the entrances muffling the tinkling of the 'old Joanna' and tipsy voices belting out songs and carols within.

On a night out, she and her friends had attempted to get into the Christmas spirit by doing the Lambeth Walk, but their hearts weren't in it and now they walked arm in arm along the middle of the street, subdued by the evidence that this was no bad dream from which they'd soon awaken. Missing their boyfriends. Missing the exuberance and all the old traditions just as Rosie was. Anxious about what lay ahead.

Freda couldn't wait to get away from London now. The spring, when she'd be posted to a farm somewhere in the countryside, seemed far, far away. Who knew what might happen before then? She shuddered at the thought of the sirens wailing, not as a practice run, but for real. The drone of heavy German bombers overhead. Running up to the Elephant and Castle to take shelter in the Underground along with hundreds of others. Perhaps, when daylight came, returning to find Granny's house nothing but a heap of rubble . . .

They were nearing the Old Justice public house. It was impossible to go far in Bermondsey without passing a pub; there were so many that locals usually gave strangers directions by naming the ones they needed to pass to reach their destination.

'Oh, I could murder a drink!' exclaimed Julie, and the others agreed. Yes, the Old Justice might look shut up from the outside, but thin slivers of light could be seen around the door frame – the air raid warden was a regular drinker there, and was turning a blind eye to the infringement, which was hardly likely to be visible from the skies in any case. The girls could hear the piano too, as the regular pianist thumped out old music hall numbers, and they knew there would be a blazing fire to warm themselves by behind a thick fire guard – a precaution against flying sparks since the interior was all mocked-up Tudor wood.

'Let's get one then!' Freda said.

It wasn't usual for groups of girls to go into pubs, but tonight the prospect was too tempting to resist. They went in, bought pints of good ale, and joined in the singing. And for a little while Freda was able to forget how lonely she was since Rosie had gone home to Somerset.

The soirée at Bramley Court was winding down – not that it had ever really got going. Eric Nash and his wife were about to leave, and Rosie could see that Maud's poor husband was itching to do the same. But Maud wasn't ready to go yet. She'd cornered Winnie now and was, as usual, complaining about anything and everything in an embarrassingly loud whisper.

'Fancy only sherry! 'Tisn't as if they'm short of a penny or two.'

'Shh! They'll hear you!' Winnie cautioned, looking around anxiously, but Lady Hastings was preparing to see Eric and his wife out and Sir James had disappeared momentarily.

'I don't care if they do!' Maud said defiantly. 'I was looking forward to a nice drop of gin and orange. An' before you say they never do spirits, it wouldn't 'ave 'urt them to splash out a bit this year seeing as there's so few of us.'

'I expect they like to keep it simple seeing as how they do all the serving themselves for our Christmas do.' Winnie was determined to stand up for their hosts. It was good of them to invite the staff into their home and wait on them for a change, and she didn't like to hear Maud running them down even if they were out of earshot.

Maud huffed disparagingly. 'An' they ruined my mince pies good and proper trying to hot them up. Gentry haven't got a clue how to use the Aga, and can't lower themselves to ask.'

'They were still nice,' Winnie ventured, trying to appease her friend. 'Your pastry's always a treat, Maud.' But her efforts went unrewarded.

'Not when it's all dried up and scorched,' Maud sniffed. ''Twould 'ave bin better to serve 'em cold than try to warm 'em up and leave 'em in the oven too long.'

'Goodnight, Mrs Mitchell. Goodnight, Mrs Hawkins,' Eric Nash called over his shoulder as Lady Hastings ushered him to the door.

'Goodnight! And happy Christmas!' Winnie called back. 'It's time we were thinking about making a move too,' she said to Maud.

'Well, I'm goin' to 'ave another sherry if there's one on offer,' Maud said. 'It's not as if we've got work tomorrow, an' we might as well make the most of it.'

'Aren't you cooking Christmas dinner for them?' Winnie asked, surprised.

'No, they're goin' over to the Edgells'. I 'spect that's why they're not 'ere tonight. Good thing too. She's a proper stuck-up one, Mrs Edgell. Just because they've made their fortune, she thinks she's better'n us.'

Winnie had had enough. 'I wish you wouldn't run everybody down, Maud. It's not nice, and when you do it in such a loud voice that they can hear . . .'

'But they bain't here!'

'I know, but you'd still do if it they were. You just don't know how loud you talk. I think you ought to get something to help you hear better.'

Maud snorted. 'If you think I'm going to make a fool of meself walkin' round with an ear trumpet . . .'

'You can get little things that go in your ear now,' Winnie said.

'Oh ah? An' where would I find the money for that?' Maud spluttered.

Voices could be heard coming from the hallway, and not those of the Nashes. Lady Hastings, yes, and another woman, equally well spoken. For all the world it sounded like . . .

'Anne!' Winnie exclaimed. 'She must have decided to come home for Christmas after all! Oh, Lady Hastings will be so pleased!'

'Hmm. Your Rosie don't look too thrilled, though,' Maud said tartly.

It wasn't that Rosie was displeased. More that she was embarrassed. It was, after all, two years since she and Anne had met, and she didn't know if Anne had ever found out what had happened between her and Julian. Or, indeed, how close the two of them were now.

Anne was wearing a calf-length camel coat, high boots, and a brown fur hat pulled well down to frame a face that was rosy from the cold. To Rosie she looked older somehow, though perhaps sophisticated would have been a more accurate description. She smiled at the guests who were still there.

'How lovely to see you all. And Rosie . . .'

Their eyes met and the layer of sophistication was stripped away. Anne looked awkward suddenly, as awkward as Rosie was feeling, and in that moment it was clear that she did know that something had been going on between her and Julian. Well, not all of it, hopefully. Oh please not that. But enough.

Rosie forced a smile. 'Anne.'

'It's been so long, Rosie!' Anne said. 'How are you?'

Rosie was saved by the appearance of Sir James.

'Anne! Darling! What a lovely surprise! We weren't expecting you!'

'Oh, Daddy!' Anne went to him, and as they hugged, Winnie, who had been all too aware of Rosie's discomfort, took the opportunity to buttonhole Lady Hastings.

'We really must be going, milady.'

'So soon?' Lady Hastings turned to Rosie. 'You'll stay, won't you, Rosie? I'm sure you and Anne would love to have a nice long chat.'

'Not tonight, milady,' Winnie said firmly.

'Well, you must come back another time, Rosemary. Not tomorrow, of course – we shall be with Giles and Jean, and Julian too, perhaps. His parents are hoping he will be able to join us.' She cast a quick glance in Anne's direction. 'I'm sure when he knows Anne is here he'll make the time, however busy he might be. It is Christmas Day, after all!'

Winnie nodded. 'It certainly is.' She put a hand under Rosie's elbow, guiding her towards the door. 'Don't worry about seeing us out, milady. I know the way – I should do! But thank you for your hospitality. It's much appreciated.'

'Oh, Mrs Mitchell, think nothing of it. It's just a small token of our appreciation for all the hard work you do for us. And of course your commitment to the WVS.' She turned to Rosie. 'Boxing Day, perhaps? Eleven, shall we say?'

Rosie floundered helplessly. How was it that Lady Hastings could turn her every request into an obligation it was impossible to refuse?

'Thanks again, milady,' Winnie said, and ushered Rosie to the door.

'That was a surprise, Anne turning up,' Winnie said as she and Rosie walked back to their cottage. 'Mind you, I'd have thought she'd have come home for Christmas anyway.' Rosie was silent. 'You didn't want to see her, did you?' Winnie went on.

'Not really,' Rosie admitted.

'Well, you mustn't let Lady Hastings bully you into it then. She can be very overbearing at times.' Winnie paused, hunting in her bag for her door key. 'But maybe it's time you and Anne made up. It's not worth falling out with a good friend over a boy.'

A boy. That almost made Rosie smile. It was a long time since Julian had been a boy. But she let it slide.

'We never actually fell out,' she said. 'But I couldn't face either of them.'

'And now?' Winnie prompted. 'You seem to have got over whatever the problem was with Julian.'

But that of course went to the heart of the matter. It wasn't just the past that made Rosie reluctant to get close to Anne again. It was what was happening now.

If she and Anne had a heart-to-heart, she'd have to tell her that it was possible she and Julian would be getting together. He had said he missed her, after all, and that was probably the closest he was likely to come to admitting his feelings for her. But she still dreaded the thought of breaking it to Anne.

It was sad, really, she thought. They'd shared so much of their growing-up years, the laughter and tears, their hopes and dreams; even the fact that they were both in love with Julian had been a bond rather than an obstacle to be overcome. If they were ever to become friends again, she couldn't keep a relationship with Julian secret. Perhaps she should tell Anne about her feelings for him now, so that at least it wouldn't come as a dreadful shock later. She couldn't then accuse Rosie of going behind her back. But the very thought of it made Rosie feel sick with apprehension. If Anne was still in love with Julian, she would be terribly hurt. And if nothing ever came of it, she'd have spoiled their relationship for ever when there was no need.

No, it would be best to keep her secrets a little longer. Better still, she'd stay away from Bramley Court – and Anne – altogether.

Winnie's voice interrupted her reverie. 'So what are you going to do?'

'I'm not sure,' Rosie said. But she was lying.

The last of the visitors had left, and although she was not strictly on duty this evening, Polly had cleared away the used sherry glasses and was washing them up in the kitchen. Sir James had followed her and picked up a tea towel.

'Oh sir, you don't need to!' she protested, looking surprised.

'Nonsense! This is your evening off. It's a bad job if I can't help you by drying a few glasses.'

Truth to tell, consideration for the maid wasn't Sir James's only reason for absenting himself from the drawing room. He had a feeling that Frances wanted to talk to Anne alone. But he was also afraid that what she had to say might well lead to a disagreement, and he would be called upon to arbitrate. He didn't want to have to do that. Frances would expect him to back her up, and actually he agreed with her. Though Anne was a grown woman now, to him she was still his little girl, and his first instinct was to protect her. But neither did he want to upset her. She came home all too seldom these days, something he regretted. There had always been a strong bond between them – wasn't that the way between fathers and daughters, just as it was between mothers and sons? But Philip wasn't here and Anne was. Frances was determined that here she would stay and when Frances's mind was made up about something, she wouldn't let it go, come hell or high water.

No, Sir James didn't want to be drawn into this. But he

couldn't help hoping that Frances would win the day. It would be good to have Anne at home again.

'I wish you hadn't made arrangements for Rosie to come and see me, Mother,' Anne said when they were alone.

Frances bristled. 'Why so? I thought it was what you would want.'

'Exactly. You thought. I'm not a child any more, and I don't need you to think you know what's best for me.'

'But surely . . . You and Rosemary were always such good friends. Why would you not want to see her?'

'You're missing the point, Mother. When Rosie and I meet is for us to decide, not you.'

Frances sighed, exasperated. 'If it was left to you, Anne, you'd never make your mind up about anything. Well, it's arranged now. She's coming on Boxing Day and I'm sure you will be very glad that you can renew your friendship, considering she has had the good sense to come home for the duration of the war and you will be here too.'

Anne reached for a clean glass that had been left on the silver salver and poured herself a sherry.

'That's just it, Mother,' she said. 'I don't know that I will be here.'

'But we agreed. It's much safer here than in Bristol. Your gallery will be closed, and I could really use your help here. My WVS—'

'You see? There you go again.' Anne sighed and swallowed her sherry in one gulp. 'We didn't agree anything. You decided, and assumed that I'd go along with it. Look, Mother, I don't want to fall out, but I have to tell you, one of the reasons I went to Bristol in the first place was so that I could make decisions for myself.'

'Well!' For once Frances was almost speechless. 'I've never

done or said anything that wasn't for your own good. Yes, I admit I'd like to see you and Julian together. And I thought you wanted that too. As for what war work you decide on, that's your choice entirely. Rosemary is training as a nurse, but what she really wants is to work on an ambulance, and I am only too pleased to help her achieve her ambition. You could do the same. You could be a driver, she could be the attendant. You'd make a wonderful team. And since Julian is in practice in Bath, you'd see plenty of him too.' She paused, confident now that she had made an argument that Anne would have to see was the perfect solution.

Anne closed her eyes momentarily, then sighed and shook her head. 'You simply can't help yourself, can you? And if I came home, it would be just the same as it always was.'

'So?' Frances spread her arms wide. 'If you don't come home, what will you do? You'll be called up for service, you know that, don't you? Pushed into whatever cubbyhole they decide. Much better that you take the initiative.'

'Which is just what I intend to do.' Anne raised her eyes to meet Frances's. 'I've decided I'm going to join the WAAF. In fact, I've already put in my application, and as soon as my job packing up the gallery comes to an end, I shall begin my training.'

Chapter Eleven

For Rosie, Christmas Day had been overshadowed by anxiety. She was dreading having to face Anne and although Winnie had said she shouldn't let Lady Hastings bully her, Rosie didn't feel she could risk offending her. Since she was Winnie's employer and her husband owned her cottage, that really wasn't wise. Nevertheless, the prospect filled her with dread.

She wondered if Anne was as reluctant as she was to meet. If so, perhaps she might cut her visit short and go back to Bristol. It was Rosie's only hope. But on Boxing Day morning Anne's car was still parked where she had left it, close to the house, and Rosie steeled herself for the inevitable, watching the hands of the clock move inexorably towards the appointed time. Ten o'clock. A quarter past. She was dressed now in her best day frock, but she felt anything but ready. Her heart was thudding and her stomach tied in knots as if the breakfast she'd managed to eat had curdled and given her indigestion.

She was in her bedroom applying a touch of lipstick when she heard a knock at the front door, and Winnie called up the stairs to her. 'Rosie! Can you come down? Anne's here.'

Her stomach jolted again. Oh my God. She'd assumed her ladyship had meant for her to go to Bramley Court, not that

Anne would come here. And had she mistaken the time? Perhaps Frances had said ten, not eleven.

'Coming,' she called, and headed for the stairs.

Anne was in the hallway. She was wearing the same coat, fur hat and boots as when she'd arrived on Christmas Eve.

'Anne!' Rosie greeted her. 'I thought I was supposed to come to you.'

'That was Mother's plan,' Anne said drily. 'But I thought we could go for a walk instead.'

'Oh – yes, good idea.' Probably Anne didn't want her mother eavesdropping on their conversation. 'I'll just get my coat.'

'You'll need it,' Anne said. 'The sun's nice, but it's cold and frosty.'

It certainly was. As they emerged into the brittle sunshine, the bitterly cold air stung Rosie's cheeks.

'I thought we could walk down towards the woods,' Anne suggested.

'Why not?' The frosted grass crunched beneath their feet as they stepped onto the lawn.

'It's good to see you, Rosie,' Anne said. 'It's been so long. Mother tells me you're at St Mark's, training as a nurse.'

'Yes. For the time being.'

Although she had decided not to mention Julian yet, Rosie realised this was an ideal opportunity to tell Anne that she was hoping to transfer to ambulance work, as an attendant or even a driver, and that Julian might teach her to drive, but somehow she couldn't bring herself to seize it.

'What about you?' she asked instead. 'You'll be coming home to help your mother out with her WVS, I expect. She's roping everyone in. She's even got Mum involved, though I think Maud Hawkins is proving something of a challenge.'

Anne laughed shortly. 'You could say that. I do think she's

met her match in Maud. But no, I won't be coming home. I've decided that when everything has been finalised at the gallery, I'm going to join the WAAF. The Women's Auxiliary Air Force.'

Rosie stopped walking, looking at her old friend in amazement. 'The WAAF! Goodness!'

'Don't sound so surprised,' Anne said. 'It makes perfect sense to me. Philip is in the RAF, remember – a pilot. I felt I wanted to do something to support him. In communications, perhaps. You never know, I might get to hear his voice if he's flying and reporting back.'

'But what if . . .' Rosie hardly liked to put into words the very first thought that had occurred to her.

'You mean there's always the possibility I might hear that he's missing? Or worse?'

Rosie shivered. 'That would be just so awful . . .' Her voice tailed off; she didn't even want to think about it.

'At least I'd know,' Anne said, and Rosie was surprised all over again at the strength that lay beneath her seeming vulnerability.

'Mother is horrified, of course,' Anne went on. 'She wants me here. So that there's at least one of us she can still control.'

Rosie felt a moment's sympathy for Frances.

'I'm sure that's not it, Anne. She just wants you to be safe. I imagine an airbase, or wherever you'd be working would be a prime target for the Germans. As likely to be bombed as a city with docks and aeroplane factories.'

'You don't know the half of it,' Anne said, bitterness creeping into her tone. 'But enough about me. Mother tells me that when you're fully trained, you're hoping to become an ambulance attendant. She even suggested I could become a driver – that we'd make a good team. Then, when she discovered that wasn't going to happen, she said she was going to get Julian to give you some more driving lessons so that *you* could be an ambulance driver. I can only think that's a form of blackmail. Don't you agree?'

Her eyes, hard and challenging, met Rosie's and colour that had nothing to do with the cold frosty air and everything to do with guilt and shame flamed in her cheeks.

'Anne, I am so, so sorry,' she began. 'It really was only a stupid fling, but it was very wrong of me to go behind your back, and I'm very ashamed of myself.'

Anne raised an eyebrow. 'A fling? For Julian, maybe. But not for you – you wanted it to be far more than that. You've been in love with him since we were children. Don't deny it.'

'I can't. But so have you! Surely you remember—'

'That we both said we were going to marry him when we grew up? Of course I do.'

A lump rose in Rosie's throat for those two little girls and their dreams. Dreams that they should have left behind long ago, before they could shatter a friendship.

'I never meant to hurt you, Anne. You must believe that,' she said desperately, reaching out for Anne's hand, but Anne pulled away, stiff and remote.

'Don't worry about it, Rosie. Recently I've discovered I really don't care any more. I blame him as much as you – more, actually. He apologised profusely, begged me to give him another chance, and more fool me, I did. I forgave him and we made a fresh start. But recently I discovered he's been cheating on me again. From the time I took him back, from what I can make out. And not just with one woman. He's a philanderer, Rosie. He can't help himself. So if you want Julian, you can have him, with my blessing. Mother won't be best pleased, of course. She's set on making a match between us. But that's too bad.'

'Oh, Anne . . .' Rosie was almost speechless, and Anne went on.

'The field's clear for you now – if you still want him. That's really all I wanted to say.' She turned abruptly and began walking back towards the house, her back straight, her head held high.

Rosie turned to follow, but Anne's purposeful stride told her she didn't want her to. And quite honestly, Rosie didn't want to either. She was in shock, trembling, scarcely able to take in all the things Anne had said. She needed to be alone for a little while to recover herself and process it all. She turned in the opposite direction and headed blindly for the woods.

She should be happy that Anne was leaving the way clear for her to pursue her heart's desire. But oh, the emptiness, the regret – grief almost. Whatever she might have gained, she had lost her childhood friend for ever. And somehow, at this moment, that was what mattered most of all.

Anne wasn't ready to go home yet either. She wasn't ready to face her mother, who had been steely cold since their confrontation, or her father's loving concern over the rift between the two women who meant the most to him. Anne felt guilty about the things she'd said to Frances, and thought it would have been better to break the news of her decision to join the WAAF over the telephone. Perhaps then she would have been able to keep her cool, rather than giving vent to the resentment that had built up over the years.

But more than that . . .

She went to her car and slid into the driver's seat. Tears filled her eyes and ran unchecked into the collar of her camel coat. She absolutely couldn't go into the house until she had her emotions under control. She didn't want anyone to see her crying. She needed time to recover from what she'd just done. In spite of everything, she was still in love with Julian, and now, if the relationship between him and Rosie began again, she would have lost her oldest friend too.

There was no such luxury as a Christmas break for the bomb experts. In time of war it was business as usual. They had enjoyed a turkey dinner, brought in in sealed tins by some volunteers from the local WVS, but then it was back to work on the final plans for the bombs they hoped would be successful in blowing up the bridge that was their target. Their only concession to the festive season was to have a broadcast of a carol service playing in the background.

On Boxing Day it was much the same, but they'd made sufficient progress for Major Jefferis to tell them to take the evening off and go to the White Swan for a drink or two. Sometimes he joined them, but not today. He was still too engrossed in checking and finalising the day's work.

When Clarke and the other three who made up the 'drinking clique', as they were known to the more sober and serious engineers, reached the pub, they were surprised to find it much quieter than usual. The locals must be spending the evening with their families, they surmised.

Once they were settled with their usual pints and chasers, the talk inevitably turned to the war. One piece of good news was that a squadron of the Australian Air Force had arrived in Britain today, but – not so good – there were rumours that a decision had been made in Berlin to occupy Denmark. Where the intelligence came from, no one could be certain, but given the way Hitler was invading other countries that surrounded Germany, it was horribly plausible that he would be set on fanning out into Scandinavia.

'Jefferis knows a lot more than he's letting on,' Stan Beck, dark and good-looking, said in a low voice. Though the bar was almost empty and there was no one within earshot, they were still talking quietly, mindful as always of the importance of tight security.

'I wouldn't be surprised,' agreed Ian Crombie, a red-haired Scot of about Clarke's age. 'It's no good trying to pump him, though. Whatever he knows, he'll keep it to himself.'

'As he should,' Clarke said. 'I'd trust that man with my life.'

'You do know he's got the Military Cross, don't you?' Steve Green, a little older than the others, wiped a dribble of beer foam from his top lip with the back of his hand.

'No, I didn't.' But Clarke wasn't really surprised. From what he'd seen of the major, he would almost certainly meet any situation with bravery. 'How did that come about?'

'He used to be an expert in building roads and bridges, it seems,' Steve explained. 'Back in '22, he was in India. His job was to open up a passable way through the mountains to connect a couple of settlements, and he got the work done despite the fact that they were under regular fire from enemy snipers.'

'Building bridges, and then working on ways to blow 'em up.' Ian took a long pull of his beer. 'Ironic that, don't you think?'

'The best credentials, though,' Clarke said. 'If you know your structure, you know where the weak points are.'

The conversation moved on, and the men had almost finished their second pints when the pub door opened and to their surprise none other than Major Jefferis himself came in.

'Good Lord!' Stan muttered under his breath, and Clarke was very glad they were no longer discussing the major. There would have been some red faces if so.

Jefferis nodded to the four men and went straight to the bar, where he ordered a pint and a whisky. He brought them over to the table and the men moved around to accommodate the extra chair that Clarke had pulled across.

'I'm not too late then?' he said, brusque as usual.

'We'll be here till closing time,' Stan said. 'We weren't expecting you, though.'

'No, but I've got some news for Sutherland.' Jefferis took a pull of his beer and looked at Clarke. 'HQ called.'

'So they work over Christmas too then,' Stan commented. Major Jefferis ignored him.

'You're to go back to Somerset. The first batch of prospective agents have finished the vetting procedure and will be arriving to start their training shortly.'

Clarke nodded. He'd be sorry to leave the Firs. He'd enjoyed the work and the company, but he'd known it was only a matter of time before he was returned to do the job he'd been assigned to.

'Well.' Steve Green raised his glass in Clarke's direction. 'You'd better make the most of this, my son. And we'd better have another drink to send you on your way.'

'He's not going just yet, though, is he?' Ian Crombie said.

'Don't turn down a good excuse to have another pint, Crombie.' Stan Beck drained his glass and pushed back his chair. 'Brown ale? Or a short this time?'

Jefferis waved to him to sit down. 'I'll get these. No, it'll be a week or two before he leaves us, I'm told, but with a war on – who knows?' He looked at Clarke. 'You've done good work, Sutherland. You'll be missed.'

Clarke knew it was the highest praise he could expect from the major, who would never gush false appreciation as so many ambitious and self-important officers did. And he was grateful for it.

'Thanks,' he said. 'I'll miss you all too.'

* * *

Winnie had been desperate to know how the meeting between Rosie and Anne had gone. But when her daughter got back, she guessed from the look on her face that it had not gone well.

Against her better judgement she ventured a tentative 'How was it?' but Rosie was not forthcoming.

'Well, we talked,' she said shortly, and disappeared upstairs without even stopping to take off her coat. Best to leave her, Winnie thought, but an hour later when Rosie had still not reappeared, she decided to take the bull by the horns. She didn't want this to drag on until dinner time – Winnie still called the midday meal 'dinner', even though at the big house they called it 'lunch' or 'luncheon'. Boxing Day dinner was Rosie's favourite – she liked the cold cockerel, bubble and squeak and the remains of the home-made stuffing even more than the hot meal on Christmas Day – but neither of them would be able to enjoy it with whatever had gone on between her and Anne hanging over them.

Rosie's bedroom door was closed. Winnie knocked, and when there was no answer, she called, 'Are you all right, my love?'

'Yes, I'm fine,' Rosie replied, but her voice was thick with tears, and Winnie decided to go in anyway.

Rosie was sitting on her bed, looking out of the window, so that her back was towards the door. 'I'm fine, Mum,' she repeated when she realised Winnie was in the room.

'Come on, love. Come downstairs,' Winnie urged.

Rosie turned to face her then, and Winnie could see that her eyes were red and puffy.

'Please, Mum, just leave me alone,' she said miserably.

'I can't. Not when you're like this,' Winnie said. 'Why don't you tell me about it? You'll feel better if you do. Bottling it all up only makes it worse.'

Rosie's eyes brimmed with fresh tears and she bowed her head, one fist pressed against her mouth. 'I can't,' she whispered. 'I'm so ashamed. And I just don't know what to do.'

'Course you can tell me,' Winnie said. 'I'm your mother. You can tell me anything. I won't judge you.'

She went around the bed and sat down beside Rosie, patting her free hand and then covering it with her own.

'Come on, love. I can make a good guess anyway. So just tell me.'

And Rosie told her.

'Well, that's much as I thought,' Winnie said as Rosie came to the end of her narrative. 'I guessed Julian Edgell was behind it. He was the reason you went off to London, too, wasn't he?'

Rosie nodded. 'Oh Mum, I've made such a fool of myself. I really thought . . .'

She broke off. Even now, she couldn't bring herself to tell her mother the full truth of what had happened that last night. She was still so ashamed, even more than she had been for seeing Julian behind Anne's back. Still cringed at the memory of how she had been so swept along on a tide of heightened emotion that she had totally humiliated herself. She'd spent almost two years trying not to think about it, so painful was it. But now she was remembering. Every moment of heady desire and exhilaration, and the crushing shock and shame of discovering she'd got it all wrong.

It had started when Julian had been at medical school in Bristol. Rosie invariably worked at the garage on a Saturday – it was always the busiest day of the week. The café was open in the morning and people who'd been to market stopped off for a cup of tea or coffee, while those lucky enough to own cars came in to fill up with petrol so they could take their family out for a run the following day, especially now that spring was here and there was warmth in the sunshine. Rosie had been almost run off her feet by the time she left at five. She was making her way home up the hill when a car passed her and came to a halt a few yards ahead, and Julian wound down the window and called to ask if he could give her a lift. He must be home for the weekend!

Excitement at seeing him bubbled in her veins like sparkling champagne, and she was glad that today she was dressed for helping out in the café and not wearing her oily overalls.

'That was lucky!' he said as she slid into the passenger seat. 'That hill's a drag at the best of times, and it's really hot today.'

'I don't mind usually, but I've been on my feet all day and I'm tired,' Rosie admitted. 'So thank you!'

'My pleasure. It's been a long time since I've seen you, Rosie. You never seem to be around when I'm at home.'

'I do work on Saturdays. But I don't go far on Sundays.'

'I imagined you'd be out gallivanting with your friends.'

Something in the way he said it, and the sidelong glance he gave her, made her think he was angling.

'I do usually go out with the girls on a Saturday night. To the pictures, or a dance. But I don't think I'll feel much like dancing tonight after the day I've had,' she added.

'So why don't I take you out for a drink so we can catch up,' he suggested. 'Unless you're too tired, of course.'

Rosie's heart leapt. 'I expect I'll be recovered after I've had a cup of tea and something to eat,' she said as lightly as she could manage.

'Good. I'll look forward to it. I'll pick you up – how does half-seven sound?'

'Sounds fine.'

He stopped the car outside her mother's cottage. 'I'll see you then.'

'OK.'

As he drove on towards the big house, it was all Rosie could do not to turn and watch him go. But she didn't want him to see her looking. Didn't want to give away how excited she was feeling. But oh my goodness! She could scarcely believe it. She was actually going to go out with Julian! It was beyond her wildest dreams. Suddenly she wasn't tired any more. She skipped up the path to the cottage like the spring lambs that gambolled in the fields bordering the grounds of Bramley Court, her heart singing.

For Rosie, the whole evening had a dreamlike feel to it. They'd driven out into the countryside and stopped at a hostelry that according to Julian had once been a coaching inn. He was obviously familiar with the place, leading her straight into a bar with padded seats in inglenooks, and a log fire blazing in the big hearth – although the spring day had been pleasantly warm, a chill had set in when darkness began to fall.

He'd asked her what she'd like to drink, and she didn't really know what to say – she wasn't used to going to pubs or drinking alcohol. He'd suggested a 'rum and black', and she'd said that yes, that would be lovely, and then been pleasantly surprised to discover the 'black' was short for blackcurrant, which sweetened the sharp kick of the spirit.

She knew they'd talked, but couldn't remember afterwards much about what they'd talked about. She knew she'd asked him if his mother didn't mind him going out when he was only at home for what was left of the weekend, and he'd replied, 'No. Why would she?' She'd also asked if he ever saw Anne, since they were both in Bristol, and to her relief he'd said, 'Sometimes,' but not elaborated. And he'd asked her about what she was doing and she'd rattled on far too much about her job at the garage. It was that that had led to the part of the conversation she'd never forget.

'So has this Mr Bendle taught you to drive?' he'd asked.

She'd laughed. 'Not really. Unless you count the time he let me move a car out of the way so he could bring the one he was servicing out of the workshop.'

'And did you manage it?'

'Yes! Though it was only from one side of the yard to the other.'

'Well done.' His eyes met hers, and there was something of a challenge in them. 'How would you like me to teach you to drive properly?'

'Oh!' For a moment she was too startled – and delighted – to know what to say. 'Oh, that would be amazing! But you're not home very often.'

'I could come out sometimes in the evening.' He smiled. 'I don't spend all my time studying, you know. Perhaps not as much as I should.'

'I wouldn't like to be the cause of you failing your exams,' she said quickly.

'Don't worry. That's not going to happen,' he assured her, confident as ever. 'So how about it?'

'All right. Thank you,' she said.

The rest of the evening had passed Rosie by in a blur of disbelieving delight, and all too soon the landlord was ringing a brass bell and calling 'Time!' and then they were driving home, the headlights of the car cutting a swathe through the unlit lanes.

When Julian drew up outside Winnie's cottage, he swivelled to face her.

'So shall we make a date for your first driving lesson? How does Thursday evening sound to you?'

Rosie was startled all over again that this was really happening – and so soon.

'That would be fine,' she managed.

'Can you walk down to the main road? I'll meet you there at about eight.'

She nodded. 'I'll be there.'

She should have realised then, of course, that he didn't want to be seen by anyone from the big house. But if even an inkling of doubt had crossed her mind, it was obliterated by what happened next.

He kissed her.

Only a brief light touch of lips and his hand covering hers, but enough to make her head spin and her heart beat so hard she could hear its echo in her ears.

'I'll see you then,' he said, and she climbed out of the car and watched as the tail lights disappeared in the direction of the road that linked Bramley Court and his own home, Pridcombe House.

For Rosie, the weeks that followed were the happiest she could remember. They met most weeks down on the main road, always on a Thursday. Julian would drive until they reached a spot where it was safe for her to take over, and he coached her gently through the basics – gear changes, reversing, cornering, and the rules of the road. Later they would stop for a drink at one of the hostelries they passed, and then he would drive to what he said was the entrance to a disused quarry, where he'd pull in under the trees and they would cuddle and kiss, longer kisses than that first time, deeper, even more exciting. Little by little his caresses became more intimate, until that fateful night when everything had escalated to red-hot passion.

She'd scarcely seen him over Christmas and she wasn't sure whether he was even at home. But he had appeared on the doorstep on New Year's Day, bearing a lump of coal that he held out with a laugh and an apology that he hadn't been able to get away to 'first-foot' when the clock had chimed midnight last night. She'd invited him in, and when Winnie had tactfully left them alone, he'd pulled a little box tied with a ribbon out of his pocket and given it to her. 'A late Christmas present,' he'd said. She'd opened it to reveal a silver heart-shaped pendant on a delicate chain, and she'd thought her own heart would burst.

'It's beautiful!' she'd whispered, tears of joy stinging her eyes, and he'd fastened it around her neck and kissed her, hastily and warily, in case Winnie should come back into the room.

'Just like you,' he'd said.

And she'd believed, really believed that this was for ever, and not spared a thought for Anne.

It was a few weeks later that all her dreams had turned to ashes, a cold, clear night when the moon slanting through the bare branches lit the spot where they always parked to something close to daylight and glinted on the silver pendant that she now wore every day. She was feeling a little woozy; tonight she'd had three rum and blacks instead of her usual two, and it had gone to her head, so that she'd relished the moment when he undid her buttons, kissed her mouth, her throat, her breasts. And when he slid up her skirt, her desire had mounted to meet his, pulsing through her body. She'd known where this was leading, but she no longer cared. She desperately needed to be close to him, as close as a man and a woman could be.

'I want you,' he'd whispered urgently, his breath hot against her cheek. And 'Yes! Yes!' she'd moaned in response.

He'd drawn back slightly then, looking down into her face. 'Are you sure, Rosie?'

'Yes!' And then she'd uttered the words that had ruined everything.

'I love you, Julian.'

Jennie Felton

She knew, the moment she had said it, from the way the mood changed instantaneously, that she'd made a dreadful mistake.

'Hang on,' he said. 'Rosie, you don't think . . .? Look, I thought you knew. I really like you. I've enjoyed giving you driving lessons, and I've enjoyed . . . well, being with you. You're different to any other girl I've ever known. But hey, don't go all serious on me!'

'But Julian . . .' Her hand had gone to the pendant at her throat, panic replacing passion. 'I'm sorry . . . I shouldn't have said that. I didn't mean it.'

'Oh Rosie, I think you did,' he said. 'And I'm glad you said it. It's brought me to my senses. Look, I'm sorry too, if I've been leading you on.' He moved away from her, sitting up, rearranging his clothes. 'I didn't mean to. But I have to make my feelings clear now. I don't want anything happening because you're under the misapprehension that I have intentions towards you.'

Rosie was crying now, and it only added to her humiliation. 'Take me home!' she whispered through her tears.

He started the engine without another word, reversed out of the clearing, put his foot down when they reached the main road. It was only when he stopped outside the cottage that he spoke.

'I think it would be better if we didn't see one another again, Rosie. Best for both of us.'

It was then that she'd realised the significance of him wanting always to meet her at the end of the drive, and it was what he'd just said that had opened her eyes to what she'd refused to see before. *I've enjoyed being with you. You're different to any other girl I've ever known. But hey, don't go all serious on me!* He didn't want Anne's mother or father to see her getting into his car. Didn't want them to tell Anne. Winnie had been right all along. It was Anne or someone like her that he'd be happy to get serious with. He was probably dating her when he was in Bristol. Rosie meant nothing to him but what people called 'a bit on the side'.

She'd known then she couldn't face either him or Anne again. Couldn't bear to see them together and couldn't bear the shame of what had just happened. She'd fled to London, fully intending to put it all behind her and start afresh. But it hadn't happened, and now here she was again, making the same mistake, falling into the same trap. Kidding herself that Julian had feelings for her.

But perhaps this time he really did. Perhaps he'd been shocked when she'd left so suddenly and never come back. Perhaps he'd missed her and wished he'd never said those things to her. And something had gone very wrong between him and Anne, that was clear. Anne had said she didn't want him; that, in as many words, Rosie was welcome to him . . .

Her head spun.

'Oh, Mum, I just don't know what to do,' she said wretchedly.

Winnie reached out and patted her hand. Though her eyes were troubled, she was her usual pragmatic self.

'Has Julian said anything to you about carrying on where you left off?'

'He did mention giving me lessons so I can drive an ambulance.'

'Hmm. I wouldn't think that was very wise under the circumstances. Why don't you have a word with Mr Bendle? He'll have time on his hands, what with so many cars being off the road. If Julian really wants to start seeing you again, he'll find another way. And if he doesn't . . . well, you'll know you've got to forget all about him.'

Her mother was right, Rosie knew. Waiting for him to make

a move that couldn't be misinterpreted wouldn't be easy. Her feelings for him ran too deep. But it was the only way.

She wiped her eyes and blew her nose.

'I'll try, Mum,' she said.

But she knew that this time she couldn't run away. For her mother's sake she had to stay here and brazen it out. And Anne had left the door open for her.

Chapter Twelve

Now that Christmas and New Year were over, things began to return to what had been the 'new normal' since the declaration of war.

Anne had returned to Bristol to finish the packing of the gallery's priceless items and seeing them safely stored in the church crypt, where they would remain for the duration of the war, and to pursue her application to join the WAAF.

Frances, frustrated by her failure to persuade Anne to come home, had immersed herself once more in her WVS work, and Clarke was sharing his final ideas with the group at the Firs before leaving for Somerset to prepare for the arrival of the first prospective secret agents.

Rosie was back to working regular shifts at St Mark's and still facing the same thankless duties. And Freda was both surprised and delighted to learn that in a few weeks' time, she would be posted to a farm not far from Hillsbridge to begin work as a land girl.

Meanwhile, the war seemed almost as far away as ever. According to the reports on the wireless and in the newspapers, most of the action seemed to be taking place at sea, where several ships had been sunk by magnetic mines and U-boats, while in faraway Uruguay the Germans had scuttled their own warship when she became trapped by British ships. The Russians had invaded Finland, but the expected advance by the Germans into France had not materialised. It had been dubbed the 'phoney war'.

Winnie had even received a letter from Don. They were on the French–Belgian border, he wrote, and most of their time was spent digging trenches and weapon pits along the Maginot Line – whatever was that? Winnie wondered. The weather was cold and miserable, nothing much was happening, and Don was disgusted that Lord Gort, the British CO, was second in command to what he rudely termed 'a Frog'.

Winnie had shaken her head at that. 'A Frog' indeed! She'd thought she'd brought her children up to be more respectful than that to their elders and betters, but she wasn't going to dwell on it. She was just happy to know that for the moment at least he was safe.

Apart from worrying about Rosie's love life, Winnie's main concern was that the first wave of rationing had come into force a week after Christmas. Like everyone else, she'd been issued with a ration book, and was supposed to register with shops so that the retailer could mark off the coupons as they were used.

'I s'pose we'd better do it quick sharp,' Maud had said to her, and they'd decided to go into town together on the Saturday.

Winnie usually liked to shop in the market for butter, cheese and bacon, but neither she nor Maud was certain how the system was going to work, and they thought it might be safest to register with shops that would be open all week long. Maud was in favour of doing the lot in the Co-op, which comprised enough different departments to cater for pretty well anything, but Winnie preferred to go to Fred Thomas's butcher's shop for her meat, which she'd heard would soon be added to the list of rationed foodstuffs. For one thing, rightly or wrongly, she trusted Fred more than she trusted the men who worked behind the butchery counter in the Co-op, and for another, she liked to support him. There were folks who wouldn't go into his shop because of his stutter and the way his hands shook. Maud, for one, wasn't keen. 'You never know, he might have a fit or some'ut,' she'd said. Maud had a horror of people who suffered from epilepsy.

That Saturday, though, Winnie managed to persuade her to venture into Fred's shop, and was very soon wishing she hadn't. Fred was slicing liver for a customer who was in front of them, and Maud shuddered, turning her head away and grimacing. As if that wasn't bad enough, she'd said in that same loud whisper that had embarrassed Winnie so at the first WVS meeting, 'He's gonna cut his finger off in a minute! He shouldn't be using a knife like that, not the way he is.'

The woman who was buying the liver turned and glared, but Maud was unabashed.

'Well, 'e shouldn't. It's not hygienic. He could be bleeding all over that liver and you'd never know.'

'Maud, hush up!' Winnie said.

'He can't hear me. He's deaf, isn't he? From all the guns and explosions.'

'You're the one that's deaf,' Winnie said tartly. She caught the eye of the customer and shook her head, disassociating herself from her erstwhile friend.

'Well, sorry I'm sure, but I can't get me meat 'ere,' Maud said. 'You can do what you like, Winnie, but I'm goin' to the Co-op.' And to Winnie's relief, she huffed out.

Throughout all this Fred had given no indication that he could hear every word, but Winnie knew better. His hearing wasn't so impaired that he was unable to make out what a loud-mouthed woman was saying just a couple of feet in front of him. When the other customer had paid for her purchases and left, she took her opportunity to apologise.

'I'm so sorry about my friend, Mr Thomas, but she can't stand the sight of blood. She's very squeamish.'

Fred, who was wiping down the counter, looked up.

'Sh-sh-she shouldn't come in a butcher's shop then, should she?' he said mildly.

'No, she shouldn't.' Winnie didn't want to make things worse than they already were by going on about it. Just as long as Fred knew that Maud's opinions were her own, and she didn't agree with them.

'I'd like to register with you, Mr Thomas. For me and for my Rosie. She's back home, living with me,' she said. 'Then I'll have some ham. How much am I allowed?'

Fred Thomas wiped his hands on his striped apron, and adjusted the straw boater he always wore in the shop.

'Three ounces each if you want the c-c-cooked. An extra ounce if it's not.'

'Oh, cooked, please. I don't want to have to do it myself. It's hardly worth it, is it, for that little bit and it wouldn't be as nice as how you do it.'

'Right you are.'

A juicy-looking ham was already on the bacon slicer. Fred spread out a sheet of greaseproof paper, cut a couple of slices and showed it to Winnie.

'Is that all I get?' she asked, dismayed.

'I reckon that's th-th-three ounces. I'll pop it on the scales, and you can see.'

Sure enough, when he arranged the weights, the scales seemed perfectly balanced; in fact, if anything they were tilted a bit to the generous side.

'Oh my goodness,' Winnie groaned. 'And that's got to last me a week?'

'You've got your Rosie's allowance too, don't f-f-forget.'

'I think I'd better save that. Me and Rosie will have to share. What about bacon?'

Fred Thomas shook his head. 'Sorry, Mrs M-M-Mitchell. It's either ham *or* bacon. You can't 'ave both.'

Winnie's heart sank. She should have known. 'Well in that case, I'll have to use Rosie's allowance as well,' she said wretchedly.

Fred wrapped the ham and replaced the joint in the slicing machine with a side of bacon. But after he'd cut and weighed it, he gave a quick furtive glance around the shop, empty now apart from Winnie, and slipped a couple of extra rashers onto the meagre pile before hastily wrapping it up and placing it on the counter beside the package of ham.

'Oh, Mr Thomas,' Winnie began, overcome with gratitude. 'Thank you! But you shouldn't—'

A look from the butcher stopped her in her tracks, and she realised another customer was coming into the shop.

'S-s-sorry I can't give you any m-m-more, Mrs Mitchell,' he said, scribbling some figures on a clean sheet of greaseproof paper with a thick black pencil and turning it towards her so that she could see what she owed.

'Well, it's not going to last long,' she said, playing along. 'But thank you anyway.'

'Awful, isn't it?' the new customer said, joining her at the counter.

'Awful,' Winnie agreed, handing over the two ration books to Fred and counting out her money.

Fred crossed off the coupons with the same thick pencil and passed the ration books back to her.

'S-s-see you again then, Mrs Mitchell,' he said, tipping his straw boater to a jaunty angle on his sparse greying hair.

'Yes, and thanks again, Mr Thomas.'

What a nice man he was! she thought as she left the shop. She couldn't expect him to do it again, of course, but she could always live in hope.

She smiled to herself, rather glad that Maud had walked out in a huff. Fred wouldn't have done what he had if she'd been there. And he sure as daylight wouldn't have done the same for her.

You're a fool to yourself, Maud, she thought. And avoiding the Co-op, she went into the grocery store on the corner of the street to register there too.

Driving back to his base in the Mendip Hills, Clarke made a slight detour from the most direct route so that he could pass through Hillsbridge. As soon as he turned off, he remonstrated with himself for giving in to a whim. The chance that he might see Rosie Mitchell would be a bad bet if he was checking odds on a horse race. But he didn't turn around. The compulsion to keep going was too strong.

Coming at the town from a different direction, he was able to see a little more of it than he had before. After descending yet another hill with fields on either side, he passed a pub, some large houses and some terraces, and, when the road levelled out into the valley, a pit yard above which head gear towered, an official-looking building, and a subway running under one of the two railway tracks that bisected the town. The road then followed the railway embankment on his nearside, while on the other he saw a cake shop, a bakery and a wooded area. At its end, the road met the one from Bath that he'd driven that day when he'd first arrived in Somerset, and he turned onto it and bumped across one of the two level crossings.

The town was busy this morning: shoppers with baskets and canvas bags, children clutching ice-cream cornets – ice cream in January? he thought. But he supposed whoever made and sold it needed to do business all year round to survive. A dog darted across the road in front of him and he braked sharply and saw a young woman grab the animal by the scruff of its neck and administer a smack to its rump. But it wasn't Rosie, and before he knew it, he was climbing again, up the steep hill, away from the town.

But the extra minutes the detour had added to his journey had been worth it, he thought. He was learning more about the place she called home, getting a feel for it. And he'd be back. If – when – he got a break from his duties.

He put his foot down and headed out into the countryside towards the Manor and whatever awaited him there.

Had he come into town from the Bath direction, Clarke might well have spotted Rosie crossing the road and walking down to Bendle's garage. She hadn't seen Julian since before Christmas, but she was determined that when she did, she'd be ready to tell him she didn't need him to give her driving lessons, as Mr Bendle had offered to teach her. At least that was what she hoped.

As always on a Saturday, Brenda had opened the café. Through the window Rosie could see customers sitting at the little tables with their checked cloths, and Brenda herself clearing used cups and saucers onto a tray. Rosie waved to her, and Brenda gave a little wave back. 'I'll be in later,' Rosie mouthed, and hoped that Brenda understood what she was trying to convey. She didn't want her to feel slighted.

In the workshop, she found Mr Bendle under the bonnet of the most peculiar vehicle she had ever seen. The front half was a car right enough, but the back had gone, the chassis covered with canvas. It must be one of those that had been converted into ambulances, she realised, and felt a little thrill of excitement. Perhaps one day soon she would be working in it, or one very like it.

'Well, well, if it isn't our Rosie!' Mr Bendle emerged, straightening up and wiping his hands on his greasy overalls. 'We are honoured!'

If Rosie hadn't known him well, known that he didn't mean anything by the sarcasm, that it was just his way, she might have been put off. But she did know him, and he knew that she wouldn't be in the least offended by his greeting.

'Is that an ambulance?' she asked, nodding at the vehicle, which had not so long ago no doubt been someone's pride and joy.

Mr Bendle nodded. ''Tis, ah. Can't say I'd fancy gettin' carted off in it, though. Too cramped fer my liking. An' whoever did the alterations made a pretty mess of things. Shouldn't have touched the engine at all. But they've gone an' done summat, and it's left to me to find out what an' put it right. Anyway, wot brings you 'ere today?'

'I've got a favour to ask,' she said.

'Oh ah, an' wot's that?'

'If you can't help me, you can say no. I'll understand.'

'Come on, girl, out wi' it.'

Rosie took a deep breath and told him.

'Well, good fer you, girl,' he said when she'd finished. 'Course I'll give you a few lessons, though it gets dark early, don't forget. You'd do better in the daylight, to start with at any rate. Would tomorrow afternoon suit?'

'That would be amazing,' Rosie said, surprised and delighted. 'I've got a day off tomorrow.'

'An' so 'ave I – if I can sort out what some silly bugger's done to this engine. Come down about three-ish and I'll see what I can do.'

'Thank you so much!' Rosie said. 'I'll be here.'

'You won't be drivin' this one, though.' He patted the wing of the converted car. ''Tis more than my life's worth to let anything happen to this. I got the contract, you know, to look after the new ambulances. Not sure 'ow, but I'm well pleased, I can tell you.'

'You got it because everybody knows you're a good, reliable mechanic,' Rosie said. 'Now I'll just pop into the café and say hello to Mrs Bendle, and leave you in peace. And thank you again.'

'Don't you worry yer head, it'll be a pleasure.' Mr Bendle grinned at her and ducked back underneath the raised bonnet of the converted ambulance.

As things turned out, it seemed Rosie had sorted things out with Dick Bendle just in time. As it was a Saturday, Matron had decided to divide up the shift between her and Flo Jennings, another orderly, Rosie taking the second half from four until eight.

As she took the bus to Bath, she was feeling buoyed up and positive. Her driving lessons were arranged and she could rely on Mr Bendle to make a good job of teaching her. And she was determined not to dwell on the fact that a part of her still wished it was Julian.

She'd been pleased, too, that a letter from Freda had arrived by second post, and delighted with the news it contained. She'd known, of course, that Freda had volunteered as a land girl, and thought it would suit her down to the ground. But she could have been sent almost anywhere in the country. Rosie could scarcely believe she was going to be nearby, and that alone had been enough to cheer her. She'd really missed her friend, missed having someone of her own age to do things with and, even more importantly, talk to about absolutely anything. Yes, she could talk to her mother, but it wasn't the same. There were things she couldn't bring herself to tell Winnie. She didn't have to watch every word with Freda, and she knew she wouldn't be judged. Freda might be a bit short sometimes, but at the heart of things they understood one another.

With any luck they'd be able to meet up in their spare time to do some of the things they used to do, if with the war on there was anything happening. She couldn't see why the cinema would shut down – the boy who cycled from the Palladium in High Compton to the Palace in Hillsbridge with the reels of film the two cinemas shared was too young to be called up and the man who showed them too old. And if there was an air raid, they could always take shelter in the subway that ran under the railway lines. And spring and summer would be on the way soon and they could just go for walks . . . Yes, Rosie was really looking forward to having Freda close by.

The hospital was much quieter than it was in the week, as any patients who were well enough had been discharged. All that was required of Rosie was to make sure Flo had done a thorough job when she'd cleaned this morning and hadn't left any fluff under the beds, and that the patients' toilets were respectable – no unflushed lavatories and no soap scum in the sink. She would also do the rounds with the tea trolley and serve the early-evening meal when it was time.

Tonight they served it a bit early as the kitchen staff were anxious to get away and Sister wasn't on duty to snap that routine was routine and should be adhered to, and the staff were paid to be here until it was all done. Rosie knew that the adenoidal and not very bright kitchen assistant had a date with her boyfriend, a young man who'd been turned down for active service on medical grounds, and so she offered to help with the clearing up. She was just putting away a stack of clean plates that had been left to dry in a rack beside the sink when to her complete surprise Julian came into the kitchen.

He was the very last person she'd expected to see today – as far as she knew, none of his patients were on the wards, and it was almost unheard of for a doctor to drop in for no reason on a Saturday evening. In spite of herself her pulse began racing as it always did when she met him, either arranged or not. She froze, the pile of plates balanced between her hands, and Julian approached her, arms outstretched.

'Hey, let me take those. Where do they go?'

'Here . . .' She indicated a shelf in one of the wall cupboards. 'Be careful! They're heavy.'

'I think I can manage them,' he said drily. 'But that shelf is far too high for you to reach.'

'I was going to use the step stool . . .'

'Well, now you've no need.' He put the pile of plates onto the shelf she'd indicated and turned to her. 'Right, that's better.'

'I didn't know you had any patients here now,' Rosie blurted, totally thrown by the unexpected encounter.

'I don't. I came to see you.' He looked around. 'Where's the kitchen maid?'

'She's gone home. I told her I'd finish up here.'

Julian raised an eyebrow. 'I wouldn't have thought that was part of your job.'

'Maybe not, but she's got a date. And I haven't got much else to do.'

'I see.' He sounded disapproving. Then his tone changed. 'So we can talk here uninterrupted, then? I've got something to tell you.'

'What?' Her already jangling nerves were now on high alert, but his next words took her completely by surprise.

'You're to start a trial as an ambulance attendant next week.'

Her eyes widened in disbelief, all awkwardness and caution forgotten, and Julian smiled, that smile that had always made her heart turn over.

'I had a word with the head of department. Told him you were wasted here.' That smile again. 'And so you are. Washing and drying dirty dishes . . .'

'Oh, Julian, thank you! That's amazing news. What do I have to do?'

'Report to the ambulance station at St Mark's on Monday, and they'll take it from there.'

Her head was spinning. 'What do I wear?'

'You'll be measured up for a uniform once they sign you on permanently. Until then, you can continue to wear your nursing uniform along with the appropriate Air Raid Precautions badge. You'll be based here at St Mark's, but it's highly likely you'll be working hours that don't coincide with the bus timetables. Mother has agreed that you can have the use of her car now that Frances has got one of her own to replace the one that was requisitioned. So I think it would be a good plan to start those lessons right away. We don't want you driving into any more gateposts,' he added drily.

'Oh, it's all right,' Rosie said. 'My old boss at the garage is going to teach me.'

'Well!' Julian looked surprised – and yes, a little hurt. 'I was rather looking forward to it.'

'I'm sorry, but I thought you'd be too busy.' Now that the moment had come, Rosie didn't know whether she was relieved or regretful that she'd only just today made the arrangements.

'Well, in that case I'll have to think of some other way to see you, won't I?' Julian said with a rueful smile, and Rosie's heart leapt. Her mother had said just that – that if he really was interested in her, he'd find some other way. But she honestly didn't know how to respond, and he went on, 'It won't be this week, though, I'm afraid. You're right, I am up to my eyes in work, and although Dr Hamilton's sharing the load now, he's just come down with a nasty case of influenza. But when things ease . . .'

'Yes, of course,' Rosie said.

'I must go now.' He reached out and squeezed her hand. 'I'm glad that I caught you to give the good news. See you soon, Rosie.'

He disappeared into the hospital corridor, leaving the door open behind him, and Rosie just stood for a moment, a hand pressed to her mouth. She was delighted, of course, that she was going to work on the ambulances instead of being a glorified skivvy. But her emotions were running riot. Did Julian really want to see her? Was he really still overworked at his practice? Or was he just saying it to keep her sweet, and there was nothing wrong with his partner at all?

She didn't know what to think. Meeting him like this and the things he'd said had stirred up all her old feelings, and once again she could feel that treacherous quiver of hope.

'Damn you, Julian Edgell!' she said aloud. And finished putting away the clean cutlery.

Chapter Thirteen

'Ah, there you are, Mrs Mitchell.'

Lady Hastings had found Winnie in the drawing room, where she was dusting the grand piano and the ornaments, a trinket dish and framed photographs, that were lined up along the top. Time was when no one would have dared leave them there; in Sir James's father's day, he had played so enthusiastically that they would have been shaken off by his thundering and not always tuneful chords. These days, however, no one played it, not since Philip and Anne had given up the lessons they'd taken as children.

It was a depressingly cold and damp February morning and Winnie had been forced to light the gas lamp in order to see what she was doing. She turned now, the duster still in her hand. 'Milady?'

'Leave that and come and sit down.' Lady Hastings waved the fat manilla folder she was holding in the direction of one of the easy chairs. 'There's something I want to ask you.'

Winnie did as she was bid, hoping fervently it wasn't Rosie her ladyship wanted to talk to her about. Ever since Anne and Rosie's acrimonious reunion, she'd been half expecting Lady Hastings to raise the subject with her, and dreaded it. She didn't want to get involved. But the manilla folder was a good sign – her ladyship used them for her WVS paperwork. That would be much safer ground, though she was puzzled as to what Lady Hastings could want to discuss with her in the middle of a working day. Though Winnie was a loyal member, she'd never yet been singled out for anything of any importance.

'As you know,' her ladyship began, 'I'm planning to raise funds to aid the war effort, and in particular the need for more Spitfires. They're wonderful little fighter planes and many more will be needed for the defence of our country. Since Philip is a pilot in the RAF, it's a cause close to my heart, and I think it would be most appropriate if we, the people of his home town, could raise enough to provide at least one. The Hillsbridge Spitfire.

'To this end, I've decided to launch the project with a dance, all proceeds to go to the fund. James will make a substantial donation to start it off, and I feel sure that people all together enjoying a pleasant evening's entertainment will be the ideal backdrop to engendering a spirit of community, a desire to work together in the interests of us all.'

She paused to give weight to her words, which sounded to Winnie very much like a prepared speech. She nodded enthusiastically, as she felt sure was expected of her, but couldn't quite understand where this was all leading.

'Now, I'm already well ahead with the preparations,' Lady Hastings went on. 'I've booked the town hall for Easter Saturday – the twenty-third of March. I've persuaded the Paget Press to print advertising material and the tickets at no charge – they are happy to do that as their contribution to the fund – and I've applied for a licence to sell liquor. Catering for light refreshments will be done by a small committee under the capable leadership of Mrs Bendle.'

That'll get Maud's goat, Winnie thought . . .

'However, so far I have not been able to engage the services of a band to play for the dancing, and a dance without music would be rather pointless, don't you agree?'

Realising the understatement was meant to be droll, Winnie smiled dutifully. 'Certainly would, milady.'

'So.' Lady Hastings became serious once more. 'This is something I am hoping you can help me out with, Mrs Mitchell.'

'Me?' Winnie exclaimed, taken aback.

'Indeed. The problem is that conscription has stripped the most popular local dance bands of their key musicians, and those that are left don't feel able to take bookings, even in a worthy cause. The exception to this paucity of talent is the High Compton Accordion Band. I'm given to understand that at least half its members are well over the upper age limit for conscription, and I'm sure they would appreciate being able to contribute to the war effort – ideally free of charge. Now, if I remember rightly, your late husband's brother is their conductor, and it occurred to me that you would be the best person to make an approach.'

'Oh!' Winnie bit her lip. 'I don't know that he's their regular conductor. And I haven't seen much of him since Ern died.'

'Nevertheless . . .'

Winnie was in a quandary now. The truth was, she'd never seen much of Charlie Mitchell. He and Ern had fallen out long ago, over some perceived slight of Charlie's wife, Ada – a thoroughly unpleasant woman – and she didn't relish the thought of contacting him now, much less asking a favour of him. But she couldn't tell Lady Hastings that. It was private family business.

'He works for the LMS railway company, I understand,' Lady Hastings said. 'If he's a driver or a fireman, I suppose it might be difficult for you to know when would be the best time to get hold of him. But . . .'

Winnie was tempted to take this way out, but she didn't like lying. Charlie had been a goods train driver once, but something had happened that had seen him demoted all the way back to being a cleaner. It wasn't only Ern he'd upset, she'd guessed.

'He works in the sheds,' she said.

Lady Hastings nodded, satisfied. 'Ah, maintenance. Good. I'm happy for you to take the rest of the day off so that you can go and seek him out.'

There was nothing for it, she'd just have to bite the bullet and speak to Charlie, Winnie thought. But she'd put it off as long as she could.

'I'll finish up here, and then I'll go after I've had my dinner,' she said.

When Clarke had arrived back at the Manor, he had discovered that a new arrival had been seconded to the unit to assist him. According to Firkins, the powers-that-be had decided that explosives was too wide a topic to be covered by one instructor alone. While Clarke was well aware that there was more than a grain of truth in this, he couldn't help feeling aggrieved that it had been done in his absence, and without any reference to him. He knew this was ridiculous; if a decision was made by those who ranked far higher than he did, he would have no say in the matter, but it still rankled, not helped by the fact that he didn't like the new man.

He couldn't put a finger on exactly why he felt this way. Sergeant Holder had never been openly disrespectful, but it was as though beneath a thin veneer of civility he was sneering at both Clarke and the arrangements he'd put in place for the working of the section. He was prone to telling risqué jokes and ribald stories, but that was par for the course, especially for the lower ranks. He spent too much time in Firkins' office for Clarke's liking, leading to speculation that he was secretly reporting back to the major. Clarke hoped this wasn't the case; a snitch in the camp was the last thing he wanted. But Holder's record in the bomb disposal unit was faultless as far as he could tell, and he seemed keen to be accepted by the other instructors. Yet Clarke couldn't shake the feeling that not only did he dislike Dennis Holder, he didn't trust him either.

Mistaken though he might be, he was going to keep a close eye on the man.

After just a week in her new role, Rosie's driver, Paddy Murphy, had reported that he was more than satisfied that she was well suited to the job, and she had been taken to ambulance head-quarters to be issued with her new uniform. Since she was slimly built and of average height, it hadn't been difficult to find a greatcoat – a double-breasted style in navy blue wool – that fitted her. It had a red ARP badge sewn onto the lapel, but she'd also been given a white metal one to be pinned to her collar and a woollen cap. For the time being she was to continue wearing her nursing uniform dress, but she'd been measured up for a woollen jacket and skirt, and given how cold the weather was, she couldn't wait to get them. This morning she'd shivered as she cleaned the ambulance, wiping down every surface and piece of equipment and sweeping and washing the floor, though by the time she'd finished, the hard work had warmed her up somewhat.

As she emerged, shrugging into her greatcoat, she found Paddy leaning against the ambulance and smoking a cigarette. 'All done?' he asked.

Paddy was a pleasant man in his late fifties, an experienced attendant as well as a driver, and she was lucky to be paired with him, even if he did leave all the menial jobs to her. His Irish brogue reminded her of the man who had rescued her from the thugs on Paddington station, and he had the same sort of wicked twinkle in his eye. From the beginning they had got on famously, so that the times they were idle passed quickly with jokes and chit-chat. She also liked his brisk efficiency when they were attending emergencies. It bolstered her confidence.

Now, it seemed, a call-out was imminent. A nurse was hurrying towards them across the yard, a slip of paper in her hand.

'Sure, that was good timing!' Paddy ground the butt of his cigarette out on the tarmac with the toe of his boot and winked at the nurse. 'What have you got for us then?'

'There's a problem with a birthing.' She handed him the scrap of paper. 'Here's the address. The poor woman's been in labour for far too long, and the district nurse thinks it's time to get her here.'

'Are you ready for this?' Paddy asked Rosie as they climbed into their seats. 'You never know, moving her might hurry her along. D'you fancy playing midwife if the wee one makes his appearance while we're en route?'

Rosie felt a twinge of anxiety. Yes, she'd been trained. Yes, she'd watched from the sidelines as a baby was delivered. But was she competent to do what was necessary if the baby really did come before they got the mother back to the hospital?

Paddy laughed at her expression. 'I'm joking you. The district nurse will come with us, I wouldn't wonder.'

'I can manage if she doesn't!' Rosie protested, more confidently than she felt.

'Sure you can.' He let out the clutch and the ambulance shot away from its parking space like a runner in the Derby, the bell clanging. Rosie experienced a little thrill of excitement. She wasn't stuck on the wards any more, frustrated and bored. She was actually doing something useful and fulfilling.

Julian, and the fact that she hadn't heard from him in the last weeks, was forgotten as she hung onto the grab strap and wondered what this call-out – and the next – would bring.

The petite grey-haired officer who was interviewing Anne following her application to join the WAAF looked up from the sheaf of paperwork on the desk in front of her.

'You were at finishing school in Geneva, I see. Does that mean you speak French?'

'I do, yes.'

'Fluently?'

'Well . . . yes.' Anne was a little puzzled as to why that should be relevant, unless it was something that would be useful if she was assigned, as she hoped, to communications.

The officer didn't enlighten her, simply moved smoothly on to other questions, which Anne surmised were designed to probe her capability and character traits. She answered as truthfully and concisely as she could, and a few minutes later the officer shuffled the paperwork together and looked up, removing her spectacles.

'I think that will do nicely for today.'

'And . . .?' Anne broke off. She was anxious to know if she would be accepted, but to ask outright might be seen as presumptuous.

As if she knew exactly what Anne had been about to say, the officer smiled.

'We'll let you know our decision very soon. But in the meantime, I will say that in my opinion you are a very capable young woman, and well suited to the service. Thank you for applying, and for coming along today.'

'Thank *you*.' Anne shifted her bag onto her shoulder and got up, feeling cheered. It was inevitable that there had to be some discussion before she was officially appointed, but from what the officer had said, that was probably just a formality.

Already she was bubbling with excitement and just a touch of nervousness as to what her new life would hold. She'd be doing her bit for the war effort, she'd be in the same service as her brother, she'd be well away from her mother's annoying habit of trying to run her life for her, and best of all she'd be leaving behind the turmoil and heartache of loving a man she couldn't trust.

Winnie couldn't put it off any longer. When she'd at least made the big house look respectable, she had gone home and made herself a sandwich with just a scrape of butter and a spoonful of home-made gooseberry jam. She'd have liked a slice of ham, but she'd used the last of it in the packed lunch she'd made up for Rosie. She checked their ration books. Yes, there was just enough left to buy another couple of ounces. She'd go to the butcher's shop later. But first she needed to speak to Charlie. She put on her coat, picked up her bag and set off towards town.

The sheds were on a railway siding on the far side of the track, and when she stepped inside, the noise of men working on the engines and shouting to one another was deafening. The corrugated-iron roof amplified it, she supposed. When they spotted her, the men stared curiously, but she couldn't see Charlie among them. One stopped what he was doing and came towards her, wiping his filthy hands on an equally filthy rag.

'What can I do you for, missus?'

'I wanted a word with Charlie Mitchell,' she said. 'I'm his sister-in-law.'

'Yeh, I'd'a know that,' the man said. 'You b'aint in luck, though. He don't work 'ere no more.'

'Oh.' Winnie was a bit taken aback. 'Where's he working now, then?'

Jennie Felton

The man shrugged. 'I don't rightly know. He left in a bit of a hurry.' He turned to a couple of other men who were working nearby. 'Do either of you know where 'e went?'

Both men shook their heads. 'Could be he's labouring for one of the builders,' one said. 'Or road sweeping for the council.'

Winnie could see she was getting nowhere. 'Thanks anyway,' she said, and left the shed feeling very fed up. The only place she could be sure of finding him was at his home, and that was a good step away, on the other side of Hillsbridge. There would be no point going now; if Charlie had found another job, he'd be at work. But to go in the evening meant a special journey, and a long walk there and back. It wasn't a prospect she relished, but she couldn't see any alternative. She'd call in at the butcher's, then go home and have a bit of a rest to set her up for the extra exercise she could have done without.

She checked her watch – almost two o'clock. By the time she got there, Mr Thomas should be open again after the lunch hour. She crossed the main road, went through the subway beneath the railway line and walked along the street. As she'd thought, just as she reached the shop, Mr Thomas was turning over the sign that hung on the door. Seeing her on the step, he opened the door and held it for her.

'Afternoon, Mrs Mitchell. I don't often see you in here in the week.'

'No, but I had some business in town, so I thought I'd kill two birds with one stone,' Winnie said.

'So what can I do for you?' He was back behind the counter now.

'I'd like a bit of ham. Just a couple of slices.'

'You're in luck.' He nodded in the direction of the slicing machine. 'I've only got that bit left – there's been a run on it the

184

last couple of days. I don't get my next delivery until tomorrow, so it'll be Thursday before it's cooked and ready.'

'Well, I'm glad of that. Otherwise I'd have come all the way into Hillsbridge on a fool's errand.'

'That would have been a shame.' Mr Thomas began turning the handle on the machine.

A thought occurred to Winnie. 'It was Charlie, my late husband's brother, that I came into town to see, but he's not working at the railway sheds any more, and nobody there could tell me where he's gone. You wouldn't happen to know, I suppose?'

Mr Thomas shook his head. 'Sorry, I don't.' He put the small slices of ham on a sheet of greaseproof paper and brought it over to the counter. 'I could ask his wife when she comes in next – that's usually on a Friday. But I can't make no promises.'

'Oh well, it was worth a try,' Winnie said, resigned. 'I thought if you knew, it might save me a journey up to his house.'

'That's a long way for you to have to go,' Fred agreed, looking concerned. 'Important, is it?'

'Well, yes. It's not for myself. It's Lady Hastings wants me to see him. She's organising a dance to raise funds to buy a Spitfire – the Hillsbridge Spitfire, she's calling it – and she wants me to ask Charlie if the accordion band could play for it.'

''Tis no good you asking Charlie, then,' Mr Thomas said. 'He hasn't got anything to do with it any more. Took the hump over something and walked out. Don't ask me what, but you know Charlie.'

'Oh.' Winnie didn't know whether to be sorry, or glad that she didn't have to make the approach to her brother-in-law that she'd been dreading. 'That's that then, I suppose.'

'I . . . I m-might be able to help you.'

'Oh? How's that?' Winnie said, surprised.

Mr Thomas looked a bit bashful. 'Well . . . I p-p-play the p-piano for them.'

She was even more surprised. She'd never seen the accordion band performing; she would have liked to have gone to one of their concerts, and suggested it a few times to Ern when he was alive, but he hadn't wanted to. He was reluctant to see his brother, she'd surmised. And since his death, she hadn't fancied going on her own. But she'd never have guessed that Fred Thomas might be a member. She wouldn't have thought he'd be able to play an instrument with his trembly hands. But you never knew. Life was full of surprises.

'So do you think . . .?' Not knowing how much influence he had when it came to the band's engagements, she was a little unsure about how to proceed.

'When's this dance anyway?' the butcher asked, and she recovered herself.

'Easter Saturday. At the town hall. Oh, Mr Thomas, I'd be so grateful, and I know Lady Hastings would be too. Most of the bands are missing key players because they've been called up . . .' Again she broke off, realising she was being less than tactful.

'So we're a last resort?' Mr Thomas said mildly.

'Oh no, not at all.'

He smiled. 'Don't worry, I'm not offended. I know we'm a bunch of old f-farts.'

He was wrapping the ham now. 'Look, Mrs Mitchell, this is all bits and pieces. I'm not going to charge you for it – it would only have gone in the bin anyway – and I don't want you to use up your coupons on it.'

'Oh, Mr Thomas, I can't let you do that . . .'

'Well, have a bit of tongue to go with it, then. That's not on rations yet, so you can put your book away.'

'That would be nice.' It was the least she could do, she

thought, getting out her purse. Rosie wasn't keen on tongue, but she was quite fond of it. A nice thick slice with a bit of mustard, yes, she'd enjoy it.

'I'll be in on Saturday as usual,' she said, counting coins out onto the counter.

'And I'll let you know if we can manage the dance on Easter Saturday,' Mr Thomas said.

'Thank you so much.'

Full of hope, Winnie left the shop. Suddenly the long walk home didn't seem nearly as onerous. What a nice man Mr Thomas was. For the first time it occurred to her that he'd hardly stammered at all, except when he'd been a bit bashful about being a pianist. Could it be that he felt comfortable with her?

Oh, don't be such an old fool! she told herself. But it was with a spring in her step that she set out for home.

Rosie, too, was feeling elated. She and the midwife had supported the distressed mother-to-be to the ambulance and made her comfortable, but they had scarcely pulled away from her terraced house on the northern outskirts of the city when everything happened very fast. Perhaps it was the jolting of the ambulance that had persuaded the reluctant baby to put in an appearance, as Paddy had suggested it might, and they had still not reached the hospital when the head could be seen. Moments later the midwife was cradling the baby in her capable hands as he slithered out into the world. 'You have a little boy,' she'd told the exhausted mother as she passed him to Rosie.

By the time Rosie had cleaned his face of the caul that covered it, wrapped him in a towel and laid him in his mother's arms, she had been close to tears. It wasn't professional to get emotional, she knew. But a new little life entering the world was awesome, and she counted herself lucky to have witnessed it.

When they'd arrived at St Mark's and opened the ambulance doors, a porter and a nurse had arrived with a trolley, and mother and baby had been conveyed into the hospital. It was then that the midwife, who had seemed rather curt to Rosie earlier, turned to her with a smile and a nod. 'Well done. I don't suppose you've ever delivered a baby yourself. But you were right on the button.'

For Rosie it was praise indeed, and she couldn't wait to finish her shift, go home and tell Winnie about her momentous day.

Chapter Fourteen

The weeks leading up to the dance were busy and eventful.

The day after Winnie had talked to Fred Thomas, she saw his butcher's van drive past the cottage and park on the drive leading to the big house. As she watched, Mr Thomas climbed out and approached the front door. He wasn't wearing his boater this evening, or his stripy apron, but a sports jacket and trilby hat. He'd come with news for Lady Hastings, she guessed. She would have liked to be the first to know if her efforts had borne fruit, but of course Mr Thomas wouldn't have known she lived in the cottage he had just passed.

Winnie stayed by the window, watching, the minutes ticking slowly by. She hoped he wasn't stammering too much, but that Lady Hastings would be kind and pretend not to notice if he did. She could be so sharp if something annoyed her. But if Mr Thomas had good news for her and her problems with a band were solved, surely she wouldn't want to do anything to upset him.

At last he emerged, turned his van in the widest part of the drive, taking care not to run onto any of the flower beds that surrounded it, and juddered away from the house. As he came closer, she could see that, though clean and well kept, the van was far from new. But at least it got him around. She supposed as a tradesman he was entitled to a petrol ration.

About to turn away from the window and finish clearing up the remains of her dinner, she was staggered to see the van pull up beside her gate, the door open and Mr Thomas climb down. Oh my goodness, he was coming up the path! Anxious as she was to find out what he'd had to say to her ladyship, Winnie was horrified; any moment he was going to knock on her door, and here she was still in her work dress and a pinny. But there was no time to do anything about that now. Running a quick hand over her unruly hair in a vain attempt to tidy it, she answered the door as soon as he rapped with the knocker.

'Mr Thomas!' she said, feigning surprise.

'I-I've just been up to see Lady H-H-Hastings,' he said. 'I didn't know you lived here till she told me or I'd have c-c-come to you f-first.'

'Oh, you weren't to know,' Winnie said. 'It's nice of you to think of me, though. I have been wondering . . .'

''Tis all f-fixed,' he said. 'Her ladyship's going to get the post-ers printed now. They're all ready bar the name of the b-band, so now she knows we'll play, that can go ahead quick sharp.'

'That's wonderful!' Winnie said, delighted.

'I think Lady Hastings were pleased.'

'I'm sure she's very relieved,' Winnie said, and then, on impulse, 'Can I offer you a cup of tea? The kettle's on the boil . . . well, it always is in my house.'

'That would be n-nice,' Mr Thomas said. 'Her ladyship did offer me a drink, but I wouldn't 'ave felt comfortable 'avin' one up there.'

'Come in then. But don't mind the muddle. I'm still clearing away my dinner things.'

She led the way into the kitchen and moved her plate and water glass onto the oilcloth-covered cupboard beside the sink. 'Sit down, do, Mr Thomas.'

She made the tea and poured cups for them both.

'Do you take sugar?' she asked.

'T-two, please. Though I sh-shall have to cut down when it goes on rations.'

Winnie added two generous spoonfuls of sugar to his cup. 'You should open a grocery department on the side,' she said with a smile.

'That's not a bad idea,' he agreed, stirring his tea.

Winnie sat down, blew on her own tea and took a sip.

'So what's the plan for the dance? Does Lady Hastings want anything special in the way of music?' she asked, hoping her ladyship hadn't been too demanding. Mr Thomas swiftly set her mind at rest.

'A bit of a mix, really. Some modern, some old-time. The sort of programme we usually play. And Betty Crook – she's our singer – will do a couple of numbers too. But you can still dance to those, she don't mind.'

'I'm looking forward to it,' Winnie said. 'Though I'll be stuck in the kitchen, I shouldn't wonder, sorting out the refreshments and making tea for the teetotallers. Are you teetotal, Mr Thomas?'

He grinned ruefully. 'Not a chance. Not for my late wife's want of trying, mind you. But I like me pint too much.'

'Oh dear, you've lost her, have you?' Winnie realised she knew nothing about Mr Thomas beyond that he was a nice man and a very good butcher. Living so far out of town meant she was out of touch with Hillsbridge folk, though she'd learned a lot more since she'd joined the WVS needlework bee.

'Back in '35,' he said. 'She got a bad dose of flu. It went to her chest and that was that.'

'I'm sorry. It's hard, isn't it,' Winnie sympathised. 'My Ern's been gone three years now, and I still miss him every day.'

'You've just got to get on with it, though, haven't you?' Mr Thomas sounded resigned, but the sadness was there in his eyes and his voice.

'Very true,' Winnie agreed. 'I expect you're glad you've got your music.'

'The band was my saviour when I lost her.' There was still a faraway look in his eyes. 'We never had a family, you see. We'd have liked one, but it never happened. At least you've got your daughter, haven't you? Lovely girl. She used to fill up my van when the petrol got low. Haven't seen her lately, though.'

'No. She's training as an ambulance attendant. And I've got a son, too – Don – but he's in the army. In France now. I'm worried to death about him, I can tell you.'

'You must be.'

They chatted for a while longer, then Mr Thomas pushed his cup to one side and got up. 'Well, thanks for the tea, Mrs Mitchell. But I mustn't take up your time any longer.'

'It's been a pleasure,' Winnie said, and then added impetuously, 'Why don't you call me Winnie? I know I'm not young any more, but "Mrs Mitchell" makes me feel like a proper old granny.'

The moment the words were out, she wondered if she was being too forward, but Mr Thomas smiled.

'Right you are. And I'm Fred.'

As she saw him out, Winnie felt lighter than she had done in a long while. And it occurred to her once again that Fred Thomas had hardly stuttered at all once they'd got into a conversation and he'd relaxed. Perhaps he'd enjoyed the interlude as much as she had. She rather hoped the opportunity would arise to do it again sometime.

Rosie and Paddy Murphy had had a busy day. They'd attended an elderly lady who had fallen in her kitchen and was unable to get up; since she lived alone, it was fortunate a neighbour had found her and called an ambulance. She'd hit her face on a kitchen worktop as she fell and gashed her forehead, but even more concerning was that Rosie suspected she'd broken her hip. Between them she and Paddy had managed to get her onto a stretcher and into the ambulance, and they'd taken her to the Royal United, which was more suited to diagnosing and treating her than St Mark's. While they were there, they'd received a call to a toddler who was choking on a grape – they'd be in short supply soon if you could get them at all, Paddy had observed. Rosie had managed to make the boy cough it up but decided he should be checked out by someone with more medical expertise than she had, so it was back to the hospital.

And so it had gone on, one call after another, some serious, some what Paddy called 'time-wasters'. If it was this busy now, what would it be like if there was an air raid? Rosie wondered.

It was late in the afternoon when Rosie began to be concerned about Paddy. She'd noticed that his driving, usually first class, had become rather erratic, and he was squirming in his seat every so often as if he was in pain. 'Are you all right?' she asked him, but he waved her concerns aside. 'Sure I'm fine. Just a bit of indigestion, that's all. I ate my pasty too damned quick.'

It was true. He had gobbled it down – a cold, suety pastry filled with chunks of tough meat and undercooked potato that he'd bought from Joe's Café, a trailer in a lay-by at the side of the road. A call had come in and he had finished it while driving, showering his uniform with flakes of unappetising pastry. No wonder he had indigestion.

What was hopefully going to be the last job of their shift was to take home a farmer who had been brought in early this morning after a cow he was milking had kicked out and broken several of his ribs. He'd been under observation all day, and the doctor in attendance had wanted to keep him in overnight in case complications arose – an internal injury, perhaps – but the farmer was adamant that he had to get back to the farm. He'd already been away too long, and he needed to make sure his animals were being well cared for by the farmhand he dismissed as 'not quite all there'.

They'd made the long drive out into the country and bumped their way up a rough track to the farmhouse. The farmer's wife, wearing trousers tucked into wellington boots, had come hurrying out of a barn and squelched across the muddy farmyard to greet him rather impatiently. 'I thought you was dead and buried, the time you've bin!' But she took his arm and helped him up to the house.

When the door had closed after them, Paddy had started the engine and nursed the ambulance back down the rough track. But Rosie, concerned, thought there was more to the way he was weaving about than simply avoiding the ruts. She hesitated to mention it again; Paddy was the sort who hated a fuss. But as they drove along a narrow lane and he hit the bank, she felt she could keep silent no longer.

'Paddy, why don't you pull in and have a rest when there's a gateway,' she said.

'Sure didn't I tell you, I'm fine!' he snapped. But at that moment he hit the bank again with such force that Rosie thought they were going to turn over.

'P'raps I'd better,' he conceded. 'This pain's getting worse.'

There was a gate leading into a field not much further along the lane and the bank had been flattened here to allow access. Judging by the churned-up mud, it was obviously used frequently, but Rosie was just glad that Paddy was going to have a rest. When she got a good look at him, though, she was alarmed to see the sheen of sweat that ran from his receding hairline all the way down to his shirt collar, and she didn't like the way he was rubbing his arm, either. This was far more than indigestion caused by a stodgy pasty. Rosie thought it was far more likely he was having a heart attack.

She experienced a moment's panic. Supposing his heart stopped! She'd been trained in the Silvester method of resuscitation, but to administer that the patient had to be flat on his back with room to manipulate his arms from his sides to a position where they were stretched out above his head, and there was no way she could do that in the cramped front of the ambulance. On the point of calling in to headquarters for assistance, she hesitated. Paddy needed urgent treatment, and heaven alone knew how long it would take for a doctor or another ambulance to reach them out here. She wasn't even sure exactly where they were and wouldn't be able to pass on accurate directions. The quickest way to get help for him was to drive to the hospital. But clearly Paddy wasn't fit to do that. There was nothing for it. She hadn't yet been given the necessary test that would allow her to drive, but it was no time to worry about that.

'If I get out, can you shift over into my seat?' she asked, already climbing down into the mire that had been churned up by tractor tyres.

'What?'

'Move over, dammit, Paddy! I'm going to drive.' She was relieved when he managed to drag himself from his own seat to what had been hers, but the fact that he'd actually done what she'd told him wasn't a good sign. The effort had made him breathless too, and he was gasping for air.

'Just hang on, Paddy. Don't you dare black out on me.'

She started the engine and tried to pull away, but for agonisingly long minutes the ambulance wheels spun in the thick mud.

She jumped out again, opened the back door and yanked a neatly folded blanket off the bed. Laying it down directly behind the rear wheels, she ran back and climbed into the driving seat, where she engaged reverse gear. To her relief, she felt the wheels move just enough to lift them out of the rut. She pressed down hard on the accelerator pedal and the ambulance lurched back onto the lane.

'I thought I was gonna have to push,' Paddy said, a weak attempt at humour, but it cheered Rosie. If he could still crack a joke, he could make it back to the hospital, she thought. Hoped. Prayed.

'Can you tell me the way until we're back on the main road?' she asked.

'Ah sure, you can't miss it. Just keep going right . . .' But his voice was breathy and strained as if he was struggling to speak at all.

Rosie drove as fast as she dared, even radioing in to warn St Mark's that they were on their way and that Paddy would need immediate medical attention. She completed the journey safely, and in record time, and as she turned in through the hospital's main gate, she saw a nurse and a porter waiting outside with a trolley stretcher. A white-coated figure emerged from the doorway – a doctor, ready and waiting in case he was needed to begin immediate treatment.

As the porter made for the rear of the ambulance, Rosie threw open her door and yelled, 'He's in here!'

The porter detoured to the passenger side, followed by the nurse, and Rosie leaned across to open the door. But it was immediately clear that although – thankfully! – Paddy was still breathing, he couldn't summon the strength to get out of the ambulance himself.

'Give me a hand here!' the porter instructed.

Rosie swung Paddy's legs out and levered him forward so that the porter could take his weight, and between them he and the nurse got him onto the trolley and set off at a run for the main doors of the hospital.

For a few minutes Rosie remained where she was, uncertain as to whether she could trust her legs, which were shaking uncontrollably. Then she climbed down cautiously and stood leaning against the ambulance, head bowed, eyes closed, taking deep breaths to steady herself.

'Well, well, if it isn't Florence Nightingale herself!'

Her eyes flew open at the sound of the familiar voice.

Julian! Rosie wondered if she was hallucinating. She hadn't expected him to be at St Mark's today; if she'd thought about it at all, she would have assumed he would be taking his afternoon surgery or still out on house calls. But here he was, not dressed for doing a ward round, but wearing a sports jacket and cavalry twills.

He nodded at the ambulance. 'And driving too, I see.'

'I had to,' she said defensively. 'Paddy was taken ill.'

'Well, it's a good thing you didn't try to get into the hospital by way of the pedestrian access this time,' he said.

Quite suddenly Rosie's delayed shock erupted into anger. 'It's not a laughing matter,' she flared. 'Paddy is having a heart attack. I thought he was going to die.'

'I'm sorry . . .' Julian looked uncharacteristically thrown by her outburst.

'So you should be!' she returned. 'It was awful, Julian. He frightened the life out of me.'

'Are you all right?'

'I will be. As soon as I know Paddy is going to be OK.'

'He's in good hands,' Julian said. 'And you did well.' When she remained silent, he went on, 'How are you getting home?'

'On the bus, of course, but not until I know Paddy's going to make it.'

'You haven't got Mother's car?'

'I'm not sure she trusts me with it.'

'Then I shall take you. You're in no fit state to go by bus.'

Again! This was getting to be a habit, Rosie thought. But after the day she'd had, she really didn't relish the idea of taking the bus.

'Are you sure?'

'No problem. Frances wants to see me anyway. Something about this dance she's organising, I think.'

'In that case . . . thank you. But I do want to find out how Paddy's doing first. And I need to make sure the next crew have arrived for their shift.'

'They have. And I honestly think I should get you home. Look, Frances will let me use her telephone to call St Mark's when I'm ready to leave, and I'll stop off at the cottage and update you. How does that sound?'

'OK. Thank you.' Rosie felt too wiped out to argue. And she really shouldn't delay Julian if he was expected at the big house.

'Come on then. My car's just over there.'

They drove in silence for a while, but Rosie was puzzling over something.

'How did you come to be at St Mark's?' she asked.

'I can pick up the ambulance frequency on my radio. I was on my way to Hillsbridge when I heard you call in. Then I heard St Mark's call the Royal to ask if John Whetherley was available. They knew from what you said that your driver was having a heart attack, and Whetherley is the top man in his field. So I made a detour.'

'Mr Whetherley!' Rosie said, impressed.

'Yes, so you can stop worrying.'

That would be easier said than done, she thought. But for the moment the anger she'd felt at Julian's flippant response to what had happened was quite forgotten. Once again she was falling under his spell.

Julian had dropped Rosie at her mother's cottage and continued on to Bramley Court. He'd ring the hospital for news, he'd told her, and let her know what they said. Rosie told Winnie what had happened, and when they'd had their tea, she went to the front window to watch for Julian. The wait seemed endless, and she hoped and prayed it didn't mean that something awful had happened. But at last there he was, knocking on the front door. She hurried to open it.

'Well?' she asked anxiously.

'All good. He's holding his own. I'm sorry if I've been a while, but I needed to see Mother before heading back to Bath, so I made the call from there so as to be able to give you the very latest update.'

'He's really going to be all right?' Rosie was very relieved, but still anxious as to how things would progress.

'So far. And as I said before, he's in the best possible hands. And in the best place. He's been transferred to the Royal so that he can be under Whetherley's care.'

'Thank you – for everything,' Rosie said. 'I'm sorry I was in such a tizzy.'

'A tizzy? Were you?' he teased. Then, 'Oh, by the way, I told Mother her car will be in safe hands if she lets you borrow it. And that there really was no need for me to give you those extra driving lessons. Now, I must go.' He turned, raised a hand. 'See you soon.'

And then he was gone.

What a day! Rosie thought as she watched his tail lights

disappear down the drive. Her emotions were all over the place. Anxiety, delayed shock, a little bit of pride in herself. And beneath it all that sliver of hope was growing brighter. Surely Julian wouldn't have done or said the things he had unless . . . Was he making an attempt to rekindle what they had once shared? And this time, not in secret. Not behind Anne's back . . . No, she mustn't think like that! But she realised it would be very hard not to.

Anne had been waiting anxiously to hear if she'd been successful in her application to join the WAAF. Now that the art gallery treasures had all been moved to the safety of the church vault, she was at something of a loose end. But when the letter arrived, rather than simple confirmation and an order to report to one of the training centres, it asked her to telephone the recruiting office for a further appointment. Puzzled, she did so immediately, and the young woman who took her call booked her in to report there at 11 a.m. two days hence.

She made the journey into the town centre still wondering why she needed to be seen again. The recruiting office had previously been a menswear shop, and was situated between a newsagent's and a shoe shop. Now recruitment posters and a model Hurricane occupied the window space that had once displayed suits and jackets on plaster dummies. The front office where the receptionist was positioned behind a desk was small, and Anne expected to be directed through to the section that had been partitioned off to form an interview room. Instead she was instructed to take the stairs to the first floor, which had become offices.

Little light filtered in through the small barred windows, and the landing was almost as dim, but a petite uniformed figure was standing outside the only door that was open, and Anne recognised the officer who had interviewed her previously. She held the door wider as Anne approached. 'Mr Green will see you now. Please go in, Miss Hastings.'

She stood aside for Anne to enter the office, where a man faced her from across a big, worn desk. He rose to greet her and she saw that he was not wearing uniform but a dark suit, white shirt and a tie that looked regimental. A folded handkerchief peeked from his breast pocket. Why was he in civvies? Anne wondered. Only his handlebar moustache and Brylcreemed hair gave any suggestion that he might be an RAF officer. The female officer didn't follow her in, but closed the door, leaving her alone with Mr Green.

'Miss Hastings. Thank you for coming. Do sit down.' He indicated a hard upright chair that had been set at right angles to the desk.

Anne took the chair, straightening her skirt so that it wouldn't ride up over her knees, and Mr Green sat back in his rather more comfortable chair and reached for a pipe that lay in a big glass ashtray on the desk.

'Flight Lieutenant Marley doesn't care for me smoking,' he said conspiratorially, 'but you won't mind, will you?'

'No, of course not.' Who was she to argue? Especially as she had begun to quite like a cigarette herself since she had left home.

'Now, I'm sure you are wondering what this is all about,' he said when he had got the pipe going and sweet, aromatic smoke curled into a ray of sunlight that was shining in through the window.

'I am rather,' Anne said.

'I'll explain in a moment. Perhaps first I can ask you a little about yourself. You were at finishing school in the French-speaking part of Switzerland, I understand.'

'Yes.' Why this interest in where she had gone to school? Anne wondered.

'So you speak French?'

'Yes.' The WAAF officer had asked her the same question. She must be headed for comms, Anne thought.

'You skied, I expect?' Mr Green was speaking now in French.

'Yes, and I still go back a couple of times a year in the season.' Anne followed his lead and replied in French.

'And what about other sports? Athletics? Hockey? Tennis?'

Though she was growing ever more confused, Anne answered truthfully, still speaking in French as he was. 'I play tennis, and of course I did play hockey at school. I wasn't much good at athletics, though. Well, at least not the high jump or sprints. I did like cross-country running, though. I couldn't go very fast over short distances, but I could keep going.' She smiled slightly. 'Actually I came third out of thirty on school sports day one year.'

'Well done you!' The officer reverted to English. 'And you're in good health? There's nothing you missed out when you applied to the WAAF?'

'No. I wouldn't do that. A sniffly cold is all I've suffered for years now, and everyone gets colds in the winter, don't they?'

'Indeed they do.' He laid his pipe, which had gone out, in the ashtray and retrieved a packet of Players from one of the desk drawers. 'Would you care for a cigarette, Miss Hastings? I think I am going to have one.'

Anne was beginning to think that she really could do with one. 'Thank you.'

The officer lit first hers and then his own cigarette with what looked like a solid silver lighter. He blew a perfect smoke ring into the ray of sunlight and sat forward, elbows on the desk, chin resting on one big fist. 'So. To business. I understand Flight

Lieutenant Marley had you sign the Official Secrets Act when she first interviewed you. I must emphasise that what I'm about to say to you is covered by that. Nothing that passes between us must go beyond these four walls. I know that you have volunteered for the WAAF, but you are being considered for quite a different role.'

Anne frowned. 'What—'

'Be careful.' He pointed to the cigarette burning away between her fingers. She jumped, took a puff, coughed, and stubbed it out in the big glass ashtray.

Mr Green raised an eyebrow, then continued. 'As I'm sure you know, the Germans have taken control of certain European countries, and are planning to invade and occupy France. If – or rather when, in my opinion – they are successful, there are groups of French patriots who intend to fight them to the bitter end. It's the job of my department to assist them, help them to set up resistance cells, keep them supplied with what they need, even lend our expertise in blowing up bridges and railway lines, that sort of thing. But we need people who are fluent in French – as you clearly are – to liaise between them and us. In fact you seem to fit the bill on all counts, which is why I believe you would be most useful to us.'

'Useful?' Anne echoed, stunned. 'You mean you want me to go to France as some sort of secret agent?'

The big man smiled slightly. 'Broadly speaking, yes. Exactly what role you would be best suited to would be decided during your training, should you agree to run with this. But before you make any decision, I must warn you that going into enemy territory is highly dangerous, no matter how well prepared you are. The Germans will be anxious to dispose of those they consider a threat, and will stop at nothing to root them out. If an agent falls into their hands, their prospects are dire. I'm talking torture here, Miss Hastings, as well as incarceration and execution. So I would advise you to think about this very carefully before we proceed any further.'

Anne's head was whirling. This was all so unexpected. So totally overwhelming.

'What about my application to join the WAAF?' she asked.

'That's already going through. You will be given the rank of flight officer. And, incidentally, should you decide to take the path I'm suggesting, you will be given a codename. So perhaps you could also think about whether there is a French name you would like to be known by.'

'My mother's name is Frances,' she said. 'Perhaps I could be Françoise.'

'Good.' He nodded approvingly. 'And your accent is excellent, by the way. That will be very important if you are to pass yourself off as a native and blend into the background.'

He ground out his cigarette in the ashtray and reached for his pipe once more. 'Take as long as you need to come to a decision. It shouldn't be taken lightly. When you have, or if you have any further questions, let Flight Lieutenant Marley know, and she will contact me. But please remember – in the meantime you must behave as normal, and you must not tell anyone, even your nearest and dearest, about this meeting, or what you have been asked to do.'

'I understand.' Realising the interview was at an end, Anne rose, and Mr Green went with her to the door, where he shook her hand.

'Good luck, Miss Hastings. I'm sure you will arrive at whatever is the right decision for you.'

She left the office in a daze. This wasn't what she'd expected at all. But to be chosen for something so vitally important to the war effort was a huge honour. Could she do it? Mr Green was right, of course. She must think carefully before she did anything rash. But even the thought of danger was exciting. Frightening, yes, but exciting. It was her chance to show the world – and especially her mother and Julian – that she wasn't that timid little girl any more. An opportunity to stretch her wings and fly. She thought she already knew what her decision would be.

Chapter Fifteen

By the middle of March, the first prospective agents had arrived at the Manor: three men, one of whom was half-French, and two young women, both recorded as officers in the FANY – the First Aid Nursing Yeomanry. This, Clarke knew, was their cover, and they were known only by their codenames, Jeanne and Marie.

Although the two girls were sharing, all eight bedrooms were now occupied, and with a parachute instructor due to arrive, Firkins faced a dilemma. The para, it seemed, didn't have a permanent base but moved from training centre to training centre as required. How long he would be here was an unknown; it would depend on how quickly the trainee agents became proficient enough to be dropped safely into France. But while he was here, he would need accommodation. Firkins' first suggestion was that Dennis Holder should move in with Clarke, but Clarke was having none of it. His dislike of Holder had grown even stronger since the girls had arrived. He was disgusted by the crude remarks Holder made about them, and the lecherous looks he gave them. He disliked spending any time at all with the man, and he certainly wasn't going to have him invading his personal space.

'This is going to be an ongoing problem,' he told Firkins. 'I suggest we convert one of the downstairs rooms into a bedroom.'

'Oh yes, and which one?' Firkins enquired sarcastically. 'The men won't be too pleased to lose their recreation room, and I'm not vacating my office.'

'That's in half of what used to be the library,' Clarke said. 'The racehorse trainer had the partition put up so as to create a storage space, as well you know. We don't use the other half.'

'Because it's full of junk!' Firkins retorted.

'So we clear it. Between us it shouldn't take long.'

'It's very small.' Firkins seemed set on insisting Clarke share his room with Holder.

'The para's only going to be here for a couple of weeks at a time. All he needs is a bed and enough room for his kit. And you've already arranged with that furniture shop in Shepton Mallet to deliver a bed. I don't see the problem.'

In the end Firkins had been forced to back down, and Clarke, Dave Thompson and Colin Stewart had worked tirelessly to clear the small storage room of the boxes of equine food supplements, medications and miscellaneous equipment that were stacked against all four walls, leaving only a narrow aisle for access. Not wanting to have to contend with Holder, who would be more of a hindrance than a help, Clarke had instructed him to take the trainees to the firing range, where he could test their skills with small arms.

'This is bloody hard work!' Stewart complained, returning grubby and sweating from the barn where they were depositing the boxes. 'I can see why the horse man decided it was easier to leave all this stuff here and buy new. Especially since I suppose it's the owners of the horses who will be paying for it.'

'You want to get fit,' Thompson told him with a smirk. 'A cushy job like yours is doing you no favours. And this is a damned sight easier than setting up the assault course. Now that *was* a challenge.'

'Very true,' Clarke agreed. The assault course had been put

together alongside the river that ran through the estate and ended in a large lake. They'd piled logs, made tunnels out of oil cans, and fashioned a rope bridge. 'You should have left it for the recruits – it could have been part of their training.'

'Good plan,' Thompson agreed facetiously. 'Shall we go down and dismantle it when we've finished here?' and the others rounded on him with pithy rejoinders.

Just as they had finished, a furniture van pulled onto the forecourt and two beefy men unloaded a cast-iron bedstead and a mattress.

'We could've done with them earlier on,' Thompson remarked as the men carried the bedstead effortlessly inside.

When they had left, Firkins, who had supervised the installation with his usual pomposity, joined the trio.

'Well, it will have to do, I suppose,' he said, waving a hand to indicate the newly cleared room. 'And just in time. The parachute chap is arriving tomorrow.' He turned to Clarke. 'You'll have to go to Bath and pick him up, Sutherland. He doesn't have a staff car; they're all in use now. His train gets in at ten twenty-five.'

'That's Bath Spa, is it?' Clarke asked, all innocence.

'You know damned well it is.'

'There are two railway stations in Bath, that's all. Bath Spa and Bath Green Park,' Clarke reminded him.

High spots of colour rose in Firkins' cheeks. 'Very well, I'll check,' he said shortly.

'If you would. I don't want to go to the wrong one.' Clarke was fairly sure it would be Bath Spa – Green Park catered mainly for more local routes – but he was enjoying winding Firkins up.

Nevertheless, he was rather pleased Firkins had chosen to single him out for what the man probably thought was an imposition. To get to Bath, Clarke would have to drive through

Hillsbridge, and that was something he was more than happy to do.

I'll find you yet, Miss Rosie Mitchell, he thought, and smiled to himself.

Lady Hastings was fuming. She had been running through her checklist of things that still had to be done in preparation for the dance when she'd received a telephone call from the WVS regional commissioner to inform her that evacuations were to begin again, and this time Hillsbridge was to receive sixty children from cities deemed to be at risk when the Nazis started a bombing campaign. She understood the reasoning behind the government's decision and agreed it was wise to take precautions. But it was the date the children were due to arrive that was frustrating and annoying her: 26 March. Just three days after the dance, and with a bank holiday weekend in between. If she was to be sure that everything was in place it needed to be done at once, and she was still knee-deep in arrangements for the dance. The posters were all up now, and fliers had been posted in the windows of almost every shop in Hillsbridge and High Compton. Mr Thomas had agreed to allow his butcher's shop to act as an impromptu box office and had reported that tickets were selling well. But there was still a great deal of behind-the-scenes organisation to be taken care of and she just couldn't see how she could handle both projects at once.

She slammed down the telephone and went in search of Winnie, finding her on her hands and knees polishing the sides of the stair treads, where they were not covered in carpet.

'Can you spare a minute, Mrs Mitchell?'

Winnie gathered up her cloth and tin of wax polish – she couldn't leave them here for someone to fall over – and followed Lady Hastings into the library.

'I may need you to take on some extra duties with regard to the Spitfire dance,' her ladyship said without preamble. 'I've just been informed I have to make arrangements to receive sixty child evacuees on Easter Tuesday, and with only a week's notice that is going to have to take precedence. This couldn't have come at a worse time, and I can tell you, I'm not best pleased.'

''Tis a bit inconvenient,' Winnie agreed. 'But at least you've got a list of all those as volunteered to take a kiddie in, haven't you?'

'Yes, but they'll all have to be contacted, and the letters need to go out straight away if they're to get them before the bank holiday on Good Friday. And some of them may have changed their mind, so more may have to be found to replace them. I just don't see how I can get it all done and ensure the dance goes off satisfactorily.'

'Take one thing at a time, that's what my Ern would have said.' Winnie had a pretty good idea of what was coming – and she wasn't best pleased either. She really didn't want to be lumbered with chivvying up the WVS members who had taken charge of the various aspects of the arrangements for the dance, and she had no idea how she could help with the evacuees.

'Couldn't you ask Mr Edgell to get one of his typists to send letters out to all them who said they'd take a child?' she suggested. 'They could do it in no time, and get it in the post straight away. I expect one of them goes to the post office every day. And you could get something in the local paper. It's news, after all – they'd do a good spread as well as an advert, I shouldn't wonder.'

'That's a good idea,' Lady Hastings conceded. 'But the paper's going to be coming out a day early this week. Friday is a bank holiday, remember.'

'Then you'd better get on to them quick sharp, hadn't you?' Sometimes Winnie surprised herself with the things she dared say to her employer.

'I will.' Lady Hastings was recovering something of her usual decisiveness. 'I'll make some calls immediately.'

Winnie nodded, satisfied. It hadn't taken her ladyship long to regain her can-do attitude. And with any luck Winnie could avoid the jobs she'd been afraid her ladyship was going to foist on her. The one thing she wouldn't have minded doing was if Lady Hastings had wanted her to take some message to Mr Thomas the butcher. She'd really enjoyed their chat. Never mind, now that meat was on ration and she was registered with him, she had a good excuse to go into the shop whenever she was in town. It wasn't much fun not being able to buy what you wanted, but 'every cloud has a silver lining', as Ern used to say. Winnie returned to polishing the stairs with new vigour.

Clarke left in good time to meet the train the parachute instructor was going to be arriving on. Firkins had provided him with only the sketchiest information – whether he was being deliberately cagey or if it was all he'd been given, Clarke didn't know. Apparently the man was a sergeant in the army air corps and his name was Taylor. He would be in uniform, Firkins went on, so it should be easy enough to identify him among the other disembarking passengers. Clarke wasn't so sure about this. Now that Britain was at war, there could be any number of soldiers travelling about the country.

As he approached Hillsbridge, he slowed, keeping a sharp lookout for a certain young lady, though he had to admit the odds of spotting her were long ones. What he did see, however, was a poster affixed to the trunk of a tree on a small traffic island in the middle of the road, and his interest was aroused by the word 'Dance' that was emblazoned on it in large black capitals.

A dance. Surely if it was being advertised here, it must be being held locally. Might Rosie Mitchell be going to it? There couldn't be much going on in the way of entertainment for young women of her age under the present circumstances. It might be his best chance of finding her again. But sandwiched as he was between a delivery van and a bus, he couldn't stop to read any of the details, which were in much smaller print. He'd have a look on the way back, he decided.

As he rounded the bend, he saw that the level crossing gates were closed, with a couple of vehicles already queuing on the road ahead. He was checking his watch, hoping that he wasn't going to be held up for long, when he saw the driver of the delivery wagon in front of him stick out his arm to indicate he was turning right. He pulled across into a street that branched off the main road, and on impulse Clarke followed him. He didn't think he would be going far out of his way; it looked as if the street was horseshoe shaped and led around a central block of shops, rejoining the main road on the far side of the tree where the poster hung.

Clarke passed a gents' outfitters, a newsagent's, a double-fronted store displaying pedal cycles, and a chapel; then directly in front of him, on the far side of an open square, he saw an impressive two-storey building with a couple of steps leading up to double doors. And glory be, notices were displayed in glass-fronted cases to either side. From this distance he couldn't see what they referred to, but he guessed that this must be the town hall, and they could be advertising local events.

He drove straight across and stopped facing the billboards. One of the notices definitely said 'Dance'. He was about to get out of the car to have a closer look when a loud honking made him almost jump out of his skin. He wheeled round. The bus was right behind him and the driver was gesticulating angrily. Only then did he see the bus stop signs, two of them. This must be the central stopping place for the town, he guessed. He raised his hand in apology to the driver and quickly reversed along the side of the square. The passengers disembarking from the bus were now blocking his view of the poster, so he got out of the car, walked along the pavement and was rewarded by what he saw. The dance the poster was advertising was being held here in the town hall on Easter Saturday, with all proceeds going towards a fund to buy a Spitfire.

Yes! Clarke couldn't see that he would be required to give classes in explosives on a Saturday evening. Intensive as the course would be, there had to be some respite for both the trainees and the instructors. Come hell or high water, he was going to make it to Hillsbridge for the dance.

As the train emerged from the darkness of Box Tunnel into brittle spring-like sunshine, a passenger who could scarcely have been more different to the paratrooper who sat in the opposite corner of the carriage felt a smile of pure happiness curve her lips and lift her heart.

Somerset! Freda hadn't realised until that moment just how much she'd missed it. Green fields stretching away from the rail track on both sides, trees and hedgerows beginning to burgeon with new leaf. Cows clustering in gateways, lambs gambolling or suckling from their mothers. Soon they would be a part of her life – or she hoped they would. She didn't know if the farm she was bound for was livestock or arable, but she didn't care much. She was coming home.

She left her seat, past a mother nursing a toddler on her lap, and clambered over the long legs of the soldier in the corner of the carriage. He'd fallen asleep almost as soon as he'd boarded the train in Swindon, and she hoped he hadn't missed his stop. In the corridor she lowered a window so that she could breathe in the familiar scent of the countryside. And yes, she could smell it, the freshness that came from grass after a shower of rain, even if it was tainted with the smoke from the engine. And the less pleasant rather sweet odour of silage. Even that delighted her.

The route was reasonably familiar to her from the times she'd visited Granny before she had become too ill to be left alone and Freda had gone to London to take care of her, and the occasions too when she'd returned to visit her parents, though that hadn't been for a long while now. Not far to go. They'd soon be pulling into the platform at Bath Spa. She went back to the carriage to retrieve her suitcase from the rack so as to be ready.

The soldier had woken up now and moved his outstretched legs to let her past. When he saw her struggling to retrieve her suitcase, he got up.

'Here, let me help you.'

'Thanks. It is pretty heavy.' She watched enviously as he hefted the suitcase as if it weighed nothing at all. If she was going to work on the land, she'd need to build up some muscle of her own, or she'd be of no use to anybody.

With the same ease he carried it into the corridor and she followed. He set it down and returned to the carriage, but a few minutes later, when they pulled into the station, he was back, a kitbag slung over his shoulder.

'I'll get it out for you, but then you'll have to find a porter. I have to look out for someone.'

'Thanks,' she said again, grateful that she wouldn't hold up the other passengers waiting behind her to disembark.

There was a porter a little further along the platform, and she waved to try to attract his attention, but he was looking the other way. When the soldier reached him, he stopped and said something to him, and the porter headed in her direction with his trolley.

'Where to then, miss?'

'I need to get to the taxi rank.' In the letter she'd received from the farmer, he'd told her to take a taxi and he'd pay the driver when they arrived. Petrol was too scarce to use his ration on unnecessary journeys.

As they headed to the station foyer, Freda got out her ticket and also a half-crown, and when the porter left her just outside the entrance, where a couple of taxis were waiting, she pushed the silver coin into his hand. She wasn't used to tipping, and she didn't know how much he would expect, but when he touched his cap to her and pushed the coin into his pocket, she guessed she must have got it about right.

The driver of the first cab in the line leapt out and approached her, eager for his fare. He took her suitcase, opened the boot of the car and heaved it inside.

'Right. Where d'you want to go?'

Freda fished the farmer's letter out of her bag and read out the address, written in bold capitals at the top of the first page, though in reality she had no need to do so. She'd committed the details to memory, but all the same it was better to be safe than sorry.

'Rookery Farm, Westerleigh.'

The cabbie opened the rear door of his taxi and held it wide for Freda to get in. Then he climbed into the driver's seat and they were off.

It's really happening, Freda thought, excitement bubbling up inside her. Would she ever go back to Granny's house in London? Would there even be a house to go back to when this war was over? But she wasn't going to worry about that now. She couldn't wait to begin work that didn't mean sitting at a typewriter all day, work that would be in the open air. And best of all, within reach of Hillsbridge.

* * *

Lady Hastings poured herself a large gin and tonic – how on earth could people drink it with orange squash? – and settled back into her favourite chair. What a day! But she was more than satisfied with what she had accomplished.

The journalist on the local weekly newspaper had been pleased to be able to report the imminent arrival of the evacuee children, and had promised there would be a piece in this week's *Hillsbridge Echo*. She was also going to include a mention of the Spitfire dance on Easter Saturday as a reminder for those who hadn't yet bought their tickets. And Giles Edgell had agreed to get letters to the families who had offered to take in children typed up and mailed today for a promised next-day delivery.

She'd also managed to get hold of Julian, and he'd assured her that he'd arranged emergency cover so that he could support the dance, and would most certainly be there.

'Papa is making a generous donation and he'd never forgive me if I didn't come along,' he had said. 'Besides, it might be my last chance to see Anne before she's posted away. She is still set on joining the WAAF, I suppose?'

'I'm afraid so,' Lady Hastings said bitterly. 'I've done my best to dissuade her, but she's adamant it's what she wants. Because her brother is an RAF pilot, I imagine. But you might well have better luck if you speak to her. Tell her you don't want her to go; how much you'll miss her.' She paused a beat. 'You *don't* want her to go, do you?'

'Certainly I don't! Since I left Bristol I haven't seen nearly enough of her, and I must confess I was hoping that if she did war work of some kind locally we'd be able to meet far more often.'

'Oh, Julian dear, do please do your best. For all our sakes. You two are so perfect together. She adores you – you do know that, don't you?' Lady Hastings paused to let her words sink in, then went on, 'But maybe I'm making assumptions I shouldn't.

My only excuse is that I really don't want her to go. I'm already out of my mind with worry for Philip. If I have to worry about Anne too . . . Wherever she's based would almost certainly be a target for enemy attack. My little girl, in danger of losing her life . . .'

'I'd worry about her too,' Julian said. 'Rest assured, Frances, I'll do everything I can to persuade her to stay in Hillsbridge.'

Now, cradling her gin and tonic, Frances hoped that Julian would succeed where she had failed. And that he wouldn't tell Anne that she'd given him a little nudge in the right direction.

At just after nine that evening, Freda was climbing the stairs to bed. 'Early to bed and early to rise' was obviously the motto to live by on a farm. But she didn't mind one jot. She was, in any case, very tired and couldn't wait to get into the big bed with its patchwork counterpane. But she was in good spirits, and as she undressed and laid out clothes ready for the morning, she thought back over what had been a momentous day. Everything here was perfect, just perfect . . .

The farm had turned out to be everything she could have hoped for, and more, set in the heart of the Somerset countryside. A long dirt track led between fields, and in one of them she'd seen a tractor moving slowly in a straight line. She had guessed it might be planting seed for the new season's crop of some foodstuff or other.

The farmhouse itself was big, square and built from local lias stone. It looked well maintained, unlike some. But she was taken by surprise by the man who emerged from the house as the taxi came to a stop in the farmyard. She'd imagined that the farmer would be middle-aged, or even elderly, with a weatherbeaten face and thinning hair hidden beneath a battered trilby hat. But this man was no more than mid thirties, with a full head of dark hair and muscled arms, and a tan that no doubt lasted from one summer to the next showing beneath his rolled-up shirtsleeves.

He greeted her with a nod and turned to the business of retrieving her suitcase and settling up with the cabbie, then, as the taxi pulled away, he turned to her.

'So you're our new land girl. Do I call you Miss Dobbs, or are you OK with your Christian name?'

'Oh yes, of course. It's Freda.'

'And I'm Ted Holland. You can call me Ted, or Farmer, I don't mind which. Let's go in and you can meet my mother.'

Carrying her suitcase, he led the way into a big flagstoned kitchen where a buxom older woman in a shapeless jumper and skirt was stirring a pot on an open range. She turned, still holding the spoon.

'Glad you're here, missy. We can certainly do with some help. We've lost all but one of our hands – George Griffin – to the army, and he's gettin' on a bit now. It's too much for just him and our Ted, so I hope you don't mind hard work.'

Mr Holland senior must be dead, Freda guessed. 'I've got a lot to learn, but I'll do my very best,' she said.

'Well I hope so, or you'll be sent packing. But don't worry, we'll keep you well fed if nothing else.' She turned back to the pot. 'You like a beef stew, I hope?'

'I do. And it smells delicious.'

'Should be. Meat from one of our own cows, and home-grown vegetables.' She gave the stew a last stir and put the spoon down on a plate on the counter. 'You can get on with whatever you've got to do, Ted. This won't be ready for another hour or so. I'll look after our young lady. Show her her room an' all that. I expect you'd like to freshen up after your journey, miss.'

She lifted Freda's suitcase as easily as the soldier had done and led the way up the stairs and along a landing, then threw open a white-painted door.

Freda had been astonished by the size of the room beyond. She had expected to be shoehorned into a box room or even an attic. A fire was burning low in a small fireplace; the room hadn't been used lately and needed airing, Mrs Holland explained. A patchwork quilt covered the bed, and the rest of the furniture – a marble-topped wash stand, dressing table and double wardrobe – was heavy oak and quite old, Freda guessed.

'Make yourself at home,' Mrs Holland said, putting the suitcase on the bed. 'Bathroom's just across the landing.'

It hadn't been difficult for Freda to do just that. She'd enjoyed good food; the beef stew was delicious, as was a supper of bread, cheese and pickles. Mrs Holland and her son didn't waste words, but she didn't mind that – in fact she rather liked them for it. She'd known too many people who were overfond of the sound of their own voice, and there was something quite reassuring about the Hollands. And this bed . . . She sank into it, loving the softness of the feather pillows and mattress.

Yes, she was going to be happy here, she thought. She could feel it in her bones. The work might be hard, but she was determined to enjoy it. And she had something to look forward to as well. In the last letter she'd received from Rosie, her friend had suggested that she try to get to Hillsbridge on Easter Saturday, when a grand dance was being held in the town hall. *I'd love it if you could come with me*, Rosie had written. *It would be like old times.* Just how she was going to get there, Freda wasn't sure, but she wasn't going to worry about that now. Her eyes were drooping, her head sinking into the pillow, and she was drifting, drifting into a deep and dreamless sleep.

Chapter Sixteen

The day of the dance had finally arrived. Although Frances had everything organised, she still rechecked every single detail. A barrel of beer and bottles of soft drinks, gin, whisky and mixers behind the bar – she'd been lucky to get the spirits, she knew, but a persuasive word with the publican who'd supplied the beer had done the trick. The tea urn was set up in the kitchen, together with the necessary crockery, and Brenda Bendle had assured her the refreshments were all in hand – crusty bread fresh from the bakery, butter, tasty cheese courtesy of Fred Thomas, and pickles, home-made and donated. Fred had also been to see her the previous evening to finalise arrangements for the accordion band to arrive in good time to set up on the stage. And the cash float for the bar and another for any ticket sales on the door were stored in biscuit tins in the kitchen for safe keeping until they were needed.

When she eventually returned home after satisfying herself everything was in place, she found to her relief that Anne had arrived. She'd been worried that her daughter might not turn up.

'I'm so glad to see you, darling,' she said, giving Anne a quick kiss, and was surprised when Anne responded with a hug. Their relationship wasn't usually tactile. Perhaps it was because it could be a long while before they were together again, Frances thought, and hoped fervently it might be a sign that Anne could be persuaded to change her mind. For that, she was relying on Julian to work his magic.

'Shall we have a cup of tea before we have to get dressed for the dance?' she suggested.

'Or perhaps something stronger!' That was Sir James, who had appeared in the doorway and overheard the conversation.

'Definitely something stronger,' Anne said, and again Frances wondered if she was having second thoughts.

She smiled, satisfied, feeling far more confident that what she had planned, with Julian's help, might actually bear fruit.

Freda, too, was looking forward to the dance. This morning Ted Holland had taken her with him to fetch the cows in for milking, and she'd sat beside him while he demonstrated the technique for squeezing the cows' udders into the big metal pails. When they were done, and the cows had been turned loose into a field, they'd returned to the farmhouse to find a cooked breakfast awaiting them. Bacon, egg, sausage, fried bread . . . It was years since Freda had seen such a feast, and she'd enjoyed every mouthful. Then, over toast and marmalade and hot sweet tea, she, Ted and his mother had sat chatting, and for the first time they'd asked her questions about her background.

'You sound local,' Mrs Holland had said.

'That's because I am.' Freda had gone on to explain that her home was in Hillsbridge.

'Good Lord!' Mrs Holland said, astonished. 'Do your family know you're here, so close?'

Freda nodded. 'I wrote to tell them.'

'So they'll be expecting to see you,' Farmer Ted said.

'At some point, yes. But only when I have some time off.' Freda was anxious he shouldn't think she'd be shirking her duties.

He drained his cup and pushed it towards his mother for a refill. 'No time like the present,' he said. 'You're not yet into a regular routine, and when you are, believe me, I shall be working you till you drop. I could take you over this afternoon if you like. I have to get fuel for the tractor.'

'Oh, that's kind.' But already Freda's thoughts were skittering to the dance Rosie had told her about. Did she dare mention it? Nothing ventured, nothing gained, she decided.

'Actually, there is something . . .' she said tentatively, and went on to explain about the dance. 'I could stay with my friend Rosie. But I don't want you to think I'm taking advantage, and I'm not sure how I'd get back tomorrow.'

'Ted could fetch you, couldn't you, Ted,' Mrs Holland said.

Raising an eyebrow, Ted grinned at Rosie. 'See how under the thumb I am? Now she hasn't got my father to boss about, she does it to me.'

'Oh, please – I don't want you to put yourself out!' Freda said, embarrassed, but Ted was having none of it.

'I'll take you into Hillsbridge this afternoon and pick you up tomorrow morning. You'll miss milking, mind,' he teased. 'But none of them will be expecting you. Do you want to use the telephone to make a call?'

'No, it'll be all right,' Freda said. She'd often stayed with Rosie in the old days when they'd been out together, curled up in Rosie's big three-quarters bed and chatting long into the night. As for her parents, she knew they would be at home for the rest of the day once her mother got back from her Saturday-morning trip to the market, and knew too they would be delighted to see her.

She was delighted herself. It would be nice to surprise Mum and Dad, and she couldn't wait to tell Rosie all about the farm. For the moment, at least, the war seemed a long way off.

* * *

Clarke had his plans in place. Dave Thompson, Colin Stewart, and Roy Taylor, the parachute instructor, were going to come to the dance with him, all pleased at the prospect of some light entertainment that wasn't simply a pub crawl, and some girls to flirt with.

So far Clarke hadn't told the others about Rosie, but he decided now that he should. As they chatted over a cup of tea and a plate of scones, the perfect opportunity arose.

'Let's hope all the pretty girls haven't gone off to do war work,' Colin was saying. 'It would be a bit of a let-down if it's nothing but pensioners and old married women.'

'Well, I haven't mentioned it before, but there is one I'm hoping to see,' Clarke said. 'I met her on the train when I came down from London. Trouble is, I think she might be spoken for. As Hillsbridge was on my way, I offered her a lift, but there was some chap waiting for her in Bath. A real prick, too.'

'That's a pity,' Dave sympathised, and Colin suggested there was every chance the chap might have been called up by now and was out of the picture.

Roy, the para, joined the conversation. 'That's a coincidence. There was a bonny lass in my carriage when I was on my way here. If I hadn't fallen asleep the minute I sat down, I might have been in with a chance, but I didn't wake up until we got to Bath. Remember, Clarke? I pointed her out to you. She was getting into a taxi when we went out to your car.'

Clarke nodded. 'Bonny's the right word for her,' he agreed, but he was thinking of Miss Rosie Mitchell.

'Never mind. Plenty more fish in the sea,' Dave said.

'So what's the plan?' Colin asked, and after some discussion they decided to stop off for a drink at a convenient pub on the way to Hillsbridge and arrive at the dance about an hour after it was due to start. By then things should be in full swing and they wouldn't be quite as conspicuous, inevitable since they would be in uniform.

Their duties for the day were finished now, so when the last scone had been eaten and the pot of tea was empty, Clarke went in search of Firkins to tell him of their intention. He wouldn't be best pleased, but what the hell? Crossing swords with him had become the norm, and really Clarke couldn't care less.

Rosie had got the bus home when she finished her shift. She was tired, and as she got off at her stop and started the long walk along the lane, she was almost wishing she could have had a quiet evening rather than going to the dance. But she couldn't let her mother down, and Lady Hastings would never forgive her if she didn't put in an appearance.

The days were beginning to lengthen and it wasn't yet properly dark. As she neared the driveway that led to the estate, she saw a figure approaching from the opposite direction and startled. No! It couldn't be! But for all the world it looked like Freda.

Her tiredness forgotten, Rosie quickened her pace, and as the distance between them closed, she could see she was not mistaken.

'Freda!'

'Rosie!'

They fell into one another's arms, hugging like long-lost sisters.

'What a surprise!' Rosie gasped. 'Are you coming to the dance?'

'I hope so. If your mum doesn't mind me staying overnight.'

'When has she ever?' Rosie said. 'She'll be so pleased to see you! Come on. Let's get indoors, and then you can tell me all your news and I can tell you mine.'

* * *

Frances was to pick up Winnie at half past six. Anne would follow later with her father. Winnie had been surprised but delighted to see Freda, and pleased, too, that Rosie would have some company at the dance. She couldn't imagine Rosie would be a wallflower, but single men would be in short supply, and it wouldn't be so bad if the girls were together. If needs be they could always dance with each other, as they used to sometimes in the old days.

She made tea for them, and when it was time, she got her coat and bag and looked in on the two girls, who were in the kitchen, chatting.

'I'm off then.'

'Right, Mum. See you later.'

'Make sure you wear some sensible shoes,' she cautioned. 'You can take your fancy ones in a bag. You don't want to have to be walking home in those.'

Rosie laughed. 'We know, Mum. We've been to plenty of dances in the town hall and walked home afterwards.'

'Well, since then you've been to plenty of dances in London, I expect, and I daresay it's different there. And wear a coat. It's nice enough now, but it'll get cold later on.'

'OK, Mum. OK!' Rosie said. 'We're grown women, remember?'

Winnie sniffed. 'And still my daughter.'

'Go, Mum,' Rosie said sternly. 'You don't want to keep Lady Hastings waiting.'

As the door closed after Winnie, Rosie and Freda looked at one another and giggled.

'Come on then, let's go and get ready,' Rosie said, getting up.

The two girls went upstairs to her room, happy simply to be together.

* * *

It looked as if the dance was turning out to be a tremendous success. Besides the tickets that had already been sold, Gracie Parker, who was on the door, was kept busy with people who hadn't already purchased one.

From the moment the accordion band began playing, Rosie and Freda barely had time to catch their breath. Eligible men were in short supply, and most of their partners were widowers and those whose wives had not been able to join them for one reason or another. After forty minutes or so, they went to the kitchen to see if Winnie needed any help, but she assured them everything was in hand.

'Just go and enjoy yourselves,' she urged them, and they did as they were told.

As they went back into the main hall, Rosie whispered to Freda, 'I'm just going to powder my nose. Are you coming with me?'

'Better not. There are a couple of empty seats. I'll grab them while I can.'

When Rosie emerged, it looked as if Freda had been right. When the last dance had ended, everyone had gravitated towards the available seating. Rosie took the chair Freda had saved for her, and the minute she sat down, Freda grabbed her hand.

'You chose just the wrong moment to go to the lav,' she whispered. 'Julian Edgell's here!'

Rosie's heart missed a beat. 'Where?'

'I think he went into the committee room. I expect Sir James has got a bottle of his best Scotch in there. The toffs won't be slumming it at the bar, you can bet. But I'll tell you who is. Another bit of excitement you missed.'

'What's that?' But Rosie was too busy wishing she'd put off her visit to the cloakroom. She wanted Julian to know she was here, and hopefully he would ask her to dance.

Freda waited a beat or two, assuming a tantalising look, before replying.

'Four chaps in uniform. I didn't get a good look at them, so they could be as ugly as sin for all I know. But hey! At least they're young and fit. What I can't understand is what they're doing here. The nearest army camps are on Salisbury Plain, aren't they? And the RAF are in Wiltshire, I thought.'

'Yes.' But Rosie was keeping an eye on the door to the committee room, willing Julian to appear. The band had struck up a foxtrot, though, and her view was now obscured by dancers.

As it ended and the floor cleared again, Freda caught sight of the four young servicemen standing beside the bar with their pints of beer and grabbed Rosie's arm.

'There they are! But that one – the ginger one – I'm sure that's the chap who was on my train. Oh!' She broke off, flustered. 'He's looking!'

'I expect he is,' Rosie said shortly. 'Sizing up his chances.'

Joe Marshall, the town clerk, who was conducting the band tonight, picked up the microphone and faced the hall. 'One last dance, then we'll take a short break and you can enjoy your refreshments. So, ladies and gentlemen, take your partners for a barn dance.'

'Bother!' Freda sounded disappointed. 'I was hoping for a nice slow waltz.'

'Trust you.' But truth to tell, Rosie had been hoping much the same, except that it would be Julian who appeared as if by magic and swept her into his arms.

In fact it was Cliff Evans, chief of the volunteer fire brigade, who manifested in front of her, his not inconsiderable bulk blocking her view of the four servicemen and, more importantly, the door to the committee room. She forced a smile as he led her onto the dance floor, while Mr Wright, the boot mender, did the same with Freda.

The circle was almost complete when the band struck up, and a few stragglers hastily squeezed in where they could. To Rosie's horror, she saw that just a few couples ahead of her now was one of her old school teachers, Mr Burden, whom the girls in her class had christened 'Creepy'. As far as she knew, no official complaints had ever been made about his behaviour, but his lascivious looks and double entendres had made them all uncomfortable.

She felt that revulsion now just as she had then. As the women moved forward and the men back, she'd be forced to dance with him. It might only be one short repetition of the steps until she moved on, but the thought of being so close to him was repellent. And before she knew it, he was next in line. There was no way she could avoid him.

As they met, his clammy hand seized hers, his arm slid around her waist, and he was looking sideways at her with *that look*, the one she remembered so clearly and which made her skin crawl. She gritted her teeth, staring straight ahead and praying for the moment when she could escape. As he twirled her underneath his arm, she caught the stench of stale body odour and thought she was going to be sick.

Just then the music stopped and Joe Marshall spoke into the microphone again. 'Let's slow it down now, and we'll make this a waltz – a gentleman's excuse-me.'

The band struck up again in three-four time and – horror of horrors – she was face to face with Creepy Burden. One sweaty hand clasped hers, the other wound tightly around her waist. He clearly had no intention of letting her go any time soon.

And then someone was behind him, tapping him on the shoulder. Creepy ignored them, smirking and tightening his hold on her.

'*Excuse me*, I said. Sure, you can't hog this dance with the prettiest girl in the room.'

The voice, the Irish accent, the authority took Rosie back to Paddington station. It couldn't be, surely?

'All right, all right, no need for that.' Perhaps, since the IRA were known to be dangerous, it was the accent that persuaded Creepy Burden to release her, and she looked up into the face of her saviour, half smiling at her, that slightly crooked smile that crinkled his very blue eyes and produced the cheeky dimple.

'Rescuing you is getting to be quite a habit, Miss Rosie Mitchell,' he said, but instead of taking her into a hold for the waltz, he laid a hand in the small of her back and guided her to the side of the floor.

'We're not dancing?' Rosie was so startled to see him again those were the only words that sprang to mind.

His smile broadened. 'Not while it's an excuse-me. I'm not risking losing you again now that I've found you. Later, perhaps?' His eyes met hers with a lazy, questioning gaze. 'If my luck holds, that is.'

With almost everyone on the dance floor, there were plenty of unoccupied seats and he led her to the ones that were nearest. 'Will this do?'

'I was with my friend.' Rosie waved in the general direction of where she and Freda had been sitting, but she was no longer there. 'She must be dancing.'

'I expect she is. My friends have been arguing over her ever since we arrived. They knew you were spoken for.' Then, seeing her startled look, he went on, 'Ah, don't be worrying. I'm not making assumptions. It's the man who met you at the station I'm talking about. I thought I saw him when we came in – late, I'm afraid. It's not easy dragging my mates away from a public house, indeed it's not.'

'You mean Julian Edgell.' Rosie could feel hot colour rising in her cheeks.

'I'm guessing you won't be wanting other company if *Doctor* Edgell is here,' Clarke said with sarcastic emphasis, referring to Julian's hoity-toity response when he had addressed him as 'mister'.

A sudden thought occurred to Rosie. It could do no harm to let Julian think she was with someone else. It might even make him jealous.

'He's just a friend, that's all,' she said.

'So you wouldn't mind if I joined you?'

Rosie hesitated, wondering if that would be taking it a little too far.

'And sure, it looks as if my friend and yours will be doing the same,' Clarke went on, nodding towards the dance floor, where the waltz was ending and the soldier was steering Freda back to her seat, his arm around her waist. 'We could make it a four-some if we can commandeer two more chairs.'

'What about your other friends?' Rosie asked, panicking a little now.

'Ah sure, they're big enough and ugly enough to take care of themselves. They're happy with a drink in their hands, Miss Rosie Mitchell.'

Defeated, Rosie gave up.

Ten minutes later, the four of them were sitting around one of the small tables that had been brought out as soon as the floor was clear, with plates of bread, cheese and pickles, fresh pints of beer for the men and cider for the girls. Just how Clarke had managed it Rosie wasn't sure, but he certainly gave the impression of being a man who could control almost anything.

Freda was pink with pleasure, telling Rosie excitedly that this really was the man who had helped her with her suitcase, and

Clarke responded, admitting that by some strange coincidence he had met Rosie too on the train.

'Is there a single pretty girl left in London?' he asked with a wicked twinkle. 'Or does Hillsbridge have the monopoly?'

'It's my home, but I'm here to work,' Freda said between nibbles of cheese. 'I'm in the Land Army, and as luck would have it, they've posted me close enough for me to see my parents – and my best and oldest friend.' She nodded at Rosie.

'Less of the old!' Clarke admonished her with a wink at Rosie. 'So what are you doing for the war effort, Miss Rosie—'

'Will you stop calling me that,' Rosie interrupted him. 'Just call me Rosie like everyone else does.'

'OK. Rosie. Now will you answer my question?'

'She's an ambulance driver,' Freda said. 'She trained as a nurse, and then she was an ambulance attendant, and now she's driving. That's right, isn't it, Rosie?'

Rosie nodded, a bit embarrassed.

'I'm impressed,' Clarke said. 'Did they teach you?'

'To drive? No, not really. But when my driver had a heart attack, I . . . well, I took over and got him to hospital. And with him off sick, and no one to take his place, they gave me the job and I've been driving ever since, with another girl, Molly Doughty as my partner. So it was a bit of a fluke really.'

'You'd already passed your driving test then?' Clarke asked.

'No. I'd had some lessons, but by the time I was ready to take my test, petrol was rationed and it had been suspended anyway. One of the hospital bosses tested me on the ambulance and gave me the all-clear.'

'Well done you,' Clarke said.

Freda was growing impatient. 'What I want to know is what you and your friends are doing here, and why you're all wearing different uniforms.'

Clarke and Roy Taylor exchanged glances. Then Clarke said, 'That's for us to know and you to find out.'

'But we can't, can we, if you won't tell us,' Freda pointed out.

'There you are then. Men of mystery.' He turned back to Rosie. 'So you were a nurse before the war?'

'No, I worked in a garage. Then when I was in London I was a waitress. I've only just done my nursing training.'

'A garage. That's where you learned to drive, I'm guessing.'

'Yes.' It wasn't the whole truth, of course, but Rosie wasn't going to go into details. 'It's a long story,' she said apologetically.

Clarke and Roy Taylor lit cigarettes and they chatted some more, inconsequential small talk. Then Mr Marshall walked out onto the stage and took the microphone again.

'Ladies and gentlemen, may I have your attention? Before we recommence the dancing, Sir James Hastings would like to say a few words.'

He waved towards the wings, and Sir James appeared from behind the heavy red velveteen curtain. Mr Marshall handed him the microphone and began clapping, encouraging the audience to join in.

As the applause died away, Sir James began to speak.

'Firstly I would like to thank you all for coming along tonight to support our project – to raise funds to purchase a Spitfire. I hope you are having an enjoyable evening.

'Secondly, and most importantly, I must thank my dear wife for the tireless work she has put in to make tonight happen, and to make it the success it undoubtedly is.' He glanced towards the wings and held out a hand. 'Frances.'

Lady Hastings appeared and strode towards her husband, nodding her acceptance of the round of applause that accompanied her. As it died away, Sir James spoke again.

'I must also offer my heartfelt thanks to the accordion band, who are giving us the benefit of their time and talent this evening free of charge, and the traders who have so generously donated the food and drink that you have just enjoyed.' He went on to list the businesses, and yet another bout of clapping echoed round the hall.

'Now, as you no doubt know, this is a cause close to our hearts, since our dear son Philip is an RAF pilot. Who knows? He may one day fly our very own Hillsbridge Spitfire. To this end, I have made a sizeable donation to start off the fund.' He produced a cheque from his breast pocket and waved it aloft. 'My dear friend and neighbour Mr Giles Edgell has matched my donation. Unfortunately he and his good lady wife are unable to be with us tonight, so he has entrusted his donation to me, and here it is.'

He fumbled in his pocket again and with a flourish drew out another cheque, then glanced at both and added with an apologetic smile, 'Actually, this is my cheque, and this one Mr Edgell's.'

This produced a dutiful titter from the floor of the hall, and Rosie whispered, 'I bet he did that on purpose.'

'But we can't see it from here,' Freda objected. 'Nor how much it's for.'

'Now.' Sir James waved the two cheques aloft. 'I am going to ask my daughter, Anne, and Mr Edgell's son, Julian, to present these to my wife so as to officially open the fund, which will I'm sure be showing a healthy balance thanks to all of you who have bought tickets and patronised the bar this evening.

'One last thing. Julian Edgell is a medical practitioner, so if any of you have twirled around too many times or consumed a little more refreshment than is strictly wise, you can be assured you are in safe hands.' He waited for the laughter to die away and continued, 'Dr Julian Edgell and Miss Anne Hastings.'

Another gesture to the wings and Julian appeared from behind the curtain. Of Anne there was no sign. Julian smiled, and raised his arms in a helpless shrug as if to convey amused exasperation. Then he disappeared behind the curtain for a moment, and reappeared leading a reluctant-looking Anne by the hand.

Rosie's heart plummeted. They looked for all the world to be an item. Or was this staged, like Sir James's mixing up the cheques, put on for the entertainment of the audience?

Clarke was gazing at the stage, frowning, but Rosie didn't notice. She was unaware of anything but Anne, hand in hand with Julian now and smiling. They parted briefly as Sir James handed them a cheque each and they presented them to Lady Hastings. But the worst was yet to come.

'I have one more announcement to make,' Sir James said into the microphone. 'A very special one. This evening Dr Julian asked me for my daughter's hand in marriage, which I was only too delighted to give. And happily my dear Anne has accepted his proposal. Our two families, already close, will become even closer when Miss Hastings becomes Mrs Edgell. I shall miss her greatly, but I know she will be in good hands, and I wish them a long and happy life together.

'Ladies and gentlemen, please raise your glasses and join me in congratulating the happy couple and echoing my good wishes for their future.'

'Hip, hip . . .' A man's voice rose from the back of the hall, and the entire audience joined in. 'Hooray!'

Everyone, that was, but Rosie. She sat stunned and silent, fighting the tears of shock and dismay that were all but choking her. This time her hopes and dreams were well and truly shattered.

Julian was going to marry Anne as her mother had always

predicted. Anne hadn't meant a word of what she'd said at Christmas – that she was done with Julian and Rosie was welcome to him. And Julian had been leading her on, just as he always had.

It was over. Rosie felt as if her whole world had come to an end.

Chapter Seventeen

Looking back afterwards, the rest of the evening was little more than a blur to Rosie.

The two men had left her and Freda at one point to go to the bar for fresh beers, and returned with a rum and black for Freda and a gin and orange for her. While they were gone, Freda had turned to her, shaking her head sympathetically and squeezing her hand – Rosie had confided to her earlier that judging by how he'd treated her recently, she had high hopes for a relationship with Julian.

'Oh, Rosie, I'm so sorry! You must be devastated.'

Scarcely trusting herself to speak, Rosie had managed a single word. 'Don't.'

But Freda had been unable to resist one last platitude.

'He's not worth upsetting yourself over, Rosie.'

Although she meant well, it hadn't helped one jot, but somehow Rosie managed to pull herself together. Though the hurt was a physical ache in her stomach, and though her heart felt as if it was breaking, she was determined to put a brave face on it.

They danced, she and Clarke, Freda and Roy Taylor, and each time she saw Julian and Anne dancing close together, a fresh dart of pain pierced her like a sword. But she averted her eyes, met Clarke's, strikingly blue, and forced a smile.

Time seemed to drag now, the hands on the big wall clock moving so slowly it seemed they had stopped altogether. But eventually, when they pointed to almost midnight, Mr Marshall announced the last waltz. The band began to play and the lady vocalist crooned the words.

> Who's taking you home tonight
> After the dance is through?

'That's me, I hope,' Clarke said in Rosie's ear. 'I have a car. I'll drive you and Freda home – I expect Roy will come too – and then I'll come back for the others.'

'Thank you.' Rosie didn't have the strength to argue, and in any case all she wanted was to be somewhere she no longer had to pretend and could cry out her heartbreak in private.

At that very moment, she spotted Julian and Anne dancing cheek to cheek, and over Anne's shoulder Julian saw her too. For a fleeting second their eyes met, and it seemed to Rosie that he was looking disgustingly smug.

She was never entirely sure what got into her then. Fury, certainly. He'd been playing with her, just as perhaps he always had. Defiance. She wouldn't let him see how much he'd hurt her. And a sudden recognition that Clarke was a very attractive man. Something of a mystery, yes. He and his friend seemed determined not to appease her and Freda's curiosity. But also a safe haven. He'd rescued her not just once, but twice. The horrible incident on Paddington station had been an obvious assault, and coming to her aid might have been what any chivalrous man would have done. But tonight was far less clear-cut. She'd been desperate to escape the clutches of her one-time teacher, and somehow he'd spotted her discomfort and acted on it. The hand that had held hers was cool and firm, not flabby and sweaty, and the

237

other, placed firmly in the small of her back, felt good, protective, cocooning her from the crush of couples around them, and from Julian's cruelty.

She glanced in his direction again; he was still looking at her, even as he held his wife-to-be in his arms, and instinctively she moved closer to Clarke, her chin resting against his broad shoulder. Let Julian see she didn't need him, with his flattery and duplicity! Clarke responded, holding her tightly. She breathed in the maleness of him and quite suddenly was more aware of him than ever. Perhaps it was the soft lighting and the gin working their magic, but she felt light-headed and graceful as their feet moved in perfect harmony, hers following his with unprecedented ease.

As the waltz ended, he dropped a light kiss on her forehead. Her skin tingled where his lips touched, and a tiny dart of sharp pleasure twisted deep inside her. Then, as the band played the National Anthem, he stood to attention and, like almost everyone in the room, sang along.

He spoke to Roy about his suggestion that they would take Rosie and Freda home, then excused himself to find his other friends and tell them of the slight change of plan. While he was gone, the two girls went to the cloakroom to collect their coats and outdoor shoes. Rosie made a detour to the kitchen to tell Winnie that she and Freda were leaving.

Winnie gave her a pat on the arm and a deeply sympathetic look, but to Rosie's relief made no mention of the engagement announcement.

'That's fine, love,' she said. 'You go. Lady Hastings will bring me home when we've finished clearing up here.' Then her eyes went to Rosie's feet. 'But do change your shoes, there's a good girl.'

'It's all right, Mum,' Rosie said. 'Clarke is taking us in his car.'

'Clarke?' Winnie was looking alarmed now. 'Who's Clarke when he's at home? Not one of those soldiers, I hope.'

'Yes. He's an officer, I think.' She'd noticed the insignia on his uniform.

'Oh, Rosie, for goodness' sake be careful!' Winnie warned. 'You can't trust servicemen, and you don't know him from Adam.'

Rosie had never told Winnie about the incident on Paddington station; she hadn't wanted to worry her. But now . . .

'I've met him before,' she said. 'He came to my rescue in London when a gang of louts were molesting me. And I travelled all the way home with him on the train.'

Winnie sighed, shaking her head. 'Good Lord, whatever next! You've never said.'

'And that's not all. Tonight he rescued me from that creep Mr Burden, so I'm sure I can trust him,' Rosie told her.

'Well, just be careful,' Winnie warned again. 'After what happened tonight . . .' she nodded in the direction of Julian and Anne, who were accepting congratulations from numerous people, 'you'd be putty in anyone's hands.'

At the allusion to the devastating announcement, Rosie felt tears stinging her eyes, and angrily blinked them back.

'We'll be fine, Mum, honestly. But if we're not home when you get in, you have my permission to call the police,' she added in an attempt to lighten the moment.

'Hmm!' Winnie snorted. 'Any harm would've been done by then.'

'Night, Mum.' Rosie managed a tight smile, and joined Freda and the two men, who were by now waiting at the door.

'Where's your car, then?' she asked with forced brightness as they went down the stairs and out onto the pavement.

'Just along here.' Clarke pointed ahead of them. He'd been

careful tonight not to park at the bus stop, though he hadn't thought any would be running at this time of night.

In fact there was quite a queue waiting, men mostly, while the womenfolk were occupying the wooden benches that were placed at intervals along the front wall of the town hall.

As Clarke opened the driver's door and leaned across to unlock the one for the front passenger seat, Roy opened it wide and gestured to Rosie to get in.

'We'll go in the back,' he said.

Dave and Colin emerged from the shadows.

'Don't be too long.'

'We're timing you, mind . . .'

In two unrepeatable words, Clarke told them to get lost, and a few jokes that Rosie guessed were equally unrepeatable were thrown back at him, though since Clarke had started the engine she couldn't actually hear them.

'Don't mind them,' Clarke said. 'They've had a drop too much to drink.' He reversed fast but accurately. 'But you'll have to tell me the way, Rosie. I haven't a clue where you live.'

'Straight ahead,' Rosie said, 'then turn right at the main road and keep on over the two level crossings . . .'

She continued to direct him, and when she told him to turn off the lane they were on and into the drive that led to Bramley Court, Clarke whistled softly.

'This leads to a grand house, surely?'

'Yes, but I don't live there.' Surprising herself, Rosie actually laughed. 'My father was the gardener and we have a cottage in the grounds . . . Just here.' She pointed, and Clarke's one permitted headlight picked out the little building with its small square of garden and picket fence. He braked, and turned off the engine.

'We'll see you safely to the door.'

'There's no need,' Rosie said, panicking a bit. 'We're fine now.'

'Don't be such a wet blanket, Rosie!' admonished Freda, who was snuggling up to Roy in the back seat.

'You two go on if you like,' Clarke suggested, and Rosie's throat tightened.

Freda and Roy climbed out of the car and disappeared into the shadows beyond the picket gate.

'I have a confession to make, Rosie,' Clarke said.

Rosie's first thought was that he was going to tell her he was married, and unexpectedly she experienced a feeling of disappointment. But to her surprise he went on, 'I came to the dance in the hope I might see you again. I saw the posters when I drove through Hillsbridge a few days ago and thought it was possible you might be there. So now you know – our being here tonight was no accident.'

'Oh!' Rosie said, taken aback.

'I wasn't even sure you weren't spoken for,' he went on. 'And when we arrived and I saw the chap who met you at the station was here, I thought he must be with you. But it seems I was mistaken. He really is just a friend.'

'Yes.' The tears were threatening again.

'So.' Clarke paused, a long, pregnant pause. 'Now that I've found you, and you're not promised to Dr Whatever-his-name-is, can I see you again?'

Rosie's first instinct was to turn him down. Then the imp of rebellion crept into her again, and with it the realisation that her mother was right. She knew absolutely nothing about this man.

'Perhaps. If you tell me where you're based and what it is you're being so secretive about.'

She felt him go away from her. 'I can't, Rosie. At least not until I know you a good deal better, and maybe not even then.'

'I have signed the Official Secrets Act,' Rosie protested.

241

'So have I, and for the time being I have to stick to it to the letter.'

'So you don't much care whether I agree to go out with you or not,' Rosie said, a bit miffed.

'Actually, I do care very much. For some unknown reason I've wanted to see you again ever since I set eyes on you. But I can't, and won't, talk about what it is I'm doing. All I can tell you is that it's nothing immoral or illegal, and it's in the interests of the war effort.'

Rosie hesitated, and realised she wanted to believe him. But . . .

'I'm not sure I'm ready to believe what any man says. Not after . . .'

'What happened tonight – the good doctor and the surprise announcement? He's led you on, is that it?' When Rosie was silent, he went on, 'If it's any comfort, I wouldn't believe anything he said either. He's an obnoxious bighead, full of his own importance. And then tonight you found out he's going to marry someone else. Don't deny it, I saw your face when you heard the news.'

'For a complete stranger you seem to think you know an awful lot about me,' she said defiantly.

'It was pretty clear you were shocked. And not best pleased.'

'It was that obvious?' Rosie asked bitterly. 'Stupid of me to care. It's not the first time he's hurt me. But this time I really thought . . .' She broke off. Why was she explaining herself? Telling a man she scarcely knew her deepest secrets? But the tears were pricking again, and somehow it was a relief to let it all out.

'I've been such a fool! I've wasted the whole of my life because I've been blind. And I don't think I can trust my own judgement any more.'

'Oh, Rosie.' He leaned over and took her hand. 'Not all men

are like him, I promise you. And for what it's worth, I do understand. Once upon a time – a long while ago – I was badly let down by someone I cared for very much, and I gave up on relationships with women. And then . . .' he paused, 'I met you.'

Rosie looked up. It was too dark to see his face clearly, but from the earnest note in his voice more than his actual words, she was tempted to believe him. In that moment she made up her mind. If only to show Julian Edgell she didn't give a fig that he was going to marry Anne Hastings.

'All right,' she said.

Silence stretched between them, then Clarke said, 'You've changed your mind? You will see me again?'

'Yes.'

She sensed him relax. 'Next Saturday?'

Rosie was flustered again. 'I don't know. I work shifts. I'd have to check.' Realising he thought she was making excuses, she went on, 'Is there a telephone I could reach you on?'

'I can't give you the number,' he said. 'It would be more than my life's worth. Could I call you? At the hospital where you're based, perhaps?'

She thought quickly. 'I'm on a day shift at the moment, but that could change when the rota comes out tomorrow. If we don't get called out on a shout, I should finish at six. I'll know by then, and I'll wait by the phone in the ambulance depot.'

'That number's not top secret?' he asked, joking, she imagined.

'No.'

'And you know it?'

'It's easy. Just the code for Bath and four digits.'

He leaned across, opened the pocket in the dashboard and took out a notepad and pen. 'Write it down for me.'

She did so, and handed the pad back. He tore off the top sheet, tucked it away and leaned across once more to replace pad and pencil in the dashboard pocket. As it clicked shut, he slid an arm round her shoulders, pulling him towards him.

His mouth was firm yet gentle on hers, with no expectation of reciprocation. But to Rosie's surprise, the same little thrill she'd experienced when they were dancing pulsed deep inside her, and she found herself kissing him back. He wasn't Julian. Dear Lord, he wasn't Julian. But she needed this with every fibre of her being.

A sharp rap on the window startled them apart, the driver's door was thrown open from the outside, and Roy's face appeared.

'What the hell are you two up to? Freda's getting cold, and Dave and Colin will be wondering if you've left them stranded.'

'I thought you'd be keeping Freda warm,' Clarke said equably.

'And so I have been. But there's only so much a man can do, and you're cosy enough by the look of it.'

'Sorry . . .' Rosie opened her door and began climbing out.

'Night, Miss Rosie Mitchell,' Clarke teased. 'See you soon, I hope.'

As the car turned and pulled away, Rosie watched it go, her emotions churning. Then she pushed open the picket gate and walked up the path to where Freda was waiting.

Anne Hastings, still wearing the dress she'd worn to the dance, sat on the edge of her bed and stared at her reflection in her wardrobe mirror, silently asking her other self all the questions that were racing through her head, and seeing only the tension in her clasped hands, tight shoulders and frowning face.

What in heaven's name had happened this evening? None of it made any sense.

She thought back to the moment it had begun. When Julian had asked her to marry him.

They'd been in the drawing room at home, her mother and father having left them alone – on purpose, she now thought. It had come as a complete shock to her when he had gone down on one knee and proposed. For a moment she had been elated – all her dreams were coming true! Then the uncertainty had come flooding in.

'Julian . . . I don't know what to say,' she'd managed, still trying to process this unexpected turn of events.

He'd smiled up at her, that smile that could charm the birds from the trees. 'Just say yes, and make me the happiest man alive.'

'Let me draw breath! And do get up, for heaven's sake.'

He did, but led her to the love seat, where he'd sat beside her and taken her hand.

'Why now?' She wasn't sure why she had asked that question, except that she was incapable of thinking straight.

'Because I love you, Anne, and I want you to be my wife,' he said earnestly. 'We've always known that we were destined to be together, haven't we? And with this damned war, who knows when there will be another chance. I want you here, safe. Then hopefully we'll make it through and we can spend the rest of our lives making one another happy.'

The ice around her heart had begun to melt a little then. For all her determination, he still had that effect on her. But she'd meant what she'd said to Rosie at Christmas. He'd cheated on her with her oldest friend. Could she ever trust him again?

'What about Rosie?' she asked.

Julian frowned. 'What about her?'

'You cheated on me with her. You might be doing it again for all I know. With both of you working in Bath, you'd have plenty of opportunity.'

'Oh, Anne – I admit it, and I'm truly sorry. But that was more than two years ago. I promise you're wrong to think I've been unfaithful to you since. It's you I want, and only you.'

Anne was torn now by indecision. Though she'd made up her mind to forget him, it wasn't that easy when she was still in love with him. But she still wasn't sure that he was telling her the whole truth.

'You've taken me by surprise, Julian,' she said. 'I need a little time to think it through. You know I'm joining the WAAF?'

'Yes, and I'm not happy about it. Airbases will be targets for enemy bombing. I really don't think it's a good idea, any more than your mother does.'

At the mention of her mother, Anne had stiffened, without really knowing why. She definitely shouldn't rush into this. No matter what her heart was urging, she would listen to her head.

'I'm sorry, Julian. I'm really happy and flattered that you should ask. But I do need to think about it.'

'Your father has no doubts.' There was an edge now to Julian's tone.

'That's Daddy all over.' She smiled faintly. 'He's the eternal optimist. But I need a little time to be sure in my own mind.'

'Very well,' he said reluctantly. 'I respect that. But I know I can make you happy, and I hope you will arrive at the same conclusion.'

They'd left it there. Her father had given her a quizzical glance as she and Julian had emerged from the drawing room, and her mother had looked thoughtful. Anne had smiled, but said nothing, and excused herself to go to her room.

When she had come downstairs, dressed and ready for the dance, it was to find her father on the point of leaving.

'I thought we were going together,' she said.

Sir James had smiled. 'And I thought it was much more

fitting for you and Julian to arrive together. He's just making some phone calls to ensure he's not needed back in Bath – though don't worry, I'm sure he won't be.' He patted her hand. 'I'm delighted for you, my darling. I know the two of you will be very happy. He asked my permission earlier, and of course I was only too delighted to give it.'

'But Daddy . . .' Anne began to protest, but Sir James didn't let her finish.

'We'll talk about it later. Your mother will be wondering where we all are, and you know how important this evening is for her.'

At that moment Julian appeared in the hallway, having apparently overheard the last part of the conversation.

'You go with your father, Anne. I still have a couple of calls to make. I'll see you there.'

Anne wasn't sorry. She didn't want him pressing her for an answer. And she decided not to mention it again to her father. There would be time enough when this evening was behind them. Or so she'd thought.

It had come as a complete shock to her when Julian had dragged her on stage and her father had announced their engagement. Somehow Daddy must have got hold of the wrong end of the stick. But there was no way she could rebut the announcement here, in front of all these people, and make fools of both her father and Julian. She'd have to go along with it for now or she would cause them the most dreadful embarrassment.

How she'd got through the rest of the evening she didn't know. While she smiled and accepted congratulations her head was full of unanswered questions. Why? Why had Julian chosen this evening to propose to her? Why was he now behaving as if she'd accepted? Was he really so sure this public announcement would influence her decision?

She'd got the answer to that question when he'd driven her home.

'So it looks as if I will be able to buy you a ring now, darling. I'm sorry I didn't have one to give you when I proposed, but I'm afraid it was a sudden decision I made when Frances told me you were joining the WAAF. I couldn't bear the thought of losing you.'

'Did you tell Daddy I'd accepted your proposal?' Anne demanded. 'Were you trying to force my hand?'

'No, of course not!' Julian sounded indignant, but Anne had the distinct feeling there was something he wasn't telling her. Daddy had clearly believed they were engaged; the pride in his voice and on his face would have told her that even if she hadn't known that he would be incapable of deliberately making a false announcement. But her mother . . . her mother . . . Anne remembered that her look had been more satisfied than anything else, and the first little seed of suspicion was sown and took root.

'I'm sorry, Julian, but you are still going to have to wait for my answer,' she said flatly as they arrived back at Bramley Court. 'And if you don't mind, I'm going straight to bed.'

'Good plan. I have to drive back to Bath now, to be ready for tomorrow's early surgery. I'm sure you'll feel much more positive in the morning,' was Julian's reply, and although she was relieved, it struck her as very odd that he should be dashing away.

Now, in the sanctuary of her bedroom, she ran over the evening in her mind, searching for answers and becoming more and more convinced that it was her mother who was behind it all. Frances had been determined to keep her close, and as always she'd let nothing stand in her way. It would be just like her to have planned the whole thing, steamrollering any obstacles aside. Perhaps she'd primed Julian to propose after first asking her father's permission. And then lied to Sir James, told him it was a done deed and pressured him to announce it in public when there was no way Anne could object without causing a scene? Knowing her mother as she did, it was perfectly feasible.

Her only uncertainty was how much Julian had known, and what his motive was in going along with it. Yes, he always had been in Frances's pocket. The two of them were thick as thieves and he would do almost anything she asked of him. But this? Propose marriage if he had no feelings for her? The only reason she could think of was that he saw the advantages to his career and lifestyle by marrying into the aristocracy. Well, if that was it, he was going to be disappointed. She trusted him even less now than she had before.

And as for her mother . . .

Once before, when she'd taken the gallery job in Bristol, she'd defied Frances, desperately wanting to escape her mother's control and do what she really wanted to do. Now she was filled with the same determination. Frances wasn't going to run her life, especially if she had sunk to such depths to achieve her objective. Anne would show her once and for all that she was her own woman now.

Yes, she was going to join the WAAF, and neither Frances nor Julian could stop her. But more than that, she would say yes to the suggestion that had been made to her at that second interview.

She would go back to Bristol tomorrow and agree to be tested as to her suitability to be flown into France as a special agent. And if she was accepted, she would truly be beyond Frances's controlling reach.

Driving back to Bath, Julian was feeling surprisingly positive. Anne would come around, he had no doubt, and he would have cemented his relationship with the Hastings family at no real cost to himself.

He was fond of Anne, that much was true. And she would make him an ideal wife. She would be an advantage to him when it came to progression in his career and an asset socially. She would also be malleable. She'd have no choice but to accept any infidelity on his part or be shamed, and he would be free to consort with anyone who took his fancy.

Besides all this he would have the backing of Frances, a truly formidable ally, and the sponsorship of Sir James.

Not such a bad bargain, he thought. Not such a bad day's work when all was said and done. Yes, Julian felt quite satisfied with himself, and with the performance he'd put on this evening.

Things had gone pretty well, Clarke thought as he drove his three companions back to the Manor. He'd found Miss Rosie Mitchell. He'd kissed her and she hadn't slapped his face or even protested. He'd asked her out and she'd agreed to be by the ambulance HQ telephone tomorrow evening at around six to let him know if her shift pattern would allow it.

The fly in the ointment was that she was still in love with that obnoxious doctor. He'd seen it in her face when his engagement to Sir James Hastings' daughter was announced, seen her struggle to hide her dismay. He was glad, of course, that the man was out of the picture now, but he couldn't help wondering. Had she only agreed to let him take her out on the rebound? Probably. But at least it meant he was in with a chance.

What he had to do now was win her over, persuade her he was a far better bet. The fact that the fair sex seemed to find him attractive should have given him confidence, but he really couldn't understand it. He didn't think his looks were anything special, with a nose that had been broken more than once and a scar over one eyebrow. He was just an ordinary bloke, and he'd never made any special effort since the girl who had let him down so badly. Quite the opposite, in fact. And when Richard Oldfield, his colleague, married with two young children, had been blown to bits by a bomb they were defusing, it had made him all the more determined to avoid any serious relationship. Until now. When it had unexpectedly become important to him.

Small steps. Play it cool. Don't for one minute let her see it mattered to him one way or the other. Don't put any pressure on her.

Dave and Colin were teasing Roy about Rosie's friend, but it didn't seem they'd made any arrangements to meet again. Not surprising, since Roy was unlikely to be here much longer, and in any case Freda seemed the flighty type. A here-today-and-gone-tomorrow sort of girl. He didn't think Rosie was like that. But he had a long way to go before he knew for certain.

The Manor was in darkness, all the trainees no doubt tucked up in bed so as to be ready for another long day tomorrow, and Firkins too, it seemed.

'Shall we get a nightcap?' Dave suggested, and when the others agreed, Clarke went along with it. All he really wanted to do was go to bed himself, but in this company it mattered to be one of a team.

In the recreation room the whisky was passed around and risqué jokes were told. Clarke laughed along with the others. But he wasn't really listening. He was thinking of Miss Rosie Mitchell.

Chapter Eighteen

Frances and Sir James were lingering over breakfast when Anne put in a late appearance.

'About time,' Frances said sourly.

'Morning, Daddy. Good morning, Mother.' Anne sat down and helped herself to what coffee remained in the cafetière.

'Morning, my love. Happy Easter.' Sir James glanced at her over his newspaperpaper, which was spread out on the table in front of him.

After a moment's silence, Frances asked, 'So, Anne, what do you intend to do now that you won't be joining the WAAF?'

'What makes you think I won't be joining the WAAF?' Anne replied coolly.

'Well, now that you and Julian are to be married . . .'

'That won't be until the war is over, if at all.' Still Anne was icy calm.

'Does Julian know that?' Frances demanded.

'He knows perfectly well – as you do – that I haven't yet decided anything.' Anne infused her words with meaning, and the colour rose in Frances's face.

'What are you talking about?'

Still Anne refused to be ruffled. 'I told him I'd think about it, and if he told you something different, then he misunderstood me. So I'm afraid, Daddy, your announcement was rather premature.'

The newspaper rustled and Sir James frowned at his daughter.

'Oh my dear, did I put you on the spot? I'm so sorry! But your mother said—'

'I'm sure she did,' Anne said pointedly. 'And I'm sorry too, Daddy, if it makes things awkward for you.'

'Oh, don't worry about me! Everyone knows that mistakes can happen. I did think it was all rather sudden, but I was so happy for you it never crossed my mind that I was putting my foot in it.'

'Stop it, Daddy. But when I've had this cup of coffee, I really must be getting back to Bristol. I have a great deal to do.'

Inwardly Frances was seething, but she couldn't let Anne go so easily.

'I was rather hoping you would help me prepare for the evacuees. It's only two days now until they arrive.'

'I'm sure you are more than capable of arranging all that yourself,' Anne said.

'She certainly is,' Sir James put in. 'And sorry as I shall be to see you go, I'm not surprised you'd rather not be around when word gets out that the engagement was all my stupid mistake. You go, darling.'

'Thanks, Daddy. And please stop worrying! Honestly, it's fine.'

As she left the breakfast room, she wondered whether her father would question her mother as to how such a mistake had occurred, but somehow she doubted it. He'd keep quiet for the sake of peace, she guessed. And because, despite all her faults, he was still in love with his redoubtable wife.

In the event, however, the subject did arise, though not at Sir James's instigation.

'Where's she getting her petrol from, I wonder?' he said inconsequentially, and Frances snapped, 'How should I know, James? Really, these days I feel I don't know my daughter at all.'

James sighed. 'Oh, Frances. Children grow up, you know.'

'Obviously. But all this shilly-shallying about Julian. It's quite ridiculous. She'll lose him if she's not careful.'

'Perhaps that's what she wants,' Sir James said mildly. 'Either way, there's nothing you can do about it. So why not just calm down and accept it?'

'I am calm, James, considering what's happened. And I won't accept there's nothing I can do about it either.'

'My dear, don't you think perhaps you've done quite enough already?'

It was his only concession to admitting that he was well aware the whole debacle was Frances's fault.

'Just concentrate on getting ready for the arrival of the refugees,' he advised. 'They, I'm sure, will appreciate your organisational skills, and be most grateful.'

Julian's telephone was ringing. He picked it up.

'Dr Edgell.'

He'd barely got the words out when he was rudely interrupted by a furious Frances.

'What the hell happened, Julian?'

'Frances?' He had recognised her voice, and gathered too that she was far from happy. 'What are you talking about?'

'You and Anne. She's denying she agreed to your proposal, yet you gave me to understand that everything had worked out exactly as we planned. What is even worse is that she is saying she still intends to join the WAAF.'

'I know nothing about that, Frances.' He was on firmer

ground now. 'She never mentioned such a thing when I drove her home. Put her on. Let me speak to her.'

'She's not here. She has returned to Bristol. I suggest you phone her. And I expect you to sort all this out.'

'Very well. I'll try.'

'You'd better, Julian. If you know what's good for you.'

She hung up and Julian buried his head in his hands. Certainly Anne had been very angry last night, but she didn't like being in the spotlight, and he'd hoped she would have calmed down and seen sense this morning. It seemed she hadn't. The very thought of grovelling repelled him. Anne could be very stubborn when the mood took her.

Damn, damn, damn. He'd been so sure things would work out. Now it was all unravelling. Not only would he be made to look a fool, his chances of marrying into the aristocracy were fading fast. Worse, he'd made an enemy of Frances. And that was a very dangerous thing to do.

Rosie was by the telephone in the ambulance HQ at just before six that evening. She'd established that she would be on day shifts until Friday, but she'd been scheduled for a late one on Saturday, and she honestly didn't know whether to be relieved or sorry.

'I think the gin and orange might have gone to my head,' she'd said when she and Freda had talked it over before she left this morning, but Freda had urged her to take a chance on him.

'He's a dish,' she'd said. 'He's an officer, and he has a car. What's not to like? And you'd be cocking a snook at Julian Edgell too.'

'You're not seeing your paratrooper again,' Rosie pointed out.

'Well, he's none of the above,' Freda said. 'Yes, he's not bad-looking, but he's just a rank-and-file soldier, and he doesn't have a car. Anyway, I don't have to date the first bloke who asks me.'

'It might be a long time before you meet anyone else. Most eligible men have been called up, and you're pretty isolated out on your farm.'

'From what he said, he might not be around here much longer, and besides . . .' Freda smiled mysteriously, 'there might be an eligible man right there. The farmer is single, as far as I know. There's no wife in sight.'

'Oh, you never said!'

'I don't always tell you everything,' Freda said. 'But to get back to you – if you turn your officer down, you're stark raving mad.'

Rosie sighed. 'All right. All right.'

'And be sure to let me know how you get on.'

'*I* don't have to tell *you* everything either,' Rosie countered with a smile.

Now, however, standing beside the telephone, she was still feeling nervous and unsure. He probably wouldn't ring anyway. He had had quite a lot to drink last night; today he might have thought better of it, especially as she'd confided in him that she carried a torch for someone else.

Five past six. Ten past. Rosie was on the point of giving up and going home when the telephone suddenly shrilled, making her jump, and before she could stop herself, she had snatched it up.

'Hello?'

Coins clanked at the other end of the line as the caller depressed the button.

'Ah! Miss Rosie Mitchell, is that yourself?' The Irish accent was unmistakable, and Rosie felt a little shiver dart through her veins.

'Yes, it's me.'

'Sorry I'm late. I got detained, so I did. I was afraid you might have given up.'

'I almost did,' Rosie said.

'Ah, that would have been a shame. So – are you going to be free next Saturday?'

'I'm afraid not. I've pulled a late shift.'

'Right.' It was clear from his change of tone that he thought she was making an excuse, and quite suddenly Rosie didn't want him to think that.

'I'm free every other evening this week,' she heard herself say.

'Every night?' His voice was upbeat again. Teasing. 'You mean I have a choice?'

'Well, every evening but Tuesday,' Rosie amended, remembering that she would be expected to help with the evacuees if she wasn't working.

'Shall we say Friday then?' Clarke said easily. 'Now that I know where you live, I'll pick you up at about eight, if that suits you.'

'OK.' Rosie was a bit surprised. She'd expected it to be earlier. Perhaps he had further to come than she'd realised.

'And don't eat too much before then. We'll get something. There must be some decent restaurants still open in Bath, I'd think.'

Rosie was even more surprised. No one had ever taken her out to a restaurant before. Fish and chips out of the newspaper was the closest she'd ever come to that.

'I'm looking forward to seeing you, Miss Rosie Mitchell.'

'Will you stop calling me that!' she implored.

'Sure I will. When I get to know you better.'

Although she was quite alone but for the relief crew enjoying a mug of tea and a cigarette while they waited for the inevitable call to action, Rosie felt the blood rush to her cheeks. As if on cue, the admin assistant appeared, describing circles in the air, which she knew meant that the telephone was needed.

Jennie Felton

'I'm sorry, I'm going to have to go,' she said. 'There might be an urgent call trying to get through.'

'So there might. I'll see you on Friday. Eight o'clock.'

At that minute the pips sounded, indicating that the time Clarke had paid for was up and he would need to put some more money in the box.

'Bye.' It was all she had time for before the line went dead. He couldn't have been calling from a local number, Rosie thought, and wondered again why he was so secretive about where he was based and what he was doing there.

She hung up, reached for her coat and bag and called goodnight to the relief crew. Then she set out for the bus stop, and perhaps a long wait for the next bus home.

Winnie wasn't there when Rosie got home, and there was a note on the kitchen table to say she was up at the big house for an emergency meeting with Lady Hastings.

An emergency? What in the world could that mean? She was gripped by sudden panic. Had something happened while she was on the way home? An invasion, perhaps? She'd been out of contact with civilisation for a good half-hour. On the bus, travelling through open countryside, she wouldn't have heard any sirens or a wireless broadcast.

Or suppose something had happened to Don? The worst of the fighting was still in Scandinavia and Scapa Flow as far as she knew, but something must be brewing in France too or surely the British troops would have been withdrawn and sent somewhere they were needed more. But perhaps they had been, and either Don hadn't been able to write or his letter had been delayed somewhere along the line.

Your dinner is in the oven keeping warm, Winnie had added at the bottom of her note, but with her nerves jangling Rosie knew she wouldn't be able to eat a single mouthful until she knew what was going on.

She put her coat back on and headed up to Bramley Court.

As the maid showed Rosie into the library, Winnie looked up, surprised. She, Lady Hastings and several other WVS members were seated in a circle of chairs, drawn up in the centre of the room.

'Rosie, what are you doing here?' Winnie asked.

'I'm worried. What's this emergency? Have we been invaded?'

It was Lady Hastings who answered her. 'If we were about to be bombed, my dear, we wouldn't be sitting here enjoying a glass of sherry. Perhaps you would care for one?'

'Oh, no thank you.' Rosie was embarrassed now for having interrupted the meeting, and in any case she didn't think sherry on an empty stomach was a good idea.

'Pull up a chair anyway. Now that you're here, I think you may be able to help. You are a trained nurse as well as an ambulance driver, and the reason I called this meeting is that I am most concerned for the welfare of the young evacuees. By the time they arrive, they'll have had a long and tiring day and they'll no doubt be upset. Do you think you could arrange for an ambulance to be in attendance?'

'Oh, I don't know about that,' Rosie said. 'It's really not my decision.'

'Surely you could put a good word in for us?' Lady Hastings persisted. 'I've spoken to Dr Hamilton, but he was no help, though he did say he'd be on call if he was needed, and I've wasted hours on the telephone to ambulance control. Nobody seems to realise how vulnerable these children are – or care, for that matter.'

'I'm sure that's not the case,' Rosie replied. 'But taking an ambulance out of service for a whole evening . . . It may not be needed here, but there could be a real emergency elsewhere.'

'But I am responsible for the welfare of the refugees,' Lady Hastings insisted, unable as always to see no further than what *she* wanted.

'I'll ask,' Rosie said. 'But I have to be honest, I don't think it will be agreed to. If it would help, I could be there to assess any child who appears to need medical attention. Then, if necessary, I could make a call and an ambulance would be sent.'

Lady Hastings sniffed. 'That will have to do, I suppose. I'll speak to Fred Thomas. Ask if we can use his shop as a first-aid centre. He, at least, is always willing to help wherever he can.'

Rosie was not at all sure that a butcher's shop was the right place for a distressed child, but she wasn't about to argue.

Winnie spoke out. 'I think that's a very good idea, milady. Mr Thomas is a very nice man and I'm sure he'll be agreeable.' Glancing at her, Rosie saw that her mother's cheeks had turned pink beneath the Bourjois face powder she used when she was dressed to go out.

'I certainly hope so,' Lady Hastings said with feeling, and returned her attention to Rosie.

'I can rely on you to be there then, can I, Rosemary? The coach is due to arrive soon after seven.'

'I'll get there just as soon as I can,' Rosie said. 'I don't finish my shift until six, and then I have to catch the bus home.'

'Hmm.' Lady Hastings didn't look happy, and when she spoke again there was reluctance in her tone. 'I suppose there's nothing for it but for me to contact Julian, see if he can help. He might even come to Hillsbridge himself and pick you up on the way so you wouldn't have to wait for a bus.'

Rosie bridled. She certainly didn't want to see Julian Edgell, let alone ride in his car.

'No thank you. I'll come by bus if you don't mind.'

'You'd best go home and eat that pie before it spoils,' Winnie said, anxious to prevent an altercation between her daughter and her employer.

'I'll do that,' Rosie said. 'And don't worry, Lady Hastings. I won't let you down.'

'Thank you, Rosemary,' Lady Hastings at least had the good grace to say. 'I'm relying on you.'

Rosie left then, annoyed by her ladyship's demands but thinking about her mother's pink cheeks when she'd spoken out about Mr Thomas. It had been puzzling her how Winnie seemed to manage to always get extra bacon or ham when rationing was so tightly controlled. Now she couldn't help wondering. Was there something a little more than butcher and customer going on between her mother and Fred Thomas?

Well, if there was, it had to be a good thing. If Winnie had a man friend, Rosie wouldn't be so worried about her being alone. And she was sure it was what her dad would have wanted too. He'd always taken such good care of his wife. Quiet, steady, a man of few words, but always there when she needed him, a rock to cling to in a stormy sea.

Rosie thought that Fred Thomas was cut from much the same cloth. And found herself hoping that something might come of their friendship.

Anne wasted no time in relaying her decision to the powers-that-be and was astonished by the swiftness with which they moved. She was to report to an assessment centre the following Monday, and the tests she would be subjected to would last no more than a few days. If she was successful, she would move to a training centre, where she would learn to use a radio, which would apparently be concealed in a small attaché case, and be trained in unarmed combat as well as the use of small arms and longer-range weapons. She would also be taught how to parachute from an aircraft.

To Anne, this was the scariest thing she could imagine. Would she ever be able to launch herself into nothingness? And if she did, would she remember how to get the parachute to open? The very thought of the ground rushing up at her made her stomach turn over.

You can do it, she told herself. Hadn't she once been afraid to even vault over a gate or turn a somersault over the bar of the roller that was used on the tennis court until Rosie had shown her how easy it was and patiently encouraged her until she'd dared to do it? She could still remember how excited she'd been when she'd finally let herself go and landed on her feet; how she'd wanted to do it again and again, not caring that she must be displaying her knickers to anyone who might be watching. This would be just the same. And she was no longer that scared little girl. She was a grown woman who'd gained self-confidence. If she could defy her mother, she could do anything.

But it wouldn't end there. If she passed the test and then satisfied the instructors who would train her, and if France really did fall to the Germans, the final parachute drop would be into real danger. Mr Green had made that clear. But she wouldn't think about that now. One step at a time. And if she was chosen, she was determined that she would gather her courage, do everything that was asked of her, and take pride in herself and in knowing that she was deemed good enough to carry out the daunting task of assisting the French resistance in their efforts to thwart the invading enemy.

On Tuesday evening, when Rosie's bus home passed the market square at just after 7.30, there was no sign of the coach that was bringing the little evacuees to Hillsbridge, and the only children she could see were those who had come with their mothers and fathers and were chasing one another around the forecourt of the George Hotel. But certainly quite a crowd had gathered, talking in little knots as they waited. As the only official stop in Hillsbridge was the one in front of the town hall, she had to remain on the bus and then walk back. But still there was no sign of the coach.

She looked for her mother among the crowd, which seemed to be getting as restless as the children, and spotted her talking to Fred Thomas, but before she could join them, Lady Hastings bustled up to her.

'You're here then, Rosemary. I have no idea what's delaying the evacuees, but it can't be good for the poor children. When they do arrive, I'd like you to keep a close eye on them and take any that look to be in need of attention to Mr Thomas's shop. Ah!' she broke off. 'That could be them now.'

Rosie followed her gaze to the main road from Bath and saw a charabanc coming down the incline into the centre of town.

Lady Hastings lifted a megaphone she was carrying and bellowed into it.

'Mr Thomas! Join me, please! Everyone else, move back. Clear a space, please! The coach has to park.'

The crowd jostled back towards the George; the parents of the children who were still running around called to them and scooped them up. The coach pulled off the road, the door opened and a woman with a clipboard got out and spoke to Lady Hastings. After a short exchange, Lady Hastings raised her megaphone again.

'Those of you who have already agreed to take a child, please come forward!' and as the volunteers tried to find a way through the throng, she bellowed again, 'Let them through!'

'This is a bear garden!' Rosie whispered to Fred Thomas, who had come to join them.

'I'm going to finish up stone deaf if she don't stop shouting through that thing,' Fred replied, looking as if he might be regretting his decision to volunteer his shop as a first-aid station.

To their relief, Lady Hastings lowered the megaphone and handed it to a lady who must be a friend of hers judging by her fur coat, which gave off a strong odour of mothballs. Instead she picked up a clipboard and pen and went to speak to the woman who was evidently in charge of the other end of the operation. After a short conversation, the woman went back up the steps of the coach to stand in the space beside the driver's cab, and Lady Hastings took up position on the road beside them. As the children began to emerge, the lady in the fur coat lined them up in front of those who had volunteered to take them in.

As she watched, Rosie was transported back to the scenes she had witnessed in London. These might have been the very same children, with their little cases and bags of possessions, all looking frightened, and some tearful. At least none appeared to be in need of medical attention. Some were in pairs, the older ones shepherding their younger siblings, while one girl of no more than ten or eleven was surrounded by three little ones, who were clutching at her coat. Who would be willing to take in a family of four? Rosie wondered.

Still holding her clipboard, Lady Hastings took her loud hailer in the other hand and began calling out the names of those on her list – quite unnecessarily, in Rosie's opinion. Given where they were standing, the volunteer hosts were well within earshot.

What followed sickened Rosie. She'd learned at school the way captured men, women and children had been forced to parade in front of prospective customers who would buy them as slaves, some of whom even wanted to inspect their teeth before making their selection. This seemed to her to be little better. She'd described the event as a bear garden – now she thought that a cattle market would be a better description.

Inevitably it was those who were clean and well dressed who were selected first, girls chosen over boys. Their names were crossed off the list and they departed, their luggage, such as it was, carried by the adult members of the family that had offered to take them in. It was those who looked as if they came from the slums who were left, dejected, heads bowed, snuffling into the sleeves of their much-worn coats. The sight saddened Rosie, and she wished she could escape, but she couldn't. She had to remain here until the last of the evacuees had been found places to stay.

The list of volunteers had been exhausted; now it was up to those who were undecided or had come as spectators to step up to the plate. Thankfully some did, though there were long pauses in the process while they considered or discussed things with their partners. Gradually the crowd thinned and the line of needy children diminished until there was just one boy of perhaps twelve or thirteen left. He was skinny, bony wrists exposed as the sleeves of his coat were far too short for him. His hair had clearly been cut by the pudding basin and his face was pockmarked and splattered with angry red spots. He glowered as he waited, but Rosie could see he was fighting back tears.

Suddenly a voice rang out from among the remaining onlookers.

'I'll take him!' It was Winnie.

Rosie was surprised – and a little dismayed. It was just like her mother to take pity on the lad, and for that she was proud of her. But she wasn't sure it was wise. How could they be sure he wasn't a wrong 'un who would cause endless trouble, perhaps even steal from them?

She caught at Winnie's arm. 'Mum, are you sure?'

'Course I am!' Winnie said staunchly.

It was then that, to everyone's surprise, Lady Hastings intervened. They couldn't know that she had always intended to take a child if there were not enough offers of accommodation.

'Thank you, Mrs Mitchell, but I'll take him myself.' As ever, her tone conveyed that she was not to be argued with. 'But I'm sorry, you and Rosie will have to walk home. With the boy as well as Lady Goodman, I'm afraid I won't have room for you.'

'Oh, we don't mind,' Winnie said. 'I'm just grateful . . .' She broke off, not wanting to admit in front of the boy that she had been worried as to how she would manage, Rosie guessed.

But the most priceless thing was the expression on the face of the lady in the fur coat. Utter horror at the thought of having to ride in the same car as a street urchin, who might well have a headful of fleas and goodness knows what other germs beside.

Lady Hastings raised her megaphone one last time, for the benefit of the few remaining stragglers.

'Thank you all for coming. And goodnight.'

'What in the world can her ladyship be thinking?' Winnie asked Rosie as they started on the long walk home.

'More to the point, Mum, what were you?' Rosie replied. 'Thank goodness she stepped in is all I can say.'

'Well, yes, I must admit I had a few qualms,' Winnie admitted. 'But I couldn't bear to see that poor boy standing there all by himself thinking nobody wanted him, and he'll be well looked after up at the big house.'

'He'll be cleaned up, treated to new clothes and made to toe the line,' Rosie said with a smile. 'His mother and father won't recognise him when he goes home!'

But she was thinking that her opinion of her ladyship needed some serious revision. What Lady Hastings had done was kind. Overbearing she could be, and she'd no doubt enjoy drilling some manners into the lad, but there could be no doubt that her heart was in the right place.

Chapter Nineteen

At last spring was arriving. After the long, hard winter, it was heartening to see daffodils and primroses in bloom, and sprigs of pussy willow, the long drooping loops of golden chain, and cascades of white flowers on the blackthorn trees. But the WVS needlework group was still hard at work knitting socks and scarves, which were needed for the soldiers in Scandinavia, the Royal Navy sailors, and those on merchant ships, which had now been armed and officially declared 'vessels of war'.

'This oiled wool is rubbing my fingers raw!' Brenda Bendle declared as she turned the heel of one sock at the weekly group meeting, and Winnie glanced down at her own hands, where the skin was cracked and bleeding. Goodness knows, doing the weekly wash in the bitter cold of winter did enough damage without the chafing of the harsh, stiff wool. But she wasn't going to complain. She'd had a letter from Don saying he was still in France, on the border with Belgium, and still working to strengthen the Maginot Line. She hadn't known what that meant until Fred Thomas explained it to her when she'd gone into his shop. It was a wall of fortifications that France had built after the Great War, stretching from Basle in Switzerland along the border with Germany to stop any future invasion. The trouble was, it was vulnerable along the Belgian border. 'Oh, I see,'

Winnie had said, though she was still foggy as to what exactly Don could be doing.

She didn't want to bother Fred with further questions, and had simply been grateful that for the moment at least Don appeared to be safe. Thank goodness he hadn't been sent to North Africa! She'd read in the *Mirror* that fighting was still going on between the British and Australian forces and the Italians and Germans there.

Although she was still a bit concerned that Rosie was going out with a soldier she barely knew, she was also pleased that she had something to take her mind off Julian.

'I suppose she'll be all right,' she'd confided to Fred.

'Course she will,' he had said. 'Your Rosie has got her head screwed on the right way.'

'I'm not so sure about that.' Winnie couldn't help thinking she'd lost it completely over Julian Edgell.

'Look, she was in London . . . what, a couple of years? You didn't know what she was doing then, did you? And she came home safe and sound,' Fred had said, and Winnie had had to smile. That was just what her Ern would have said.

A thought suggested itself to her. When Fred had called in on her the evening he'd been to see Lady Hastings, she'd really enjoyed his company, and said he must come again. Taking her courage in both hands, she said, 'Why don't you come to mine for that cup of tea on Friday? That's when she's going out with this chap.'

'Well, yes, why not?'

And so it had been arranged. Now, her knitting needles clacking, she felt pleased with herself, but also nervous. Yes, she and Fred got on very well, but she could still scarcely believe she'd actually invited him to her house. What would the other women in the needlework group think if they knew? There'd be talk behind her back for sure. Colour rose in Winnie's cheeks as she thought of it. But why shouldn't she? And she wouldn't be so worried about Rosie if Fred was there to take her mind off it.

In fact, she was already looking forward to Friday.

At Bramley Court, Frances had her hands full. Sir James had been a little surprised when she'd brought the evacuee boy home with her. She'd said she'd only do so as a last resort, as she didn't want any distractions from her organisational work for the WVS. But as always, he'd taken it in his stride. He'd made a cup of tea for the lad, whose name was apparently Billy Crossley, found some cheese and a fruit cake that Maud Hawkins had made this morning, and sat with him at the kitchen table while Frances was bustling about sorting out the sleeping arrangements. But his attempts to have a conversation with the boy had failed miserably. No matter what he asked, whether it was about his home and family or how the journey here had gone, the answer was the same. A few mumbled words. Billy would then relapse into silence, slumped over the table, slurping his tea and cramming cake into his mouth as if he hadn't eaten for days. Sir James could see very well why no one else had been prepared to take him, and he was proud of Frances for stepping in.

For the next couple of days she had no time to think about the failure of her plans for Anne and Julian. Her first challenge had been getting Billy clean. She'd run a hot bath, left him with soap, a loofah and towels and told him to be sure he washed his hair and scrubbed himself all over. She'd kept watch outside the door to ensure that when he emerged wearing one of Sir James's bath-robes, he was at least presentable. He was – more or less. She'd organised places at the local schools for him and the other evac-uees, and taken him to Bath to buy new clothes. Luckily he wasn't a fussy eater and wolfed down the healthy meals Maud made for him; Frances was determined to get some flesh on his bones.

'Goodness me, you'd scarcely know he was the same lad!' Sir James had commented.

'I've only just started,' Frances retorted. 'He still has to learn his manners. And wash his hands and face without having to be told. Believe me, he's a work in progress.'

Sir James could only be thankful that his wife had a new project to concentrate on. Hopefully it would keep her fully occupied so that she didn't do anything to further damage her relationship with Anne.

Unbeknown to either James or Frances, Julian had tried several times to get hold of Anne, without success, and he was beginning to wonder if she had already left Bristol for her WAAF posting, wherever that might be. He hoped not. If only he could speak to her, apologise and work his charms on her, the situation might yet be saved.

It wasn't only the loss of his chance to marry into the aristocracy and his falling-out with Frances that was eating away at him. It was that when there was no wedding, he would look a fool in front of half of Hillsbridge. That really hurt, as did the blow to his pride. Julian was used to being able to attract any woman he set his sights on, Rosie Mitchell being a prime example. He had no doubt he could have her again if he so wished. Yes, he'd seen her snuggling up to the chap in army officer's uniform, but he was fairly sure that was only a reaction on her part to the announcement that he was going to marry Anne. Their paths would almost certainly cross at the hospital before too long, and he thought he might well make some advances towards her when they did. If he could get nowhere with Anne, it would go some way to restoring his confidence in himself.

Once again he picked up the telephone and dialled Anne's number. Once again his call went unanswered. Was she there and deliberately ignoring the ring tone? Should he go to Bristol and knock on her door? But he couldn't bring himself to do that. She'd probably reiterate that she needed time to think – or worse, tell him she was sick of being pressured, and turn him down flat. An outright rejection would only cause more damage to his already dented self-esteem.

The best thing he could do was wait, he decided. There would be other chances, and in the meantime he'd amuse himself with Rosie – unless someone as suitable as Anne entered his orbit. Bath must be full of young ladies of breeding. It was that sort of place. And his profession made him especially eligible.

He poured himself a generous whisky, topped it up with a splash of water, tuned the wireless to a station that was playing classical music and sat down with every intention of putting the whole wretched business out of his mind.

As Anne let herself into her flat, she could hear the telephone ringing, but by the time she reached it, it had stopped. Briefly she wondered who had been calling. Her mother probably, and Anne had no desire to speak to her. But supposing it had been something to do with the arrangements for her upcoming suitability course for training as a secret agent? Unlikely, she told herself. Only the previous day she'd been at the local WAAF headquarters being given details of the location of the testing centre and kitted out with the uniform that completed her cover here in England.

She was wearing it now, and as she caught sight of herself in the long hall mirror, she couldn't help smiling with pride. Amazingly, it fitted her perfectly, and the soft muted blue suited her fair complexion and dark blonde hair and almost matched the colour of her eyes. She'd been visiting some of her friends here in Bristol to say her goodbyes, and she knew they'd been impressed.

'Just look at you, Anne!' Diana, whom she had worked with at the gallery, had exclaimed. 'I'd volunteer for the WAAF too if I thought it would suit me that well!'

'We'll have great uniforms too,' Rachel, Diana's flatmate, had assured her. 'I'm looking forward to the little frilly cap.'

Anne had raised her eyebrows questioningly and Diana had explained that the two of them were joining the Royal Naval Nursing Service. 'We're off next week too. And we called at your flat to see you yesterday, but you weren't there.'

'Because I was getting kitted out.' But of course Anne could say nothing about what she was really doing, and for the first time she felt a twinge of loneliness. Was this what it was going to be like from now on? Lying to her family and closest friends? But she wasn't going to change her mind now. Whatever the future held, she was determined to embrace it.

On Friday evening, both Rosie and Winnie were jittery.

'What time did you say your soldier was picking you up?' Winnie asked.

'His name's Clarke,' Rosie said. 'And I'm expecting him about eight.'

Winnie looked anxious. 'Well, I imagine Mr Thomas will be here before then.'

'Don't worry, I'll make myself scarce.'

'There's no need for that. But Rosie, be careful, won't you?'

Rosie gave her a straight look. 'You too, Mum,' she said mock-seriously.

'As if!' Winnie scoffed.

Moments later, there was a knock at the door.

'Oh, that'll be him now, I expect. Now, Rosie, you haven't forgot he stutters a bit, have you? For goodness' sake, don't stare if he does.' Winnie sounded flustered.

'Don't worry, I won't,' Rosie assured her.

Winnie ran a hand over her hair, unruly as usual, though she had combed it not ten minutes ago, and went to answer the door. Rosie hesitated, unsure what she should do. Should she make herself scarce, as she had said? Or would that seem rude? In the event, she still hadn't decided when she heard her mother say, 'Oh, come in, do, Mr Thomas. I've got the kettle on,' and the butcher appeared in the doorway.

'Well, if it's not R-Rosie!' he greeted her. 'N-nice to see you, m'dear.'

'She's going out in a bit,' Winnie said.

Rosie smiled at him. 'You too, Mr Thomas. But Mum's right, I am going out. I'm expecting a friend quite soon. I hope you won't think I'm avoiding you.'

'Course not, m'dear. I'm just pleased you're back home. I expect your mother was worried about you being in London at a time like this.'

'She still worries about me now,' Rosie said drily.

'I'm s-sure she does. That's what mothers do.'

'Sit down, Mr Thomas, and I'll get that pot of tea.' Winnie bustled into the kitchen.

'Actually, I worry about her too,' Rosie said when Winnie was out of earshot. 'I don't like to think of her alone, especially now, with the war and everything. That's why I came back from London.'

Fred Thomas nodded. 'I know. It's n-not going to be a p-picnic. The last war was bad, but at least folk at home were safe.' He shook his head. 'Not this time.'

Winnie was back with the teapot, complete with a tea cosy

she'd knitted herself, stitching a little doll onto the top so that it formed her skirt.

'Hadn't you better be getting yourself ready, Rosie?' she said, and Rosie took her cue.

'I had, actually. I hope to see you again soon, Mr Thomas.'

And with that she escaped upstairs, where she could watch for Clarke from her bedroom window. The nerves were knotting in her stomach now, and she really didn't know why. She'd been out with plenty of chaps in London and never felt like this. She'd caught it from her mother, she thought, and smiled, realising Winnie had been feeling much the same.

It'll be fine, she told herself. Just as long as he turns up . . .

And realised she would be very disappointed if he did not.

She need not have worried. Just after eight, she saw the beam of a single headlamp light the driveway and pull up behind Mr Thomas's van. She already had her coat on; she grabbed her bag and ran down the stairs.

'I'm going, Mum!' She had the door open by the time Clarke was halfway up the path.

'Mum has a visitor,' she said by way of explanation, not wanting Clarke to think she'd been watching out for him for any reason other than to avoid disturbing Winnie and her guest.

'I wondered who the van belonged to,' Clarke said easily; then, noticing the wording on the side of the van, 'A butcher! That's just the sort of visitor you want now that meat is rationed.'

'Oh, it's not black market or anything like that!' Rosie said hastily. 'He's just a friend.'

'Don't worry, I'm not going to report it to the police,' Clarke joked.

'I should hope not!'

'No, it's good your mother has some company,' he said,

275

serious now, as he executed a three-point turn in the drive and accelerated away. 'I think you told me on the train that she was widowed and your brother is in the army.'

'Yes.' Rosie was surprised he'd remembered. That was six months ago now. 'She's worried to death about Don, of course. But at least she's had a letter from him just this week, saying he's still in France, on the border with Belgium, and nothing seems to be happening. "The phoney war", he called it.'

'Hmm.' Clarke was silent for a moment, then went on, 'I know it's not what you want to hear, but the war is far from over. You can bet your bottom dollar the Germans are busy working out a strategy. It's not going to be quiet for long.'

'No, I don't suppose it will be,' Rosie said flatly.

'It's good that they're strengthening the defences on the Belgian border, though. The original Maginot Line is pretty impenetrable. Concrete fortifications, tunnels, underground bunkers, minefields, gun batteries – you name it. And millions of tons of steel embedded in the earth. It was started after the Great War, and they were working on it right up until four or five years ago. But the last stage – the Belgian border – was left vulnerable. And if Hitler invades France, as he's almost certain to do, that's the way he can get in without too much trouble.'

A shiver ran up Rosie's spine. *The way he can get in.* And Don was right there . . .

'I'm sorry, Rosie,' Clarke said, sensing he'd upset her. 'I just think it's better you're prepared for what is almost certainly coming. France will be overrun and will surrender. They'll have no choice. And then Jerry will turn his attention to Britain. We can only hope that we can stop him from overrunning us too. But this is supposed to be a nice evening out. Let's not talk about the war any more.'

'Yes, let's not,' Rosie agreed.

'So tell me about your day.'

'Fairly quiet really. But we did have one difficult call. An elderly lady had fallen in her kitchen and couldn't get up. It should have been pretty straightforward; the trouble was she had fallen against the door, and it would only open a couple of inches. The neighbour who'd found her hadn't been able to get in, and neither could we. Every time we attempted, she was screaming in pain, and we guessed she'd broken her hip.'

'Poor woman. So what happened?'

'We had a look round and found that the kitchen window was open, just a bit. I managed to get my hand inside and lift the arm – you know the one with little holes where the peg goes through. Then Molly, my partner, gave me a leg-up and I squeezed through.' She smiled. 'Trouble was, it was right over the sink and I fell in.'

'Oh dear.' Clarke was trying not to laugh. 'Did you get wet?'

'Worse. Not only was there a bowl of soapy water, but everything she'd used for breakfast was piled up on the side. Teapot. Half a cup of cold tea. And the remains of a bowl of porridge. Can you imagine the mess I was in? Wet, sticky, my uniform covered in tea leaves. And there was smashed crockery all over the floor. I thought I was as stuck as the patient! Then I had to try and move her out of the way of the door so that Molly and the neighbour could get it. There was no way I could do that without dragging her by her shoulders, and that was a slow job because she was in so much pain. Anyway,' she concluded, 'we managed it in the end. Got her on a stretcher and took her to hospital.'

'What an exciting life you lead,' Clarke said drily. 'Nothing so entertaining has happened to me today – and if it had, I wouldn't be able to tell you about it.'

Rosie huffed a breath. 'That is so annoying! I just hope it's nothing illegal.'

'Stop trying to pump me. You won't get anywhere. My lips are sealed, so they are.'

'One of these days I'll worm it out of you.'

'You mean this isn't the last time I'll see you?'

'Oh!' Rosie had spoken without thinking. 'That depends on whether you behave yourself,' she said, and realised she was flirting.

'We'll see about that. But I can't make any promises,' Clarke said, responding in the same spirit.

They were on the outskirts of Bath now, passing the turning that led to St Mark's hospital and on the long descent to the town.

'Is there a restaurant you can recommend?' Clarke asked.

'Not really.' The only one she could think of was a vast place on the leafy square near Green Park station. She and Freda used to walk past it when they'd come in on the train on their way to the Palace of Varieties. They'd look in at the windows and see smartly dressed people sitting at tables that were laden with crystal and silverware, a rosebud in a little vase in the centre. She wasn't dressed for that sort of place. And she shrank from the thought of having to use the right cutlery and glassware. 'There's a café I know, though. I've had fish and chips from there and it was really nice.'

'I was thinking of treating you to something a bit more special than that,' Clarke said.

Rosie took her courage in both hands. 'Honestly, that's what I'd like. I'm not used to fancy places.'

'OK. If you're sure. Where is this place?'

'I'll direct you. We should be able to park quite close.'

The café was in a little side street that branched off the square where the restaurant Rosie had baulked at took up most of the south side. From the outside it looked like a fish and chip shop, but Rosie had glimpsed a room beyond when she and Freda had gone in to buy a piece of battered cod and a portion of chips that they would eat sitting on a bench beneath the big tree in the centre of the square.

A bell jangled as Clarke opened the door. There was a small queue at the counter, but Clarke stood to one side of it, and a woman enveloped in an enormous white apron appeared.

'Do you have a table free?' he asked.

'Reckon we can squeeze you in. Come this way.' She led them into the room Rosie had noticed on her previous visits. 'There you are.' She pointed. 'Over in the corner. Will that suit you? I'll be back in a minute to take your order.'

The table was small and square, covered in green oilcloth and with a salt cellar and a bottle of vinegar in the centre. Clarke held out a chair for Rosie and sat down opposite her.

'So what do you recommend?'

'Oh, the cod,' Rosie said without hesitation. 'The batter is really crispy. And the chips are to die for. Isn't that smell making you hungry?'

'It is.' It was true. He hadn't eaten since a sandwich at lunchtime, and the aroma of hot fat and fish was tantalisingly good.

Rosie had relaxed now, and was able to enjoy the rest of the evening. The fish and chips was every bit as good as she remembered, though she still thought it tasted better out of a greaseproof wrapping and a sheet of newspaper, and without a doubt Clarke was good company. They finished their meals with dollops of ice cream and cups of tea, and Clarke smoked a cigarette. He paid the bill, and they left into a fine March evening with the hint of a frost to come. Spring wasn't quite here yet.

They went for a walk around Bath, passing Sally Lunn's teashop and the abbey, and Rosie pointed out the Empire Hotel, which had been taken over by the Admiralty just before the outbreak of war. They found a public house and went in for a drink,

Jennie Felton

Clarke ordering a beer for himself and a gin and orange for Rosie without even asking her. He remembered! she thought. Well fancy that! Then they made their way back to where he had parked the car and drove home.

When they reached the cottage, Rosie was surprised to see that Fred Thomas's van was still parked outside, but she didn't say anything.

'So when will I see you again?' Clarke asked.

'I'll be on a late shift all next week. But I should be free on Saturday.'

'Can I ring you again at the ambulance HQ?'

Rosie bit her lip, considering. 'I'm not sure. I don't think we ought to make a habit of it. But I'll be free every morning. I could use a phone box . . . Oh, but you won't give me your number, and I haven't a clue what the phone box number would be.'

'I'm sorry, I can't, Rosie. Look, I'll take a chance on it and turn up next Saturday. And if you're not here, I'll drive into Bath and pretend I've been taken ill,' he joked. 'I should enjoy being ministered to by a pretty ambulance driver.'

'Don't you dare!' Rosie responded, aiming a playful blow at him.

Clarke didn't miss his opportunity. He seized her arm and pulled her towards him. But once again there was nothing about his kiss to alarm her. It was warm and gentle, and once again Rosie felt herself responding. As little tremors of excitement twisted deep inside her, she parted her lips and the kiss became deeper, full of promise. Until Clarke pulled slightly away.

'So I'll see you next Saturday – hopefully.'

'Hopefully.'

'Goodnight then, Miss Rosie Mitchell.' He kissed her again, and Rosie found herself wishing it would last for ever. But all too soon it was over. He straightened, opened his door and got out, coming round to open hers.

'Come on. We don't want your mother thinking I've abducted you.'

There was one more light kiss and then he was gone. Rosie walked up the path into the house. The kitchen was in darkness, but light was showing from the partly open doorway of the little sitting room.

'I'm home!' she called, and Winnie answered her. 'In here, love!'

Her mother and Fred Thomas were sitting in the two easy chairs that faced one another across the fireplace, and Rosie couldn't help thinking how comfortable they looked.

'Did you have a nice time?' Winnie asked.

'I did,' Rosie said, and it was no more than the truth.

'Good. I'm glad to see you home safe, though.'

Fred Thomas got up. 'I'd better be going, Winnie. I didn't notice the time.'

'No more did I, Fred.' They were on first-name terms, Rosie noticed. 'You must come again. Perhaps for a meal.'

'I'd like that. And I'll bring a nice bit of steak, if I've got any.'

It seemed she wasn't the only one who'd enjoyed the evening, Rosie thought. And was amazed that something they'd both been nervous about had turned out so well.

Chapter Twenty

The country house to which Anne was to report for her assessment and initial training course was set on the edge of the North Yorkshire Moors. She had been looking forward to seeing a part of the country she barely knew, but as the train she'd been told to take travelled slowly through the rugged countryside, stopping at every station or halt, she realised just how isolated Bratley Grange must be. Unsurprising, she supposed. The powers-that-be wouldn't have chosen a location that might be a target for a bombing raid, but all the same, used as she was now to the bustle of Bristol, it seemed to be a desolate place.

At last she saw the sign she'd been watching for, and as the train slowed, she lifted her small case down from the rack. She climbed out onto a platform that was deserted but for an elderly stooped man in porter's uniform, and another young woman who was stepping down from the first of the three coaches. For the moment Anne didn't pay her any attention. She was on the lookout for the man she'd been told would meet her at the station. Perhaps he was waiting outside, she thought, and made her way down a slope, through a gate in a white picket fence to a tarmacked area behind the waiting room and the stationmaster's office.

It was empty except for an ancient-looking trailer that

appeared to have been abandoned. Anne glanced at her watch and then at the sky, which was already beginning to darken in the west. Given the speed they'd been travelling, she couldn't imagine the train was early.

'Are you going to Bratley Grange?'

She swung round to see the other young woman coming towards her. She was about her own age, Anne thought, with shoulder-length copper-coloured hair and wearing an emerald-green coat.

'Yes,' Anne said. 'Are you?'

The young woman nodded. 'I was told I'd be met at the station, but there doesn't seem to be anyone here.'

'No, there doesn't,' Anne agreed. 'And no taxi either.'

'Well, there wouldn't be out here in the wilds.'

'They'll be here soon, I'm sure,' Anne said with more confidence than she felt. 'Look, since we're both clearly here for the same reason, let's introduce ourselves. I'm Anne . . . oh, no, I don't think I'm supposed to say that. I'm Françoise Perez. And you are . . .?'

'Nicole.' The young woman winked conspiratorially. Although she had a faint northern accent when speaking English, her French accent was perfect. 'Will we be the only ones, do you think?'

'I've no idea,' Anne admitted. 'Or what we're going to be tested on really. They don't give much away, do they?'

Nicole fixed her with a straight look, though there was a twinkle in her eye. 'Loose talk costs lives,' she said.

Anne twinkled too. Already she liked this girl. 'Be like Dad, keep Mum,' she countered.

The silence was broken suddenly by the sound of a motor engine, faint, but growing steadily louder.

'Oh good. That sounds like our transport now,' Anne said.

But to her surprise, it was a battered pickup truck that appeared and parked next to the trailer. A stocky man with a shock of white hair climbed down from the cab, and Anne approached him.

'Excuse me, are you looking for us?'

'Sorry . . . what?' He squinted at them, his eyes screwed up in his weather-beaten face.

Her heart sank. She should have known this couldn't be their transport.

'Someone was supposed to meet our train and take us to Bratley Grange,' she said. 'I was hoping that might be you.'

The man huffed. 'Not me. Bratley Grange, eh? The place the government's took over?'

So, not so secret then. But Anne supposed it was inevitable it had got out to the locals.

The man looked from one to the other of them. 'I could take 'ee if thee be stuck,' he said. 'I be going that way.'

'Oh, thank you so much!' Nicole said, delighted. But Anne was not so sure.

'Do you think that's a good idea? If our car turns up and we're not here, we'll be off to a bad start.'

'Or we could be left waiting here for hours. And this gentleman already knows the Grange has been taken over for government business, if that's what you're worried about.'

'Well, if you're sure . . .'

'You're very kind, and you've saved our bacon, Mr . . .?'

'Dowdy. Frank Dowdy. Just let me get this hooked up.' He went to the trailer, pulled it to the rear of the pickup and attached a tow bar. 'Climb in then. It'll be a bit of a squash.'

He wasn't exaggerating. With Mr Dowdy taking up more than his fair share of the bench seat, there wasn't room for both the girls.

'One of you'd best get in the back,' he said.

Anne and Nicole looked at one another. The rear compartment looked filthy and smelled worse, and neither of them fancied arriving at Bratley Grange in such a state.

'If we put our cases in the back, you could sit on my lap,' Anne offered.

Somehow they settled themselves, hoping it wasn't too far to their destination, and with a jerk, a rattle and a crunching of gears, they were off, travelling along a narrow road through a vast expanse of moorland, where the gorse and heather were beginning to bloom. To one side they could see craggy outcrops in the distance; on the other a stream ran.

As they approached a crossroads, Mr Dowdy slowed to almost walking pace. 'Hold onto your hats, ladies,' he said, and took a sharp turn onto a road that was no more than a lane. As the truck jolted, Nicole almost lost her balance and fell against Anne, squashing her into the seat.

'Is it much further?' she asked as she righted herself.

Mr Dowdy didn't reply. He was staring intently at the road ahead.

'Here's yer lift, I reckon,' he said, and as Nicole turned to look, Anne got a view over her shoulder.

Fifty yards or so in front of them a black car was almost blocking the lane. The bonnet was up, and a man was bent double over it. Mr Dowdy drove on a few more yards, then got out of the cab and walked forward to speak to the man, who straightened up, wiping his hands on a handkerchief. The girls could see now that he was wearing a tweed jacket over what looked like brown corduroy trousers.

'That must be our driver,' Nicole said. 'He's broken down.'

'It explains why he didn't turn up. But we're stuck now,' Anne added. With the car blocking most of the lane, she couldn't see how the pickup and trailer could get past.

Mr Dowdy, however, seemed to have come up with an answer. He and the driver got behind the car and with considerable effort managed to push it onto the scrub that bordered the lane. Then they both walked back to the truck, where Mr Dowdy pointed to the trailer. Looking none too happy at the state of it, the man climbed in.

'They'll 'ave to get a mechanic out,' Mr Dowdy said, restarting his engine and manoeuvring past the broken-down car. 'Nothing to be done there.'

The girls exchanged glances. They could have been stuck out here in the wilds for hours. But they couldn't help feeling sorry for their driver, squatting in the filthy trailer. Goodness only knew what sort of state he'd be in by the time they reached their destination.

Bratley Grange was an impressive two-storey house, with a further three turret rooms rising from the roof, set in several acres of parkland.

'You'll have to walk from here,' Mr Dowdy said as the pickup came to a stop at the end of the drive. After thanking him, the girls scrambled out, relieved to be able to stretch their aching limbs, and he passed their cases down to them. Their driver clambered out of the trailer, dusting himself down.

'Sorry about that, ladies. The engine just conked out and I couldn't get it going again.'

Another man, slightly built but with a military bearing, appeared from the house and came to meet them. He was probably in his mid to late forties, Anne judged, smartly dressed, and with a neatly trimmed moustache and a short-back-and-sides haircut.

'What the hell happened, Evans?' he demanded. 'And where is your car?'

'Where it broke down, sir. I'll ring the garage and get someone out to pick it up.'

'Yes, do that.' The military-looking man turned to address
Anne and Nicole. 'This hasn't been the most auspicious beginning to your time here, has it? But I hope things can only improve
from now on. I'm Frederick Ashman, and you are . . .?'

'Our real names or . . .?' Nicole asked.

'The name of your alter ego. It's something you must get used
to, so we'll start as we mean to go on.'

'Nicole.'

'Françoise.'

Ashman picked up their suitcases. 'Let's get you settled in,
then. You've missed tea, I'm afraid, but dinner will be served at
nineteen hundred hours. Your room is ready for you, and I
expect you'd like to freshen up after your journey and unpack
your things.'

He led the way into a large hallway, which was curiously
bare. The floor was tiled, but there were no rugs, and as they
climbed the curving staircase, Anne noticed that the brown
stain on the treads extended only six inches or so from a paler
central strip. There must have been stair carpet laid here, she
thought, but presumably the previous occupant had had it
removed and the government, or whoever had taken the house
over, hadn't had it replaced.

She had rather hoped she might have been allocated one of
the turret rooms, from which she imagined the view would be
spectacular, but Frederick Ashman directed them along a landing on the first floor and threw open a door.

'This is your room. You'll be sharing. I hope you don't mind
that?'

'No . . . no.'

'That's absolutely fine.'

Anne wasn't used to sharing a bedroom, and was glad it was Nicole who would be her roommate. She felt that she knew her already, and the two of them could become friends.

Dusk had fallen now, and Ashman put down their suitcases and ignited a gas mantle that hung in the centre of the room. 'No electricity out here, I'm afraid,' he said. 'We have our own supply of gas canisters, and it seems to work well enough. I doubt it will be bright enough for you to be able to read, but I'd recommend an early night in any case. You have a couple of very busy days ahead of you. Now, I'll leave you to it, and I'll see you at dinner.'

'Come on sweetie, just a drop more.'

Freda wriggled the bottle of milk at the lamb's mouth, and to her relief he took the teat and began to suck again, nestling against her.

She'd seen him born last night. Farmer Ted – or just Ted, as she now called him – had taken her out to the lambing shed, where the ewe was in labour, and she'd watched with growing anxiety as the hours had ticked away and the ewe had become ever more distressed as she strained fruitlessly against the birthing pains.

'I'm going to phone for the vet,' Ted had eventually said. 'If anything happens while I'm gone, just take the lamb gently and lie it down right there. Don't try to do anything else till I get back.'

Freda had nodded, but nerves were tightening in her stomach. Yes, she wanted this to be over, but she was desperately afraid that she might have to deliver the lamb herself. She'd already watched Ted bring several others safely into the world, but she wasn't at all confident that she could do the same.

Trembling, she tried to calm the distressed ewe, stroking her head and massaging her belly, but all that emerged was a tiny foot.

'All right, Freda?' Ted was back. Freda breathed a sigh of relief.

'Did you manage to get hold of the vet?' she asked anxiously.

'No, dammit. He's out on another call.' He took a close look at the ewe and shook his head. 'Can't leave this any longer.'

'What are you going to do?'

'What the vet would've. Look, if you want to go . . .'

'No. I'll stay.' She was determined to see this through to the bitter end, but at the same time was trying to prepare herself for the worst.

'If you're sure.' He rolled his sleeves up above his elbows.

Her stomach churning, Freda watched as the scene unfolded and with Ted's assistance the tiny lamb emerged, covered in blood and mucus. Ted wrapped him in a towel and handed him to Freda while he tended to the ewe, and as she cradled him she marvelled at the new life she was holding in her arms and prayed that he would survive his long and difficult birth.

Her prayer had been answered. The lamb had lived. But despite Ted's best efforts, he had been unable to save the ewe.

Back in the kitchen, Ted's mother was waiting with a tin bath, hot water and more towels, and she took the lamb and cleaned him up while Ted and Freda washed at the kitchen sink.

'At least we've got this one,' she said as she wrapped him in a dry towel.

'Yes.' But Freda could see Ted was beating himself up for not having been able to save the ewe.

Mrs Holland must have seen it too. 'You did yer best, Ted. I doubt the vet could have done more.' She carried the lamb over to Freda, who was sitting in a chair beside the Aga, still chilled to the marrow and seemingly unable to get warm. 'No point upsetting yourself, m'dear. Things don't always work out the way you'd like, and you'll have to get used to it. Now d'you want to hold this one while I make a pot of tea?'

Freda's teeth were chattering too much to reply, but she had nodded and held out her arms.

'He's your baby. I'm countin' on you to look after him,' Mrs Holland had said.

Now, once more sitting in the chair beside the Aga, bottle-feeding the lamb, Freda experienced a glow of satisfaction. Yes, she was sad that the ewe had died, but having the lamb placed in her care more than made up for it. She'd hated every moment of what had happened last night, but it was all experience and would stand her in good stead. Like all of life, the rough had to be taken with the smooth, and although she had been here only a short time, she already knew this was the life she wanted. For the duration of the war, and afterwards.

At dinner, Anne discovered she was one of six young women who were being assessed. They made one another's acquaintance over a meal of vegetable soup, cottage pie and baked apples, served up by a buxom woman in a white overall, her hair covered by a net, which made Anne think she might also be the cook. One of the other girls was French, the others all from different parts of England, and all had assumed French names. Anne was sure she'd never remember all of them.

Frederick Ashman ate with them, and Anne discovered he was a colonel and the officer in charge here. She also learned that the car that had broken down had already brought two of the other girls to Bratley Grange before it had given up the ghost on its way to collect her and Nicole, while a taxi had been sent for the other two.

'I hope the car won't be out of commission for too long,' Colonel Ashman said. 'Having to use taxis will eat into our budget, and unfortunately they are not always reliable.'

When the meal was over, they stayed and chatted for a little while, but they weren't late to bed, and Anne fell asleep almost as soon as her head touched the pillow.

Next morning they were woken bright and early for a breakfast of porridge and toast, and Colonel Ashman told them that today they were going to tackle an assault course. He introduced a burly soldier – a Scottish sergeant major named Stewart – who was to put them through their paces, and left them with him.

The very sight of the sergeant major unsettled Anne, and as he barked instructions in a Glasgow dialect she could scarcely understand, she became more apprehensive. They were to be divided into two teams of three, and the course consisted of a series of obstacles that would lead them to a riverbank. There they would be expected to devise and construct a way to cross the river.

'We'll get our clothes in a terrible mess!' Nicole whispered, and the sergeant major overheard her.

'Ye'll be kitted out, ye daft wee thing! Clothes and footwear in the chests.' He indicated two large wicker trunks stacked against the wall behind them. 'Find what ye need, get changed and back here. Ye've got ten minutes. Be late and ye'll fail the test.'

The girls all scrambled to the trunks. One contained stout boots and plimsolls, otherwise known as 'daps', and the second an assortment of Aertex shirts, shorts and combat trousers. Anne selected a shirt, trousers and boots that looked as if they would fit her. With no time to go back to their rooms, the girls all rushed to the downstairs cloakroom. They left their daywear in untidy heaps and pulled on the items they'd chosen. Anne's boots were squashing her toes – she must have judged them to be larger than they actually were – but she couldn't change them now. She'd just have to manage.

Stewart was checking his watch as she got back to the room

with only moments to spare, and somehow all the others managed it too. At any rate, no one was disqualified, and Anne wondered if he really would have failed anyone who didn't meet his deadline. But none of the girls had been ready to take the chance.

'Right. Away we go,' Stewart barked.

He led them out of the park and into the open countryside that lay beyond. The ground was uneven and stony in places, covered with rough undergrowth in others, and the assault course looked to be a daunting prospect, the first obstacle a wall of wire netting stretched between two poles.

Stewart pointed at Anne. 'Ye'll be one team leader, and ye' – he indicated a red-haired girl whom Anne thought was called Babette – 'will be the other. Choose your team members – you first, Françoise or whatever your name is.'

Anne was staggered to have been selected and not a little apprehensive, but she knew to refuse would be a black mark against her. She looked the others over and, feeling guilty at not choosing Nicole first, pointed to a sporty-looking girl she thought would be the greatest asset to her team. This was no time to be sentimental. It was every girl for herself.

When the teams were complete – Anne had also chosen the girl codenamed Edith –a starting pistol was fired and they were off. Stewart followed, watching them, and was joined by another man, but most of the girls were too engrossed to take much notice.

As she struggled to climb over the netting, Anne wished she had chosen plimsolls rather than the sturdy boots. It wasn't easy fitting the thick toecaps into the spaces between the criss-crossed wires. She gritted her teeth and persevered, eventually reaching the top. But the boots had cost her valuable time; she was next to last. The leaders were already racing towards the next obstacle, and the only way Anne could think of to catch up was to jump.

Her heart missed a beat when she looked down; the ground seemed horribly far away, but she took a deep breath and launched herself into space.

In that moment, trying not to look at the drop beneath her, she caught a glimpse of Stewart and the other man. Tall, dark, a stranger. Then she lost sight of them as the ground came rushing up to meet her.

To her surprise, it was quite soft. She landed easily, automatically bending her knees and rolling, then leaping to her feet and setting off in pursuit of the leaders. As she'd admitted at interview, she was no sprinter, but with the exception of the sporty-looking girl she'd chosen for her team, the others weren't either, and by the time they reached the next obstacle – a long, narrow tunnel – she wasn't far behind. A competitive streak she hadn't known she possessed took over, and she found she was actually enjoying herself.

The last obstacle was a pit that had been turned into a veritable mud bath. By the time the girls reached the other side, they were caked in it. And the path to the riverbank was not much better. Even more daunting was the river itself. Much wider than Anne had envisaged, and fast-flowing after the winter rains had drained down from the moors above. Randomly scattered along the bank were items that could be used to construct some sort of crossing – barrels, wooden planks, ropes and so on. The girls huddled in their teams, trying to work out a plan, but nothing seemed feasible. They just couldn't see how they could build a bridge to the other side – not one that would support them anyway.

It was Edith who came up with the idea. She'd spotted a tree on the opposite bank with a rope hanging from one of its stout branches, presumably fixed there by children who came here to play.

'Look – that's for swinging across!'

'Yes, but we've got to get to it first,' Anne pointed out.

'Don't worry. I'll swim over and fetch it.'

'You can't! There's a really strong current!' Anne said, horrified at the thought of placing one of her girls in danger.

'And I'm a really strong swimmer,' Edith countered. 'I was working as a lifeguard on the beach at Brighton before the war.'

Anne could scarcely believe it. The girl looked as if a strong wind would snap her in two, and Anne thought perhaps she had chosen her name because, like Edith Piaf, she was a little sparrow. But if she'd been a lifeguard, she must know she was capable of what she was suggesting.

'OK,' she said. 'But as soon as one of us swings across, the rope will be on the wrong side of the river again. And are we sure it's secure enough to take our weight? And the branch? What if it's rotten?'

'I'll test it when I get over there,' Edith said, pulling off her boots. 'If I fall in, I can swim back and we'll just have to think again.'

As the other team struggled to rope barrels together, Edith stripped off her shirt and scrambled down the riverbank, then struck out in an impressive front crawl, revealing long, strong muscles in her arms and shoulders.

The plan worked perfectly, and the other team, still a barrel or two short of what was needed, stopped what they were doing.

'Cheats!' one shouted.

'Are we allowed to do it like that?' Marie asked anxiously.

'We're here, aren't we?' Anne said encouragingly, although she wasn't entirely sure if they had broken the rules.

Stewart joined them, alone now, and they held their breath. But thankfully they weren't disqualified or told to go back and find another way to get across, and the sergeant major actually praised them.

'Hmm. Unconventional, but at least you used your initiative,' he growled, and Anne felt a glow of pride that she'd overcome the first hurdle. This afternoon they were to be tested on their French conversation, and tomorrow there would be an interview with a psychologist. But for the moment she could relax, enjoy a hot shower and prepare herself for what was to come.

Frances was getting ready for a visit from the WVS district coordinator, who was coming to check that no problems had arisen with the evacuees. She dressed in a smart black wool suit and white silk blouse, tidied her hair and applied a little lipstick. Checking her appearance in her dressing room mirror, she decided to pin a brooch to her lapel. The diamond one would be perfect against the black wool. She got out her jewellery box and opened it, but the brooch didn't seem to be there. Then she remembered. She'd last worn it on the dress she'd chosen for the dance, and she'd returned home too tired to put everything away. She'd undressed in her bedroom, put the brooch in a trinket saucer on the top of the tallboy, and hung her dress over the back of a chair. The dress she'd rehung in her dressing room closet next day, but she'd forgotten all about the brooch.

She went into the bedroom to fetch it, but to her dismay there was nothing in the trinket saucer but a couple of hairpins. What had happened to it? Had she put it somewhere stupid, half asleep as she'd been? But no, she clearly remembered thinking it would be safe in the saucer.

As she puzzled over it, she heard the front doorbell ring. The coordinator was here. No time now to look further for the brooch. That would have to wait for later. She straightened her jacket and went downstairs.

* * *

The girls were lined up outside the library door, waiting their turn to be called in for their French language test.

First in was the redhead, Babette. The other girls clustered around the door, hoping to hear what was being said, but without success. The wood was far too thick and heavy. As she came out, she rolled her eyes and pretended to fan herself. 'Wow! Dreamboat or what?' she whispered, and added, 'He *is* French, I think.'

'*Entrez!*'

They all fell silent as the summons came from within the library, and the next girl in line stepped forward and went in. When she came out, she was blushing, and nodding to indicate that she agreed with Babette. Anne was somewhat sceptical. They were getting overexcited, she thought. But when it was her turn, she had to admit they hadn't been exaggerating. He rose to greet her, tall, dark, with conker-brown eyes. Could this be the man she'd glimpsed when she'd launched herself off the wire obstacle? she wondered.

'*Assis-toi.*' His voice was deep, his accent one of a French native, and possibly aristocratic. But she was too busy concentrating on what he was saying and her own fluency to give it another thought. It was, after all, some time since she'd been to France.

She was surprised then when suddenly he asked her if she knew Charente. She did, of course. One of the friends she'd made at her Swiss finishing school had lived in Angoulême, and she'd spent several long holidays there with her.

'*Oui. J'ai une amie à Angoulême. J'avais l'habitude de lui render visite assez souvant,*' she replied.

'I thought so,' he said, and still speaking in his native language, he went on to explain that Charente was his home and he had recognised a trace of the local accent in her speech. Anne relaxed as they chatted about the district, the cathedral at Angoulême, the river and the wooded hillsides, the vineyards and the cognac distilleries.

Finally he rose and held out his hand. 'Thank you, Françoise. I hope we may meet again.'

'Goodness, you were in there a long time!' Simone said when Anne emerged.

'Was I?' She'd been so absorbed in the conversation it hadn't occurred to her.

And of course when the last girl had been interviewed, Anne could have no inkling that the handsome Frenchman had been discussing her with Colonel Ashman.

Rosie had discovered she'd been right in thinking she would be working on Saturday evening, and was wishing she had some way of letting Clarke know so that he wouldn't have a wasted journey. But she was in for some disappointing news.

On the Friday she was a bit late getting to the hospital – there had been an accident on the Bath road, partially blocking it, and a policeman was controlling the traffic. Rosie had wondered if there had been any injuries and if the day crew had been called out. If so, they'd been and gone. But when she finally made it to work, she found them still in the ambulance bay.

'Sorry,' she said. 'My bus got held up by an accident.'

'Pity.' Wesley Tudgay, one of the day-shift drivers, was shrugging into his overcoat. 'There was a call for you. Some chap.'

'Oh no!' Rosie groaned. How unlucky was that?

'He left a message for you, though. Said he won't be able to make Saturday. Oh, and he doesn't know when he'll be able to see you again.'

For a moment Rosie couldn't think straight. 'Nothing else?'

'No, that was about it. Goin' out, were you?' But already he was heading for the door. He must have waited especially to give her the message.

The telephone rang. She rushed to it, hoping perhaps it was Clarke again. But no. A woman had had a bad fall in the town. An ambulance was needed. Rosie found Molly, her partner, in the rest room and together they set off. But her head was spinning and she felt sick with disappointment.

Clarke had said he didn't know when he'd be able to see her again. What did that mean? That it was over, just when she'd thought it was going so well? Or had something happened that was beyond his control? She just didn't know. But she couldn't think about it now. She had to concentrate on the job in hand. Her mouth set tight, her hands gripping the steering wheel, she pulled out onto the road.

Chapter Twenty-One

Be careful what you wish for.

As night fell over the army camp on the French–Belgian border, Clarke stood outside his tented accommodation smoking a cigarette and thinking how well that maxim applied to him. Important though he knew it was to have agents trained and ready to go into France to support the resistance groups that had begun preparing for a German invasion, he had still wished he could be out in the field himself.

Those that can do, those that can't teach. Another saying that seemed entirely appropriate. Except that he could. He'd proved himself time and again. And he had felt restless and resentful that he had been safe in a secret location in the heart of the English countryside where no bombs were likely to fall.

But when the call had come out of the blue, the timing was all wrong. If Rosie wasn't working, he should have been with her, and he'd had to let her down. He only hoped that the man he'd spoken to at the ambulance HQ had given her the message – he didn't want her to be waiting for him, wondering why he hadn't turned up as he'd said he would. And he hoped too that he'd made it clear that he wasn't sure how long he'd be in France, but that he'd be in touch when he got back. Could be, of course, that she was on a late shift and wouldn't have been able to keep their date either, but that was small comfort.

He ground out his cigarette in the springy turf with the toe of his boot. No sense fretting over something he couldn't change. Better to concentrate on what he'd been brought here for. It wasn't going to be easy, and the sooner he could get it done, the sooner he'd be back in Somerset again. He went into the tent and retrieved the folder of plans he'd been given at the Wiltshire airfield from where he'd been flown out.

This bridge was quite different to the one they'd been designing an underwater device for in Shropshire. It crossed the river that flowed along the border with Belgium. He'd been out to take a look at it this morning, and understood why the powers-that-be wanted it rendered impassable. Sturdy, stone-built, and supported by pillars that had been embedded deep into the earth, it would easily take the weight of the tanks and transporters the Germans would employ if they took Belgium and wanted to cross the border into France. Which they undoubtedly would. But by its very nature it was going to take an enormous amount of explosive to bring it down.

A plane droned overhead. From the sound of the engine it was a German plane. Clarke opened the flap of the tent and looked up into a clear, starry night. No other planes were in sight, and he guessed this was a scout, checking out the lie of the land and taking photographs.

It was just such a night as this that the bombers would come to back up the land invasion, or perhaps to prepare for it, and the hairs on the back of his neck rose. If he was still here when they came, the army camp would be a prime target. He might never go home. Never see Rosie again. Never be able to explain why he had been unable to keep their date tonight. Never be able to tell her how he felt about her.

He loved her, he knew that now. But she might never know it.

He gave himself a mental shake, lit another cigarette and went back to studying the plans of the bridge and its substructure, searching for the weakest point. He had to get this done and get home. As soon as was humanly possible.

Despite searching high and low, Frances still had not found her missing brooch, and she was beginning to wonder if Billy Crossley, her evacuee, might be behind its disappearance. She packed him off to his room every day when he got back from school to change out of his uniform and do his homework – she'd provided him with a desk and chair so that he could concentrate without any distractions. She always left him alone for at least an hour before checking on his progress; plenty of time for him to wander about upstairs, which might account for how little he had to show her.

Had he gone into her bedroom, seen the brooch in the trinket tray and stolen it? But why? He would have to go to Bath to exchange it for cash; there were no pawnbrokers in Hillsbridge, and she was sure Mr Reakes, the jeweller, would report it if he was offered something so obviously valuable. But she wouldn't put it past the boy to simply take it with the intention of selling it when the opportunity arose. She'd been given very little information about his background, and she couldn't get him to talk about it, but quite clearly it was less than salubrious, and taking things that didn't belong to him might very well be bred into him.

What could she have been thinking to take him in? she asked herself. But then she'd known he would be too much for Winnie to handle, while she herself never could resist a challenge.

Frances considered whether she should confront him with her suspicion and decided against it, for the moment anyway.

She had no proof whatsoever that he'd stolen the brooch, and if she accused him wrongly, the progress she was trying to make in building a relationship with him would be scuppered, perhaps permanently. Better to wait a bit and see if it turned up. If not, she would have a word with him, and if it turned out that he *had* taken the brooch, she'd haul him down to the police station and get Sergeant Meadows to give him a stern warning, a first step to make him realise the seriousness of thieving.

She'd also leave a few things lying about and see if they disappeared too. Better still, cash. She fetched her purse, took out two ten-shilling notes and some silver – florins, shillings, and a half-crown – and took them up to her room. She weighted down the notes with an antique candle snuffer and set the coins none too tidily on top, as if James had simply emptied his pockets and left them there. She found herself hoping that none of the money disappeared. Hoping that she was wrong, and the brooch would turn up too. She wanted very much to believe she could steer this awkward and poorly raised lad towards a brighter future.

Rosie was more hurt than she would have believed possible by Clarke's abrupt message and disappearance. It could mean only one thing, she felt sure. He didn't want to see her again. She'd thought that after the shock of Julian's engagement to Anne, nothing could ever touch her again. But perhaps that was just it. Besides the pain of knowing she'd lost him for ever, her self-esteem and confidence had taken a severe hit. Clarke's attention had gone some way to restoring that. Now she felt totally worthless. If he could simply discard her like an empty chip wrapper, there was no hope for her. Ever.

Winnie had tried her very best to lift her spirits. 'I'm sure there's a good reason for it, my love,' she'd said when Rosie had told her about it. 'There is a war on. And you did say he kept very quiet about what he was doing.'

'Exactly. As you pointed out, I don't know a single thing about him. He could have a wife and children for all I know. He could be a German spy. Or a spiv, making money out of the black market.'

'Well, there could be a wife,' Winnie conceded. 'I've got to say that's what concerned me most. But a German spy? Or a black marketeer? Oh, I don't think so.'

Rosie had shrugged wretchedly. 'What does it matter anyway? I'm not likely to ever see him again.'

'And you'll pick yourself up and go on,' Winnie had assured her. 'If he's been misleading you, he's not worth worrying over.'

But her words did nothing to lift Rosie's spirits. Even Molly, her new partner, noticed it.

'What's up with you?' she asked. 'You look as if you've lost a shilling and found a farthing.'

'Nothing. I'm fine,' Rosie said sharply, and Molly thought twice about continuing the conversation.

A few days later, when Rosie was sitting alone at a corner table, toying with her meal of corned beef and a jacket potato, she was interrupted by a voice coming from behind her.

'Is this seat taken?' Julian, with a tray of food, smiling his most charming smile and indicating the chair opposite her.

'Why?' she asked sarcastically.

'You look lonely. I thought I'd join you. May I?'

Perhaps he'd noticed she was looking miserable and assumed it was because of him. Rosie shrugged. 'It's a free country.'

Julian put his tray down on the table. 'Don't be like that, Rosie. I thought we were friends.'

'Don't,' Rosie said. 'Just don't.'

He sat down anyway. 'I haven't seen you lately. It would be

good to chat and you can tell me how you're getting on. Though from what I hear, you're very highly thought of. As you deserve to be.'

Rosie was making a great play of concentrating on her meal, though she had completely lost her appetite, and after a minute or so's silence Julian said, 'You do know it was me who recommended you, don't you?'

Rosie put down her knife and fork and met his eyes, challenging. 'What would Anne have to say if she knew you were buttering me up?'

He assumed a puzzled look. 'Anne? Why would she object?'

'I'd have thought it was obvious.'

Julian sighed. 'Ah. I assume you're referring to the announcement James made at the dance. Didn't you know? That was a stupid misunderstanding. I'd have thought it was all over Hillsbridge by now.'

Rosie didn't know whether to believe him or not. 'Well, I haven't heard it.'

'Hmm.' Julian's lips tightened for a moment. 'Perhaps Frances doesn't want to make James look a fool. Or perhaps the whole thing was at her instigation. She's always been most anxious for a match between Anne and me, and you know what she's like when she sets her heart on something. It wouldn't surprise me if she misled James deliberately to force our hand. Anyway, the truth is that I haven't seen Anne since that night. The last thing I heard was that she was very keen to join the WAAF, and I think she must have already left Bristol.'

'Oh, right.' Rosie didn't honestly know what else to say.

'If she has, Frances will be furious,' he went on.

'She's taken in an evacuee, a boy from the slums by the look of him, so I think she has her hands pretty full. Did you know about that?' Rosie asked.

'No, I didn't. You can see I'm totally out of touch.' Julian shook his head. 'We really must meet up for a drink sometime and you can fill me in on everything that's going on in Hillsbridge.'

Rosie was staggered. How dare he? She was still suspicious of his claim that the engagement announcement had been a mistake. It seemed very convenient to her, and she was sure Sir James would never have announced it unless he believed it was true. But then again, Frances could be very devious. Rosie wouldn't put it past her to cook up a mad scheme like that if she thought it would get her what she wanted. But if Julian thought he could blow hot and cold with her and then expect to worm his way back in with his undeniable charm, he was very much mistaken. Whatever the truth of it, he'd been all over Anne at the dance, and she hadn't forgotten the smug expression on his face when their eyes met on the dance floor. No matter that she wanted more than anything to accept his invitation. No matter that whatever he'd done, however he'd behaved, she was still in love with him. She wasn't going to be taken for a fool again.

'I don't think that's a very good idea, Julian,' she said. 'Not yet, anyway.'

She pushed back her chair, leaving Julian gaping, and left the canteen.

It was the hardest thing she had ever done.

One of the notes had gone. It was several days now since Frances had laid her trap and she had started to think – to hope – that she'd been wrong to suspect Billy of stealing. But she'd decided to leave it a little longer so as to be sure. James had chastised her over it, saying it was wrong to put temptation in the boy's way, but he hadn't told her outright to remove the money. She'd known he wouldn't. It wasn't his way to lay down the law. And now . . .

She checked again that the two notes hadn't got stuck together. They were crisp and new, and that could sometimes happen. But no. There was only one ten-shilling note where she'd left two. She stood for a moment, debating with herself the best way to play it, then made up her mind. There was no time like the present. Billy needed to know that what he had done was wrong and that she wouldn't tolerate it.

Fuming though she was, she knocked on his bedroom door as she always did in an effort to teach him good manners by example, then walked in. Instead of being at his desk studying, he was sprawled on the bed leafing through a crumpled copy of *The Dandy*, presumably once owned by a classmate.

He leapt up, stuffing the comic beneath the pillow. 'I've finished my homework, honest.'

'We'll talk about that later,' Frances said stiffly, then fixed him with a hard stare. 'Have you been into my room, Billy?'

'No, miss!' he said indignantly, but the hot colour flooding his cheeks told a different story.

'Don't lie to me, Billy. I know you have,' Frances said sternly.

'I just . . . wanted to 'ave a look . . .'

'Is that all? I think not.'

Billy looked down at his feet, scuffing the edge of the bedside rug. 'I didn't do nothing. Honest.'

'Honest?' Frances scoffed. 'I don't think you know the meaning of the word. You took some money, didn't you? You might as well admit it.'

'You can afford it,' Billy muttered.

'That is quite beside the point. And you stole my brooch too, didn't you?'

'Wot brooch? I don't know nothing about no brooch!'

'I think you do. That disappeared from my room too. I gave you the benefit of the doubt then. But now you've admitted to

306

being a thief. Don't you know stealing is wrong? Didn't your mother and father teach you anything?'

Billy raised his head, defiance blazing in his eyes.

'I ain't got no father . . . well, not any more. Just Uncle Seamus, an' all 'e's good fer is 'ittin' the bottle. And me and me ma too.'

Frances stiffened. 'This man beats you?'

Billy shrugged. 'Course 'e does. When 'e's drunk.'

'And your mother?'

'She ain't there much. She's out, all tarted up. But if she don't bring much money 'ome with 'er, then yeah, 'e'll give 'er wot for.'

Frances was staggered. Billy's background was far worse than she'd imagined. No wonder he had no moral standards. And no wonder there had been next to no information on the form she'd been given by the evacuation coordinator. She'd be having words with her. She should have been warned. But it was too late for that now.

'Sit down, Billy,' she said. 'I think it's time you and I had a talk. You're not in Bethnal Green now, and we do things differently here. And one of the things we don't do is take things that don't belong to us. What did you want the money for anyway?'

Billy shrugged. 'Just so I could get a comic of me own. An' a twist of sweets, an' a packet of five Woodbines.'

Frances made up her mind. 'I can't allow you to keep the note you stole, but if you return it, I'll give you enough to buy sweets and a comic. And I'll see about getting you a little job of some kind so that you can earn a few shillings of your own. But not if you are going to spend it on cigarettes. And not if you continue to take things that don't belong to you. Do I make myself clear?'

Billy nodded, then fished the ten-shilling note out of his pocket and handed it to her.

'Thank you,' Frances said. 'Saying thank you is something

else we do. And just one more thing. I imagine you've disposed of my brooch by now, but if you continue to steal from me, I shall have no option but to escort you to the police station and tell the sergeant about it. He won't treat you as kindly as I do, I assure you. So please don't let me down.' She paused, giving him another of her stern looks. 'For now, then, I'll fetch you some money and we'll say no more about it.' She left, closing the door after her.

Back in her own room, she stood for a moment letting it all sink in and wondering if what she'd done was the best way of dealing with the situation. She had no proof Billy was responsible for the disappearance of her brooch, whereas with the money she had been on solid ground, and she intended to make him understand that here he couldn't get away with the sort of habits he'd no doubt learned in that dreadful home. To be firm but fair. And to hope that in time she could make a difference. It would be a long and rocky road, and she must expect plenty of pitfalls along the way. But if in the time he was here she could teach him right from wrong, and that it paid to be upright and honest, it would be well worth while.

She picked up the florins and the half-crown and returned to Billy's room.

'Here you are,' she said, handing them to him. 'Now, let's take a look at your homework.'

'Morning, Mr Thomas.'

'Good m-morning, Mrs Mitchell. And what can I do for you this f-fine morning?'

'Half a pound of sausages, please.'

When Winnie had got to the counter, there was still a customer behind her, a woman she recognised as the curate's wife, and she had stepped aside, indicating the other woman should go first. 'I'm not sure what I want yet,' she'd said, but the truth was she was hoping to have a chat with Fred, and she couldn't do that when there were other customers waiting to be served. At least, not without making it obvious.

'Nice and f-fresh, these are,' Fred said, cutting four sausages off a string and putting them on the scales. 'Made 'em last night.'

'Lovely,' Winnie said. How was it, she wondered, that they'd got on so well the other evening, but now, in the shop, she felt flustered and tongue-tied, and Fred was stuttering a bit. As he wrapped the sausages, she opened her bag, got out the ration books and put them on the counter. But instead of picking them up, Fred disappeared into the back room and emerged with another package, which he put down beside them.

'What's this?' Winnie asked.

Over her shoulder, Fred's eyes went to the door, then he grinned sheepishly. 'I promised you a bit of steak, remember? It's not for frying, mind you, it's chuck, but it'll make a nice stew.'

'Oh, Fred, you shouldn't!' Winnie protested.

He checked the door again. 'If I remember rightly, you promised me a meal next t-time,' he said innocently. 'Nobody's going to report me for eating me own meat, are they?'

Winnie felt a blush creeping up her neck. 'No, I don't suppose they will,' she said. 'When d'you fancy having it then?'

'Soon as it's ready.'

'The day after tomorrow?'

'Fine.' His face changed. 'Put it in your bag now.'

Realising someone must be coming into the shop, Winnie got out her purse. 'So what do I owe you, Mr Thomas?'

Whew, that was a close one, she thought when she'd paid and left. Gert Bennett was one of the worst gossips in Hillsbridge, and she could just imagine what she would go round saying if she suspected anything. She had to laugh, though. She felt more like a youngster than a frowsty old widow. It was a very long time since she'd felt like that, and it was all thanks to Fred Thomas.

Anne was still waiting for the letter that would give her instructions for joining an SOE training school. She couldn't understand it, and she was becoming anxious. Colonel Ashman had given her to understand that it would be almost immediate. Had something gone against her and they'd changed their minds? Her heart sank at the thought, and she realised she was going to be very disappointed if that was the case. She'd thought this was her chance to prove what she was capable of, to her parents but also to herself. She wanted to feel proud. To make them proud.

So where was the letter? Lost in the post? That would be a disaster. But there could be any number of reasons for the delay, she told herself. A watched pot never boils. Just forget all about it and then it will come when you're not expecting it.

But it wasn't that easy. Any easier than it had been to turn her back on Julian Edgell.

Chapter Twenty-Two

As days and then weeks passed with no word from Clarke, Rosie resigned herself to never hearing from him or seeing him again. That he should dump her in such an abrupt way still stung, and she felt curiously empty. Once or twice she was tempted to relent and agree to meet Julian, but she told herself to forget both of them. Neither of them was worth fretting over. And it would be a long time before she trusted a man again.

She buried herself in her work, taking on extra shifts when cover was needed, and took a more advanced course in first aid and nursing so as to be better qualified to treat patients before conveying them to hospital. She met Freda once or twice when her farmer brought her into Hillsbridge, and was pleased that she seemed so happy. The life she was leading now had brought roses into her cheeks. But Rosie thought she was glowing on the inside too, and she remembered what Freda had said on the night of the dance – that there might be an eligible man right on her doorstep. Rosie had caught sight of him when he'd come to pick Freda up, and she'd thought he did look rather nice. But Freda hadn't mentioned any developments in that direction – perhaps she was being tactful – and Rosie hadn't asked. The last thing she wanted was to be reminded of her own double failure.

Even her mother was doing better than she was, she thought

wryly. But it pleased her that Winnie's friendship with Fred Thomas was progressing so well. He'd come for an evening meal twice more, providing liver and a piece of belly pork. And he'd taken Winnie out for a drive to the Chew Valley lakes one evening – he was able to get petrol because his van was used for his business, Rosie supposed. Winnie seemed happier than she'd been since losing Ern, and Rosie was glad for her. But she couldn't stop thinking about Clarke, wondering who he really was and what had happened to him. And whether she'd ever see him again.

One morning towards the end of April, as she arrived for her shift, the telephone was ringing. Since she was right by it, she answered. 'Hello. Ambulance Headquarters.'

And a voice with an unmistakable Irish lilt said, 'Rosie? Is that you?'

Clarke had arrived back from France under cover of darkness the previous night. The job had taken much longer than he'd thought – or hoped – it would. After a couple of failed attempts, he'd succeeded in blowing up the bridge he'd been sent to destroy, but it was far from being the only one the Germans would be able to use to get into France if they took Holland and Belgium. Using the same plan, he was able to destroy another – fifty yards of concrete and tarmac had come crashing down, making the bridge impassable – and he'd been preparing to move on to the next when a message had come through that he was needed back in England.

Before leaving, he'd taken a look at the remaining bridges, worked out what he thought would be the best way of rendering them useless to an invading army, and apprised a French general of his recommendations. But he wasn't entirely confident his advice would be followed. The general was as pompous and self-important as any he had met before, and expressed his opinion that his forces would be perfectly capable of ambushing a German advance now there were two fewer bridges to cover. Clarke didn't like it at all, but he'd done what he'd been sent to do and it was not his place to question a French general. That would be up to someone much higher up the chain of command.

The plane that had been sent to pick him up had landed in a field close to the Manor before taking off again, and Clarke had walked the last half-mile only to find the doors of the house locked. Hadn't they been told he was returning tonight? Fuming, he banged on the door until a light came on and he heard the bolts sliding back and the key being turned in the lock. He'd expected to be asked to identify himself, but he wasn't. The door was opened by Firkins, wearing a greatcoat over his pyjamas.

'Weren't you expecting me?' Clarke had asked brusquely.

'I forgot.' Firkins' tone was similarly short.

Like hell you did, Clarke thought. 'So why have I been called back?' he asked when the door was locked and bolted once more.

'Haven't you been told?' Firkins snorted.

'I wouldn't be asking if I had, would I?' Clarke retorted.

'Well, the CO will be here in the morning. He'll enlighten you.' Firkins turned away and ascended the stairs.

Whatever it was, it had rattled his cage, Clarke thought, and he was in no doubt now that Firkins had locked him out deliberately. But he was too tired to think about it tonight. He'd gone to the recreation room, poured himself a large whisky and taken it with him to bed.

The colonel had arrived next morning while Clarke, Dave, Colin and Dennis Holder were at breakfast. Firkins was absent, and Clarke had asked the others if they knew what was going on, but they were as much in the dark as he was. All they knew was that Firkins had been in a foul mood ever since the colonel had visited a couple of days earlier. And clearly his temper had not improved in the meantime.

'You're wanted, Sutherland. My office – now,' he barked, poking his head round the door and disappearing again.

A few moments later, Clarke knocked on the office door and went in to find the colonel sitting behind the desk, with Firkins standing beside him. He rose from his chair as Clarke entered the room, a portly figure with a neatly clipped moustache, and wire-rimmed glasses resting on a stubby nose.

'Good morning, Sutherland. You had a good journey home, I hope. Now, has Firkins filled you in regarding the changes we are making here?'

'No, sir,' Clarke replied.

'I was leaving that to you, sir.' Firkins was trying to excuse himself, but his disgruntled tone clearly wasn't making a good impression on the senior officer.

The colonel huffed slightly through pursed lips, then addressed Clarke. 'Well, the fact of the matter is that Major Firkins is relocating to a new posting. You are to take charge here with immediate effect.'

Clarke was startled by both these statements. So this was the reason he'd been called back from France. But why? Had Firkins done something to disgrace himself? Or was there some other reason entirely?

There was no way he could ask the questions, however, so he settled for a simple 'Very good, sir.'

The colonel turned to the man himself. 'I'm leaving it to you, Firkins, to ensure the handover of responsibility goes smoothly. Apprise Sutherland of what his duties will entail. Then you can take a few days R&R and report to your new posting on Wednesday next. Thank you for your service here, and now you may leave us.'

'Thank you, sir,' Firkins said stiffly. He clicked his heels, saluted and left the room.

'I expect you are wondering the reason for this,' the colonel said when the door had closed after him.

'Well, yes, sir, actually I am,' Clarke admitted.

'I'm afraid I'm not able to give you much in the way of explanation myself, but let's sit down and I'll tell you what I know,' the colonel said. He returned to the chair behind the desk, and Clarke pulled up a plastic upright that had stood in the corner of the office.

'Firkins is not best pleased, I gather,' the colonel began, 'but this is not my decision. It's come from on high. All I was told was that I was to have him relocated and you brought back from France to take over from him here. Apparently you will be contacted with further instructions as soon as I report back, so don't go too far from a telephone.' He pushed his glasses higher on his stubby nose. 'The only conclusion I can draw from the lack of clarity is that this is related to some top-secret operation. The running of this training centre, perhaps. I take it you have no idea what that might be?'

'None, sir.' Clarke would have liked to add that Firkins was universally disliked and no one would be sorry to see him go. But, of course, he didn't.

The colonel had left then, returning to his car and the very attractive young ATS chauffeur, whose looks had no doubt played as much of a part in her being given the job as her driving ability.

Although his brain was still buzzing with unanswered questions, Clarke decided his first priority was to try to get a message to Rosie before he needed to leave the line free for the call from the hierarchy that he'd been told to expect. He took the telephone from its cradle and dialled the number of the St Mark's ambulance station. And was surprised and delighted when the call was answered and he recognised the voice.

'Rosie? Is that you?' he asked.

'Clarke?' Rosie could scarcely believe her ears.

'Indeed it is. Sure, I thought you'd have forgotten all about me by now.'

'I thought *you'd* forgotten about *me*.' Rosie tried to keep her voice light. She didn't want to let Clarke know just how dejected she'd been since his disappearance.

'As if!' Clarke scoffed, then became serious. 'Look, I'm sorry I could only leave you a message before I left, but I had no choice. Orders are orders.'

'Where are you?' Rosie asked.

'Back at base now. And before you ask, I can't tell you any more than that.'

'But where have you been?'

'I can't tell you that either. Or when I'll be able to see you. But I'll be in touch. I'll phone again. Or you never know, I might just turn up at your door.'

'I wish you would!' Why had she said that?

'You're all right, though?'

'I'm fine.' She'd recovered herself a little.

'Good. Look, I can't stop to talk now, but I'll try not to disappear again, I promise.' And he was gone.

Rosie was trembling. Her head spinning. At least he'd called her. But had he meant what he said, or was he just stringing her along? What had he been doing that was so secret he couldn't tell her? Was it really something confidential connected to the war effort, or was there something he was hiding? Could she trust him? She just didn't know.

Best to simply forget him, she told herself. And tried to push her conflicting emotions to one side and concentrate on the day ahead of her.

The call Clarke had been expecting came just before midday, and it was no surprise that it was the commanding officer of his section of the Secret Intelligence Service – Section D – who was on the other end of the line.

From the outset it was clear that he was taking care not to be explicit; the line should be secure, but it wasn't unknown for telephonists to listen in on calls.

This had all happened, he said, as a result of a request made by 'a mutual friend'. 'I know you and he got on very well when you were in London, and he was most grateful for your help,' he went on. 'Now he is wondering if you could train one of his staff, and insistent that you are just the man for the job. There are so many charlatans about, and he knows you won't let him down.'

Clarke knew immediately to whom the CO was referring. 'Of course,' he said. 'It will be a pleasure.'

'So when would it be convenient to begin?' the CO asked.

'If I could have a week to sort things out at my end, everything will be ready.'

'Good. I'll let him know, and make the necessary arrangements.' The call was over.

Clarke replaced the receiver, got out his cigarettes and lit one, drawing on it deeply. From the little that had been said, no one eavesdropping would have had any idea what they had been talking about. And by the same token, there were things Clarke still didn't know, such as the name, or even the gender, of the person he was to train. But the CO's derogatory remark about charlatans at least explained why Firkins was being moved. His shortcomings had been noted in high places.

At least it hadn't been difficult to decipher the identity of the 'mutual friend'. That could only be the man he'd educated in the use of firearms and explosives when he'd still been based at St Ermin's Hotel in Westminster – Paul Clermont, heir to the Baroncy de Clermont in Charente. He guessed that Paul wanted him to take care of the training of a British special agent to join a resistance cell he was organising, something they'd discussed over their drinks and snacks in pubs and bars. Clarke had often wondered how Paul was getting on. Now he was wondering about the agent he had selected, and what cover he had arranged for them. Would he make contact with Clarke himself? He supposed he'd find out eventually. In the meantime, his thoughts returned to what he knew of the Frenchman.

Paul Clermont had seen the warning signs early in 1939: Germany was once again a threat to France. The estate to which he was heir was afforded some protection by forest and mountainous regions to the west, but he knew there were many weak points along the Belgian border where the Maginot Line had been left unfinished. If Holland and Belgium fell, the way would be clear for the invading troops. There was always the possibility, too, that they might come directly, through the Ardennes. The French would fight, of course, aided by their British allies. But if they were overwhelmed and forced to surrender, occupation would swiftly follow, and he and his fellow countrymen would be prisoners in their own land, at the mercy of their captors.

But it wasn't in Paul's nature to give in so easily. He'd called a number of his like-minded friends together, and in smoky back rooms and bars they'd made plans to form a group of resisters, with Paul as their leader.

He knew, though, that they couldn't do this alone. Willing they might be, but none of them had the expertise to blow up bridges and railway lines or carry out any of the other suggestions they'd proposed so enthusiastically. They needed specialist help.

After some thought, Paul contacted the British Foreign Office and was invited to London to discuss his plans, no doubt helped by the fact that he was part of the French aristocracy. There, in the strictest confidence, he learned that an organisation known as the Secret Intelligence Service had been set up immediately after Germany had invaded Austria to investigate, among other things, the use of sabotage and propaganda. He was given an address in central London, and it was there that the major general in charge had introduced him to Clarke Sutherland.

He'd spent two weeks training with Clarke. He'd also been given radio equipment and shown how to use it, and received some advice on the use of secret codes to communicate safely with other members of his team. But it was Clarke himself he was most impressed with, both his knowledge of and experience in his speciality, and his character and personality. If ever he needed someone to have his back, it would be Clarke. He counted him as a friend. He liked his easy manner, too, and the fact that he never boasted of his achievements, as many men would have done.

When the major general had offered to send a British agent to join him when the training programme was up and running, he'd accepted gratefully. Not only would it be advantageous to have someone on board who'd been taught all aspects of resistance, but it would also help with communications with their allies.

'As soon as everything is in place, we shall be starting short courses to assess the suitability of our volunteers,' the major general had said. 'Would you like to come back and observe? It may be you'll see just the right person to fit in with your group. Then, if they've passed the tests and completed the training programme satisfactorily, we could see about getting them to join you.'

'Thank you. I would,' Paul had replied. And thought that if he was lucky enough to find just the sort of agent he was hoping for, he could arrange for Clarke to take charge of their training.

Back in France, he'd given it serious thought. The most important thing was to provide the agent with a cover story that would stand up to the sort of interrogation that was likely to be commonplace if they were living under the heel of the jackboot. The chateau had a vast complement of servants, and the estate, which was famed for its excellent cognac, employed production workers as well as those who tended the vineyards. But many of them had been called up to serve in the French army now, and a man who fell into that age bracket would stand out like a sore thumb.

It was then that he had his eureka moment. Claudette, nanny to his two young daughters, had left to work in a munitions factory, and Elise, his wife, was struggling to care for them herself without the help she was used to. The major general had said they were recruiting women as well as men; perhaps there was one who could pass herself off as a nanny. He contacted London and outlined his idea, which was favourably received. But it would be some months before the vetting began and the courses were fully up and running.

As time passed and winter began to turn to spring, Paul had become more and more anxious. The phoney war wouldn't last for ever; sooner or later the Germans would turn their attentions back to France, and if his plan was to work, the new nanny would need to have been accepted into the household if suspicions were not to be aroused. And then, finally, the call had come. He'd packed a bag and headed across the Channel once more, and there, in a country house in the English countryside, he'd found the perfect fit.

'The girl – Françoise,' he'd said. 'She's plucky and accomplished, and she would fit in perfectly. She even speaks French in the dialect of our region. Just one thing. Can she be trained by Major Sutherland?'

He was disappointed to learn that not only was Clarke not the commanding officer of the training centre, but he was in France at present, working on the Maginot Line.

The assessment unit major had puffed on his pipe, deep in thought, and said he would speak to the D Section major general. From then on, things had moved fast. The major general had telephoned Paul, saying he was arranging for the girl he had chosen to do her training with Clarke in Somerset. He'd gone on to say that the CO there, Major Firkins, was not noted for his competence, and appeared to be universally disliked. He would pull some strings, have Firkins transferred, and get Clarke back from France.

Paul had thanked him profusely, and asked when Clarke would be back; he'd like to see him and explain exactly what it was he wanted. He had found himself a hotel room, enjoyed a trip to the theatre – amazingly, shows were still being staged as if nothing had happened – and a few drinks. Not cognac, though. Anything he chose would be vastly inferior to the famed de Clermont produce that he'd grown up with. Then he'd settled back and waited for the word.

At last! When the official-looking manilla envelope dropped through her letter box, Anne snatched it up eagerly, then hesitated, overwhelmed by nervousness.

Perhaps it wasn't the news she'd been waiting for. Perhaps it was a rejection, and she'd have to take up normal WAAF duties, whatever they might be.

Well, that wouldn't be so bad, she tried to tell herself. It might be a very interesting job. But in her heart of hearts she knew she'd be dreadfully disappointed. She really wanted to do something special, prove herself. And she loved France and the French people; wanted to be able to do something to help them if, as seemed inevitable, they were forced to live under the thumb of the Germans.

Steeling herself, she tore open the envelope, and was suffused with excitement as she read the contents of the letter. In a week's time she was to report to a training camp at a manor house situated on the Somerset Levels.

Yes! She punched the air triumphantly. She'd done it! Just as long as she could pass the tests that would follow her training, she would be accepted into the Special Intelligence Service.

Chapter Twenty-Three

Although Frances had set several more traps for Billy to fall into – money and small items of jewellery left where he would easily find them – as yet he hadn't been tempted. She still hadn't been able to find her brooch, and was still suspicious, but didn't want to mention it again to the boy without further proof of his dishonesty. Instead, determined to keep the spirits of local folk high, she spent the last week of April making arrangements for May Day to be celebrated as it always had been in the past. This year the town council, who normally took care of it, had too many other things on their minds, so Frances took charge. She arranged for the maypole to be erected in the field that adjoined the church primary school's hall, and prevailed on Fred Thomas to get at least some of the accordion band to play for the children to dance around it, and later to entertain those adults who might want to stay on into the evening. Winnie and some other WVS members, helped by Dimsie, who had recovered sufficiently to return to light duties, would provide lemonade for the little ones and tea for the adults, and Frances had enlisted Billy's help and that of a couple of his classmates to set out chairs around the perimeter of the field.

She was determined this would be an event that would provide a happy respite from the dark days they were living through.

* * *

The event had gone every bit as smoothly as Frances had hoped and Winnie was actually enjoying the festive atmosphere. The little girls in their party frocks with garlands of flowers in their hair had delighted the not inconsiderable crowd that had gathered – mothers, grandmothers, aunts and older cousins. When the last ribbon was entwined round the pole and the applause had died down, they'd run about the field, heady with excitement. And when the accordion band had struck up again, a pleasing number of adults had joined in the dancing. It was good to forget for a while that Denmark had surrendered and fierce battles were being fought in Norway and Iceland. And although as far as she knew Don was still in France, which could well be on the agenda for capture, Winnie was relieved that the phoney war hadn't yet ended.

What she didn't know was that within two weeks everything would change. Winston Churchill would succeed Neville Chamberlain as prime minister, and German soldiers would invade Holland, Belgium and France, while enemy bombers and fighter planes would provide them with cover in the skies. Soon the war would be on their very doorstep, grim reality would kick in, and any jollity would be a distant dream.

Clarke had taken the opportunity presented by a week when he would be free in the evenings. He'd phoned Ambulance HQ, checked Rosie's duty roster with the man who had answered his call and left a message with him that he would come out to see her at seven o'clock that evening.

As he drove to Hillsbridge, he had wondered just what sort of reception he would get. Rosie wouldn't have been best pleased with the brief message he'd left her, or his unexplained absence. She might well send him packing, and he couldn't blame her. So when he parked outside the cottage and knocked on the door, he was prepared for anything.

It opened. 'Oh, you came,' she said, unsmiling. 'I thought you might let me down again.'

'Rosie. I am so sorry. I only got back last night, and I called you the first chance I got, but I didn't know then when I'd be free. As soon as things were sorted out, I called again, but you were out on a shout, so I left a message . . .'

'And expected me to be waiting, at your beck and call.'

'Not at all. I've driven out on the off-chance that you got my message, half expecting you to tell me to take a running jump.'

He saw her face soften slightly, but she hadn't been ready to let him off the hook so easily.

'I've thought about it, I can tell you. You're too ready to claim you can't give me any answers because of the Official Secrets Act. You know I've signed it too, so I don't understand what the problem is.'

Clarke took a moment, thinking. It was common knowledge that work was going on to strengthen the Maginot Line – how could it be otherwise?

'If I tell you where I've been, will that satisfy you?' he asked.

'I suppose it would be a start,' she had said grudgingly.

'OK.' He looked around to ensure there was no one within earshot. 'I was sent to France to blow up some bridges on the Belgian border.'

Rosie groaned. 'Oh, Clarke, that's hardly a secret! My brother is there with his regiment. Why couldn't you just have told me?'

He smiled faintly. 'I suppose I take these things too far. Am I forgiven?'

She was wavering, he could see. 'As long as you promise there'll be no more secrets,' she said.

Clarke's stomach had clenched. There were some things he

absolutely couldn't tell her. Where he was based, and what his role was there. She might have signed the Official Secrets Act, but she wasn't a member of the SIS. But to refuse would almost certainly mean losing her.

He crossed his fingers in his pocket. 'No more secrets. You can trust me, Rosie.'

'I hope so,' she said.

'And will you come out with me now, or have I had a wasted journey?'

She'd sighed. 'There's an event tonight in town. A maypole, and dancing. Mum's there, helping with the refreshments.'

'And you'd like to go to that?' He'd grinned wickedly. 'I thought you might fancy fish and chips again.'

'We have a very good fish and chip shop right here in Hillsbridge.'

'Not as good as the one in Bath, I'm willing to bet.'

'Every bit as good.' She'd smiled, the first proper smile of the evening, and it had lifted his heart. 'I'll just get my bag.'

They'd made it just in time to see the girls dancing around the maypole, and Clarke spotted Sir James and Lady Hastings watching from the other side of the field. But of their daughter and her fiancé there was no sign, and he thanked his lucky stars for that.

They danced, and it felt so good to have her in his arms again. As dusk fell, Rosie shivered.

'I should have brought a cardigan. It's been such a nice day I never thought, but once the sun's gone . . .'

'So why don't we get that fish and chips and we can eat in the car.'

'It'll leave an awful smell,' Rosie cautioned. 'I've got a better idea. Mum won't be home for ages – as long as the band's play-ing, people will want to stay on, and she'll have to help with the clearing-up afterwards. So why don't we take it home and eat in comfort?'

'Sounds like a good plan to me,' Clarke said.

There was quite a queue at the fish and chip shop, but eventually they made it back to the cottage with their newspaper-wrapped bundles and sat down to eat.

'I have to admit, this is pretty good,' Clarke said, breaking off a chunk of crispy batter. 'But I'd have to taste the ones from Bath again before I could pick a winner.'

Rosie, her mouth full of chips, just laughed.

'What about it then?' he suggested, hoping to make the most of the evenings this week when he would be relatively free. 'How does Friday sound to you?'

Rosie had finished her mouthful of chips. 'Sorry, I can't. This is the last of my day shifts.' But she didn't suggest another day, and even though he probably wouldn't have been able to make it, Clarke wondered if she was making excuses.

When they'd finished eating and cleared up, he checked his watch. 'I think I should be going.'

'OK.' She went with him to the door, and he risked putting his arms around her and pulling her towards him, half expecting her to pull away. But she didn't. He kissed her, and after a moment she responded with a hunger that both thrilled and warmed him. But this was no time – and certainly no place – to take things further when her mother might well open the front door at any moment. He cooled the temperature of the kiss and held her slightly away from him, aware of the desire in her eyes.

'Next week, then?' he suggested, making up his mind that by hook or by crook he would make sure he was free.

'I'm not sure,' she said. But she lifted her face to his for one last kiss.

'So I'll call you.' He was feeling elated now.

Oh, Miss Rosie Mitchell, there's a fire in you somewhere, he thought as he walked to his car.

It wasn't until he was halfway back to the Manor that he remembered the promise he'd made her. No more secrets. That was a tough one. But he'd cross that bridge when he came to it. He couldn't, wouldn't risk losing her again.

Rosie watched Clarke turn and drive away, her emotions swinging from elation to doubt and back again.

Yes, she fancied him – more than a little. The little tics of excitement in her stomach and her racing pulse were testament to that. There was something about him that called to her in a way she'd never experienced before, not even with Julian. Yes, she'd wanted Julian, loved him – still did. But that was an obsession that ruled her heart; this was physical, and she couldn't understand why it should be so. She liked Clarke too. Liked his strength and masculinity, his easy manner and the way he could make her laugh. Liked his Irish brogue and those very blue eyes in a face that while attractive was not classically beautiful as Julian's was. But she still wasn't sure she could trust him. Couldn't understand why he was so reluctant to share anything about himself and his circumstances. She was still none the wiser about where he was based and what he was doing there.

She sighed, tried to put her doubts to one side, and went back into the cottage.

The young lady who had come into Julian's surgery was not one he recognised as a patient. In fact he couldn't remember ever having seen her before – and he was pretty sure that if he had, he wouldn't have forgotten. She was slim but curvy in all the right places, with chestnut hair swept into a victory roll and falling in waves and curls to her shoulders, revealing a heart-shaped face, startlingly green eyes and full lips painted scarlet.

'So what can I do for you, Miss . . .?' He indicated a chair to the left of his desk and swivelled round to face her.

'I'd rather not give my name.' She lowered her eyes, and long dark lashes brushed her cheeks. 'My husband doesn't know I'm here, but it's him I've come about. A delicate matter.'

'Which would be?'

She hesitated, and crossed her legs, shapely and encased in sheer silk stockings. As her skirt tightened across her thighs, Julian couldn't help but notice the little round bumps of her suspender buttons and rather thought he was meant to.

'Would I be right in supposing there are certain problems in the bedroom?' he asked.

She nodded. 'I'm so sorry – this is very embarrassing . . .'

'Not at all.' He gave her the benefit of his most understanding smile. 'You would like something to improve matters, I expect.'

'Oh, that would be such a relief . . .' Again her voice tailed away. She smoothed her skirt down over her knee with her left hand, and Julian saw a sapphire, almost too large to be the genuine thing, on her third finger. Was it obscuring her wedding ring? Or wasn't she wearing one?

'No problem,' he said. He pulled his prescription pad towards him, took up his Parker pen and wrote 'AOT' in clear capitals, followed by the indecipherable scrawl doctors were famous for. 'The pharmacy next door will dispense this for you. They are very discreet, and you can depend on their policy of confidentiality should they recognise you. If you squeeze two or three drops of the liquid into a drink of your husband's twice a day – hot or cold, it doesn't matter – you should notice a marked improvement in a week or so. If not, come back and we'll try something else.' He drew another pad towards him and scribbled on it. 'Since I am unable to bill you by post, I'd be grateful if you would see my receptionist on your way out and pay her the five shillings.'

As the surgery door closed after her, Julian tapped his pen against the desktop, a satisfied smile spreading across his face. At last a very suitable and very attractive young woman had entered his orbit. He suspected the problem she had outlined had been a trumped-up one. But if that was the case, he was surprised she'd mentioned a husband. Perhaps it had given her the chance to be charmingly coy. Or maybe, given that he'd been unable to see a wedding ring on her finger, he didn't exist at all.

But either way he was confident she would be back. If she'd come on purpose to make his acquaintance, she wouldn't waste the opportunity to see him again. And if there really was a husband with certain embarrassing problems, she would take Julian up on his promise to try another solution. The drops he'd given her wouldn't work at all. The letters he'd written at the top of the prescription would take care of that. The pharmacist would know all too well what they meant.

AOT. It stood for Any Old Thing.

The new intake of trainees were due to arrive at the Manor all on the same day, though on different trains that would get into Bath Spa at various times. Clarke had contacted a taxi firm and booked a large enough vehicle for all six for when the last of them was due to arrive, and suggested the others get a hot drink and something to eat in the station café while they waited.

The arrangement went off without a hitch, and just before two in the afternoon the minibus pulled up outside the Manor. Clarke went out to meet them – three men and three young women. As he welcomed them, taking a special interest in Françoise, the girl Paul had asked him to take under his wing, he had the feeling he'd seen her before. Then he remembered. When he and Paul had met up, his friend had told him Françoise came from the aristocracy, and with a sense of shock Clarke realised she was none other than Anne Hastings. Why on earth would she be training to go into France as a special agent when she should be preparing for her wedding to Julian Edgell? He must be mistaken, surely!

When they'd freshened up and unpacked their bags the new trainees assembled again for afternoon tea and their first briefing. Everything about Françoise tallied with his memory of Anne Hastings. Fashionable clothes, blonde hair cut in a sharp style that had echoes of the flappers of the roaring twenties rather than following the current fashion for bangs, waves and curls. But he was still puzzled as to why she was here, and he ran through the briefing on autopilot. This could make things very difficult for him where Rosie was concerned; he'd promised her no more secrets. If she found out that he had known that the girl who was going to marry the man she was clearly in love with had been dropped into occupied France, he had no idea how she would take it.

Well, there was nothing he could do about it now. He'd just have to find a way to deal with that problem if and when it arose. For the moment he had to oversee the training of six volunteer agents whose lives might lie in his hands, and in the case of Françoise see that it was completed as soon as possible. He must put everything else to the back of his mind and commit himself fully to his duty.

Winnie went into the kitchen, where a disgruntled Maud was rolling out pastry for vegetable pasties. Sir James had been insistent that she should make meals using only their own produce wherever possible.

'I don't know what it's coming to,' she grumbled. 'Cornish pasties with no meat. We'm all goin' to fade away before this is over. Let's just hope Churchill can do summat about it now he's in charge.'

The news had broken the previous day that Neville Chamberlain had been forced to resign and Winston Churchill had become prime minister.

'Just fancy,' she went on, 'they're callin' him Winnie. Same as you.'

Winnie said nothing. The change of government leadership had almost passed her by. There were other items in the news that she found much more worrying. German paratroopers had invaded France, Belgium, Luxembourg and Holland and there was fierce fighting. The phoney war, it seemed, had come to an end. Belatedly the Belgians had begun blowing up bridges, but from the grave tone of reports both on the wireless and in the newspapers, it was unlikely to stop the German advance. And Don was right there on the border.

'What's up with you?' Maud demanded, flicking more flour onto her pastry board, and Winnie snapped.

'Don't you listen to the news unless it's something that concerns you?' she flared. 'The Germans are all over the place. Seems there's no stopping them. And my son is right there in the firing line.'

Maud looked abashed, but only for a moment. 'It'll be all right now Churchill's in charge,' she said. 'You'll see. He'll get it sorted out. And then we can all enjoy a proper Cornish pasty again.'

In the days that followed, bad news came thick and fast. The only thing to raise hopes briefly was that the Dutch had defeated German paratroopers in a battle for the Hague, but they were quickly dashed. Luxembourg became the first country to fall, and Holland, which had set up a government-in-exile in London, quickly followed. There was fierce fighting in Belgium, and when Churchill visited Paris to meet with the French premier, he was told that as far as France was concerned, the war was as good as over.

Paul Clermont must have been of the same opinion, as Clarke received an anxious phone call from him asking if Françoise was ready to be sent to join him. It was imperative that she should be in place in his household before the area came under German control.

Clarke realised he must move things on as fast as possible, though it would leave no time for him to see Rosie until Françoise's training was completed satisfactorily. He had arranged for the parachute instructor, Roy Taylor, to come during their first week, and Françoise had successfully mastered the technique for landing safely, though one of the other girls had been blown off course and sprained an ankle badly, which would put her out of action for the time being. He also made some adjustments to the syllabus so that the basics she would need were covered first. They could track back to the finer points later if there was time. Luckily she was a fast learner and spent any free time either practising map-reading or Morse code and the use of a transmitter, or with her nose in an instruction manual. But he couldn't agree to sending her until he was completely satisfied she was ready.

He'd got to know her better when he'd helped Dave Thompson out with the unarmed combat classes and discovered she wasn't at all what he had expected. Upper class she might be, but there was no side whatever to her and he wondered what on earth she was thinking to become engaged to such a despicable man as the doctor. He'd also taken over her firearms training from Dennis Holder. Shooting straight seemed to be the one thing that didn't come easily to her, and Holder hadn't helped, ridiculing her and telling her she was hopeless instead of encouraging her. Under Clarke's tuition, her aim with small arms had improved steadily, and he hoped that if she could only master the technique of steadying the rifle while lying flat on her stomach, she'd reach the level needed to pass the final test.

As her two weeks' training neared its end, the news from the Benelux countries was very bad indeed. The Allies were being driven back towards the Channel, and Churchill had instructed the Admiralty to make plans for a mass evacuation. Since most of the action in France now was in the north and east, Clarke thought it would be relatively safe to drop her in Charente, where she would be met by Paul and members of his group. He made the necessary arrangements, and then called Françoise to his office, where he explained what was planned for her, and that she had been specially chosen because she was familiar with the area where she was to operate. During the first week, a female officer had come to measure her up for clothes with French labels sewn into them, and Clarke told her the same woman would be coming back and bringing them with her, and that she would also go over every detail of Françoise's cover story with her. Additionally, he had booked her an appointment with a dentist, who would replace any fillings in her teeth with the gold ones the French used, and she joked she was more afraid of that than parachuting into an enemy-controlled country. That, he told her, was to be under cover of darkness on Saturday 25 May.

What he didn't tell her was that the Allies were now completely surrounded, with nowhere to go but the beaches surrounding Dunkirk. He didn't want to exacerbate the fear and apprehension she would almost certainly be experiencing now that her moment had come. She'd learn of it soon enough when she was settled into the hub of Paul's resistance unit, the Château de Clermont.

While the trainee agents at the Manor were purposely cut off from access to both newspapers and the BBC broadcasts until they were ready to be sent to France, there was no escape for those in the outside world. The horrifying headlines shrieked at them from their morning papers, and the news reports on the wireless, doom-laden though they were, made for compulsive listening. Like everyone else in the country, the residents of Hillsbridge could talk of little else.

Winnie was one exception. She carried her terrible fear and dread for her son like an invisible shield, hugging it to herself as if by refusing to discuss the danger he was in she could somehow stave off the reality of it. And Frances was another. She was desperately worried for Philip, as she guessed that fighter planes would be sent to do what they could to protect the British and French troops, who were surrounded and helpless. But she chose to bury herself in her work with the WVS, planning new ways of raising money to reach the target to buy a Spitfire, and encouraging Billy to take advantage of the opportunity to make something of himself and leave the slums of London behind him for ever.

Freda was worried about the threat of the war coming closer to their shores for quite a different reason. Her house in London wasn't far from the docks, and if the expected air raids began, it was quite possible that it would be hit. The thought of her beloved grandmother's home reduced to rubble was a horrible one, not to mention all her precious belongings that she'd been forced to leave behind.

She confided her fears to Ted and his mother after they'd listened to the latest depressing news on the wireless, and was touched when Mrs Holland patted her hand and said, 'Don't worry, love. You'll always have a home here with us.' She'd thanked her, but although she loved it here in the country and hoped she could continue with farm work when the war was over, nothing would quite be able to make up for losing her roots and her precious memories.

As for Rosie, she could only chastise herself for being so harsh on Clarke. She'd heard nothing from him since May Day and did her best to pretend to herself that she didn't care. Yet one night she dreamed she was dancing with him, his arms around her, her face pressed into his shoulder. When she woke, there was a sort of magic aura surrounding the memory of the dream that stayed with her all day. Did it mean he was going to call her? she wondered, and when he didn't, she cursed herself for being such an idiot. It was just that he was the only man – apart from Julian – she'd ever really enjoyed kissing, that was all. It meant nothing.

Julian was no longer paying her any attention either, and she suspected he had a new love interest. But that didn't bother her. She'd made up her mind she was finished with men for good. She couldn't trust any of them. Especially Julian Edgell.

Chapter Twenty-Four

As she turned the pages of the *Daily Mirror* and was confronted with yet more pictures of the horror that was unfolding on the beaches of northern France, Winnie's hands shook and the black cloud of desperation that hung over her tightened its iron grip. The port of Dunkirk in ruins, destroyed by heavy bombing. The clouds of thick smoke rising from a ship that had been hit. Columns of uniformed men making their way through the dunes or hiding from the strafing and bombing as they were besieged by enemy forces. Some jostling four abreast on the wooden boardwalk of the breakwater to reach a rescue ship, where they used ladders and planks to get on board. Others were attempting to climb the substructure, and still more were wading through the surf to reach a boat. Their faces were hidden by their tin hats. However she strained her eyes, there was no way she could discern if Don was among them. Was he one of the lucky ones already on their way home across the Channel? Was he still among those trapped in this hell? Or had he been shot by a German soldier or killed by a German bomb?

Winnie had not been blessed – or cursed – with a vivid imagination, but here in the newspapers it was all laid out before her eyes, and when she closed them, she could see it still, hear the explosions and the cries and curses, feel the fear and sheer panic. Nothing helped, nothing could, until she had news of her son. She wasn't sleeping. She couldn't eat. She was sustained only by endless cups of tea and Fred Thomas's support. He'd been in the trenches in the last war. He understood. And she thanked the Lord for his friendship. Her usual optimism was drowning in a sea of mud, and she didn't know how she could have survived without him.

'What will be will be,' he'd said, reminding her so much of Ern that the tears had started to her eyes. His pragmatism was somehow far more comforting than those like Maud who tried to tell her everything would turn out well and she'd soon have Don home. They were talking rubbish; at least Fred wasn't trying to pull the wool over her eyes, treat her like a child. There was nothing for it but to wait – and pray. Winnie was on her knees more often than she had been in years. Begging, pleading, bargaining. Take me, Lord, but save him. I've had my life. He deserves his.

It was a plea only another mother would understand. But heartfelt. Truly meant. If only she knew Don was safe, she would die happy.

Anne's training had been intensive, much of it on a one-to-one basis while the other girls had been taught mainly as a group. One day, after a shooting session that had been, as far as Anne was concerned, an unmitigated disaster, she'd asked Clarke the reason.

'Is it because I'm especially stupid that I'm having most of my lessons alone?'

'Not at all,' Clarke had replied.

'Then why?'

'Let's sit down. I think it's time I put you in the picture. A French resistance leader in Charente asked for an agent to be sent to him to facilitate the working of his group. He came to England to sit in on preliminary training courses, and yours was one. He decided you would fit the bill perfectly. You speak French with the local accent – he conducted the language test with you – and he was most impressed with you in every respect.'

'Oh!' Anne was flabbergasted. The Frenchman all the girls had been swooning over!

'His request for you to be chosen was acceded to at the highest level, and also for me to oversee your training. The urgency is because Paul – Monsieur Clermont – is anxious for you to join him as soon as possible. Your cover is that you will pose as nanny to his two young children, and he wants you to be accepted by the local community before the Germans reach the south. That's the reason I've prioritised your training, and I must say you're very quick to learn. Apart from your accuracy with a gun,' he added with a wry smile. 'But don't worry, I have no doubt we'll have our very own Annie Oakley by the time I've finished with you.'

Anne was speechless, trying to take in everything he'd told her.

'So how do you feel about all this?' he asked. 'You haven't changed your mind about going to France, I hope?'

It was a moment before she could find her voice, and Clarke waited, looking anxious. Then she gathered her wits.

'Of course not,' she said emphatically. 'It's what I volunteered for. And I'm flattered that Monsieur . . . ' She hesitated. 'Clermont . . . Clermont thinks I'll be taken for a local. I only hope I'll live up to his expectations, and you may be sure I'll do my very best to make sure that I do. But how do I get there?'

'Don't worry, all the arrangements will be made for you. You'll be flown in, and that's when you'll get the opportunity to show off your parachuting skills. You did very well at those lessons, I understand. Now, perhaps we'd better get on with our target practice.'

'I think we should,' Anne said faintly, and she picked up the rifle from where it lay beside her, resolute in her determination that it wasn't going to beat her.

Within a few days she'd made amazingly good progress, and Clarke notified Paul that she was ready to join him. Everything happened very fast then, and before she knew it, the flight had been arranged and she was packed and ready to go. The other girls had been incredulous – and a little jealous – but they knew better than to ask questions, and on the night she was being picked up, they all went with her to the field where a transport plane waited, and wished her good luck when it was time for her to board.

A feeling of unreality surrounded her now and apprehension was making her stomach churn. But she was determined not to let it show, and tried to live in the moment. First the flight. Bumping over the rough ground as the aircraft gathered speed, then rising gradually until it levelled off. Half sitting, half lying against the fuselage, opposite several wooden crates with parachutes attached that prevented her from seeing anything else. When the RAF sergeant on board brought her a welcome Thermos of tea, she asked what they were doing there and he explained they were supplies Paul Clermont had asked for. When they reached their destination, they'd drop off the supplies first, then go around and it would be her turn.

Her stomach clenched at the thought, but when the moment came, she found herself unexpectedly calm. As she squatted beside the gaping hole, she saw the flicker of tiny lights far below – the welcoming party were here. She'd known they must be when the two RAF sergeants had dropped the crates. Now she watched for the small light above the hatch to turn from red to green. When it did, the sergeant wished her luck and heaved her clear.

At first her senses were numbed by the buffeting of the cold night air, which took her breath and brought tears to her eyes. Then her parachute opened and she was floating like a piece of flotsam in a whirlpool, with the ground rushing up to meet her. As her feet touched, she flexed her knees and rolled as she had been taught, but the wind still filling the billowing silk dragged her over the rough ground like a rag doll.

For a moment she lay stunned, then she saw a pinprick of light bobbing towards her and wondered if she was seeing stars before realising it was the beam of a torch.

'*On se revoit.*' *We meet again.* Anne shaded her eyes and looked up to see the man who had attended her tests at the training centre. 'Paul Clermont,' he said. '*Et tu es Françoise.*'

'*Oui.*' She was too breathless to say more.

He helped her up, unstrapped her parachute. 'Let's get you to the chateau,' he said, still speaking French, as she guessed they would from now on.

He led her across the large open space towards a copse where three or four men were gathered around the dropped crates that had been hidden among the trees. Paul spoke to them briefly, then took her to where a small car was parked out of sight of the road beyond.

'I use my wife's little runaround for this sort of thing,' he explained. 'It's less conspicuous. The only people who are aware I'm organising a resistance cell are the ones I can trust. When the Germans arrive – as they will before long – we'll know who's with us and who are the collaborators.'

Also concealed beneath the trees was a large van. 'I'm lucky enough to have a baker friend,' he added. 'He'll transport the supplies your plane dropped tonight, and I shall hide them in the wine cellars among our best cognac.'

'What . . .?' Anne stopped herself, her head so full of questions she didn't know which to ask first.

Paul started the small car and pulled away. 'I'll fill you in on all you need to know in the morning. For now, I think you need a drink and a comfortable bed.'

Clarke had made up his mind that as soon as he knew Françoise had arrived at her destination safely, he would contact Rosie. The urgency of Françoise's training and his additional responsibilities now that he was in charge at the Manor had left him no free time for personal matters. These were desperate days, and his duty to his country and the war effort had to take precedence. But given Rosie's reaction to his largely unexplained absence when he had been in France, he was concerned that he might well have lost all credibility in her eyes. Worse, it was all too likely that there would be other times in the future when he would have to disappear without explanation, perhaps for weeks on end. He'd thought seriously about the 'no more secrets' promise she'd extracted from him, and knew that if he broke it, that would be the final straw. He decided that when – if – he was able to meet her again, he would tell her at least something of where he was and what he was doing. As long as everything about him was a mystery to her, there was the danger that she would draw the wrong conclusions one way or another.

He was worried for her too. Things were looking very bad indeed in northern France, and he knew her brother was there with his regiment. A hospital ship was already on its way, but the waters along that coast would be too shallow for it to get close to the beaches, and the government were arranging for a fleet of small boats to evacuate as many men as possible, with cover from fighter jets. He hoped and prayed Rosie's brother would be among them, but with the colossal numbers involved and the likelihood that they would come under attack from the Luftwaffe, many would not make it home safely.

He should have had a free week or two before a new batch of volunteers arrived, but when the present trainees were tested, one of the two remaining girls had fallen down badly on her small-arms firing. He'd put it down to nerves, but that concerned him too. He decided he would give her one last chance – plenty of instruction and practice, and he'd look after her himself; he didn't want Holder destroying what was left of her confidence. But he also arranged for the psychiatrist to examine her again – he couldn't afford to pass her if there was a chance she would crack under pressure in the field. It would do no harm for her to have a day off to rest and relax, or perhaps have some extra sessions with Colin Stewart practising her communication skills – that was something at which she excelled.

Once he'd made the arrangements with Colin, he telephoned the ambulance HQ. They were getting used to him calling now, and even ragged him about it. 'Yer lady love? She's out on the road with her pal.'

'So she'll be free this evening?'

'She won't be working. More than that I can't vouch for.' But the man said it jovially and Clarke didn't think he was implying she had turned her attentions elsewhere.

'Can you tell her I'll see her at about half past seven?'

'Wilco.'

'Thanks.' The arrangement made, Clarke returned to the mound of paperwork that seemed to grow every day like bread dough as the yeast did its job. He was beginning to see why Firkins had always been in a black mood.

* * *

Frances had been summoned to the secondary school by a very irate headmaster. When she pulled up in the road outside the main entrance, the school secretary was waiting for her in the lobby.

'What is this all about?' Frances demanded, though she could hazard a guess. She was on the board of governors, but she didn't think this had anything to do with extra funding.

'Captain Perkins will explain.' The secretary looked most uncomfortable, and she hastily escorted Frances along the narrow corridor to the head's office.

The headmaster rose as she entered the room. He was a tall, spare man who still retained a military bearing along with his liking to be known by what had once been his rank.

'Lady Hastings,' he greeted her. 'Please accept my apology if I was rather short on the telephone, but my patience has been sorely tried for a number of weeks now.'

'I presume you are talking about my evacuee boy,' Frances said, taking the chair on the opposite side of the worn wooden desk.

'I'm afraid so. I assure you, Lady Hastings, I have made every allowance possible for the boy's behaviour given his circumstances, but the time has come when I really must speak to you about his behaviour. He is a most disruptive influence in class, has no regard for rules and no respect for his teachers. He is also of a violent disposition. Once again this morning he has been fighting – a scrap that I am assured by witnesses was started by him, and which could well have resulted in the boy he picked on being seriously injured. Were you aware he was in possession of a flick knife?'

'Good gracious, no!' Frances was shocked.

The headmaster slid open one of the desk drawers, produced the offending weapon and laid it on his blotter.

'The evidence,' he said gravely. 'If Mr Jenkins hadn't been in the playground at the time and intervened, I dread to think what might have happened. I cannot risk having a boy with such tendencies in my school, Lady Hastings. Has he ever shown any sign of it while he has been with you?'

'No. Never,' Frances said. 'Yes, he can be difficult, but he's never given me cause to think he might progress to something like this. In fact, I thought I was making headway with him. He comes from a very unsatisfactory background, I'm afraid, and although I've been strict, I actually feel sorry for him. He's had a hard life, with no discipline and no role model.'

'Very likely. But still . . .' Captain Perkins shook his head.

'Could you not give him another chance?' Frances asked. 'If you wish, I will take him home with me now and give him to understand that if his behaviour doesn't improve, he'll lose the opportunity to better himself in life. And naturally I will confiscate this knife and take full responsibility for him.'

Captain Perkins sighed and was silent, thinking things over. Eventually he nodded.

'Very well, Lady Hastings. But if there is no improvement, and certainly if there is any repeat of today's occurrence, I shall have no option but to expel him.'

'I quite understand,' Frances said stiffly.

Captain Perkins rose, went to the door and called to the secretary to fetch Billy Crossley from the staff room, where he had been left under the watchful eye of the sports master. He came into the office wearing a rebellious expression, but when he saw Frances there, his eyes dropped to the floor. He might have no respect for his teachers, but Lady Hastings was a different kettle of fish entirely.

He listened to her, sullen but silent, as she told him how disappointed she was in him, and to a lengthy lecture from the headmaster, which concluded with him being suspended for the rest of the week.

And he would certainly be hearing a great deal more from her once she got him back to Bramley Court.

The Westminster mantel clock was just chiming the half-hour as from the window Rosie saw Clarke pull up outside the cottage and walk down the path. Right on time, she thought. At least he couldn't be accused of lack of punctuality. As for anything else, she wasn't sure. But she couldn't escape the feeling of relief that had washed over her when she'd been given the message that he would see her this evening. Not just because she was glad he hadn't disappeared again, but because she would be able to get out of the house for a few hours.

The atmosphere here had been growing more and more claustrophobic ever since the operation to rescue the British Expeditionary Force from the beaches of Dunkirk had started. Rosie was dreadfully worried too, of course, for her brother's safety, but it was exacerbated by the heavy dark cloud that constantly enveloped her mother, and she worried that Winnie was going to make herself ill. The anxiety was etching itself into her face, grooves and hollows that hadn't been there before. Her eyes were haunted, she wasn't eating properly, and Rosie doubted she was sleeping either. Yet still she was restless, forever scrubbing and sweeping, polishing the brasses, anything to keep herself occupied. But when she sat down with her knitting, her hands shook so much that she dropped stitches, and the ball of wool kept rolling off her lap and onto the floor.

Luckily Fred Thomas had come for his tea today, and he'd stay with Winnie until Rosie got home, so she wouldn't be alone. It was only when she was with him that she seemed to be able to relax a little. Thank goodness for Fred! They were in the kitchen now, so Rosie called out to them that Clarke was here and went to open the door.

'Well, hello, stranger,' she greeted him, making an effort to sound cheerful. 'You've decided to treat me to the best fish and chips in Bath, have you?'

'I'm glad I can get some things right,' Clarke said ruefully. 'It's a nice evening, though, and I thought maybe we could find a country pub where we can sit outside and make the most of it.'

A pulse jumped in Rosie's throat. Country pubs were a reminder of her outings with Julian. But she swallowed and forced a smile. 'That sounds good to me.'

'You're ready, then?'

'Yes.' She was wearing a cotton cardigan over a full-skirted floral dress and peep-toe shoes. 'It's nice not to have to bother with a coat. Just let me say cheerio to Mum and Fred.'

She went along to the kitchen and popped her head round the door. 'I'm off, then. I won't be late back.'

'All right, love. Just come home safe.'

'Your mum's friend is here quite a bit then?' Clarke asked when Rosie had closed the front door after them.

'A lot more often than you.'

'Ouch!' He pulled a wry face. 'Look, Rosie, one of the reasons I suggested a table outside a country pub is that I want to talk to you. I think I owe you some explanations.'

Her eyebrows shot up. 'Really? I thought your lips were sealed.'

He cast her a sidelong look, and there was a wicked twinkle in those very blue eyes. 'Not always.'

Rosie felt herself blushing at the double entendre, but managed a pert 'I should hope not!' before continuing:

'You know pretty well everything about me and I think it's time to redress the balance.'

Clarke executed a three-point turn behind Fred's van. 'There's a pub that I pass on my way here that looks quite nice. Just outside your twin town's boundary – what's it called?'

'High Compton. But I don't know which way you come into Hillsbridge,' Rosie said pointedly.

'Well, I come down the steep hill . . .'

'All the hills into Hillsbridge are steep.'

'OK. From the direction of Shepton Mallet.'

'Just the other side of High Compton, then.'

'A white building, set back from the road?'

'Yes.'

'The Cross Hands,' Rosie said, relieved. Julian had never taken her there. But she'd gone there a few times with a friend who was in their ladies' skittles team, when she'd sat in the alley drinking gin and orange and watching the balls skim down the lane and topple the skittles.

She knew too that there was a beer garden at the rear, and she pointed to the door leading to it when she and Clarke went into the lounge bar.

'Shall I go on out and reserve a table?' she asked when he had ordered and the barman was getting their drinks. He nodded, and she went out onto the lawn and chose a table in the far corner. She guessed that if Clarke really was going to give her some answers to her questions, he wouldn't want to sit anywhere they were likely to be in close proximity to other customers.

'Good choice,' he said when he joined her bearing Rosie's favourite gin and orange and a pint of beer for himself, and she wondered if it might have come from the Edgells' brewery. Their beer was sold in all the local pubs and clubs, she knew.

For a few minutes they sat quietly, enjoying the scent from the nearby rose bushes and the song of the birds in the trees behind them. Swifts were darting in and out of the eaves of the pub; Rosie pointed them out to Clarke. 'You always know summer's just around the corner when the swifts come back.'

'I'd like to think they'd bring peace with them, but somehow I don't think that's going to happen,' he said.

'No.' Rosie didn't want to think about the war. For the moment she just wanted to enjoy the tranquillity and try to forget it was happening. But there was little chance of that.

'Is there any news of your brother?' Clarke asked.

She shook her head. 'Nothing yet. Mum and I just keep praying, but . . .' She shrugged despairingly. 'The waiting is just awful. The not knowing. Mum is taking it very hard. I'm really worried about her. I don't know what will become of her if we don't hear something soon.'

'I'm sorry,' Clarke said, but he didn't offer any platitudes and she was glad of that. She was tired of being told that everything would turn out right. There would be thousands of grieving families before this was over.

He lit a cigarette, blew the smoke into the sweet air of early evening and took a long pull of his drink. 'So. You want to know who I am, where I'm living and what I'm doing here.'

'I thought you said you couldn't tell me,' Rosie said. 'All top secret, you said.'

'Which is the truth. I shouldn't be telling you anything at all, but I'm trusting you, Rosie. It's vital that you keep anything I say to yourself. You mustn't tell anyone. Not your mother – not anyone. Every precaution has been taken to ensure not a word of this gets out. You do understand that, don't you?'

She nodded, the seriousness of his tone almost making her believe him before he had spoken a single word of explanation. 'As I told you before, I've signed the Official Secrets Act,' she said. 'Not that what I'm doing is secret. But it's binding on me all the same. You can trust me, I promise.'

'OK.' Though there was no one within earshot, he moved his metal-framed garden chair closer to hers, rested his elbows on the table and looked directly at her. 'As you know, I'm an army officer, but I specialise in explosives and firearms. And I'm in Somerset for a very particular purpose.'

'You're not going to blow bridges up here, surely!' Rosie exclaimed before she could stop herself, imagining that perhaps he was preparing to destroy river crossings to slow a German advance as he had done in France.

Clarke smiled slightly. 'Not here, no. It's more complicated than that.'

'Then what . . .?'

He stubbed his cigarette out in a large red ashtray emblazoned with the logo of one of the giants of the brewing world and took another long pull of his drink.

'Just listen, Rosie, and don't ask questions until I've finished.'

He went on to tell her about the training school on the Somerset Levels where he and other instructors were preparing men and women to go into occupied France to aid the resistance – the Maquis. And that now he was not only giving training in his own speciality, but he had also been put in charge of the place.

'When we're running a training course, I'm not always able to get away. On top of that, I now have to see that everything is running smoothly, keep on top of the paperwork and so on,' he finished. 'And if something crops up – such as when I was needed in France – then I might be deployed elsewhere at a moment's notice. There's nothing set in stone about any of this. Which is why I decided to explain myself to you.' He reached for her hand. 'Now that I've found you again, Rosie, I don't want to lose you. And I thought if you knew the truth you'd be less likely to put me out with the rubbish if I'm not always able to contact you.'

Rosie hardly knew what to say. All this was almost unbeliev-able, as if she'd stumbled into an Alice in Wonderland world. But she found herself wanting to believe him.

'I won't bin you,' she said lightly. 'As long as you keep treat-ing me to fish and chips.'

He smiled, more relaxed now. 'So why don't we make a date for it? I should be free every evening next week.'

'Oh.' She bit her lip. 'I won't be finishing work until ten.'

'So I'll come and pick you up and we can go straight down into Bath. The chip shop will still be open.'

'But if I get a shout just before the end of my shift, I might not be back.'

Clarke lit another cigarette, blowing the smoke into the dusk that had fallen while they talked. 'That's OK. I'll wait. We should still make it before the chip shop closes. And if not . . .' that wicked twinkle again, 'I'm sure we can find some other way to amuse ourselves.'

Rosie laughed. 'You are wicked, Major.'

'I certainly hope I get the chance to be.'

She pulled a straight face. 'We'll see about that . . .'

Chapter Twenty-Five

The evacuations from Dunkirk had come to an end on 4 June, but no word had reached Winnie as to whether Don had been among the survivors. A week later, Paris itself was under threat, and Churchill went to meet Charles de Gaulle and Marshal Pétain to discuss the situation. But still no news. And so it went on. The French troops had abandoned Paris and German tanks had rolled down the Champs-Élysées to the Place de la Concorde; the Italians, who had joined the conflict, were attempting to take control of the Alps and Nice; and eventually, on 22 June, France surrendered. Rosie, dreadfully worried for Don, tried hard to prepare herself for the worst, yet somehow a little flame of hope still burned within Winnie, refusing to be extinguished. 'I'd know if my boy was dead,' she insisted, displaying some of her old spirit. Rosie hoped with all her heart she was right. If Don never came home, she didn't know how her mother would ever recover.

Billy had somehow managed to stay out of trouble, though Frances wondered how long it would last. Some of what she'd said to him must have gone in, she thought, and he'd realised that if he didn't change his behaviour he would lose the comfortable billet where he enjoyed privileges few other evacuees were afforded. Yes, she had placed them all in suitable accommodation with families who would dedicate themselves to making them feel at home, but for the most part they were working-class people who had no spare cash for luxuries, even with the allowance they got to help with the children's keep. Frances had provided Billy with a wardrobe of new clothes and shoes as well as things he could amuse himself with – a kit to build a model of a tall ship, a dartboard, and an air gun that would shoot both darts and pellets. It was a risk she thought worth taking as she wanted to build trust between them, but she'd given him a stern warning that the gun was not to leave the house and grounds, and if he ever tried to shoot at anything other than the dartboard or the pile of tin cans Cook had supplied, she would confiscate it just as she had the flick knife.

She had also secured a newspaper round for him. At the moment it was only the Sunday papers he was delivering – the newsagent in town had regular boys for the rest of the week, but he'd lost his Sunday boy and had been having to do the round himself. The job provided a bit of pocket money for Billy, which hopefully would mean he wasn't so tempted to steal, and the discipline would be good for him. If he didn't blot his copybook, she hoped that when one of the daily boys left, he'd be able to step into his shoes.

Freda had settled in at the farm and now felt quite at home. Ted had used some of his petrol allowance to take her to London and collect the most precious of her belongings that she'd had to leave behind. She still worried that Granny's house might be destroyed when the bombers came, but as there was nothing she could do about it, she did her best to forget it. And she was so happy in her work it wasn't too difficult.

The lamb she'd bottle-fed for the first few weeks of his life was now suckling from a ewe who had lost her own lamb, but he still came to Freda to be cuddled, which melted her heart. When she'd wanted to name him, Ted had horrified her by suggesting he should be called Hotpot, since that was where he'd probably end up. 'Don't you dare!' she had cried, and seeing that he had genuinely upset her, Ted had promised that wouldn't happen. Freda had finally decided to call him Douglas, after Douglas Bader, the acclaimed RAF flying officer. He had lost both legs in a crash when he was just twenty-one, but was now regarded as an ace pilot.

Although she was still struggling to master the art of milking, Freda was now trusted to herd the cows into the milking shed twice a day and back to their field afterwards, a task she loved. She'd become expert at using a switch to hurry along the ones that stopped to nibble fresh new grass in the banks that lined the lane, and was always amused if any traffic had to wait until the herd had passed, or follow them all the way to their destination. It didn't happen often, it was true, but once Ted and his tractor had been stuck behind her, and he hadn't let her forget it.

He was also teaching her to drive so that she would be able to go into town to pick up supplies or visit her parents, as she did regularly. 'See, you're not the only one who can do it!' she'd told Rosie excitedly when she'd turned up in Hillsbridge at the wheel for the first time, with Ted sitting beside her.

She'd come to like him more and more. Nothing had happened between them, and in one way she was glad of that. She liked their easy relationship as it was, and in her experience taking it any further might well end up in awkwardness if it didn't work out. For the moment it was best to carry on as they were, though admittedly she did sometimes dare to dream.

* * *

Rosie and Clarke had been managing to meet regularly, and more often. The first rush of volunteers for training had slowed; they were now mostly women recruited from the ATS and the other services. Only one man who spoke fluent French was sent Clarke's way, and he supposed the majority of those who were either French nationals or had some close connection to France had joined de Gaulle's Free French army. Consequently he was able to arrange to be free almost any evening.

When Rosie was working a late shift, he invariably picked her up when it ended, and she was grateful not to have to wait for a bus at that time of night. But she was also enjoying his company more and more. And finding him more and more attractive. She'd discovered she didn't want to call a halt when their kisses preceded something more intimate; in fact she looked forward to it. His touch excited her. The kisses and caresses. His strength, his tenderness, the smell of him – tobacco, a whiff of petrol from his lighter, his maleness – made her want to forget all her inhibitions. But somehow they had controlled their desire and postponed what one day would be the inevitable conclusion. The moment had to be just right. Yet when he was not setting her pulse racing and her core crying out for satisfaction, she still thought about Julian and felt almost guilty, as if she was betraying him. Ridiculous, she knew. He'd been seen about town with a very glamorous young woman wearing clothes that would have cost Rosie at least six months' wages. Why should she feel guilty when he'd led her on and made a fool of her not once, but twice? But she did. A habit ingrained in her from all the years she had worshipped him.

Deep down, for all that she was attracted to Clarke in many different ways, in her heart it was still Julian she wanted.

* * *

These last weeks, Paul had been busy extending his original resistance cell into a much larger network beneath a veil of total secrecy. But when France surrendered, a demarcation line was drawn that divided Charente in two, part German occupied, part known as the Free Zone, administered by Pétain and his Vichy government. Almost all the Clermont estate fell within the Free Zone, but some vineyards were under German occupation, and the chateau itself was perilously close to the border. Since some of the likely insurgents lived in what was now occupied territory, it would be difficult and dangerous.

He'd also tightened his security. If an agent was captured, no matter how loyal they might be, they could be broken by torture. Any new cells needed to be kept separate from one another and from his central command. He had decided to hide his identity and location under codenames, and all communication would be by way of the 'postboxes' he'd identified, some in public places where a stranger was unlikely to arouse suspicion, some in dry-stone walls or hollow trees.

When Françoise had arrived, he had told her she would be the one to collect these messages. He'd taken her and the children out in his car for drives, picnics, and to various shops and town centres so that local people would become accustomed to seeing her as the nanny. When he was satisfied she wouldn't attract undue attention, he had dug out an old bicycle that had lain discarded in an outbuilding, cleaned it up, equipped it with new tyres and a pump and checked that the brakes hadn't become so rusty they no longer worked.

He'd primed his trusted agents to leave messages in the assigned places within the Free Zone so that she could practise collecting them and bringing them back to the chateau, and she'd managed to do it successfully But there was a problem with crossing the border into occupied territory.

German checkpoints, manned by German soldiers, had been established along the demarcation line. Passes were required in order to cross, and obtaining these had proved to be a nightmare. The process involved navigating the bureaucratic and security protocols established by both the Vichy government and the German occupying authorities. Paul had managed to obtain a registration number for the bicycle, but the passes were another matter entirely and he was coming up against one brick wall after another.

As it was becoming urgent to be able to establish contact with his agents in the occupied zone, where they could cause the Germans the most trouble, Paul had gone to a printer he knew and asked if he could produce some kind of facsimile pass, and the man had done his best. Paul doubted it would pass close examination, but if the border guards were bored and careless, it was better than nothing.

When he was ready, he talked to Françoise about his plan.

'I have some forged papers,' he said when he'd outlined the situation, 'but with any luck there won't be any need for them. There are gaps in the border, and not all the crossing points are manned the whole time. There are only a certain number of guards, and the soldiers on duty move from one point to another, so in theory it should be possible to avoid them altogether. But it's dangerous all the same. I'm not at all sure the papers would stand up to close examination, but if anyone can get away with it, it's you. I don't know many soldiers who can't be charmed by a pretty girl. Would you be up to taking the risk?'

Anne didn't hesitate. 'I wouldn't be much use to you if I wasn't prepared for that, would I?'

'Good girl. I'll let you know when I've got a trial run set up, and I'll make sure you've got an excuse for being there if you should encounter trouble, as well as the papers.'

Anne nodded. 'Ready when you are!'

She'd enjoyed her time with Paul's children – Béatrice, who was four, and Paulette, two years younger – and she'd found a friend in his wife, Elise, the only other one who knew her true identity apart from Guillaume, his father. But it was high time she began doing something really useful to the war effort. It was, after all, the reason she was here. That and to prove to herself she was capable of doing the job she had volunteered for. She couldn't wait.

Two days later, Anne set out on her first foray into occupied territory with a brown paper bag full of eggs that Paul had collected from the hen run, and her bag containing the forged papers in her bicycle basket. As she pedalled away from the chateau, she was feeling almost high on the adrenaline that was pumping through her veins. If this worked, there was something else she hoped she would be able to do. Perhaps, besides acting as a post girl, she might be able to set Paul's mind at rest about his mother, whom she knew he was worried about. Nancy Clermont was a very sick woman and was dependent on a vast array of medications. Paul had confided to Anne that since her doctor and the pharmacy were in occupied territory, he was concerned as to how much longer she'd be able to get her regular supplies, and it had occurred to Anne that she might be able to collect them for her. So far both Guillaume and Nancy had been a little distant with her. Doing something positive for Nancy might help them to accept her – as the nanny, of course, not her true role. But most of all she wanted to do it for Paul. And, if she was honest, to impress him.

In the short time she'd known him, she'd come to admire him wholeheartedly for his determination to resist the Nazis, and for all that he had already achieved. To her he seemed like a storybook hero – fearless, strong and, she had to admit, very handsome with his dark complexion, thick dark hair and dark brown eyes. No wonder the other girls had swooned over him when he'd tested them on their ability to speak French like a native. Anne had to admit he had much the same effect on her.

The sun was hot and bright, slanting through the poplar trees that surrounded the chateau on all sides, and by the time she reached the village, she was glad of the straw hat that Elise had loaned her and which shaded her eyes. As she pedalled along the village street, she passed several of the local people Paul had introduced her to, and waved to them. But as she drew closer to the control post on the border, nerves began to flutter in her stomach. Her first real test. She thought of the poisoned pill she'd been given to swallow if she was captured, and which was tucked securely into the breast pocket of her dress. If she failed, she might need it. In spite of the heat of the day she felt her skin turn to gooseflesh, and a cold shiver, rapier sharp, ran down her spine. She could see the checkpoint up ahead now on the arrow-straight stretch of road. A striped wooden barrier ran from one side to the other and a hastily erected wooden hut straddled the grass verge. A motorcyclist in grey German uniform roared past her, stopped at the barrier and took off again. But as she drew closer, two figures emerged from the hut, and she realised to her dismay that they were German soldiers, border guards she assumed. It wasn't just the motorcyclist doing a brief check; this crossing was manned. Nerves formed a lump in her throat and her mouth was dry, but there was no turning back. They would already have seen her.

Striving to look unperturbed, she cycled up to the barrier and came to a halt. She fished the papers Paul had given her out of her shoulder bag and handed them to one of the soldiers, sickeningly sure they would recognise them as fakes. But as she'd dismounted, her skirt had rucked up on her saddle, and the two border guards were too busy looking at her legs – suntanned and shapely – to do more than give the papers a cursory glance. The barrier was lifted and she was through, forcing herself to ride at a normal pace. If she appeared in too much of a hurry it might arouse suspicion.

She let out her breath on a sigh of relief and rode on steadily until she was out of sight of the checkpoint. When she came to a stand of trees that marked the spot Paul had described, she dismounted, hid her bicycle behind a thick bramble bush and counted her paces to the tree she was looking for. She found the hollow on its far side, close to the ground and almost hidden by a thick patch of wild garlic. She slid her hand inside, pulled out the note she'd been sent to get and replaced it with the one Paul had given her.

Now all she had to do was get safely back again. The soldiers on the checkpoint would think it suspicious if she returned too quickly. She was tempted to take the eggs back with her as evidence that she'd been to a farm to buy them; they hadn't looked inside the paper bag. But she decided against it and buried them in the undergrowth. Who knew what they'd noticed – they might realise that the bulging bag looked exactly the same as it had when she'd been let through.

She ensured the coast was clear, retrieved her bicycle and pedalled off in the opposite direction. If she rode a fair distance and back, it wouldn't look so suspicious.

She passed a farm and a few cottages, then came to a crossroads, where a lane led off into open countryside while the road appeared to be heading to a small town or village – she could see a church spire rising above a cluster of buildings. As she was now in occupied territory, she decided not to risk going that way.

There might be other German soldiers in the streets. So she turned instead into the lane and kept on until she decided enough time had elapsed and it was safe for her to go back to the checkpoint.

Once again her pulse was racing and her stomach was knotted with nerves as she approached it. Could she be so lucky twice? One crossing guard was still there, but there was no sign of his companion. As she came to a halt, he stepped in front of her bicycle, holding onto the handlebars with one hand, his gun in the other, and her heart leapt into her throat. But the way he was looking at her was more lecherous than threatening, and though he spoke in German, Anne knew just enough to understand what he wanted.

'*Gib mir einen Kuss.*' He wanted a kiss rather than her papers. But to gain time, Anne pretended she didn't understand, pulled her papers from her bag and held them out to him.

'*Nein. Nein. Einen Kuss!*'

'Please let me through!' Anne begged in French. And to her relief, the soldier relented.

'*Nächstes Mal.*' *Next time.* He released the handlebars, put his fingers to his lips and blew her a kiss. Then, smiling, he lifted the barrier and Anne wobbled through, hoping against hope he wouldn't grab her as she passed.

The adrenaline had fired her up. She quite forgot the ache in her legs and sped along the road to the chateau. She'd done it! She'd actually done it! But if next time the same guard was on duty, he might press her again for a kiss – and probably more, if they were alone. The thought turned her stomach, but she wasn't going to let that spoil her moment of triumph. It would probably be a different soldier, and if not – well, she'd just have to deal with it when the time came.

* * *

The army officer knocked on the cottage door, stood back and waited. When there was no reply, he knocked again. After knocking a third time without success, he guessed there was no one in. He stamped his feet, looking around. He'd come a long way and he didn't want to leave without seeing Mrs Mitchell.

Further up the drive he could see a big house, the only other dwelling in the parkland. Perhaps someone there would know if the woman he had come to see was away or if she was likely to be home soon. He went to his staff car, which was parked outside the gate, and told the uniformed – and very pretty – driver what he planned to do and that she should wait where she was. Then he strode towards the house, his swagger stick tucked under his arm, and rang the bell.

The door was answered by Dimsie, now sufficiently recovered to resume her normal duties, though her scar was still visible – just – above the neckline of her uniform. 'I'm looking for Mrs Mitchell, the lady who lives in that cottage,' he said, pointing back down the drive. 'She doesn't seem to be at home and I'm wondering if there is someone here who could apprise me of her likely whereabouts.'

'Ooh.' Dimsie wiped her nose with the back of her hand. 'I don't know, sir.'

'Then perhaps you could fetch someone who would?' The officer was growing impatient, but tried to avoid using the tone he would have used to one of his men. She was only a girl, after all, and, it would seem, not very bright.

'I'll see, sir.' She sounded anxious, though he couldn't for the life of him see why she should be. Perhaps it was his uniform that was frightening her. He only hoped he wouldn't have long to wait before he could deliver his news and be on his way.

* * *

Winnie was upstairs changing the bed in the master bedroom, and had just gathered up the sheets and pillowcases for laundering when Lady Hastings appeared in the doorway.

'There you are, Mrs Mitchell.' She was looking rather sombre, Winnie thought.

'Yes, here I am, milady. You'll have nice fresh sheets tonight. And we'll get these washed and out on the line in good time for them to dry.'

'Put them down, Mrs Mitchell,' Lady Hastings said.

'What . . . here?' Winnie asked, wondering whatever had got into her ladyship.

'Yes. There's someone here to see you.' Lady Hastings swallowed. 'An army officer,' she added gently.

For a moment Winnie stood, still clutching the bundle of bedding, as if she'd been turned to stone. She couldn't speak, couldn't even breathe out the air that was trapped in her lungs.

'Come on, Winnie.' It was the first time Winnie could ever recall Lady Hastings using her Christian name. She reached out, took the bedding from Winnie's arms and dropped it on the newly made bed. 'Take a moment to compose yourself. Then come with me.'

Winnie's breath came out on a gasp and her hand flew to her throat. 'Oh milady . . .'

'You can do this.'

She gulped, steeling herself. She had to be strong. Mustn't let herself down. Mustn't let Don down. The long weeks of anxiety had eaten away at her spirit, just as they had at her body. She'd lost so much weight she thought she could have stuffed a pillow down the waistband of her skirt and still had room to spare. And now it was here. The moment she'd feared. The waiting would be over. The grieving begun. Everyone knew what an officer at the door meant. But at least he must be a caring man. She knew of plenty who'd been notified of their loss by telegram or official letter.

'Ready,' she said, and followed Lady Hastings down the stairs.

The officer had been shown into the parlour. Winnie didn't know what his rank was; she'd never been able to remember what all those pips and stripes and insignia meant. But to her he looked very young. Not much older than Don. Oh God, Don . . .

'Mrs Mitchell,' he said. 'I'm here about your son, Corporal—'

'Yes. I know who my son is.' She couldn't believe the tone she was using. Or the words. It must be the shock. 'You've come to tell me he's dead, haven't you?'

A startled look crossed the officer's youthful face. 'Oh no, Mrs Mitchell. Not that.'

'What then?' She didn't understand. Couldn't take it in.

'Shall we sit down?' He glanced at Lady Hastings for approval, and she nodded.

'Of course. Mrs Mitchell has had something of a shock. I'll leave you with her.'

She left the room and Winnie sat on the edge of an easy chair, her hands clasped tightly together in her lap, afraid still of what was coming. Was he trying to break it to her gently?

'You might as well tell me,' she said. 'I'm imagining all sorts here.'

'Your son is not dead.' The officer looked at her directly and spoke with emphasis. 'He is one of those who was evacuated from Dunkirk.'

'Really?' She was still afraid to believe it. 'Then why haven't I heard anything from him before now?'

'That's what I'm here to explain, Mrs Mitchell. We didn't know who he was. Apparently he was climbing a rope ladder to board one of our destroyers when it was bombed. He was thrown back into the water, and picked up later by a fishing boat that was part of the flotilla of small boats that went to Dunkirk. He had sustained some wounds, but survived. The problem arose when we were unable to discover his identity. He was suffering from amnesia, brought on, we believe, by a blow to the head from a piece of falling debris when the ship was hit. He had no identification at all. It had been lost, either when he was in the water or before. We believe the latter is more likely because the uniform jacket he was wearing indicated he belonged to a regiment who said he wasn't one of theirs. Thousands of men got home, Mrs Mitchell; thousands are missing, presumed dead. Until his memory began to return, we were unable to notify his next of kin. And unfortunately he is still too ill to be able to contact you himself. That's why I'm here today, to speak to you on his behalf.'

Winnie was shaking her head, unable to believe what she was hearing. 'He's alive?' She said it wonderingly.

'He is,' the officer confirmed.

Slowly, so slowly, her brain adjusted to accept what she had been told, and tears began to run down her face. 'He's alive! My boy's alive! Oh, thank you! Thank you!'

'I must warn you. His injuries are severe. It may be some time—'

'Can I see him? Can I go and see him?'

'It's some distance, Mrs Mitchell. And you may not be able to spend very long with him.'

'I don't care about that! Just as long as I can see him. Where is he?'

'In one of our military hospitals, near Portsmouth.' He hesitated, then went on, 'I'm going back there now. If you could be ready in . . . say twenty minutes?'

'Oh, I don't know. I'm at work . . .' Winnie was torn.

Lady Hastings appeared in the doorway. She must have been listening to the conversation. 'That is wonderful news, Mrs Mitchell. Of course you must go.'

'But how will I get back?'

'Don't worry about that. James would come for you, I'm sure. And if he's not able to do so, then I'll come myself.'

'Oh, Lady Hastings, I can't put you to all that trouble!' Anxious as she was to see Don, Winnie didn't see how she could expect her employer to drive all the way to Portsmouth and back.

'Nonsense!' Lady Hastings said briskly. 'It's the least we can do. And if you want to stay on to be with Donald, feel free to do so.'

Winnie was becoming flustered. This was all so sudden.

'I don't think I could stay today. I can't keep the gentleman waiting while I pack what I'd need. And what about Rosie?'

'I can tell Rosie,' Lady Hastings said.

But the officer was looking at his watch. 'I really do need to get going, I'm afraid.'

'Then I'll come just as I am.'

The decision made, Winnie paid a quick visit to the lav, then fetched her bag and cardigan and followed him to his car.

Chapter Twenty-Six

July came in, sultry weather that gave Winnie what she called her 'sick headaches'. But she'd been so shocked by the state she'd found Don in on that first visit, she'd had Rosie borrow Lady Hastings' car to drive her back a couple of days later and help her find a B&B she could book into.

The nurse who had taken her to Don's ward had warned her what to expect, but it had still been a shock to see him lying there, hooked up to a drip, his head, one hand and both arms swathed in bandages, his deathly pale face peppered with scabs from wounds that had not yet healed over and which she supposed must have been caused by shards of flying glass. Worst of all, he'd stared at her blankly, his mouth working but no words coming out. Didn't he recognise her?

'Don, it's me – Mum,' she said.

'Mum?' But his voice was uncertain, his eyes screwed up as he struggled to process this information.

Winnie sat on the chair by the bed, leaned over and took his unbandaged hand in hers.

'Don't worry, my love. You're going to be fine. It'll all come back to you in time.'

'Mum.' This time he said it with more certainty. Winnie didn't know what had jogged his memory, but she'd kept talking anyway, thinking it might have been her voice that had helped.

'I'm so sorry I haven't been to see you before, love, but I didn't know you were here until today. An officer came to tell me, and he drove me down. I've been worried to death. I didn't know whether you were dead or alive, or perhaps a prisoner of war. I'm just so glad I'm here now.'

'Tell Margie.' He'd struggled to get the name out, but Winnie knew at once who he meant. Margie Hillman, the Hillsbridge lass he'd been dating the last time he had been home on leave. Winnie had never met her, but it seemed he thought a lot of her, and she hoped she hadn't found someone else in the meantime.

'I will, son. Can you tell me where she lives?'

Don's brow had furrowed again, then he nodded as if in a private conversation with himself. 'Northfields,' he said.

'Northfield Terrace, do you mean? Which rank?' There were three ranks of terraced houses over there, steepled up the hillside.

'Middle one.'

Winnie had spent a couple of hours with Don, but when the nurse came to tell her she thought it was time to let him rest, she agreed. She didn't want to leave, but she had noticed that his eyelids had drooped a couple of times, and once again he was struggling to converse. She'd definitely come back and stay for a few weeks, but she had to get home tonight; she had nothing with her but the clothes she stood up in and she knew she shouldn't leave it much longer if someone was coming to fetch her. Reluctantly she kissed Don, told him she'd see him again soon and that she loved him.

'You too,' he had whispered drowsily. Tears had stung her eyes; they were still blurry as she went to find a telephone to call Lady Hastings. Then, the arrangements made, she'd found the hospital canteen, where she'd eaten sandwiches and drunk endless cups of tea while she waited.

Now that she was staying in Portsmouth, she was restricted to normal twice-daily visiting times and the canteen had become almost like a second home to her. The hours between visits seemed endless and it was too hot and sultry for her to explore the town; though she had tried a few times, it always brought on one of her headaches. So she would sit in the canteen over her tea and a newspaper that she bought each day from the hospital shop. The news was depressing, though, especially when she read that Hitler was planning for the invasion of Britain. How did they know? she wondered. But she supposed they had their sources, and it did seem likely now that France and Belgium had fallen.

A few days later, she learned the hospital was being moved lock, stock and barrel to rural Gloucestershire. Being a naval base, Portsmouth was likely to be in the firing line when the invasion came. The move caused enormous upheaval, but Winnie was glad that Don would be nearer to home. It still wouldn't be possible for her to visit him every day, but she was sure Lady Hastings would extend her leave of absence if she was able to find somewhere she could afford to stay. It wouldn't be so far for Rosie to come to visit either.

At least Don was improving a little. Though progress was slow, his memory was gradually returning and he was no longer attached to the drip. He was cheered, too, when he received a letter from his girlfriend – Winnie had made the trip over to Northfield Terrace, explained the situation to Margie's mother and left the hospital address. She hoped with all her heart that he would be well enough to be discharged soon. But until that happened, she was going to stay close to him – she believed the improvement was because she was able to spend time with him, talk to him about things that were beginning to revive memories and bring him little treats.

Every night without fail, she said a prayer thanking the God she wasn't sure she believed in for sending him home to her. It couldn't do any harm to express her gratitude. Hopefully Don would soon be back in his own home, where she could look after him properly. She couldn't wait for that day.

The Battle of Britain, which had begun in the second week of July with attacks on shipping convoys and Welsh dockyards escalated into intense raids on RAF air bases and radar stations in the south east of England. Though heavily outnumbered the Spitfires and Hurricanes were more than a match for the lumbering German bombers and the RAF lost far fewer aircraft than the Luftwaffe. The airfield raids had caused major damage, but so far there had been no concentrated attacks on London or any other major city.

At about the same time, there were changes for the three sections of the SIS. They were amalgamating to form a new organisation, which was to be known as the SOE – Special Operations Executive. It was headed up by the Minister of Economic Warfare, and on his appointment, Churchill had told him, 'Now go and set Europe alight.'

Now that he was in charge of an agent training centre, Clarke was kept busy with top-level meetings and a new intake of students, which meant he had been unable to meet Rosie for several weeks. But when the latest course ended during the last week of July, and with a free weekend ahead, he arranged to meet her when she finished her shift at ten on the Saturday. For a change from their usual fish and chips, they ate at a café near the abbey that was still open and afterwards walked down to Pulteney Gardens, a green open space with vibrant flower beds running down to the river and weir. There was also a bandstand, and they sat down on the low stone wall surrounding it, enjoying the fragrance of the roses in the still night air, quite alone in a space that during the day would be occupied by dozens of visitors.

An aircraft engine interrupted the peace, circling overhead.

'That's a German surveillance plane,' Clarke said. 'A Henschel, I think. You know what they're doing, don't you? They're scoping out the Empire.'

'The Empire?' For a moment a bemused Rosie wondered what on earth he meant, then light dawned.

'Oh – the Empire Hotel. Of course! They must have found out the Admiralty relocated there. They're planning to bomb the Admiralty!'

'That would be my guess.'

Quite suddenly the night sky was split apart by gunfire, the flashes like exploding stars in the darkness. Rosie grabbed Clarke's hand. 'What . . .?'

'One of ours. He must have been following the spy plane.'

More flashes. This time from the enemy aircraft. 'He's firing too,' Rosie gasped.

The orbit of the two planes was widening, the Spitfire bobbing and weaving; any moment they would be directly overhead. Clarke jerked Rosie to her feet, pulling her up the steps into the relative safety of the bandstand.

'The Henschel has a rear gunner,' he explained.

As he spoke, the Spitfire swooped low, dipping beneath the German plane and firing as he did so. The Henschel slewed violently.

'Yes!' Clarke shouted, punching the air. 'I think he's got the pilot!'

Rosie barely heard what he said. The plane was rapidly losing height. For long minutes it appeared to be nosediving, then it seemed to recover, gaining height again and turning away from the Spitfire, which was returning from its trajectory over the city.

'He stalled, but he's recovered,' Clarke said, keeping up his running commentary.

But scarcely were his words out than the Spitfire came roaring back, peppering the spy plane with gunshot. Again it shuddered, again it began to fall out of the sky, this time trailing black smoke in its wake. And it was headed straight for the Parade Gardens. The wounded pilot must be aiming to make an emergency landing in the wide-open space. But it was coming in too fast, and at the last moment it pitched forward, burying its nose in the turf close to the riverbank. The Spitfire pilot dipped his wings in a salute and flew away from the scene.

Clarke was out of the bandstand in a second, running towards the crashed plane.

'Clarke – no!' Rosie screamed, all too aware this was an enemy aircraft. If either the pilot or the rear gunner was still alive, they could be armed and wouldn't hesitate to shoot an Englishman. And the smell of aircraft fuel was wafting towards her – if it ignited, the plane would be consumed by fire. Then her humanity and her sense of duty kicked in.

She was a trained nurse. Never mind that the crew were German. Never mind that they might be armed. If they'd survived, they must be in need of medical attention. She began to run after Clarke, barely noticing the small crowd of onlookers who were gathering on the road above them but remaining at a safe distance. He was beside the Henschel now, heading for the pilot's seat beneath the wing canopy.

'Is he . . .?'

He straightened up, shaking his head. 'He's gone. I'll check the gunner.'

Rosie followed him around the plane as he looked for the door that would allow access and egress, but when he found it, it refused to open. The force of the crash landing must have jammed it. He attacked it with all his strength, and after endless minutes it gave sufficiently for him to be able to wrench it partly open. 'Wait here,' he instructed Rosie, and squeezed inside.

Rosie waited, her heart in her mouth. Close to, the smell of aircraft fuel was strong enough to make her cover her mouth and nose with her hand, and anxiety bordering on panic threatened to consume her. Supposing something created a spark! The plane would go up in a fireball and Clarke was inside. But when a few minutes later he was back to tell her the rear gunner was alive but too badly injured to be able to crawl to the door, she didn't hesitate.

'I'm coming in.'

Clarke moved aside and she scrambled into the belly of the Henschel.

'Could we get him out between us?'

'Take a look at him and see if there's anything you can do for him where he is. I'll fetch the picnic rug from the car.'

Rosie wormed her way to where the rear gunner was slumped in his seat. He was bleeding profusely from wounds in his right shoulder and arm, and she feared an artery had been severed. But Clarke was right – he was still alive. He was groaning, and if his heart had stopped, so would the fountain of blood.

Swiftly she pulled up her skirt, wriggled out of her waist petticoat and rolled it into a tight wad, which she pressed as firmly as she could to the German's neck, holding it there until she heard Clarke squeezing back into the plane's belly.

'I've got to get him out,' he said when he reached her. And then, in a whisper but sounding surprisingly calm, 'You go. The plane could go up at any minute.'

Once again Rosie felt the stirrings of panic; once again she controlled them.

'We'll do it together. Can you drag him? I need to keep the pressure on his neck or he'll bleed to death.'

'I can do that while I drag him.' Clarke hooked his arms beneath the German's shoulders and lifted, and the man's groans rose to a scream of agony. 'Get out, Rosie. Now!'

There was no way Rosie was going to leave her patient. 'I'm going nowhere. I can help.'

'Lift his legs then. I've got the neck pad.'

That he hadn't argued told Rosie there was no time to spare, and she did as she was told. Together they manoeuvred the man to the exit door, and Rosie slid his legs out while Clarke held him. Then she squeezed through the gap and dropped to the ground ready to steady him. As his feet connected with the ground, his legs buckled and she was unable to save him from collapsing in a crumpled heap. Clarke swore, jumped down himself, and indicated to Rosie that she should take his legs again.

A lone man had ventured down the steps leading to the gardens and was heading towards them.

'Stay clear! It's going to go up!' Clarke shouted, and the man stopped in his tracks.

When they had got the German to what Clarke judged to be a safe distance from the aircraft, they laid him down on the grass.

Rosie could see that the blood had soaked her petticoat. The pad wasn't working. But the skirt she was wearing was tiered, with a flounce at the hem. Telling Clarke to press hard on the wound, she ripped at the flounce until it came away from the tier above, and twisted it into a makeshift tourniquet.

'We need an ambulance,' she gasped. 'Hasn't anyone gone to call them?'

As if in answer to a prayer, she heard a jangling bell coming closer, and moments later the ambulance appeared. The driver and attendant, both of whom she of course knew, came running towards them with all their equipment.

'Thank God!' Rosie whispered.

But the rear gunner's groans had stopped, and when she felt for a pulse, it was so weak as to be almost non-existent. She knelt beside him, beginning mouth-to-mouth resuscitation, but a sinking feeling inside told her it was too late. He'd lost too much blood.

'We're here now. Move over, Rosie.' It was Tony Grant. He was one of the older drivers and he was breathing heavily.

'I'll do it.' Pat Dunford, the attendant, who was considerably younger than Tony, knelt down and took over from Rosie, while Tony took the man's pulse. Rosie and Clarke stood by, watching anxiously.

With their attention concentrated on the patient, none of them noticed a flicker of flame running along the length of the Henschel.

'He's gone.' Tony straightened up, but after all their efforts to save the man, Rosie wasn't ready to accept it. She pushed Tony aside, feeling for a pulse herself. He was right. There was none. But still she screamed at Pat to continue with the mouth-to-mouth.

What happened next shocked them all into silence. There was a thunderous roar, and flames leapt from the plane into the night sky, illuminating the Parade Gardens and the funnel of black smoke that was forming a cloud above it.

The clang of another bell coming closer sounded clear above the awful crackling of the fire in spite of them all being partially deafened by the explosion. A fire engine. It squeezed through one of the archways and came to a stop on the riverbank. The firemen leapt down and began unwinding the hose. At least they wouldn't be short of water with the river so close by.

Shock was setting in and Rosie was shaking from head to foot. Clarke put an arm round her.

'Come on, Rosie. Let's get you home. There's nothing more we can do here.'

She cast one last agonised glance at the man Tony and Pat were loading onto the stretcher and covering with a sheet, then let Clarke lead her to the steps and up to the road where he had left his car. He eased her into the front passenger seat. As he started the engine and pulled away, she wrapped her arms around herself, still shivering violently. Neither of them spoke. There was nothing left to say.

The cottage was in darkness. No welcoming lights tonight. It had still been broad daylight when Rosie had left for work, and with Winnie away there was no one to turn them on. Clarke found a large torch in the glove compartment, and he lit the way as he and Rosie walked up the path. Rosie found her key and unlocked the door. At least she'd stopped shaking now. But Clarke preceded her into the house, lighting the gas lamps as he went.

'What you need is a strong drink, sweetheart,' he said, glad that he'd brought a bottle of gin and one of whisky a few weeks ago. Apart from the small bottle of brandy Winnie kept for emergencies, and which was three-quarters empty anyway, there was no alcohol in the house.

He went to the chiffonier in the living room, got out the whisky and two glasses and poured generous measures into both. Rosie, who had fetched a couple of towels to protect the sofa, had subsided onto it. 'Here. Drink this.' Clarke held a tumbler out to her.

Rosie frowned. 'Clarke, you know mine's gin and orange.'

'Tonight you are having whisky. With only a drop of water in it.'

'But I don't know if I'll like it.'

'Trust me, it will do you good. Gin will only make you depressed. It's not called mother's ruin for nothing.'

Rosie didn't have the strength to argue. He handed her the glass and sat down beside her, and she sipped the whisky warily, feeling it sting her tongue. But as it trickled down her throat, it seemed to warm her through.

'It's very strong,' she said. 'Can't I have some orange in it?'

'Orange doesn't go with whisky. And I don't suppose you've got any peppermint, or ginger.'

'There's some ginger beer in the pantry.'

'It will do you more good to drink it as it is,' Clarke said sternly. 'But just a few sips at a time. Don't try to put it away as you do your gin and orange.'

Rosie took another cautious sip.

'Feeling better?' he asked, putting his arm round her.

'A bit, I suppose. Oh, that was just so awful. That poor boy. He was so young! Barely out of school! Why, Clarke? Why did he have to die? It's just not fair . . .' Her voice tailed away.

'I'm afraid that's what happens in war, Rosie. Fair doesn't come into it. A lot of young men die before their time. Your brother was lucky. He'll probably be out of it now.'

'Lucky?' Rosie took a much more generous sip of her whisky. 'I don't call it lucky to be in the state he is.'

'But he's alive. And we were lucky too, not to have been in the plane when it went up in flames.'

Rosie shuddered. Suddenly it was all too much for her, and tears began to course down her cheeks.

'Oh, sweetheart, come here.' Clarke drew her close and she

burrowed into him, sobbing out the shock, fear and horror that had hit her like a thunderbolt when it was all over.

When at last her sobs had quietened to sniffs and hiccups, he got out a handkerchief and wiped her face gently. She took it from him and blew her nose. 'I'm sorry. I'm such a ninny.'

'You are not a ninny. You were very brave, Rosie.' He pulled her towards him again and kissed her – her hair, her still-damp cheeks, her mouth, and she felt herself responding with a fierce desire that flooded through her, blocking out the memories of the terrible events she'd lived through tonight.

She caressed his broad back, exploring the hard muscles, then moved around to his chest, undoing his shirt buttons and sliding her hand inside. It rested for a moment on his heart, and she was comforted by the strong beat beneath her palm. Then, as her desire grew, she ran her fingers through the soft covering of hair that ran down to his waist. She was shocked when he pulled back, holding her away.

'I think it's time I was going.'

'No! Why?' The rejection was a physical pain, gripping her gut. Her need for his strength, his warmth, his aliveness was a fever in her blood. 'Don't you want me?'

He disentangled himself, stood up. 'You know damn well I do! And I think it's best I go before I do something I regret.'

Rosie reached for his hand, clasping it tightly. 'Don't leave me. I can't bear it. Don't go, please!'

She saw the indecision in his face, the inward battle he was fighting, and she tugged on his hand, pulling him towards her. 'I want you, Clarke.'

Still he resisted. 'Rosie. You don't know what you're saying.'

And suddenly she understood. 'I do know, Clarke. I don't just want you. I need you.'

She tugged on his hand again, and he pulled her to her feet, swept her into his arms and carried her to the stairs. In Rosie's room, they fell onto her bed, in too much haste to undress fully. And lost themselves in the fulfilment of what they had both craved.

Afterwards they lay in one another's arms, legs entwined, yet still Rosie wanted him, her sensitised skin tingling and drawn to him as if by an invisible magnet. As she pressed herself to him, she felt him stirring again, and he was easing her out of what remained of her clothes. He caressed her with his hands and his mouth before entering her again, this time with restraint and tenderness, and Rosie rose to heights beyond anything she had ever dreamed of. At the last she cried out, her nails digging into those muscles of his back. Then she relaxed, curling herself around his body, her head resting against his broad shoulder. As she breathed in the scent of his skin, she found herself drifting in a haze of contentment and remembered pleasure.

And then, quite suddenly, she was aware of a feeling of guilt invading that contentment. At first, half asleep, she thought it must be because she had been unable to save that poor young gunner; that she had survived when he had not. But somehow that didn't feel quite right. She shifted restlessly, and as Clarke turned onto his side, pulling her close once more, she knew exactly what it was, and cringed inwardly.

Betrayal. Betrayal of Julian. Even as she thought it, she knew it was ridiculous. But she'd loved him for too long. Somewhere deep inside her subconscious mind she still saw them together. Would she never be free of him? Her happiness dissipated like smoke on the wind. She was trapped for ever in a dream that could never be.

As he reached for her, Clarke had felt her go away from him and guessed that, hardly surprisingly, her thoughts had returned to what she'd been through tonight. He was able to forget it; danger, bloody scenes, untimely death, he'd witnessed it all too many times, so that he had become almost immune to it. But she hadn't, and she couldn't. Flooded with tenderness, all he wanted now was to protect her, never again allow her to be exposed to such horror, her very life endangered. There was no way that was possible, of course. He had a job to do, and so did she. But if they were together, he could make sure she was safe at least some of the time. Love for her swelled within him.

'Marry me,' he said.

She turned her head on the pillow, looking at him in the dim light of the moon that filtered in through the open curtains, but for what seemed to him an age she said nothing. She was biting her lip, and there was something like panic in her expression. It wasn't what he wanted to see, and he felt suddenly incredibly foolish. But just now, when he'd made love to her, he'd really believed she felt as he did. He'd done nothing to force her; quite the opposite. He'd been ready to suppress his desire for her and walk away rather than take things beyond the kisses, which she seemed to enjoy. It had been her decision. She who had invited him to cross the Rubicon. And now . . .

'I'm sorry, Clarke,' she said. 'I'm flattered you should ask me, and I wish I could say yes, but I can't.'

'Why not?' He didn't know why he should have asked, and regretted it the moment the words were out.

'Oh, Clarke, you know the reason,' Rosie said miserably.

Like a lightning flash the patience he'd nurtured ever since he'd first set eyes on her erupted into ice-cold anger. He sat up, glaring down at her.

'It's that bloody doctor, isn't it? Well, I hope he makes you happy.'

Rosie sat up too, holding the sheet around herself protectively. 'He won't, Clarke. I know that now. In fact, he asked me out not so long ago, and I turned him down, if you must know. I've come to realise he's everything you think he is. Vain, self-important, and yes, a philanderer. But fool that I am, I do still love him, and it wouldn't be fair of me to marry you when I don't love you. You deserve better than that.'

Clarke's anger had died as quickly as it had flared. It hadn't just been the horror of the crashing spy plane and the deaths that had followed that had been tormenting her. She had been in purgatory for much longer than that. And despite himself, still all he wanted to do was to make her happy.

'Suppose I was to tell you I have enough love for both of us?' he said.

She shook her head. 'No. Forget about me, Clarke. Find a woman who loves you back.'

'I'm not sure I can do that any more than you can forget that bloody doctor,' he said ruefully.

A tear was trickling down Rosie's cheek. He brushed it away with his thumb and she took his hand, holding it against her chin. 'I am so sorry, truly I am. I wish I could marry you, but you must see it wouldn't work.'

'I guess. Do you want me to go now?'

The tears spilled over again. 'No. Please don't. Not tonight. Will you . . .' She hesitated. 'Oh, I know I'm being selfish and I shouldn't ask, but . . . would you hold me again? I feel so safe with you.'

Summoning up every ounce of his self-control, Clarke did as she asked, and when she fell asleep in his arms, he rested his chin in her hair. She cut up flakes of her favourite soap and dissolved them in hot water when she washed it, and now he breathed in the sweet citrus scent that would forever remind him of her, and was overcome with a despair greater than he had ever experienced in his life.

Chapter Twenty-Seven

When Rosie woke next morning, she was alone. In those first confused moments, she struggled to understand; several times when she'd stirred in the night he had still been there beside her and she had burrowed close to him, taking comfort in the warmth and strength of his body.

It hadn't been a dream, had it? He'd made love to her – the little ache in her stomach, the stickiness between her legs and her state of undress bore witness to that – but afterwards? He'd asked her to marry him and she'd refused him. Told him to find someone else, someone who truly loved him. Had he taken her at her word?

A feeling of sadness descended on her. It had been the right thing to do, she still believed that. He deserved better than a wife who was in love with another man. It just wasn't fair when he'd been so good to her, told her as much as he could about himself. And when she'd said she wished she could accept his proposal, she'd been telling the truth. She enjoyed being with him. Felt safe with him. Revelled in the electricity that sparked between them. She would miss him dreadfully if she never saw him again. But that was a sacrifice she had to make. Last night after their lovemaking, she'd felt guilt. Her gut reaction had been that she had betrayed Julian, and knowing it was ridiculous didn't change anything. He was still uppermost in her mind. A part of her loved him still and always would.

She eased aside the covers, reached for a cotton wrap to cover her nakedness, went to the top of the stairs and called Clarke's name. There was no reply. No sounds of life from the kitchen. She went down, her bare feet making the stairs creak. She was surprised he hadn't woken her when he'd left. If he'd left.

He had. She knew it when she saw the note propped up against the glass jug in the centre of the table. The roses she'd cut and arranged in it yesterday seemed to be drooping as if they were hanging their heads in sympathy. She picked up the note, written on a blank sheet of paper torn from a diary.

My dear Rosie. If you change your mind, you now know where to find me. I can only hope you will. Love always, Clarke

Tears sprang to her eyes as she read it. So he *had* taken her at her word. But he'd left the door open for her. He still wanted her. It was up to her to make the break and set him free. But hard as it was, she wasn't going to change her mind. If she did, while she was still in love with Julian, there could be no happy ending.

She refolded the note, took it up to her room and put it in her handkerchief sachet. Then she got dressed for work – she was on the day shift today – went back downstairs and made herself a cup of tea and a slice of toast.

Life had to go on. Without him.

By the end of July, Don had improved sufficiently to leave the hospital, but to Winnie's intense disappointment he was not coming home but being sent to a recuperation home in Buckinghamshire that had recently been requisitioned by the government. The original idea had been to make it a maternity hospital for evacuee women to give birth, but beds were at a premium since the military hospitals had been overwhelmed by the number of men wounded at Dunkirk and the fighting that had preceded it.

Winnie had been allowed to accompany Don in the ambulance taking him to Buckinghamshire, and had been staggered by the grandeur of his new surroundings. The vast rooms had been cleared of furnishings and divided up into wards to accommodate fifty patients, and there were even beds on the veranda, though she guessed they would have to be moved inside when the fine summer weather ended and autumn and winter set in. The mansion was surrounded by lawns, trees and shrubs and there was a lake in the grounds that Don would be able to explore when he was fit enough, but it was miles from a town or village where she could find accommodation, and she had no option but to return with the ambulance when it went back to Wiltshire.

She'd been a bit tearful when Fred had come to collect her and, typical of him, he'd offered to take her to see Don if he was still hospitalised after a few weeks. But she'd refused. She couldn't ask him to use his precious petrol to go all that way, and she didn't want him to neglect his business either. 'At least I've seen him through the worst of it,' she'd said stoically. 'And I can't expect her ladyship to let me have any more time off. She's been very good as it is, and I don't want to take advantage.'

'She wouldn't see it like that, any more than I do,' Fred had assured her, but Winnie had remained firm.

'It's best I get back to work. And Don's so much better now. His memory is still a bit patchy, but the letters from his girl help, and he's getting back to his old self. He'll do better still when I'm not there mollycoddling him, I wouldn't wonder,' she added.

'You can mollycoddle me instead,' Fred had said with a wicked grin. 'I've missed your good home-cooked dinners while you've been away. I've missed you too.'

Winnie leaned over and patted his hand where it lay on the gearstick. 'And I've missed you.'

In some ways she'd been glad to get back to her own home, her own kitchen, her own bed. But she was a bit worried about Rosie. Some of the spark seemed to have gone out of her.

'What's up with you, my girl?' she asked when she'd been back for a few days.

But Rosie was evasive and Winnie didn't push her.

'They're working you too hard, I shouldn't wonder,' she said. 'And you've lost weight. Have you been eating proper meals?'

'I'm fine, Mum,' Rosie insisted, but Winnie couldn't help noticing she'd made no mention of Clarke, or seeing him again, and she guessed that something had gone badly wrong there. A terrible shame. Though she'd had her doubts to begin with, Clarke seemed a nice chap, a darned sight better than Julian Edgell, and not so far out of Rosie's league. She just hoped it wasn't Julian that had upset her – again. But that was something else she could do nothing about.

She remembered the old saying: When they're little they're a weight in your arms, and when they're grown they're a weight on your heart. How true that was! But at least both her children were safe – for the present, anyway – and she prayed they would stay that way.

Billy Crossley had a girlfriend, another evacuee, who was staying with Mrs Wilton, one of Frances' WVS ladies. Mrs Wilton, who was married to a farmer and lived on the far side of town, had assured her that Alice Meek was a very nice girl, and in one respect Frances was hopeful that she would be a good influence on him. But she was also a bit concerned about what they might be getting up to when they walked out on these balmy summer evenings. If Billy got the girl in the family way, it would be a disaster.

That evening – the first Saturday of August – Billy had gone out to meet Alice, and Frances had spent an hour listening to the BBC Home Service on the wireless while she sorted out some clothes she could donate to a charity for needy women. Then she had settled down with Steinbeck's *The Grapes of Wrath*, which she had been meaning to read ever since it had won the Pulitzer Prize, and never quite had time.

When she eventually looked up from the pages, she was shocked to see that the hands of the mantel clock were nearing half past eleven. She'd been so absorbed by the story she'd lost track of time. For a moment she was still there in her imagination, living in the days of the Great Depression, then it occurred to her – she hadn't heard Billy come in. Was he still out? His curfew, which she imposed strictly, was eleven.

Her first reaction was annoyance. But after she'd checked with James, the anxiety as to what he might be up to began nagging at her.

'Come to bed,' James urged her – he was already wearing his silk dressing gown, and pouring himself a last tipple of his favourite whisky. 'He knows where we hide the spare key.'

Frances was having none of it. 'I'm waiting up. He's going to get a piece of my mind when he does get in.'

James shook his head. 'Poor chap. You should allow him a bit of leeway, Frances.'

'Which he'd only take advantage of,' Frances said crossly, thinking that if James took a firmer hand with Billy, he might be less trouble.

'Well, it's up to you, my dear.' James disappeared up the sweeping staircase, and a moment later she heard the bedroom door close after him.

Frances eyed the whisky decanter, which James had returned to the silver tray on the sideboard. Dammit, she'd have one herself, she decided. She could do with one. The wretched boy had ruined her pleasant, relaxing evening and her nerves were now tightly strung.

She poured the whisky into a crystal tumbler and added a little water from the pitcher that stood beside the decanter. She carried it to the parlour window, from where she could see the drive, illuminated by an old-fashioned gas street lamp that James had bought at auction years ago. But she'd left her spectacles on the occasional table beside her chair along with her book, and when a running figure appeared in the pool of light, she couldn't see properly whether it was Billy. She hurried to the front door, not wanting James to be disturbed if he rang the bell, and opened it.

But it wasn't Billy. It was a girl, still running, and now just a few feet away. She slowed when she saw Frances standing in the doorway, then hurried towards her, breathing heavily.

'Oh, your ladyship! Please! Can you come?'

Frances's stomach lurched. This must be Alice. Something had happened to Billy.

'You'd better come in,' she said. This wasn't a conversation she wanted to have on the doorstep. The girl – small and thin, her tear-stained face framed by long bright red hair – hesitated. 'This way, come on!' Frances urged her, and led her into the drawing room, where she poured her a glass of water from the pitcher.

'Sit down and drink this,' she instructed the girl, and as she did so, she saw a dark circle of hair covering the crown of Alice's head like a St Peter's tonsure. As she'd thought, that bright red wasn't her natural colouring. She'd dyed her hair, and it was now growing out. 'Now, tell me what this is all about. Billy, I presume.'

Alice nodded. She was shaking so violently that water sloshed from her glass, soaking the skirt of her cotton dress and the arm of the chair. 'It was awful! Just awful! There was a fight. It wasn't Billy's fault. But they've taken him to the police station.'

Frances didn't know what to think. It was something of a relief that he wasn't badly injured – or worse. He'd have been taken to hospital, not the police station, if he was.

'Who else was involved?' she asked.

'Oh, all of them. It was awful!' Alice said again. She was crying in earnest now, tears coursing down her thin face. 'I didn't know what to do.'

'All right. I'll come with you and find out what's going on.' Frances got up, but as she did so, the doorbell rang loudly and insistently. When she answered it, it was to find PC White, one of the local constables, on the doorstep, his helmet tucked under his arm, and the station Riley was parked on the drive.

'I'm sorry to disturb you, milady,' he said deferentially. 'But I'm afraid your evacuee boy is in a spot of bother.'

'So I gather,' Frances said stiffly. 'I've got his young lady here, very upset, I may add. Do you want to speak to her?'

'Not just now.' PC White fiddled with his helmet, tucking it more securely under his arm. 'It's you I've come for. Sergeant Meadows needs to interview the lad, take a statement, and we can't do that without a responsible adult. He's too young.'

Frances's heart sank. This was looking more serious by the minute. Any hope she might have had of getting to bed was fast receding.

'Very well, Constable,' she said. 'Let me get a coat and I'll come with you. But can we take the girl too? She's also very young, and is living with the Wiltons at Fosse Farm. We can't allow her to walk all the way there at this time of night.'

'I can take her as far as the town centre, but we're very busy with all this going on.' PC White didn't seem too pleased at the prospect.

'You'll take her out to the farm or answer to me.' Frances was at her most authoritative. 'Alice!' she called. 'Hurry up now, and the policeman will take you home.'

A tearful Alice emerged from the drawing room, wiping her face with a grubby handkerchief, and Frances ushered her out. PC White opened the rear door of the Riley and they climbed inside.

'I 'spect we'll be wanting to talk to you tomorrow, young lady,' he said, very official now that he'd overcome the first hurdle – getting Lady Hastings to come to the police station. When he'd been instructed to fetch her, he'd been somewhat overawed, and had entertained a horrible vision of having to drag her out of bed at this ungodly hour.

He started the car and drove towards Hillsbridge without saying another word.

It was almost one o'clock before a furious Frances drove Billy home. He would have spent the night in the cells had she not promised that she would ensure he was back to appear before the magistrates in the morning. Since she was almost royalty in Hillsbridge, her word was good enough for Sergeant Meadows.

'What were you thinking of?' she demanded the minute the front door closed after them.

Billy hung his head. 'Sorry, miss.'

'Sorry's not good enough, I'm afraid. And you address me as milady. I'm not your school teacher.'

'Yes, milady,' he muttered.

'I'm ashamed of you, Billy. And disappointed. Just go to bed now. But rest assured I shall have a great deal more to say in the morning.'

Still looking dejected, Billy headed off up the stairs. Frances went around turning off all the lights, then shot the bolt on the front door and followed him.

She'd hoped James would be asleep; she really didn't feel like talking tonight. But when he heard the bedroom door open, he raised himself up on the pillows. 'What's going on, Frances?'

'It's Billy, of course,' she snapped. 'The girl he's been seeing turned up at the door, and then PC White, wanting me to go with him to the station to be his responsible adult.'

'I thought I heard voices.' James sounded drowsy. 'What's he done?'

'You'd know if you'd bothered to come down and find out,' Frances said caustically. 'He's in trouble. I've got to go to court with him tomorrow. Or you could.'

'We'll see. Are you going to tell me what's happened?'

Thinking that 'we'll see' meant the court appearance would be left to her annoyed Frances still further. 'He's been charged with assault,' she said shortly. 'Alice – his girl – maintains he wasn't to blame, but all the witnesses have said he was the one that started the fight. Accused another lad of saying unpleasant things to Alice, and just went for him. Which I'm afraid I believe. He has an uncontrollable temper, James. Among other things. I wish I'd never set eyes on him, and certainly not offered to take him in.'

'You don't mean that, Frances,' James said, settling himself back on the pillows. 'You know you love a challenge, and I'm very proud of you.'

With that he turned over and was soon breathing deeply and evenly.

Tired as she was, however, it was a long time before Frances was able to fall asleep. Her world, it seemed, was turning upside down. She had heard nothing from Anne since she'd left in a huff, she was worried about Philip, the fund to raise money for a Spitfire had stalled, and now there was all this trouble with Billy. She almost hoped he'd be sent to an industrial school for young offenders and she could go back to concentrating on her WVS and ways of reaching their target for the Spitfire. But James was right. She didn't like failing, and she wasn't ready to give up on Billy yet.

Anne had become a familiar figure in the nearby village and was now tasked with almost all the communications between the members of Paul's network of resistance fighters, the maquisards, who had already carried out some acts of sabotage, such as blocking the main rail line in the occupied sector with slabs of concrete that they'd obtained from a building site and transported at considerable risk to themselves by forklift truck.

Anne knew her job was fraught with danger too, especially when she had to cross the border into the German occupied zone. But she'd discovered a few places out of sight of the manned crossings of the demarcation line, along with a reserve of courage and determination she'd never known was there during the sheltered years of her previous life. She was proud that she was doing her bit to help frustrate the enemy.

As she'd hoped, she and Elise, Paul's wife, had become close, and she'd come to accept that his parents, though clearly not entirely happy about him running his operation from their home, were prepared to go along with it in the hope that he and his band could make a difference. As for the children, they were a constant delight, and she loved spending time with them when she wasn't doing duty as a courier.

There was just one person she couldn't bring herself to like at all, or even trust, and that was the baron's sister, Blanche, who also lived at the chateau.

When Anne had first arrived, Blanche had been away visiting her son, who lived in Bordeaux, which was under German occupation. But now she had come home, complaining that she could no longer stand being under the same roof as her daughter-in-law. Exactly what they had fallen out about she didn't say, only sniffing and huffing about Marie's perceived faults, which were apparently endless.

'She's a bitter woman,' Elise had told Anne. 'Louis is her only child, and when he was just two years old her husband, Gerard, was killed in a tragic accident. Blanche moved back here to her family home, bringing Louis with her, of course. At the time Guillaume and Nancy were childless – it just hadn't happened for them – and Blanche entertained some notion that one day Louis would inherit the estate and the title. But then unexpectedly Nancy fell pregnant, and gave birth to Paul. With her hopes crushed, Blanche came to feel the world was against her. She'd lost her husband, and the woman she'd believed to be barren had borne a son who was first in line to become the next baron.

'To her disgust, Louis fell for a girl she didn't consider good enough for him, and when they married and relocated to Bordeaux she was devastated. Not only had he married beneath himself, but he'd abandoned the mother whose whole world revolved around him.' Elise shook her head despairingly. 'She's never forgiven Marie – or Paul, for that matter – and she can't move on.'

'I see.' Anne was thinking about Frances's determination that she herself should marry well, and decided that English and French aristocracy were not so different.

But there was something else that concerned her. Blanche was a wholehearted supporter of Pétain and his Vichy government, and believed that the so-called Free Zone should fall into line and collaborate. After listening to one of her long tirades over dinner, Anne had become worried for Paul. If Blanche found out what he was doing, it was possible she might denounce him to the Gestapo.

She worried too that Blanche was suspicious of her. Sometimes she caught the woman eyeing her narrowly, and she didn't like the comments she made from time to time. 'What made you feel you needed a nanny now the children are no longer babies?' she'd asked Elise. And to Anne herself: 'Should you have been out all morning on your bicycle? Didn't your charges need you?'

When she'd mentioned her concern to Paul, however, he hadn't seemed to be worried. 'She'd never betray her own family,' he had said. 'She's always been the same – anything to be disagreeable. She's all talk, nothing more.'

Anne very much wanted to believe him, but she saw Blanche as a dark, ever-present cloud all the same. And one day towards the end of August, when the whole family were at dinner, Blanche dropped her bombshell.

'I happened to meet Captain Klein this morning.'

Klein was second in command to Colonel Schultz, who was in charge of the occupied sector here.

Nancy froze, a forkful of fish midway between her plate and her mouth. 'Good heavens, Blanche! How on earth . . .?'

'Didn't you know?' Blanche said archly. 'He often slips across the border to enjoy a cup of good coffee at Pierre Manet's café. I was there with Minette du Bois. I asked him about the possibility of crossing into the occupied region to enable me to visit friends. He was very pleasant, very helpful.'

'So he agreed?' Guillaume asked, sceptically.

'Not exactly. He said it wasn't his place to authorise crossings; I'd have to go through the official channels. But he was most apologetic, and said he would put a word in for me with the colonel.'

Paul snorted. 'And you believe him?'

'Why shouldn't I? The Germans aren't all monsters. They are human beings too, remember.' Blanche turned to Guillaume. 'I think it would be politic to invite him and the colonel to dinner one evening. It would be good to have them on our side, wouldn't it? I'm sure we could expect a reciprocal gesture here and there. What do you say, Guillaume?'

'That this isn't something we should do without a lot of thought,' the baron said firmly.

'But you must see the sense of it!' Blanche persisted. 'And this is my home as much as it is yours,' she added pointedly.

'It's a bad idea, Tante. I don't want to share the dinner table with the enemy.' Paul spoke decisively, and Anne saw Elise give him a warning look accompanied by a small shake of her head. *Don't antagonise her*, that look said. Too late.

'You don't yet hold the title, Paul. It's no more for you to make decisions about who we entertain than it was for Captain Klein to grant me permission to cross the border,' Blanche said waspishly.

The conversation ended there, but Anne no longer had any appetite for the river trout she had been so enjoying. This woman was dangerous, she was sure. She only wished Paul could see it.

It was harvest time on the farm, and Freda spent long days out in the fields working alongside Ted, George Griffin and a few men from the village to get the hay cut, baled and either into the barn or built into a rick. She really enjoyed it, especially when the big carthorse snuffled into her hand as she led him along the lane at the end of the day. She was berry brown now, so unlike the pale creature she'd grown used to seeing in the mirror since she had lived in London; her hair was so long the only way of keeping it tidy was to fasten it up into a ponytail, and she sometimes wondered what it would be like to wear a skirt or dress again – and high heels!

But she had also had time to think, and she had remembered several more things she wished she had brought from London when Ted had taken her there, things she would hate to lose should the house be bombed. Photographs mostly, snapped on a little Brownie box camera and developed at the chemist's shop. And a set of chairbacks she'd been embroidering and never got around to finishing. She couldn't expect Ted to take her again, but she could go by train when she got a few days off, as she was sure to when the harvest was all safely in.

When she told Ted of her plans, he wasn't at all happy. 'I don't think you should go, Freda,' he said. 'There's a rumour that now France and Belgium have thrown in the towel, Hitler is stepping up preparations for aid raids.'

'All the more reason why I should go straight away,' Freda argued. 'And anyway, as you say, it's just a rumour.'

'A bit more than that, I'm afraid. I happened to run into Matt Bull, the *Chronicle* reporter, when I was in town the other day. He said the intelligence agencies had got wind of it, but they've put a blanket ban on all news outlets, forbidding them to publish any mention of it.'

'Oh, you know how these things snowball. I'm sure I'll be all right.' Freda wasn't going to be talked out of her plan.

And Ted was forced to admit defeat – for the moment at least.

Frances had not been best pleased when she arrived with Billy at the magistrates' court the morning after the 'affray', as Sergeant Meadows called it, to be told that his case could not be heard that day as no specialist juvenile JP could be there. He would have to go to Bath for his hearing, and as yet no date had been fixed.

She had prevailed upon the sergeant to withdraw the charge, promising that she would keep Billy on a tight leash, and eventually he had agreed, subject to his inspector's approval. He'd given Billy a severe lecture, and warned him that if there was a next time, he'd face the full force of the law and would undoubtedly be sent to an industrial school or reformatory. 'You won't like it much there,' he'd finished. 'It won't be a cushy number like what you've got with her ladyship.'

Frances had bristled. 'For the foreseeable future I shall be ensuring his life with us is far from "cushy",' she said tartly. 'Yes, he has a room of his own, a comfortable bed and good food. But I assure you his liberty will be restricted just as it would be in a reformatory school until I can trust him to behave in a responsible manner.'

But it wouldn't be easy, she admitted to herself. Yes, she could take him to school and collect him every day, but she wouldn't put it past him to slip out if the fancy took him. And keeping him in every night would make her as much a prisoner as he was.

'But I won't be able to see Alice!' he'd objected when she'd told him he would be gated for the next two weeks, and longer if he didn't behave himself.

'She can visit you here,' Frances had said, quashing all his arguments. 'Though why any girl would want your company I can't imagine.'

Billy did seem chastened by the whole unhappy business. Not so much being arrested and threatened with the juvenile court – he'd had plenty of run-ins with the law in London, Frances guessed. But being unable to meet his girl seemed to have affected him deeply. Good as her word, she allowed Alice to come to the house, and kept a watchful eye when they went for walks in the grounds.

She'd found his Achilles heel, she thought. And hoped

desperately that there would be no more trouble when she allowed him more freedom.

It seemed that the tip-off Ted's newspaper reporter had given him had been rooted in the truth. On 13 August, the Luftwaffe began another wave of attacks on airfields in Kent, Sussex, Hampshire and Essex. The RAF Spitfires and Hurricanes managed to send them packing, thanks to acquired intelligence, and a Dornier was shot down over the Thames estuary. In the next few days there were more massive attacks, but the German intelligence was somewhat lacking and only three of the airfields targeted were fighter bases.

Frances was understandably fearful for Philip, who could be flying up to four sorties a day, and she became obsessed with listening to all the wireless news broadcasts, leaving Billy more or less to his own devices. She was also worried about Anne. She had been posted to an RAF base in Lincolnshire, Frances had been told, but she hadn't received a reply to any of the letters she'd sent to her there.

The Battle of Britain, as it came to be known, was still continuing ferociously as the month drew to a close, and the Vauxhall factory at Luton was targeted, bringing the attacks perilously close to London. Once again Ted tried to talk Freda out of going to Bermondsey, but her mind was made up.

'I'll take you then,' he offered.

'You'll do no such thing. You'll be far too busy here,' Freda said firmly, and Ted realised he was fighting a losing battle.

Chapter Twenty-Eight

When Rosie began a week of night shifts on 3 September, she could scarcely believe that it was the first anniversary of the outbreak of war. Just a year? It felt to her as though it had been going on for ever. And now it seemed things were intensifying. A few bombs had been dropped on Bath the previous night, in Twerton High Street and on the football ground, and she wondered if Clarke had been right when he'd predicted that the spy plane they'd seen shot down might have been scoping out the Admiralty Headquarters. She still had nightmares about what had happened, and couldn't forget the young rear gunner she and Clarke had been unable to save. His boyish face still haunted her, and she dreaded encountering something similar in the course of her duties. But she couldn't let that stop her doing what she had signed up for. And she wouldn't; she was as determined about that as she was not to contact Clarke. She missed him dreadfully, but it would be wrong of her to lead him on when she was in love with Julian.

Her heart still raced whenever her path crossed with Julian's at St Mark's. He never now mentioned a possible meeting, but her stomach still turned somersaults at his occasional suggestive remark or if he looked at her in that meaningful way. Then one day she saw a very glamorous young woman in the passenger seat of his car, which was parked outside the hospital while he visited one of his patients. She'd heard rumours he was seeing someone, and the hurt she'd felt, though not as sharp as it had once been, was still an ache she couldn't ignore. It had proved to her that however hopeless it might be, she was far from over him. No, she had no right to harbour regrets about setting Clarke free. He didn't deserve to be second best.

To her relief, her night shift passed without incident. The air raid siren did sound once, its mournful wail echoing around the hills that surrounded the city, but not long afterwards it was followed by the all-clear, and she breathed again.

Not so the following night. Molly was on a rest day, and tonight Rosie was partnered with Paddy, who had returned to work as an ambulance attendant when he was deemed fit enough.

It was just after midnight, and she was in the rest room at Ambulance HQ when the ear-splitting alarm sounded. She'd made herself an extra strong coffee because she was beginning to feel drowsy, but a few minutes later, when the engines of a heavy bomber shook the ground beneath her feet, she was instantly wide awake. Dear God, this really was an air raid.

She dumped her half-drunk cup of coffee on the floor beside her chair and hurried outside. Paddy was already there, looking down over the darkened city, and she grabbed his arm as a bomb whistled through the air and the sound of an explosion and a flash quickly followed.

'Something's been hit!' she gasped as another bomb fell, and another, close to the river.

'We'd better get down there,' Paddy said. 'There's houses on the Locksbrook side of the river. Got your gas mask, love?'

Rosie nodded. It went everywhere with her. As she went back to collect her keys, the telephone began to ring, its shrill tone making her jump, and she picked it up, surprised the call should have come through so quickly.

'Ambulance Headquarters. How can we help you?' Rosie was surprised at how level her voice sounded when she was shaking so.

The voice at the other end of the line was cultured, crisp and calm.

'This is Mrs Forbes-Jenkins of the Linleys. From what I have just seen, I think houses in Audley Grove and Audley Park Road may have been bombed. Whether there have been casualties I couldn't say, but perhaps you could attend the scene to ascertain whether medical attention is needed.'

The Linleys. That explained it. The people who lived there were mostly well-to-do and would certainly have telephone lines in their homes.

'Audley Park Road,' Rosie repeated. 'We're on our way.'

As they drove through town, yet more bombs fell, this time on the south side of the river.

'That's pretty close to St Michael's, by the looks of it,' Paddy said. 'Didn't sound like it hit a building, though. More of a thud. The churchyard, maybe?'

Rosie didn't reply. She was driving as fast as she dared, and it required all her concentration. But she did have a fleeting thought – if the bomb had landed in the churchyard and opened up a crater where bodies were buried, some very grisly scenes would greet whoever went to investigate. Still, long-dead remains were vastly preferable to what she and Paddy might find in Audley Park Road.

As she turned into the street, it was clear that several houses had been hit. A fire engine and a police car were already in attendance, and people clad in their nightclothes were milling about. But at least the bomber seemed to have left the area. Perhaps the bomb they'd seen fall on the other side of the river was the last of the plane's load, dumped on its way home.

Rosie and Paddy climbed out of the ambulance and hurried towards the bomb sites. The fire chief and two policemen were in the garden of the house that seemed to have suffered the worst damage. The front half of the roof and the upper storey had collapsed into a heap of stone, tiles and rubble, and several burly firemen were working on it with axes and their bare hands. Someone must be trapped inside, Rosie realised, and while Paddy continued on down the road to identify anyone in need of medical attention, she crossed the small patch of lawn. As she drew closer, a woman broke free from the policeman who was restraining her and ran to where the firemen were working, hitting out at them blindly and crying hysterically.

'Hurry, please! My baby's in there!'

Rosie's heart missed a beat. The policeman had reached the poor woman and was trying without much success to drag her away, and the urgency of the situation was emphasised by the fire chief, who was yelling instructions to his men. But for the moment, Rosie's first concern was for the distraught mother.

'Let me,' she said to the policeman, and put an arm around the woman's shaking shoulders. 'It's all right, my love. Just take a few deep breaths. I know you're terribly worried, but this won't help anyone. You have to let the firemen do their job.'

Still the woman struggled, with a strength born of desperation. 'But my baby's in there. I must get him!'

At that moment another police car raced into the road. With a screech of brakes it pulled up behind the ambulance and a man leapt out of the passenger seat and ran towards them. The baby's father, Rosie guessed, and from the stained overalls he was wearing she gathered he must have been at work on a night shift when the police had arrived to tell him what had happened and rush him to the scene.

'Maurice!' The woman broke away and threw herself into his arms, sobbing.

With one problem taken care of, Rosie turned her attention to the firemen, who were attempting to clear a way through the mound of debris that had once been the front of the house. But their progress was painfully slow. Though they were all big men, it would need an army to make a path wide enough for any of them to get through, especially since bricks and plaster were still falling intermittently. So near and yet so far. But as one of them moved the searchlight they were using slightly, Rosie could see the path they were opening up more clearly, and the solution to the problem came to her in a flash. She was half the size of any of the men.

She turned to the fire chief. 'I'm sure I could squeeze through there.'

The chief shook his head decisively. 'I can't let you do that, miss. The whole lot could come down on top of you.'

'But I'm a nurse. I can at least tend to him if he needs medical attention.'

'Maybe. But my answer's still no. It's unsafe. This is a job for my men.'

Rosie's dander was up suddenly. A baby was behind that pile of bricks, timber and rubble. A baby who could be injured and would almost certainly be distressed.

Before the fire chief could stop her, she had darted to the gap they were desperately trying to widen.

'Let me through. I'm small enough to get in.'

'Garret! Hopkins! No!' The chief was racing after her, and as the men turned, surprised, to look at him, Rosie took her chance. She dropped to her hands and knees and began to wriggle into the hole. Shards of glass cut her hands, the rubble bruised her knees, and she could scarcely breathe; dust was clogging her nose and throat. But she carried on, dislodging some of the bricks as she went.

Though it could have been only a few brief minutes, to Rosie it seemed like a lifetime before she emerged and scrambled to her feet, coughing and spluttering, in what appeared to be the remains of a sitting room. A sofa strewn with dust and plaster was angled against a far corner, an overturned table to her right, a wireless lying beside it, an easy chair just visible beneath the rubble, but as far as she could see, no baby. If only they'd told her where to find him! But they hadn't, and she hadn't waited to find out. She'd just have to search for him. Just as long as he wasn't beneath the fallen masonry . . .

Think, she commanded herself, and somehow managed to still the panic that was threatening. *The air raid siren went off some minutes before the bombs fell. If there were no shelters nearby and you were alone with a baby when the warning came, where would you put him to keep him as safe as possible?*

The answer came to her in a flash. Under the stairs. But why hadn't the woman stayed with him? She must have been in the garden when the house was hit; she'd never have managed to get out otherwise. But this was no time for wondering. She had to find the baby.

She picked her way across the debris to a door that was hanging off its hinges and found herself in a passageway. One end was completely blocked, but at the other she could see the banister rising into a section of wall that looked relatively untouched as far as she could see. As she stepped across to the far side of the passage, she caught her toe on a fallen brick and almost fell, stumbling blindly into what felt like wood panelling. She inched along first one way, then the other, but couldn't find a cupboard door.

And then she heard it – a baby's cry, coming from behind her. She felt her way back along the panelling towards the pitiful wail. Rubble was barring her way, but when she stood on tiptoe, feeling above her head, there it was, a tiny gap that must be the door fitting. She began grabbing lumps of stone and plaster from the heap that was blocking the door, throwing them back along the passage until she found a handle. She kicked the last of the rubble aside and dragged the door open. The crying had quietened now to soft heart-rending snuffles, and inside the cupboard it was pitch dark. Rosie dropped to her hands and knees, crawling towards the sound, until her searching fingers encountered what felt like a wicker basket. She stopped, sliding her hands inside and touching something soft – a blanket. She got hold of the basket and wriggled backwards, pulling it with her until she reached the door.

By what light filtered through from the sitting room, she could see the baby, his little head just visible above the blanket. Her first instinct was to lift him out into her arms, but that wouldn't be the right thing to do. She needed him to be in the basket if she was to take him out by the route she had got in. She could then check him over before handing him to his mother. But it wasn't a carrycot or even a cradle. It was an ordinary boat-shaped shopping basket, presumably the nearest thing the mother had been able to find when the alarm had sounded. Realising his little lungs shouldn't be exposed to the dust and debris in the tunnel, Rosie took off her jacket and covered him with it.

As she pushed the basket in front of her into the tunnel, she heard the ominous rumble of falling masonry. She remembered the fire chief's warning – that the whole lot could come down at any time – and questioned her decision to get the baby out from his safe space. Her heart was beating so hard she scarcely noticed her own discomfort. She had to get him out as fast as she could. If the roof came down on him now, it would be her fault. In desperation, she pressed on.

And then, suddenly, the beam of a powerful torch cut through the dust-filled darkness, and a voice called to her.

'OK, I've got him.' The basket was wrenched away from her and she scrambled as fast as she could after it. Big hands grasped her shoulders; one of the firemen was lying flat on his stomach, reaching in as far as he could and pulling her towards blessed fresh air.

It was a long moment before Rosie could catch her rasping breath and ask anxiously, 'Is he all right?'

'I reckon so.' Paddy was there, lifting the baby out of the basket, and Rosie felt relief flooding through her veins.

She could relax now. The baby would be safe in Paddy's hands. She tried to get up, but the world was swirling around her, fading. Rosie had never in her life fainted before and she was determined not to faint now. But this time determination alone was not enough. She sank slowly, almost gracefully, to the ground, her back against the fallen masonry.

To her surprise, her last conscious thought was a longing not for Julian, but for Clarke.

Maud had managed to get hold of some suet and dried fruit to make Christmas puddings – she liked to make them in good time and was late this year. But in her haste to get them in the copper, she had made a dreadful mess on the kitchen floor, and Winnie was doing her best to clear up the spillages of black treacle and clumps of moist mixture when she was called to the telephone. Her ladyship had kindly allowed her the use of the Bramley Court line to receive messages from the recuperation home, so she knew it must be them who were calling, and her immediate reaction was anxiety. Had Don taken a turn for the worse?

To her amazement, however, quite the opposite was the case. He had been deemed well enough to come home, and he would be brought by ambulance at the weekend! When the call ended, she danced a jig around the room, but then, as the first euphoria began to wear off, she found herself wrestling with all kinds of unsettling questions that she'd neglected to ask.

Would he be fit enough to be left, or would she need to ask Lady Hastings for yet more time off? Where would he sleep? He certainly wouldn't be able to climb up into the attic room. Would he even be able to climb one flight of stairs if she let him have her bed, or asked Rosie to swap bedrooms so that he could have his old room back? What if they were planning to deliver a hospital bed? There wouldn't be room anywhere but the living room for one of those great cumbersome things, and even so the furniture there would all have to be moved. And might he be on a special diet? That would mean getting in things she didn't have in the pantry.

Flustered, she went in search of Lady Hastings, anxious to pass on her news straight away and hoping she might have some suggestions as to the best way to prepare for Don's arrival.

'You must be delighted!' her ladyship said when Winnie told her. 'They wouldn't let him come home unless he was well on the road to recovery. And you must take all the time you need to prepare for his arrival.'

'To be honest, that's what's worrying me,' Winnie admitted. 'I want everything to be right for him, and I don't know where to start.'

'Talk it over with Rosie,' Lady Hastings advised. 'She's medically trained. She'll know what to do.'

'That's true.' A wave of relief washed over Winnie, swiftly

followed by another thought. 'She's at home now. Perhaps . . .' She broke off, worried that she was taking advantage, but before she could even finish the request, her ladyship had stopped her with a raised hand and a smile.

'Go, Mrs Mitchell.'

'Oh, milady, that's so kind! But I was in the middle of washing the kitchen floor – it's in an awful mess,' Winnie protested.

'Cook is perfectly capable of cleaning up after herself,' her ladyship said tartly. She didn't have much time for Maud these days, not since the cook had backed out of any involvement with the WVS. 'Just go. Rosie will be very happy to hear the news, I'm sure, and she will give you all the help you need to prepare.'

'Thank you so much, milady!' And without even bothering to take off her apron, Winnie headed for home.

Rosie was at the kitchen sink, elbow-deep in soap suds, swilling out her uniform shirt, filthy from the events of the previous night. She hadn't told her mother anything of what had happened, beyond saying there had been 'a bit of an air raid'; didn't want to talk about it, and didn't want Winnie to worry either, so she'd taken the opportunity to clean up her uniform while Winnie was out of the way.

Unsurprisingly, she was still very shaky, and couldn't stop reliving the claustrophobic fear she'd felt as she had crawled through the rubble to reach the baby, and hearing the creaks that might mean it all came crashing down on them as she returned with him by the same route. She'd been praised for going above and beyond the call of duty, told she was very brave, but she didn't feel brave. If anything, she was ashamed that she'd fainted. The superintendent had told her she should take a few days off, but she was too proud for that. She was fine, she'd insisted. But she wasn't fine. Her throat was still sore from inhaling so much dust, the hot water was stinging her raw and bleeding hands, and worst of all, her nerves were jangling and her head was all over the place remembering how much she'd longed for Clarke. He was her rock, she supposed, a safe place she no longer had access to, and that made her unbearably sad.

So lost in thought was she that she didn't see Winnie hurrying up the path, and when she came bursting in, Rosie jumped as if she'd been shot.

'Mum! Whatever . . .?'

'Your brother's coming home! On Saturday! Don's coming home!'

'That's amazing!' Rosie exclaimed, but although it was, and she was delighted, it was as if all her emotions were blunted somehow. As if she'd retreated into a protective shell.

'It certainly is! But there's so much to think about to get ready for him . . .'

Still feeling oddly removed, Rosie dried her hands, set the kettle to boil, and sat down with her mother, listening to the litany of things that needed to be sorted out and offering advice where she could. But when Winnie got around to her concerns about the sleeping arrangements, she was alert enough to make a quick decision.

'He can have his old room, Mum. I can stay at the ambulance station. There are rest rooms, and it will be easier too. It looks as if we're going to be very busy, and it will save me travelling in and out of Bath every day.'

'I thought you'd be here to help me out,' Winnie protested anxiously.

'Don't worry, I've got today off,' Rosie said, deciding to take up the superintendent's offer of some recovery time. 'We'll make a start right away.'

'You're a good girl, Rosie,' Winnie said. 'I wouldn't ask if your father was still here, but . . .'

'I know.' Remembering the special relationship her mother and father had shared brought a lump to her throat. But hopefully once Don was here, Winnie would revert to her usual cheery self. There was a special relationship between mothers and sons too.

'Right, what's first?' she asked. Busying herself with the preparations would help her forget last night's trauma as well as the memory of her longing not for Julian, but for Clarke.

Anne and the Clermont family were enjoying a light lunch when Blanche made her shock announcement.

'Oh, Guillaume, I happened to see Captain Klein this morning, and Colonel Schultz too. So I took the opportunity of extending your kind invitation for them to dine with us.'

The stunned silence that followed was broken by Guillaume's fork clattering onto his plate. 'You've done *what*?'

'Invited the commandant and his second in command to dinner. When we discussed it, you were in agreement,' Blanche said in a tone she might have used to one of the children.

An angry flush had risen in Guillaume's cheeks. 'I said no such thing! I said I'd think about it.'

Blanche shrugged. 'Then I must have misunderstood you. Anyway, it's too late now. It's all arranged, and the colonel would be most offended if the invitation were withdrawn.'

Guillaume was spluttering furiously now, and Nancy, who had become very frail lately, laid a hand on his arm.

'*Chéri*, don't. You'll give yourself a stroke. You know what the doctor told you. If Blanche has invited the Germans, we will have to entertain them. We have no choice.'

'I really don't understand why you are objecting, Guillaume,' Blanche said guilelessly.

'Because I don't want them in my house. And you had no business taking it upon yourself to invite them.'

'But surely you can see it can only be advantageous to us to treat them as friends,' Blanche argued.

'Friends!'

'Better than enemies, surely? They wield all the power now, Guillaume.'

'She's right,' Elise said. 'And so is Nancy. We have no choice. You know the saying? Keep your friends close and your enemies closer. It won't be so bad. I'm sure a bottle of your best cognac will help to oil the wheels.'

Anne was horrified. Paul was away for a few days meeting with some of his group to discuss the disruption of lines of communication the Germans were using. She would have to face this without him. But what possible reason could Blanche have for flouting her brother's wishes? Simply jealousy and bitterness, as Elise had suggested? Or was she collaborating with the enemy?

'*Mam'selle?*' Anne was suddenly aware that Blanche was speaking to her. She looked up, hoping that her dismay was not written all over her face,

'*Je suis désolée.* I didn't quite catch that.'

'*Vous êtes pardonné.*' A sickly-sweet smile only emphasised the thinness of Blanche's lips. 'I said I am sure the Germans will be delighted to dine in the company of a pretty young lady. They are known as womanisers, I hear.'

'If so, I can assure you they are going to be disappointed,' Anne said shortly, hoping fervently that Blanche would go no further than mischief-making.

* * *

For once in his life, Julian's cocky self-confidence in his ability to make everything turn out the way he wanted it had deserted him. Instead of sleeping soundly after his late-night tipple of Glenfiddich, he tossed and turned, drenched in cold sweat, as he imagined the possible consequences of a disastrous evening surgery. If this got out, it would ruin his reputation; worse, he could find himself struck off the register.

Why the hell had Frances chosen this evening of all evenings to visit him? He hadn't seen much of her in the six months since her plans for him and Anne had gone awry, and he suspected she held him responsible for their short-lived engagement as well as for Anne going off to join the WAAF. He'd disappointed her, and she'd lost interest in him as a possible match for her daughter.

Anyone other than Julian would no doubt be feeling they had only themselves to blame for what had happened. Not he. The girl had been leading him on, as so many young women did.

Gwenda Hollis had come to see him with a sore throat and what she described as a bad chest. It wasn't the first time she'd been to his surgery with some minor complaint, and he suspected she was inventing excuses to see him. This evening had been no different. She had managed to be the last patient in the waiting room, and had come into his consulting room wearing her usual coy expression. In the past he hadn't risen to the bait. Gwenda came from one of the most deprived areas in Bath; not at all the class of girl he normally bothered with. But this time he was feeling a little jaded – the young lady he was supposed to be taking out to dinner tonight had telephoned him to cancel their date – and for the first time, Julian acknowledged that Gwenda really was a very pretty girl. Younger than he was used to, but with long blonde hair framing a heart-shaped face, brown eyes and curves in all the right places.

'How can I help you?' he asked pleasantly, swivelling his chair round and indicating that she should sit facing him.

As she described her symptoms, her skirt rode up above her knees, exposing a pair of shapely legs, not lost on Julian.

'You have quite a history of these infections,' he said. 'I think it's time I gave you a thorough examination to try to determine the cause of the trouble. There's a gown on the examination table. Could you get undressed and slip it on? Don't worry, I'll give you some privacy while you do.'

He followed her to the table and, with an encouraging smile, pulled the floral curtain around it. After a minute or so he asked, 'Ready?' and when she said she was, he pulled the curtain aside again and approached her, his stethoscope hanging around his neck.

'First I'll listen to your chest.' He ran the stethoscope from her neck to her midriff, silently admiring the pertness of her breasts beneath the thin cotton robe and then laying his hand on the left one, supposedly to listen to her heartbeat. 'Could you turn over onto your tummy?' he asked, and as she did so, the gown fell open, revealing firm, full buttocks. Most of his patients were anxious to keep a modicum of underwear on while being examined, but Gwenda had removed her panties, and Julian's excitement grew as he listened to her lungs, which sounded exactly as they should. Just as he'd thought. There was no sign of any congestion.

'OK.' He allowed a little consternation to creep into his voice. 'Could you turn over again? I think I need to look into this a little more closely. It would appear to be somewhat complex.'

She did as he asked, looking up at him wide-eyed. 'Is it serious?'

'I hope not,' he said, reassuring now. 'It's quite common for the fair sex to suffer from gynaecological problems, which can manifest themselves in many ways. If you would just lie back . . .

Let's have you flat.' He ran his fingers up her leg, stroking her firm thigh. 'Now, can you bend your knees and spread your legs a little? I need to do a little internal examination, but it won't hurt, I promise. Good . . . good . . .'

Now confident that Gwenda could see nothing but his head and torso, he unbuttoned his trousers while his fingers crept higher and higher, closer and closer to her hidden places, and found the dampness inside.

It was at that moment that everything had gone horribly wrong. Gwenda squealed so loudly it might as well have been a scream and pushed herself up onto her elbows. 'What are you doing?' she shrieked. 'You said it wouldn't hurt!'

Dear God, she was a virgin! Julian stepped away, hastily fumbling with his trousers. But not fast enough. The consulting room door, which Gwenda had failed to close properly after her, swung open to reveal Lady Hastings, her concerned expression turning to shock and outrage as she took in the scene.

'Julian!' Never had she sounded more forbidding.

'Frances,' he said weakly. 'I can explain . . .'

'You certainly will!' She turned to the examination table, where the frightened girl cowered, arms wrapped around herself. 'And you – it's Gwenda Hollis, isn't it? Get yourself dressed! Have you no shame?'

'But . . .' Gwenda was close to tears, hugging herself ever more tightly. 'I 'aven't done anything wrong! It was him . . .'

'Didn't you hear me? Put your clothes on.' Lady Hastings bundled up the garments Gwenda had left on a chair and threw them at her, then jerked the curtain across so that the girl was hidden from sight. When she emerged, she skittered fearfully past, not even stopping to put on her shoes but carrying them in a shaking hand, and ran out of the consulting room. Frances shut the door after her.

'Well, Julian?'

'It's not what you think, Frances. I was examining the girl for some gynaecological ailment and she became frightened . . .'

'Do you take me for a fool? I know a sexual assault when I see it. And that girl is no more than fifteen years old, if I'm not much mistaken. What in heaven's name were you thinking?'

'Frances, you've got it all wrong . . .' Julian protested weakly.

'And to think I hoped you and Anne would marry! Rest assured, Julian, I shall be reporting you to the Medical Practitioners' Standards Committee.' She turned towards the door. 'I promise you, you haven't heard the last of this.'

Now, lying awake, her words echoed and re-echoed in Julian's ears. If she did report him, he'd deny it, of course. But Frances could be ruthless, he already knew that. And unless she thought better of it when the shock of what she'd seen wore off, he was finished.

He groaned in despair, buried his head in his sweat-drenched pillow and sobbed like a baby.

Freda had left for London early on Saturday. Ted had reluctantly taken her to Bath Spa station, and his mother had provided her with egg sandwiches, a home-made Cornish pasty, a wedge of slab cake and a flask of tea. 'I've had a good breakfast and I'll be back tonight!' Freda had said, laughing. 'You feed me up as if I'm one of the cockerels you're fattening for Christmas!'

'You never know what's going to happen these days,' Mrs Holland had retorted. 'Best to be prepared.'

Not because she was hungry, but because she couldn't resist it, Freda had broken a corner off the slice of fruit cake and eaten it on the train, washing it down with a mug of tea.

By midday she was at Paddington and taking the Underground to the Elephant and Castle. As she walked down the Old

Kent Road, she was overcome with nostalgia, and the memories brought a lump to her throat. Yes, she was very happy on the farm, but a part of her belonged here in Bermondsey. She wondered whether she would ever come back again, and if she did, what she would find. Granny's house and all the old familiar landmarks gone? The pubs? The building where she had worked? The churches, the factories, the tannery?

Stop it, she told herself. *It might never happen.* But if it did, she was glad she had come back to her old stomping ground for what might be the last time.

It was the same when she unlocked the front door of Granny's house and stepped inside. A rush of emotion. But the house had been shut up for so long, an unpleasant musty smell greeted her, and the first thing she did was go from room to room sliding her hand carefully behind the blackout blinds to open the windows and remove the dead flies that lay on the white-painted windowsills.

She twisted a tap on the gas stove and was rewarded by a hiss, but when she ran the tap to fill the kettle, the first water to come out was brown and rusty. She left it running while she found the matches, lit the gas and got the tea caddy, teapot and a cup and saucer from the cupboard. She didn't have any milk, and cursed herself for not stopping to buy some, but perhaps she could use what was left in Mrs Holland's flask to lighten the tea a little – if the tap ever ran clear. Eventually it did – well, almost – and she decided that since she would be boiling the water anyway, she would risk it.

She turned on the wireless, and to her surprise that too was working. She'd thought it would need a session on the accumulator after such a long time. She twiddled the knobs before remembering there was only one station on air now – the Home Service. She and Rosie had liked listening to the Light

Programme for music and comedy, and sometimes the European music stations, but the government had closed all those down to prevent – as far as was possible – German propaganda being aired. She turned the wireless off again. The Home Service mostly broadcast news, and she was thoroughly fed up with the doom-laden tones and upper-class accents of the reporters.

When she'd eaten her sandwiches and another bit of slab cake, she went upstairs to her bedroom, taking the remains of her almost-black tea with her, and spent several hours choosing the things she most wanted and packing them into her rucksack.

It was late afternoon when she decided she really should be making her way back to Paddington. She hefted the rucksack – heavier now than she would have liked – and was making her way downstairs when the mournful wail of the air raid siren sounded. She froze. A raid! Oh, surely she couldn't be that unlucky! She waited a moment, listening for the all-clear, and when it didn't come, panic set in. What was she going to do? Did she have time to run down to the Elephant and Castle? Were there any shelters closer by? She didn't know. Oh, if only she and Rosie had erected the one the council had delivered to them just before the war started instead of leaving it leaning against the garden fence! They'd laughed about it – actually laughed! It wasn't a laughing matter now.

Briefly she considered whether she could squeeze into the tiny cupboard under the stairs, but the thought of being buried under tons of rubble should the house suffer a direct hit terrified her. The Underground would be the safest bet – if she could make it – and if the trains were still running, perhaps she could make it to Paddington after all. She took a flying leap down the last few stairs, grabbed her handbag from the kitchen and raced out, not even stopping to lock the door behind her.

She'd just made it to the Old Kent Road when she heard the deafening roar of powerful aircraft engines. It sounded as if they were flying up the Thames estuary, and a moment later the sun was blotted out as the formation came closer. Dozens of them! Heading, no doubt, for the docks.

Frantic now, Freda looked round for cover. The nearest pub was several hundred yards away and the German bombers were almost overhead now. The only shelter she could see nearby was a telephone box. She ran for it, wrenching the door open and recoiling at the stench of tobacco and urine that filled it. She covered her mouth and nose with a shaking hand and let the door close behind her. It wouldn't provide much protection, but at least she wouldn't be out in the open.

She slipped out of her rucksack harness and leaned back against the side of the kiosk. Her legs had turned to jelly, but by holding onto the shelf that housed the telephone directory, she managed to stay on her feet. Until the first explosion rent the air. And another. And another. Slowly she slid down until she was sitting on the filthy floor, curled into a ball with her arms covering her head. The explosions seemed to go on for ever, and with each one a shudder ran through her, yet in a strange way nothing seemed quite real any more. It was as if she was the central character in a horror film.

And then silence, except for the ringing in her ears and the echoes reverberating through the air. Had they gone? Was it safe to emerge and try to make it to the Elephant and Castle? Scarcely daring to breathe, Freda levered herself to her feet and pushed open the kiosk door. The smell that met her was almost as revolting as that of the telephone box. Like nothing she had ever smelled before. A potpourri of gunpowder and smoke, a huge cloud of which was forming over what she knew to be the docks, with tongues of flame leaping within it.

She reached for her rucksack, but just as she was about to make a dash for it, she heard more bomber engines approaching and dived back inside the kiosk. This time she managed to remain on her feet, but she was sobbing with shock and fear as the second wave of bombers dropped their loads. Minutes seemed like hours to Freda until the same eerie silence fell over Bermondsey, and a glow on the horizon denoted a huge fire raging somewhere near the river. Never in her life had she felt so alone, and she wished with all her heart that she had taken Ted's advice.

Ted. If she could only speak to him, it might calm her shattered nerves. He was bound to give her wise advice as to what she should do. She fumbled in her bag, found her purse and got out some change, only to find that, panicked as she was, she couldn't remember his telephone number. Stupid! Stupid! She knew it so well! She took a few deep breaths and tried to clear her mind. Suddenly it came back to her. She fed coins into the slot and dialled the number. And thank God, it was Ted who answered.

She depressed button A and heard the coins fall.

'Ted, it's me.' Her voice was shaky; she was crying again.

'Freda? Are you all right?'

'No, I'm not! There's an air raid and I don't know what to do.'

'Where are you?'

'In a phone box on the Old Kent Road. I was trying to get back to Paddington, and . . .' Her voice tailed away.

'Are you far from your house?'

'Not far.'

'Is the raid still going on?'

'It's stopped for a minute, but it did that before and then it started again.'

'Look.' Ted spoke slowly and calmly. 'If it's safe, get back to the house and under the kitchen table if there's nowhere better. Otherwise, stay where you are and I'll find you.'

'Ted, you can't . . . I'll try to get back to Paddington . . .'

'You'll stay where you are or go back to the house. I'm coming to fetch you.'

And the line went dead.

Chapter Twenty-Nine

When the ambulance bringing Don home had arrived at the cottage soon after midday, it was clear he was tired out from the journey, and Winnie was glad the ambulance driver and attendant were there to help him up the stairs to his old bedroom. Rosie was at work and would be staying at the hospital, and Winnie would never have been able to get him to bed unaided. But now, after a nap and a few hours' rest, he seemed to be recovering, and when she took him some toast, a rock cake and a cup of tea, he made short work of it.

'That's better, isn't it, son?' She was sitting beside the bed with her own tea and cake.

'Yeah. It's good to be home.' Don drained his cup.

'Good to have you here, I can tell you. Now, d'you want another cup of tea?'

'No, you're all right. I think I'll have another little nap.'

'Yes, you do that. It's what you need – that and some of my home cooking. I'm doing a roast tomorrow for dinner. Fred found me a nice bit of belly pork. I'm frightened to death it's going to get him into hot water, but he says it'll be all right. He's a lifesaver, is Fred.'

Don smiled, though his eyes were already half closed. 'It's Fred this and Fred that, isn't it, Mum?'

Colour rose in Winnie's cheeks. 'Oh, I don't know about that, son. He's just a friend, you know . . .'

But Don was already asleep.

He was right, though, Winnie thought. She didn't know what she'd do without Fred.

There had been a brief respite in the bombing in which Freda had managed to get back to Granny's house. She couldn't wait in the stinking telephone kiosk for the three hours or so that it would take Ted to reach her, and in any case she'd remembered that in her rush to leave she hadn't locked up, and if thieves or looters tried their luck there was nothing to stop them from getting in. But as darkness fell, it began again. Relentless waves of Luftwaffe bombers, guided by the light of the blazing buildings in the docks.

Now, however, as she sheltered beneath the sturdy dining table, Freda was fervently wishing she hadn't phoned Ted. She could easily have got to the safety of the Underground at the Elephant and Castle during that lull, and if the trains were still running, she could have been back in Bath by now and Ted wouldn't be risking his life coming to fetch her. If anything happened to him, she would never forgive herself. The thought of him being killed or badly injured was too awful to contemplate. And he might come all this way only to find a bomb had fallen on one of the roads on his route through the capital so that it was impassable. If he didn't arrive, she wouldn't know the reason, but would be left wondering and worrying.

The long hours seemed endless. Another bomb fell, so close that the windows rattled in their frames and the whole house shook. She ducked her head, curling into a ball beneath the table and half expecting the whole building to come crashing down around her. *Oh, hurry, Ted! Please hurry!* As if in answer to a prayer, she heard the doorbell ring, followed by a pounding with the brass knocker. She scrambled out from beneath the table, almost falling in her haste, and ran along the narrow hallway. By the time she reached the door, the bell was shrilling again, insistent and continuous. She grasped the knob, twisted it and yanked the door open.

Oh, thank God! Thank God, it was him. She threw herself into his arms, the tears she'd been managing to hold back now streaming down her cheeks. After a moment, he held her away.

'Come on, Freda. For goodness' sake, let me in!'

'Sorry . . . sorry . . . Oh, I was so worried! Are you all right?'

'Yes. But the sooner we get away from here the better. Are you ready?'

Terrified of going out into the maelstrom again, Freda raised her panic-stricken eyes to his. 'Couldn't we stay here?'

'I don't think that's a good idea,' Ted said in his familiar Somerset drawl. 'Can't risk my car taking a hit.'

'Never mind the car! What about us?'

He grinned his lopsided grin. 'I've made it this far. Reckon my luck will hold. Looks like it's the docks they're after. Get your things, my girl, and let's make tracks.'

Freda didn't have the strength left to argue. Praying he was right, she ran into the living room, grabbed her rucksack and her handbag and hurried back. Ted took the rucksack from her and started down the path. Freda heard the drone of heavy engines in the distance, growing louder with every second. She yanked the key out of the lock, reinserted it into the keyhole on the outside and turned. Then she sprinted down the path. The passenger door was open for her and Ted already had the engine running. She half fell into the seat, slamming the door after her, and for a few moments watched the clear skies for the bombers. But thankfully they didn't veer towards them. As she'd thought, they were following the river, above which the glow of the burning buildings lit the dark sky, not unlike dawn breaking on a stormy day.

Ted pulled away, heading for the Old Kent Road and the route that would take them home. Only when they reached the outskirts of London did either of them speak.

'I'm so sorry, Ted,' Freda said. 'You shouldn't have come, but thank God you did.'

He reached across and patted her hand. 'At your service, ma'am. I couldn't risk losing my best land girl.'

Warmth flooded through her. Really, Ted was a man in a million and she was very, very lucky to have been posted to his farm.

'Don't worry, I'll work harder than ever,' she promised.

On his first day back at school following the weekend, Billy sat on the bed in his room chewing on a nail that was already bitten down to the quick. Since the episode when he'd so nearly been sent to an industrial school, he'd tried his hardest not to do anything to upset the apple cart here at Bramley Court. He knew he'd been lucky to get away with it, just as he'd been lucky to be sent to live in the lap of luxury such as he'd never dreamed of. But more than that, he really didn't want to disappoint her ladyship. Yes, she could be tough. Yes, she laid down rules and expected him to stick to them, and if he didn't, the tongue-lashing she gave him stung just as much if not more than Uncle Seamus's belt on his bare backside. But you knew where you stood with her. He'd never known anybody like her before – someone he could look up to and trust. And he liked her. Admired her. Respected her even, and respect wasn't something he was used to feeling.

But today, when he'd got home, she'd been funny with him. Snappy. Cold. She'd asked him how the arithmetic test he'd been worried about had gone, but when he'd told her, it was as if she wasn't listening. He'd been so proud that he'd got seven out of ten of the problems right and he'd thought she'd be pleased that the coaching she'd given him had paid off, but she'd just nodded and said, 'Good,' in a distant sort of way. He hadn't expected glowing praise, that wasn't her way, but he'd expected more than that. Now he was searching his conscience to think what he could have done to make her like that.

He hadn't skipped school. He hadn't said any rude words that he could think of. He'd served out his punishment for starting the fight without complaint because he knew he deserved it. And he hadn't once lost his temper.

It was his temper he was most afraid of. The white mist of fury that could spring up from nowhere. He could be happy enough one minute, and the next, when something caught him on the raw, he'd explode and lay into whoever had offended him with his fists and any weapon he could lay hands on, such as the knife that her ladyship had confiscated. He'd been a bit upset about that – he liked his knife, and on the mean streets where he lived in London it had saved his bacon more than once. But she hadn't thrown it away. He'd seen it hidden beneath the utensils in the kitchen drawer, so it wasn't lost for ever, and to tell the truth he didn't think he needed it here. He could look after himself well enough without it.

No, he didn't know what he'd done for her to treat him as she did when she was punishing him. And that worried him. If he didn't know, how could he put it right?

He attacked his nail with the ferocity normally reserved for his enemies, felt a sharp pain as his teeth tore at it and tasted blood. He sucked on it so as not to get it on the yellow candlewick bedspread.

A tap on the door made him jump guiltily; the handle turned, and her ladyship came into the room.

She looked different somehow, and he couldn't quite work out why. Because of what he'd done that had upset her? Even if he didn't know what it was, he thought he ought to apologise. 'Sorry, miss,' he said – calling her that was a habit he couldn't seem to break.

'No, Billy,' she said. 'I'm the one who's sorry. I'm not my usual self, and I think I owe you an explanation.' He frowned, puzzled, and she indicated the bed. 'Do you mind if I sit down?'

'No'. He shifted along a little to make room for her.

'I'm afraid I had some news today that is rather upsetting,' she said. 'You know my son is a fighter pilot? And you know they're engaged in open warfare with the Luftwaffe? Well, we have had news that he didn't return from last night's sortie. He's officially missing in action. But I don't think I need tell you that I very much fear he is dead.'

Lady Hastings had given Winnie a few more days off to see her son settled in. On Tuesday morning, she was making a hot chocolate for Don's elevenses when there was a knock at the door and Fred came in.

'What are you doing here this time of the day?' Winnie asked, though as always she was pleased to see him. But his next words shocked her to the core.

'I've got some bad news from Bramley Court. I've just been up there delivering an order, and Lady Hastings herself asked me to let you know. Her son, Philip, is missing in action.'

'Oh my life!' Winnie pulled the pan of milk off the gas ring, her other hand flying to her heart. 'That's terrible. Is there any hope?'

'I s'pose there's always hope, but it doesn't sound good to me,' Fred said prosaically. 'The Spitfires and Hurricanes have mostly been trying to stop the enemy bombers, haven't they? I'd have thought he'd have been found if he'd come down over land. But if he came down in the sea . . .'

Winnie pulled herself together with an effort. 'I must go up and see her ladyship. She'll be in a terrible way.'

'And I must get going. I've got a few more deliveries to make, and I don't want to keep the shop shut for longer than I have to.'

When he'd left, Winnie took Don's hot chocolate in to him, and as he propped himself up on the pillows and took it from her, guilt washed over her. Her son was alive. Still groggy, but recovering. But it didn't sound as if her ladyship had been so lucky.

'I've just got to pop up to the big house,' she told him. 'I won't be long. You'll be all right while I'm gone, won't you?'

Don chuckled. 'I'm a big boy now, Mum – remember?'

And still my son, Winnie thought. 'Well, don't try getting out of bed on your own,' she warned him.

'For goodness' sake, just go, Mum!'

With his exasperated words ringing in her ears, she hurried up the drive and round the house to the back entrance, the way she always went in on her way to work. Maud was in the kitchen, peeling vegetables for a stew.

'Wot you doin' here?' she demanded accusingly. 'I thought you were s'posed to be on holiday.'

Winnie bristled, but ignored the unpleasant greeting. 'I've just heard the awful news about Philip,' she said. 'I've come to see her ladyship to offer my condolences.'

Maud snorted. 'A bit early. He isn't dead yet.'

Again Winnie refused to rise to the bait. 'All the same, I'd like a word with her.'

'Well, you'll find 'er in 'er study.' Maud had resumed her attack on a carrot. 'But I doubt she'll want to speak to you.'

Wondering why she had ever thought of Maud as a friend, Winnie headed for the study without another word. As she pushed the door open, she saw Lady Hastings seated at her desk, head resting on her hands as she massaged her forehead. Winnie stepped back hastily and knocked. Knowing her ladyship, she didn't think she would want anyone to see the distress she must be experiencing.

It was a moment or two before Lady Hastings called, 'Come!' But when Winnie entered the study, her ladyship had composed herself, and if it hadn't been for her pallor and the dark circles beneath her eyes, no one would have known that anything was amiss.

'Oh, Mrs Mitchell, it's you.'

'Yes, milady.' Winnie hovered, searching for the right words. 'I'm so sorry, and I just wanted to let you know I'm thinking of you.'

'That's very kind.' Lady Hastings managed a tight smile.

'I do know something of how you must be feeling, and I just hope things turn out well for you, as they have for me,' Winnie said.

'Yes. You have been lucky. But somehow I don't think this is going to end well in my case.' The strain was telling in Lady Hastings' voice. 'But if you don't mind, I'd really rather not talk about it.'

'Of course, I understand, your ladyship. I just wanted you to know . . .'

'And your concern is much appreciated, but . . .' She broke off, and Winnie remembered what Maud had said. She might have meant it nastily, but she was right. Lady Hastings wanted to be left alone with her thoughts, and, no doubt, prayers.

'I'll be going then,' Winnie said. 'But if there's anything I can do, be sure to let me know.'

'I will.' The same tight smile. 'Though I daresay you have your hands full at the moment.'

Once again Winnie was consumed by guilt. 'I'm never too busy for you, milady,' she managed, and backed out of the room. Poor Lady Hastings! she thought. When the chips were down, fate wasn't selective. All over the country rich and poor alike were suffering the same anxieties, the same grief. And no doubt it was the same for the Germans. They were human beings too. This wasn't their fault. It was the fault of the hierarchy, who were no doubt safely ensconced in their bunkers in Berlin. At that moment Winnie wished them all dead, and thought of what she'd like to do with them given the chance.

She left the house the same way she'd come in, walking straight through the kitchen without acknowledging Maud and closing the door behind her with a sense of relief that she was leaving the family's suffering behind.

Their midweek dinner with the German officers was every bit as nerve-racking as Anne had known it would be.

They made an odd couple, reminding Anne of Laurel and Hardy, except that this pair were not remotely funny. The commandant was Hardy – tall and overweight, with slicked-down hair, double chins and a small moustache, while the captain was smaller and thin-faced. He wore wire-framed glasses, the only departure Anne could see from her image of Stan.

Guillaume had introduced her as the nanny to Paul and Elise's children, and the captain had leaned towards her as if to greet her in the French style, but when she instinctively pulled back, he had instead offered his hand, limp, moist and, to Anne, quite disgusting. The colonel merely nodded a greeting, but his eyes lingered on her all the same.

Their pre-dinner drinks finished, Guillaume ushered the two

German officers into the salon, indicating that he would sit between them, and Blanche took the seat on the other side of Colonel Schultz. Anne was much relieved to find herself seated between Elise and Nancy. A servant poured wine and she took a sip, hoping it would calm her jangling nerves.

Guillaume was addressing Schultz. 'It's a great pity my son is unable to join us this evening. He was looking forward to meeting you, but unfortunately he has been called away on urgent business.'

'A great pity indeed.' The colonel's French was halting, and his accent almost comically bad. 'I imagine you must be facing problems given the restrictions now imposed upon you by most of France being under our control. But I hope it has not prevented you from making what I understand is your very fine cognac. I would be most disappointed if I am not able to sample it.'

'It will certainly be served later,' Guillaume promised, refraining from adding that since the best vintages were aged in the cellars beneath the chateau for anything up to fifty years, there were plenty of bottles to offset the difficulties with processing this year's grapes.

'*Très bon.* I much look forward to it.'

'I must confess, this year hasn't been easy,' Guillaume said. 'Most of our young workers were called up for military duty, and it takes the older and less fit ones much longer to do their jobs.'

'Not so old and unfit that they can't cause trouble.' Captain Klein's French was considerably better than Schultz's. His frequent trips to the coffee shop were paying off in terms of his ease of conversation, Anne thought.

'Trouble?' Guillaume repeated, looking concerned.

'*C'est rien.*' Schultz threw a warning glance at Klein, but the garrulous captain was not to be silenced.

'Last night a group of men were seen crossing the border and disappearing into your vineyard. Raising our suspicions that they were employees of yours, most likely bent on causing mischief.'

'Oh, dear me, I find that hard to believe,' Guillaume said. 'I've issued strict instructions that they are not to cross into the land that is under your jurisdiction and certainly not to cause any trouble. But I will definitely investigate this tomorrow and deal very harshly with anyone who has defied my orders. Do you want me to hand them over to you, Colonel?'

'That won't be necessary this time, Clermont. But should it happen again . . .'

'I assure you Guillaume will leave them in no doubt as to what will happen to them should they disobey him,' Blanche said in an ingratiating manner. 'You must know we are more than willing to accept you as our neighbours. Something that should be to our mutual advantage.'

The colonel smiled at her graciously. 'Exactly so, *madame.*'

But Anne's blood had run cold. She was horribly sure the men who had been spotted were Paul and his fellow saboteurs, looking for a place where they could damage the German lines of communication. Supposing they hadn't realised they'd been seen and went back tonight? The border guards would now be on high alert, and they might very well be captured.

She didn't dare glance in Elise's direction; a look passing between might not go unnoticed and would raise the Germans' suspicions. Were they here tonight on a fishing expedition? Oh, no! Please no!

Given the circumstances, Guillaume's cook had excelled herself with a menu that would have been fit for a king. Black truffles were followed by a duck cassoulet and Bordeaux canelés, a soft rum and vanilla batter in caramel pastry cooked in fluted moulds. But Anne was so nervous she was finding it difficult to swallow a single mouthful, and Nancy hardly ate anything either. Day by day she seemed to be fading away, and so far Anne had been unable to obtain the medication she needed so badly.

When coffee was served, Guillaume's butler produced and uncorked a bottle of the chateau's finest cognac. When it was poured, the commandant swirled it in the glass, sniffed it, took a sip and smacked his lips. 'Magnificent!'

'A toast is called for, don't you think?' Guillaume raised his own glass. 'To our friendship.'

Although she knew he was only doing what he thought was necessary to keep his family safe, Anne shuddered. All she wanted now was to escape. But the Germans were in no hurry to leave, and the minutes dragged by, feeling like hours.

At last the commandant rose. 'We must leave you, I am afraid. My driver has been kept already too long.'

'It's been a pleasure, and I hope we may entertain you again soon.' Guillaume too was on his feet, holding out another bottle of cognac to his guest. 'And please accept this as a token of my regard. Perhaps it will help to warm a cold evening when autumn arrives.'

At last! They were going! Anne felt dizzy with relief. But not so dizzy that she didn't follow the party out of the salon into the hallway and see the colonel kiss the hand of a very tipsy Blanche.

'*Enchanté, madame.*'

Again a shiver ran up Anne's spine. Blanche was far too friendly with the Germans for her liking. But surely she wouldn't betray her own brother and his family? Nevertheless, Anne wished she would go back to Bordeaux, where it wouldn't impact on the Clermonts if she did turn collaborator and informer.

And she said a prayer that Paul would soon be home safely.

As the door closed after the German officers, Blanche faked a genteel yawn.

'I think I'm ready to retire, Guillaume. These occasions can be so exhausting.'

'Not just for you. Nancy needs to go to bed. She looks dreadful.'

'You want me to call the maid?' Blanche asked archly.

'If you would, but if she's busy, I'll see to her myself.'

Blanche shrugged. 'I'm sure she is.' She headed for the stairs, no longer able to control the smile that was twitching at the corners of her mouth. Things had turned her way at last! Although it was never spoken of, she was certain that Paul was heading up a resistance cell and using the chateau as his headquarters. The fact that he had been absent for two days had convinced her she was right. He was almost certainly one of the would-be saboteurs the colonel had spoken of.

But now the seeds of suspicion had been sown. All she had to do was water and tend them. She hadn't quite made up her mind if she should drop hints to Captain Klein when she met him in the café, or actively seek out the colonel and tell him what she knew, all the while pretending she could scarcely bear to betray her family but felt nonetheless that it was her duty to do so. Whichever, it made no difference to her plan. She thought it quite likely that all the Clermonts would be arrested, along with that snooty little au pair or nanny or whatever she was supposed to be. And by the same token they would be interrogated and sentenced to death – if they were still alive after being tortured. But the one she really wanted to see dead was Paul. The man who had stolen her son's inheritance. With him dead, the way would once more be clear for Louis to become the next baron, and if Germany won the war, she knew she could count on the officers who would become her friends to ensure he achieved the position in society that she had always wanted for him.

Smiling broadly now, she began to prepare for bed.

As Anne had feared, Paul and his men hadn't realised they'd been spotted, and had returned that night to the place they'd found. They'd just begun unloading their explosives when a shout had gone up and a warning shot had been fired.

'*Allez vite!*' Paul had ordered, and they had scattered, racing for the cover of the woods and the vineyard.

Jean Zambussi, one of the estate workers and Paul's second in command, lived in a tied cottage close to the border, and all the men headed to it from their different directions. When everyone had reached it safely, they assembled in the back bedroom with the curtains drawn and in total darkness but for a single candle to discuss the best course of action.

Paul had suggested that given what had just occurred, it would be wise to put their activities on hold for a while and lie low, and the others had agreed, though they voiced their frustration at having been so close to achieving their object only to be thwarted. After a couple of hours, when they deemed it safe, most of the men had left for their own homes, but the chateau was much further away, and while there remained the possibility of German reinforcements searching the area, Paul hadn't wanted to take the risk of leading them there.

He was anxious, though, to hear every detail of how the dinner party had gone, so he'd left for home early next morning, hoping to be able to speak to Elise and Anne, who would certainly be up, before the others surfaced. Blanche was never an early riser, and since Nancy's health had deteriorated, she and Guillaume had taken to breakfasting in bed. Sure enough, when he arrived, he found Elise and Anne lingering over croissants and coffee; the children had run off to play in the nursery.

'Oh, Paul, thank God you're home!' Elise exclaimed as he walked through the door. 'We've been so worried about you!'

'And yet here I am. I told you I'd be away for several days. There was no need to worry.'

'Well we did! The German officer said—'

'First things first.' He kissed her. 'Is there any coffee left in that pot?'

'You're in luck,' Anne said. She fetched a cup from the chiffonier, and he sipped the coffee gratefully, then leaned forward, elbows on the table.

'So how did last evening go?'

'Stressful,' Anne said, and went on to explain what the captain had said about men being sighted crossing the border, and how they had been afraid that if Paul and his men weren't aware they'd been seen, they might walk straight into a trap if they tried again.

'Ah,' Paul said. 'So that explains it.'

'Explains what?' Elise asked anxiously.

He told them.

'Oh, dear God!' she exclaimed. 'You can't do it again, Paul! It's far too dangerous!'

'We've already agreed to leave it for a couple of weeks,' he told her. 'We have to let the dust settle before we try again.'

'I wish you wouldn't!' Elise said, and Anne asked, 'Do the others know?'

Paul nodded. 'Yes. We congregated at Jean Zambussi's and agreed on it, though some of the hotheads needed some persuading.'

'Idiots!' Elise shook her head. 'So did you all stay the night at Jean's?'

'Just me and Victor Clemence. The others made their way

home when we thought the danger had passed.' He took a sip of his rapidly cooling coffee and made a face. 'This is cold. I'm going to make a fresh pot.'

As he scraped back his chair, he heard a rustle outside the door and froze. 'Who's there?' he called.

'Only me.' The door opened and Blanche stepped into the room. 'Your mother would like a glass of milk and I've come down to fetch it for her.'

'Oh, right. There's a jug here.' Paul spoke in a perfectly normal tone, but Anne's heart was thumping. How long had Blanche been standing outside the door?

Blanche got a glass, poured in the milk and left.

Anne, who had been holding her breath, let it out on a gasp. 'Do you think she overheard what you were saying?' she asked in a whisper.

'I've no idea,' Paul said. 'But even if she did, she'd never betray her own family.'

'I'm not so sure. I don't trust her, Paul. She's very friendly with the German officers.'

He shrugged. 'Nothing we can do about it now,' he said, deliberately casual. 'I'm going to get that coffee.'

As Blanche went back upstairs with Nancy's milk, she was smiling with satisfaction. So she'd been right. Paul was mixed up with the resistance movement. And she'd heard enough to take it to Colonel Schultz. Her plan was working better than she'd dared hope. Soon her son would be heir to the title and the estate – or perhaps he'd inherit immediately if Guillaume was taken . . .

As she pushed open the bedroom door, she rearranged her features into an expression of sympathy. 'Your milk, Nancy,' she said sweetly.

* * *

Anne was on her way to deliver notes to the postboxes in occupied territory to inform the Maquis there that things had been put on hold for the present, and for the first time in a long while she was feeling jittery. As she cycled past the café, she glanced in at the window – and felt her blood turn to ice.

Sitting at a table just the other side of the glass was Blanche. And opposite her, his head close to hers, was Captain Klein.

The mail forgotten, Anne turned around and pedalled as fast as she could back to the chateau to inform Paul.

Next day, her worst fears were realised. A friend of Paul's arrived at the chateau just after breakfast with the dreadful news – Jean Zambussi and Victor Clemence had been arrested. A furious and devastated Paul confronted Blanche. 'This is your doing, isn't it?' he demanded.

'I don't know what you mean!' But she'd turned pale.

'Don't deny it. You were seen in the café with that German officer. Did you tell them that I'm involved too?'

'No!' It was true, she had not. She'd stopped short of actually naming Paul. She didn't want Captain Klein to think her utterly ruthless. But one of the men she'd had arrested would do so when they could no longer stand the torture they would be subjected to.

Paul knew it too. Knew that his whole family and Anne too were at risk, and he could think of only one way to get them to safety.

Using his radio and the code he'd been taught, he contacted SOE headquarters.

The telephone in Clarke's office was ringing. These days it seemed he was forever tied up with administrative matters instead of his preferred role – teaching the recruits as much as he

436

could from his vast knowledge of arms and explosives. Explosives was still covered exclusively by him, but he'd been forced to hand over the firearms instruction to Dennis Holder, something he was not best pleased about, but the man did seem to have mellowed somewhat and was treating the recruits with more respect. Perhaps his pride had been satisfied as he'd moved up the pecking order.

'What now?' Clarke grumbled to himself as he went to his desk and picked up the telephone. 'Sutherland.'

A young lady with a cut-glass accent spoke in his ear. 'Oh, Major Sutherland. The colonel would like to speak to you.'

A click, a moment's silence, another click, and Clarke's immediate superior was on the line.

'Sutherland. We have a situation,' he said without preamble. 'I'm sending you to France. Tonight.'

'But, sir, I have a group of volunteer trainees here,' Clarke protested. 'I can't simply—'

'That will be taken care of. I'm arranging for Major Button to look after things while you are away. He's most capable, and well versed in your specialities.'

Clarke knew Dominic Button, liked him, and knew that he was well qualified to head up the arms and explosives training. But he was at a loss to understand what was behind this urgency.

'What's going on? And why me?' he asked.

'Because you are the best man for the job. And because it has been specifically requested that it should be you.'

'To blow up more bridges?' Clarke said, a little sarcastically.

'Possibly. But it's not what makes this operation a top priority. I think I'd better explain.'

'I'd be grateful if you would, sir.'

'There has been a possible exposure of one of the top resistance men in Charente, Paul Clermont – you'll know him, as I believe you trained him in explosives. The lives of his entire family and one of our own agents could be in mortal danger, though Paul himself intends to remain in France and continue his work.'

Clarke listened with growing concern as the colonel talked, and immediately spotted a problem.

'I'm not sure the landing site is suitable for an RAF cargo plane. As far as I know it's surrounded by woods, and they drop off agents and equipment by parachute.'

'So I've been told. Which is why I've secured the use of a privately owned Beech. A recently retired chum of mine pilots one for a well-known corporation, and he has the permission of the chair of the board to fly to France and bring back the family. It's not ideal, I know, but needs must. And another thing. One of the family members is very frail. You will need to ensure she has all the care she will require from a registered medic. Can I leave that with you?'

'Yes, sir. I'll do my best.'

'Good. Then be in the field adjoining your billet at twenty-three hundred hours. I'm counting on you, Sutherland.'

As the call ended, Clarke stood for a moment deep in thought. Unexpected as all this was, he was well used to keeping a clear head in an emergency. His priority now was to arrange for someone with medical training to go along with him, and the first person he thought of was Rosie. Besides being a trained nurse, he knew she could keep a cool head in a tight corner. But he'd had no contact with her since he'd foolishly ruined everything by asking her to marry him. He'd been waiting, hoping that she would be in touch with him, but it hadn't happened, and he didn't know how she would react if he called her now. And though this provided an opportunity to perhaps cross the gulf that divided them, the whole operation was fraught with danger.

Clarke didn't like the idea of exposing her to that. But he couldn't think of anyone more suited to the job and he had a sneaky feeling that if she got to hear that he'd approached someone else first, she would be annoyed, and probably hurt that he'd passed her by.

If they managed to reach France without being targeted by the Luftwaffe, the worst would be over. Under cover of darkness they could have the refugees on board and take off in a very short time. Then it would be a matter of keeping out of the way of enemy fighters, and they should be back in the relatively safe West Country before dawn broke.

Clarke made up his mind, picked up the telephone again and dialled the number of Ambulance HQ in Bath.

As luck would have it, Rosie was in the rest room at the ambulance station enjoying a late breakfast of porridge, toast and tea from the canteen when she heard the telephone ring. Damn! If it was a shout, she'd have to leave her meal unfinished.

Paddy's head appeared round the door. 'For you, Rosie.'

'For me?' She didn't get many personal calls these days except the occasional one from home. She put down her spoon hastily, anxious suddenly. Was something wrong? With Don perhaps? Or her mother? She'd been overdoing things since he came home, Rosie was sure.

She hurried out of the rest room and picked up the telephone. 'Hello?'

The familiar voice that answered made her catch her breath. 'Rosie. I'm glad I've managed to catch you. I need to talk to you.'

'Clarke?' she said, and for a long moment nothing else. A myriad of thoughts and emotions were swirling inside her and she simply didn't know what to say. Then, 'What do you want?'

'I have a huge favour to ask of you. I'd much rather have come to see you so I could explain face to face, but it's too urgent for that. I have to go to France tonight to rescue a family whose lives are at stake, and I need to take someone with nursing training with me as one of the family is very sick. I can't pretend it's without risk; in fact it could be bloody dangerous. But knowing you, I'm sure you'd be up to it and do a good job under difficult circumstances.'

Rosie was staggered. 'You're asking me to go with you to France? Tonight?'

'Yes, tonight. We leave at eleven o'clock, and if all goes well you should be home again by morning.'

'But why? I don't understand. Who are these people?'

'Sit tight and I'll tell you. When war threatened, a Frenchman named Paul Clermont came to me to learn what he could about explosives and we became firm friends. He's now a group leader in the Maquis – the French resistance movement – and runs not only his own cell, but several satellites. Two of his men have been captured by the Germans and may well talk. Paul is the son of a family who produce one of the finest cognacs in the whole of France. He and his wife and children live in the chateau, along with his parents and his aunt. If his name is revealed they will almost certainly all be arrested, tortured and executed. Paul is insistent that he will remain in France and take his chances, but understandably he is desperate that his family should be taken to safety.'

Rosie's head was spinning. 'If he's still in France, how do you know all this?' she asked. 'He didn't telephone you, surely?'

'Ah, by all that's holy, of course not! He spoke in code, by radio transmitter, and the operative passed it on to my superior officer, who is arranging everything.'

'And who is the person who is so sick they need a nurse?'

'Paul's mother. She's not had the medical attention her

condition requires since the occupation. The chateau is in the so-called Free Zone, but the border bisects their land and travel has become difficult. So what do you say, Rosie? Are you up for this, or do I need to find someone else?'

'Oh, Clarke, I don't know!' It wasn't so much the danger that scared Rosie witless. It was that she was afraid of what might happen if she was with Clarke again.

'I promise not to make any demands on you, me darlin'.' Even at this distance he could read her mind. 'I've learned my lesson, so I have.'

For a long moment Rosie was silent. He'd keep his word, she knew. He was a man of honour. It was herself she didn't trust. These last weeks she'd missed him so much. Regretted the end of their relationship. But nothing had changed. The shadow of Julian still lay between them. Could she remain strong, resist the temptation she knew would torment her?

'Ah, Rosie, don't feel obliged,' Clarke said. 'I'll find someone else.'

In that instant Rosie knew what she was going to do. She couldn't let him fly off into danger with a stranger. She couldn't bear it if something happened to him and she wasn't there beside him.

'I'll come with you,' she said.

'Darlin', are you sure?'

'I said so, didn't I? But where is the plane picking you up? How do I get there?'

'I'll come and fetch you Do you need to go home to get some things?'

'No, I'm staying here at ambulance headquarters at the moment. Don was allowed home and needed his old room back. And I'm on duty until six this evening.'

'Can you be ready by eight?'

441

'That's plenty of time.'

'OK, I'll be there at half seven. If there's any change of plan, I'll call again. Leave a message if you're out. And thank you for being an angel.'

'I just hope I won't be one too soon!'

'I second that. See you later, Rosie.'

And he was gone.

Rosie took a deep breath and released it slowly. What in the world was she thinking? But it felt right, somehow. It was what she had to do. And it was far too late now to change her mind.

Chapter Thirty

Billy and his girlfriend had taken the bus into Bath. The farmer's wife who had taken Alice in often made trips to Bath, so Alice had come to know the town well. She led Billy across the Old Bridge and up the main street, pointing out the Roman baths as they passed, then through an arcade of small shops. When they reached the abbey churchyard, they sat for a while watching other visitors feeding the pigeons that swooped and clustered around them.

'They're making me hungry!' Alice said. 'Mrs Wilton took me to a lovely little shop where they sell buttered teacakes.'

Billy thought Alice had landed on her feet just as he had. 'You want one?' he asked.

'Too true I do! Come on, I'll show you.'

As she led him back onto the main street and into a warren of alleys, Billy was mentally assessing how much money he'd brought with him. He'd had something special in mind when he'd suggested coming to Bath. Would he have enough left to buy it if he treated Alice to the teacake?

The idea had come to him quite suddenly. He'd been really worried about 'miss', as he still called Lady Hastings, no matter how many times she told him to address her as milady. It was a habit he just couldn't break when speaking to someone in authority. But she hadn't pulled him up on it once since she'd told him her son was missing, just as she didn't seem to notice anything he said or did, and although he was glad to have more or less free rein, he couldn't help being concerned. She just wasn't the same woman at all, and strangely he missed the old Lady Hastings, with her boundless energy and command of every situation, even her scoldings.

He'd thought about the time she'd gated him for getting into that fight in town. That would have been useless at home; he'd just have climbed out of a window and faced the consequences later if he was caught. And about how shocked he'd been by her tongue-lashing when she'd accused him of stealing her brooch. He hadn't even done it! But she'd been really upset about losing it.

The brooch! Would it cheer her up if he got her a replacement? He'd looked in the window of the jeweller's shop in Hillsbridge, but all the price tags had been turned over so he couldn't see how much anything cost, and he guessed that meant they were really expensive. A pawn shop would be cheaper. There weren't any in Hillsbridge, but there would be in Bath.

Now here he was, and worrying about how far the money he'd been saving would stretch. He'd been putting away almost all of his earnings from his paper round – not just his wage from the newsagent, but the tips he was given – and he'd brought the lot with him, packed away safely in the sponge bag Lady Hastings had bought him to keep his toothbrush and face flannel in and secreted now in the rucksack on his back.

'Here we are.' Alice came to a halt outside a little café and looked at him expectantly. 'Shall we get some teacakes to take away?'

Billy knew what she was thinking and didn't want to disappoint her. 'Let's have them here. With a cup of tea.'

'Oh!' He could see she was impressed. 'I didn't think . . .'

'Come on.' He pushed open the door with its jangling bell and strode inside as if this was something he did every day.

The tea came in a fancy pot, with china cups and saucers, milk in a tiny matching jug and sugar in a bowl. The teacakes were every bit as delicious as Alice had promised – hot and crisp and oozing melted butter, a real treat since rationing. There were paper napkins beside their plates, but Billy wiped the butter from his chin with the back of his hand. Another old habit that was hard to break.

When they'd finished and a waitress in a black dress and white frilly apron presented them with a hand-written bill, Billy's heart sank. This was going to eat into what he'd set aside for the brooch. But he didn't want Alice to see that he was dismayed at the cost. He dipped into the sponge bag for a handful of coins, spread them on the table to count out what was needed, and was about to put away what remained when Alice whispered urgently, 'What about a tip?'

For a moment Billy didn't know what she was talking about. A tip?

'For the waitress!' she hissed.

Reluctantly he picked out a florin, and Alice slid it under the rim of her plate.

'Do you know of any pawn shops?' he asked when they were back on the street.

Alice shook her head. She was the one out of her depth now.

'I want to get something for Lady Hastings,' he explained. 'Her son's missing and I want to give her something to cheer her up. Let's try some of these side streets.'

As they walked over the cobbles, he took Alice's hand and she didn't pull away. 'There's one!' he exclaimed triumphantly. He pointed at the three golden balls dangling over the pavement from a metal bracket. 'They tell you that's where you can find Uncle.'

'Uncle? Uncle who?' Alice asked.

'Never mind.' Billy hastened his pace so that Alice had to almost run to keep up with him until they reached the shop window.

It was full of any manner of things. Watches, a Brownie box camera, binoculars, a walking stick with a carved handle, even a man's dress suit, white shirt and black bow tie on a hanger. And of course, jewellery. Rings, earrings, bangles, necklaces – and brooches. Billy was looking for something similar to the one Lady Hastings had lost, and spotted just the thing. A sparkling emerald surrounded by tiny diamonds.

'That's the one,' he said triumphantly. He opened the shop door and walked in, followed by an awed Alice.

The pawnbroker was a fat man with a bald head and thick pebble glasses. He eyed Billy with suspicion. 'You won't get rid of any hot stuff here, my son. I don't want the rozzers bangin' on my door.'

'I'm not here to get rid of anything,' Billy said indignantly. 'I'm here to buy.' He jerked a thumb in the direction of the window. 'It's in there. The round brooch with the shiny stone in the middle.'

The pawnbroker stopped in the act of pulling aside the dusty velvet curtain, eyeing Billy with even greater suspicion and blocking his way to the window.

'Buy, is it? Steal more likely! You must think I came down with the last shower.'

Billy glared indignantly, then pulled out his sponge bag and emptied it onto the counter. 'I got bangers an' mash – see?'

The fat man's chins wobbled and he chortled scornfully. 'Yeah, but not nearly enough. Where's yer pound notes? You'd need a fistful of those before I'd give you house room. How much 'ave you got?' He elbowed Billy aside and counted the coins into piles of half-crowns, florins, shillings and sixpenny bits. The coppers he pushed to one side, not giving them a second glance. 'Tell you wot, son. If you'm serious about gettin' a brooch, I'll show you what you can have fer that. Fer the young lady, is it?'

He winked lasciviously at Alice, then went to a cabinet and opened a drawer. 'Here. Now that's pretty, bain't it? I'll let you 'ave that for the silver. The rest's no good to me. Clog up me till, that will. 'Ere, 'ave a look.'

Billy took the brooch. It was pretty, and truth to tell he couldn't see there was much difference between it and the one in the window that he'd taken a fancy to. The central stone was much the same size, although it was a pale blue colour, and it was set in a silvery surround. He turned it over; the pin was a bit bent, but that wouldn't show, and he really didn't want to leave empty-handed.

'All right,' he said. 'Go on then.'

The pawnbroker pushed the little heaps of silver towards the back of the counter.

To Billy's surprise, Alice spoke up. 'You sure, Billy?' Billy nodded, about to put the brooch into his trouser pocket. 'Haven't you got a box?' she said to the man, who chortled again.

'Not fer that one, miss.'

'You must have one somewhere.'

Billy was turning red. He couldn't believe Alice was haranguing the pawnbroker, and he was afraid he might change his mind. But the man only huffed. 'I'll see what I can find.'

He went back to the drawer, hunted around and came out with a small white cardboard box decorated with silvery scrolls. 'Best I can do.'

The box was scuffed on the corners and around the edges, but Billy took it gratefully and slipped the brooch inside. It looked even better to him resting on the faded bit of silk that had once been purple.

'Fancy you arguing with that man!' he said admiringly when the shop door closed behind them.

'Well, you were had,' Alice said.

But Billy barely heard her. He was feeling cock-a-hoop, and he couldn't wait to get home and give miss the brooch.

Freda squelched across the farmyard, her boots making sucking sounds as she went. A rain storm in the night had turned the yard into a sea of mud and manure. She had just taken the cows back to their field after evening milking, and they weren't fussy about where they did their business.

'Time for a cuppa, I reckon.' Ted, who had been clearing up in the milking shed, was right behind her.

At the kitchen door, Freda eased off her filthy wellingtons with the help of the boot scraper.

'You'll have a lot worse than this to contend with come winter,' Ted remarked.

'I don't care.' She stepped inside in her stockinged feet. 'I love it here, and anyway, the cows will be back inside soon, won't they? So at least I'll be spared the mud the tractor's churned up in the gateway to the field.'

'True. We'll have to be getting them into their winter quarters before long.' Ted straightened up and shook the rain from his waterproof jacket. 'And I guess anything's better than having bombs falling all around you in London.'

Freda shivered. 'Oh, that was awful! I don't know what I'd have done if you hadn't come and got me. I don't think I've ever been so frightened in my life.'

'Can't say I was very happy with it.' Ted's trousers were tucked into his thick seaboot socks, and he pulled them out and followed her into the kitchen.

'You were a hero, braving it for me.'

'I wouldn't do it for everyone, that's for sure. Just my favourite land girl.' He gave her bottom a playful smack. 'Come on, let's see if there's any tea in the pot.'

A tingle of pleasure ran up Freda's spine. Last time he'd said 'best land girl'. 'Favourite' was a lot more personal. As was the slap on her bottom. But she was determined not to read too much into it. She didn't want to spoil their easy relationship. She'd had her share of romantic disasters; she didn't want this to turn into another one.

'Oh, there you both are.' Mrs Holland appeared in the doorway that led to the sitting room and the stairs. 'Kettle's on the boil. I'll make you a nice cup of tea. And then I'll get supper going.'

Freda sank into the old rocking chair that occupied one corner and sighed with satisfaction.

This was the life. She didn't want it to end. Ever.

Billy and Alice parted company in Hillsbridge. Billy usually walked Alice home, but she knew how anxious he was to get back to Bramley Court to give Lady Hastings the brooch, though she hoped her ladyship wouldn't make any scathing comments. Alice was well aware that the so-called gemstone was nothing but glass, and Billy had spent all his money on a worthless trinket.

'Are you sure you'll be all right?' he asked.

'Course I will! It's still daylight, and there will be plenty of people out and about.'

He nodded, grateful, but still feeling a bit guilty at leaving his girl so abruptly. He watched her go until she was out of sight, then headed for home at a cracking pace.

He found Lady Hastings in the sitting room. A photograph album lay open in her lap, and when she looked up, he saw that her eyes were misted with tears. She brushed them quickly away with her fingers and closed the album.

'Billy! I didn't expect you back so soon. You and Alice haven't fallen out, have you?'

'No, miss. I've got something for you.' He fished the little box out of his pocket and held it out towards her, but as she straightened up, he was shocked to see that a brooch that looked very like the one that had caused all the trouble was pinned to the lapel of her jacket.

'You've found it!' he blurted.

'Yes. It was in one of my dresser drawers. It must have fallen in and got covered up somehow. I am so sorry I accused you of stealing it. It was very bad of me to jump to conclusions, but you hadn't been here long and . . . Well, I am truly sorry and I hope you will forgive me.'

'Yes, miss. Course, miss.' He turned away, ridiculously disappointed. He might have been cleared of thieving, but she wouldn't want the brooch he'd bought for her now.

'Billy?' Her voice stopped him. 'I thought you said you had something for me.'

'It's nothing,' he said, reddening.

'I'd still like to see what it is.'

Caught between a rock and a hard place, Billy realised he had no option but to give it to her. If he didn't, she'd think he was still upset with her for not believing him when he'd said he hadn't taken her brooch. Reluctantly he extended his hand again and she took the box. 'Thank you, Billy.'

He looked at the floor, chewing on his fingernail as she

opened it, not wanting to see the expression of scorn on her face as the contents were revealed. There was a long moment of silence, then, very softly, she said, 'Oh, Billy.'

Surprised by the gentleness of her tone he looked up.

'I got it 'cos I thought it might cheer you up,' he said hesitantly. 'I know it's nowhere as nice as that one . . .' He nodded his head towards the brooch pinned to her lapel. 'But you've found it now, so I needn't have . . .'

'That was such a kind thought. And it's so pretty! I love it.' To his amazement, she set the box down on the occasional table beside her chair, unpinned the brooch she was wearing, and replaced it with the one he'd just given her. 'Look – it's perfect!'

Remembering how Alice had told him he'd been had, he said doubtfully, 'I don't think it's real jewels.'

'Maybe not,' Lady Hastings said. 'But have you never heard the expression "it's the thought that counts"? I shall treasure it for ever. Come here.'

She put her arms around him, hugging him so tightly that the metal surround of the brooch dug into his cheek. Nobody had ever hugged him like that, not even his mother, and he had no way of knowing that it was a very rare thing for Lady Hastings to do, even with her own children.

As she released him, he saw her eyes were full of tears, and he was suddenly overcome with embarrassment.

'Miss . . .'

She smiled sadly. 'Take no notice of me. Let's just say you've touched my heart.' Her voice faltered, then she recovered herself. 'Go on, off you go. I'll see you at dinner. And,' she fingered the brooch, her eyes still brimming with tears, 'have no fear, I shall be wearing this.'

* * *

Clarke was waiting outside the ambulance station when Rosie looked out of the window at 7.30. Her heart began to beat a tattoo, and her pulse was racing in time. She could scarcely believe this was happening and she'd been unable to concentrate on a single thing since Clarke had called her this morning. A myriad of random thoughts and questions were running riot in her head, and nervousness had made her jumpy at the thought of being alone with him. After the way they'd parted, there would almost certainly be an awkwardness between them even if the subject was avoided. The ease with him that she'd grown used to, and prized so much, would be gone for ever.

Would he mention that night? Should she? Or was it best avoided altogether? With a pang, she remembered the ecstasy of their lovemaking.Why, oh why, had he asked her to marry him and broken the spell? But she thought too of the things he'd said in an effort to make her change her mind. *I have enough love for both of us.* And the words tore at her heart. How badly she must have hurt him. Yet he'd stayed the night with her because she'd asked him, holding her until she fell asleep. Then left in the morning before she woke to avoid any more awkwardness, she supposed.

Yet now he'd contacted her and asked her to go with him to France. He must have been desperate to do that. But desperate for what? To be with her? To try to make things right between them? She hoped not. Much as she had missed him, she was still convinced that she'd done the right thing in turning down his offer of marriage. Until, unless, she could be sure she could forget Julian, it simply wasn't fair to him. But despite her misgivings, she still felt a small stab of pride that he should think she could do this, and somehow she got a grip on her nerves, buttoned her coat and walked out to meet him.

'Thank you, Rosie,' he said as she climbed into the

passenger seat of his car. 'I know this is a huge favour, but you were the only person I could think of who'd be capable – and prepared to do it.'

'So tell me what's going on,' she said.

Clarke pulled out onto the road. 'I really don't know much more than I already told you. That two of Paul Clermont's operatives have been captured and he's desperate to get his family out of France before the Gestapo come looking for them. He specially asked for me because he knows and trusts me, and there's some suggestion he wants me to stay on to help him with his plan to inconvenience the German occupying force.'

'You're not coming back?' Rosie said, dismayed.

'Possibly not. But the pilot will look after you, ensure you get back safely.'

'But what about you? If this Paul's cover is blown, surely you'll be in every bit as much danger as his family?'

'He plans to keep on the move,' Clarke said. 'He knows that part of France like the back of his hand, and believes he can keep out of sight.'

'That is brave, but utter stupidity,' Rosie argued. 'Don't do it, Clarke.'

He didn't answer her. Instead he said, 'There's something else I should tell you. It's quite likely that Anne Hastings will be flying back with you.'

'Anne?' Rosie was staggered. 'What's she doing in France? She joined the WAAF, and the last I heard she was working in comms.'

'That's the story,' Clarke said. 'In fact, I oversaw her training as a special agent. She's been in France ever since, working with Paul.'

Rosie swore, a word she'd learned long ago at the garage. She

453

rarely used it, and never in front of Winnie, who would have been horrified. Just now, though, it was the only one that came into her mind and was out before she could stop herself.

'Rosie Mitchell!' Clarke's tone was teasing, mock-shocked. 'I'm surprised at you.'

'Yes, well, there are things you don't know about me. And it just about sums up the way I'm feeling. Anne – a special agent! She used to be afraid of her own shadow!'

'So clearly there were things *you* didn't know about *her*.'

'And you've known all this time? Why didn't you tell me? No more secrets, we promised.'

'Well, some things are more secret than others,' Clarke said.

He swung off the road and into the car park of a country pub he used to take her to. 'Have you eaten?' he asked.

'I had a sausage roll at lunchtime – though what the sausage was made of I haven't a clue.'

'Then you'll need something. It's going to be a long night.'

'I'm not hungry!' Rosie protested, but Clarke overruled her. 'Well I am. Come on.'

As they walked into the pub, a wave of wistfulness washed over her for the happy times they'd spent here. But at least this meeting wasn't turning out to be as awkward as she'd envisioned. Clarke bought her a glass of cider – 'You can have a gin and orange when you've eaten,' he said – and a pint of locally brewed beer for himself, and ordered the pie of the day and chips. Rosie didn't think she would be able to eat a single thing, but at Clarke's insistence she decided on a hot dog, and he added another portion of chips to the order. When the food arrived, he cut cautiously into the pie.

'What the hell is this?' he exclaimed as he encountered what appeared to be nothing but a concoction of vegetables.

'I think this sausage is a bit suspect too,' Rosie said ruefully.

'But at least the bread's fresh, and there's plenty of onion and tomato sauce.'

By the time they'd finished and Rosie was enjoying her gin and orange and Clarke a tot of whisky, the last of the awkwardness had melted away. He looked at his watch.

'We'd better get going,' he said. 'I'm hoping the plane will arrive in time for me to talk to the pilot before we leave and firm up the arrangements. We can wait in my office until then. We have a full course of agents in residence, and I'd rather they didn't see us and start asking awkward questions.'

He paid the bill and they left the pub.

At the chateau, another argument was raging. The first had been when Guillaume had learned that his sister was to blame for the arrest of Paul's men.

'What the hell is the matter with you, Blanche?' he'd raged. 'You've put the whole family at risk, you know that?'

Blanche had fought back, but Guillaume refused to listen.

'I won't have you under my roof a moment longer!' he'd stormed. 'You can go to Bordeaux and make friends with the Germans there if you so wish. Pack your things. I'm calling a cab to take you to the station, and if I'm unable to get hold of one, I'll take you myself.'

The cab had arrived and Blanche had been dispatched, though it was really a case of shutting the stable door after the horse had bolted.

Still furious beyond belief, Guillaume was now venting his anger on his son and refusing to leave the chateau with the rest of the family.

'Why should I be forced out of the home that has been my family's for generations? The Germans will move in, no doubt, and they'll steal everything of value.'

'Don't you understand? They'll arrest you if you stay here. Or shoot you if you resist.' Paul was struggling to hold onto his own temper, which was being sorely tried. 'What good will any of the heirlooms be to you if you're dead?'

'The colonel won't have me shot, even if Blanche thinks I should be. He isn't so bad. We got on very well when he and the other chap dined with us,' Guillaume argued.

Paul swore. 'You sound just like your sister. That won't count for anything if they think you've been harbouring the resistance.'

Guillaume, red in the face, snorted. 'We don't even know if your men have talked. They'll have taken their suicide pills if they had any sense.'

'We don't know they had the opportunity, and we can't take the risk. You have to go with the others.'

'Please, Guillaume!' Nancy, propped up on the chaise longue, spoke in a weak voice. 'It would break my heart to lose you.'

'You see, Papa? You must go with Maman. For her sake if nothing else.'

Guillaume was silent and Nancy spoke again. 'I won't go if you don't, *mon chéri*.'

He shook his head angrily. 'Don't talk foolishness, Nancy.'

'I mean it. If you are going to die, I want to die alongside you.'

'We'll see about that.' Guillaume had no intention of giving in so easily.

'And both of you, please stop quarrelling. Supposing you never saw one another again? How can you let it end like this?'

'*Désolé*, Maman,' Paul said wearily. 'But there's still time for you to think about this carefully, Papa.'

Exasperated, he walked out of the salon, leaving them alone.

The Beech had landed in the field adjoining the Manor and the pilot turned off the engine since it was another half-hour before they were scheduled to take off. As he helped Rosie into the main cabin, all pale leather, thick carpet and stainless steel, Clarke thought that no one would mistake this for a military aircraft. He settled her, then went to talk to the pilot. He would have liked to take off straight away, but he knew that to arrive early at the landing place would put them in additional danger. If the plane was spotted coming in to land, it would give any patrolling Germans more time to reach them.

Rosie couldn't hear what they were saying, and she tried to relax into the soft leather seat, but her nerves were jangling now. She'd never flown before – why would she have? – and the very thought of taking off added to her fear that they would come under attack from the Luftwaffe.

When the pilot turned on the engine and began running through his take-off checks, Clarke came back, sat in the seat next to her and took her hand.

'It's OK, Rosie.'

'Is it?' She gave him a pleading look and he smiled at her encouragingly.

'You're amazing. Do you know that?'

She didn't feel amazing. She felt terrified, and only held onto his hand more tightly as the twin engines roared, and the plane bumped over the rough ground, gathering speed, and rose into the dark sky. When it had reached its flight path and was flying straight and level, she relaxed a little. They hadn't encountered any enemy fighters; Clarke had said they could well all be busy offering protection to the bombers that were blitzing London night after night.

Rosie was beginning to feel sleepy. It was well past her usual bedtime – unless she was working a night shift – and the gin and orange Clarke had bought for her earlier was probably having a delayed effect. She dozed, her head resting on his shoulder, only waking when the plane swerved suddenly, and rapidly lost height, and she realised Clarke was no longer beside her but once more sitting with the pilot. She leaned forward, anxious again. 'What's happening?'

'We're just crossing the French coast and Steve needs an extra pair of eyes to keep a lookout for enemy aircraft.'

'Is that why we . . .?' She broke off, peering out of her window.

'Evasive action. Yes. It's OK. They've gone now.' But he was still concentrating on the all-encompassing darkness both in front of and to his side of the plane, and his reply didn't do much to reassure her. They were now over occupied territory. She wanted to ask how much further they had to go but didn't want to distract Clarke or the pilot.

The tension was back now, stiffening her muscles, and a throb had begun over one of her eyes. She'd better not be getting a sick headache, she thought. One of those could lay her low, and she had to be alert and in command of herself if she was to do the job that Clarke had brought her to do, and do it well.

They'd regained height since they'd dropped to avoid the enemy plane, and at last Rosie could tell they were descending again, steadily this time, though the headache had now spread into her ears, an uncomfortable pressure that sent little jolts of pain into her eardrums.

'We should be over the landing site now,' Steve said. 'But where are the lights to guide us in?'

'You're sure we haven't been blown off course?' Clarke asked.

'Nah. It's as calm as a mill pond. I've only had to alter course once, after we did a little detour to avoid that scout plane.'

'So where *are* the lights?' Clarke asked. 'They had four when I came before – one on each corner of the field.'

Steve didn't answer. The moon had emerged from behind a cloud, and temporarily at least it was illuminating the field sufficiently for him to be able to see its dimensions, edged on three sides by woods and the fourth by a road. He flew a low circuit, while Clarke kept a close eye on the skies, watching for any lights that would indicate an enemy aircraft in the vicinity. 'Clear,' he reported.

'I'm going in then,' Steve said. 'We'll be safer on the ground.'

He flew back over one stretch of woods, turned so he was heading into the wind, and began his final approach. The landing was a little bumpy on the uneven ground, but the wheels were safely down and the plane slowed and came to a halt just short of a hedge that bordered the road. The moon had slipped behind a bank of cloud and the field was left in darkness. No torch beams. No sign of life at all.

'Where the hell are they?' Steve expostulated.

'I'll go and look for them.' Clarke was unbuckling his safety belt. He opened the door, climbed onto the step and jumped down to the ground. Within minutes he had disappeared into the deep shadow of the trees, only the flickering beam of his torch indicating his fast-moving position.

Rosie's nerves were jangling again. She leaned forward in her seat. 'What now?' she asked the pilot.

'We wait,' he replied.

Clarke plunged into the woods, heading in the direction of the chateau. His progress was much slower than he would have liked, hampered as he was by undergrowth and low branches, and he knew that if he couldn't find the Clermonts soon, the plane would have to leave without them. It was far too dangerous to remain here, and even now he was risking Rosie and the pilot's safety.

His great fear was that the family – and Anne – were already in enemy hands. It was the most plausible explanation for their failure to be at the landing site at the appointed time. If that was the case, there was nothing further he could do to help them, and it would also mean the Germans would be keeping a close watch on the chateau and its surroundings in case any other members of the Maquis came here looking for Paul. For all Clarke knew, he could be heading straight into a trap. But he wasn't going to let that stop him. He plunged on, ducking under branches and wrenching his feet through thick patches of bramble.

The thrum of a motor engine sounded a little further on and to his right; Clarke stopped, catching his breath, and listened, then crept cautiously in the direction of the noise. He could see the lights of the car now, but not what sort of vehicle it was. A German patrol? Or the family getting as close as they could to the landing site to save the sick mother from having to walk too far? There was a track to the landing field, he remembered, If he'd gone a little further up the field before entering the woods, he would have found it.

Sudden silence reigned as the engine was killed. Clarke crept closer – and heard voices. He couldn't make out what they were saying, but it didn't sound as if they were German soldiers. Then he heard a voice he knew. Paul! With his smattering of French he recognised the words 'Papa' and '*Vite!*' – 'Quickly!' An older man's voice replied, but Clarke didn't understand a single word of what he said.

As he broke through the last few feet of woodland, he saw the car pulled into a small clearing adjacent to the roadway. When the beam of his torch had reached them, they had all frozen, and he called out to them.

'It's me! Clarke Sutherland! We're here – and waiting!'

Chapter Thirty-One

'Clarke! *Dieu merci!*' Paul turned to the older man. 'Come on, Papa! We are not going without you.'

Clarke approached them. Besides the two men, there was a young woman he assumed was Paul's wife, holding the hand of a child, and an older woman who was hanging onto the still open door of the car for support. Anne was bent double and reaching inside. She emerged with another child, who ran to Paul, clutching at his legs.

Clarke summoned up his limited French. '*Allez vite! Dangereux pour . . .*' 'Dangerous for all of us,' he wanted to say, but the last words evaded him, and he hoped he had managed enough to convey the urgency of the situation.

Anne said something in French to the older woman, and she managed to stand for a moment unaided while Anne slammed the car door shut, then leaned back against the vehicle, her head bowed. Anne took her arm, levering her upright once more, but she was clearly dreadfully frail and unsteady. She'd never make it to the plane unaided, and would slow them all down, Clarke realised.

'I'll carry her,' he said, and as he picked her up, he was shocked at just how shrunken her body was. Dear Lord, she was nothing but skin and bone, and light as a feather in his arms. Small wonder that Paul had asked for a nurse to accompany her.

'This way.' Paul had hoisted the younger child – a little girl – onto his shoulders. He led the way to a well-beaten path, which would be much easier going than the one Clarke had struggled through, and the others followed in single file. Every so often the old man stopped, and Paul gave him a push with an impatient '*Stupide! Ne sois pas stupide!*'

After what seemed an age to Clarke, the trees became sparser and they emerged from the wood. The plane was within reach, though now facing in the opposite direction. Steve had turned in a tight circle so that they would be heading into the wind for take-off. But Clarke's relief was short-lived. Rosie was racing towards him, and her first words chilled him to the marrow.

'Oh, thank God you're here! I'm sure I saw lights up there.' She pointed to the unwooded side of the field. 'I think it was a patrol vehicle.'

Clarke swore. If Rosie was right, the Germans could well have spotted the plane and be driving around looking for a way to get into the field.

'Your patient,' he told her as he lowered Paul's mother to the ground. 'Get her to the plane.'

Without hesitation, Rosie went to the old woman, and Clarke saw the shock on Anne's face as she recognised her old friend; heard her say wonderingly, 'Rosie?'

But Rosie was all business, and he was glad he'd warned her that she would be meeting Anne. She merely nodded, took the old woman's arm. 'Come on. Let's go.'

At that moment, Clarke heard the engines of both a car and a motorcycle, so loud that he knew they must be close by, and a powerful searchlight lit the sky over the spot where Paul had left his car.

He pushed his jacket aside, reaching for the gun concealed there. 'Go! All of you! *Vite!* I'll cover you.'

Paul hoisted his daughter onto his shoulders once more and raced towards the Beech, lifting her in through the open door. The rest of the fugitives followed more slowly, Rosie and Anne supporting Paul's mother between them. They had covered about half the distance when quite suddenly Guillaume swung round as if still determined not to leave his home.

Too suddenly. He collided heavily with Elise, who was just behind him, and she stumbled and fell.

Clarke swore and started towards her, but Guillaume, his dash for home forgotten, was already helping her to her feet, and Paul too had reached her and his elder daughter. Instinctively Clarke checked the field. To his horror, he saw movement from the direction of the clearing. He swung round, and in the now fitful moonlight saw three figures emerging from the trees. 'Go!' he yelled at the rest of the party, and they headed for the Beech as fast as they could manage.

Clarke cocked his gun, then hesitated, uncertain as to his best course of action. The Germans were still a fair distance from the fugitives, but they would be armed. If he took a potshot at them now, a firefight would follow, and there would be casualties on both sides. But if they intended to take the fugitives alive with the aim of extracting intelligence from them, and didn't know he was there, he might have a chance to shoot them from behind.

As he hesitated, undecided, two shots rang out. The first hit Elise; instantly she fell again. The second caught Paul, and he too went down. Belatedly Clarke's decision was made for him. The moon was once more behind cloud, and he could no longer see the Germans. But aiming at the spot from which the shots had come, he fired, spraying as wide an area as he could, then ducked to avoid the retaliation that would be heading his way. Sure enough, bullets zinged through the air inches above his head, and from his crouched position he fired off several more rounds in the hope of drawing the Germans' fire.

Then, staying low, he scuttled towards the spot where Paul, Elise and the child had fallen.

'Where are you hit?' he asked Paul urgently.

'My leg. It's nothing. But Elise . . . Get the child to safety, Clarke.'

There was no time to waste. At any moment the moon could emerge from behind the cloud and they would be sitting ducks. He took the little girl from his friend and raced to the Beech. Rosie and Anne were crowding the doorway, no doubt trying to see what was going on. Clarke lifted the frightened child towards them.

'Françoise, take the girl. She knows you. Rosie, I need you here. Elise is badly hurt.' He turned to call to the pilot. 'As soon as we've got them on board, don't wait – just go.'

He cocked his gun and stepped down, and Rosie followed.

To Rosie, it felt as if she had fallen asleep and woken into a nightmare. She dropped to her knees in the mud churned up by the plane, taking a cursory look at the young woman. She was conscious – just – moaning and muttering something unintelligible. A great dark patch was visible across the front of her dress, and her jacket was wet and sticky. Blood. Lots of it. Under normal circumstances, Rosie would want to find out more about the injury before moving her. But this was one of those occasions when getting her to safety had to be the priority.

'Elise, is it?' she asked. 'Don't worry, you're going to be fine. But we have to get you onto the plane, and I'm sorry, it's probably going to hurt. OK?'

'I can do it.' The man Rosie assumed must be Paul was struggling to get to his feet, but it was clear he could put no weight on his injured leg.

'You can't, mate,' Clarke told him. 'Leave it to us.' He moved towards Rosie. 'You take her legs. I'll take her upper body.' He slid his arms beneath Elise's. As he heaved her from the ground, she groaned sharply, but when Rosie lifted her legs, she made no sound. Rosie thought she might have passed out from the pain and the shock.

Somehow she managed to back up the steps of the plane and set Elise's legs down gently in a space between the seats, then she fetched a pillow and positioned it under her head as Clarke lowered her torso to the carpeted floor.

'Make sure the door's securely fastened behind me,' he told Rosie, then he yelled to the pilot, 'On the count of ten, go!'

Rosie stepped over Elise carefully as Clarke backed down the steps. The door swung back briefly, and as she caught the handle, ready to secure it, he looked back up at her. 'See ya soon, m'darlin'.'

Tears sprang to her eyes. But this was no time for sentiment. She had work to do. The work Clarke had entrusted to her. Resolutely she blinked the tears away and returned to do what she could for her patient.

She was scarcely aware that they were moving until the thrust of the powerful twin engines almost threw her off balance. The plane bumped over the rough ground until the wheels lifted, and Rosie had to hold onto the nearest seat so as not to tumble backwards. But somehow this time she wasn't afraid. She was too busy concentrating on what she had to do to think of anything else. There would be time enough for that when – if – they made it home safely. And more than enough time to worry about Clarke, left behind in an occupied country and facing who knew what dangers.

For the moment, all that mattered was the welfare of her two patients.

'What's wrong with my mummy? And why isn't Papa coming with us?' Paulette, the younger Clermont daughter, raised her head and looked at Anne with troubled eyes.

'She's not feeling very well, *chérie*. But she'll be better soon. And your daddy is very brave. He's working hard to get everything back as it used to be before the war. A lovely place for you to grow up in.'

For all that she managed to make it sound reassuring, Anne was seriously worried about Elise. Supposing she didn't recover? Supposing Paul was captured and executed? If neither of them survived the war, what would become of the children? She didn't think their grandmama was long for this world, and the only other relatives they had, as far as she knew anyway, were their grandfather and his obnoxious sister. She glanced back at Elise, still lying on the floor while Rosie pressed a pad against the wound to stem the bleeding.

It was unbelievable, she thought, that they should have been thrown together after all this time under such circumstances. It had come as a tremendous shock when they'd got to the landing site and she'd seen Rosie waiting there for them. For a moment she'd thought she must be hallucinating, that all the stress since the arrest of Paul's men had driven her a little crazy. But it wasn't a hallucination. It really was Rosie.

What on earth was she doing here? Paul had told her that Clarke Sutherland, the man who'd trained her, would be on the flight, so seeing him had come as no surprise to her. He'd also told her that someone with medical training would be on board, but he hadn't said who. Perhaps he hadn't known, and even if he had, he wouldn't be aware that she and Rosie knew one another.

Anne had known, of course, that Rosie was working as an ambulance attendant, but she couldn't understand why she had been sent on this rescue mission. Was it possible she was SOE too, and nursing was her cover story just as the WAAF was Anne's?

But she couldn't be an agent; she didn't speak a word of French, wouldn't even have learned the rudiments at the board school. Oh well, it would all become clear when they were safely home. *If* they made it . . .

Anne's thoughts turned to her own future. It hadn't been mentioned; Paul had had far too much on his mind to even think about it. They hadn't yet been told where they would be housed when they got back to England, only that it was being taken care of by the same officer who had arranged for them to be flown out of France. All she hoped was that it wouldn't be anywhere in the vicinity of her home. She didn't want to return to her mother's domination, especially since she would come under a barrage of questions as to why she hadn't been in touch for such a long while. And she absolutely didn't want to be anywhere near Julian.

Another thought occurred to her. Had Julian and Rosie got together when she herself was out of the picture? Knowing him as she did, for a social climber and a snob, she thought it was unlikely. A fling in his wild youth was one thing, but now he was older, he'd be thinking of a suitable marriage. When she'd turned her back on him, he would have begun looking around for a well-connected replacement, a bill Rosie could never fit. Really, he'd treated her despicably, leading her on even though he didn't have any long-term plans for her. Selfish bastard!

No, she didn't want to see Julian ever again. In fact, if she was honest with herself, what she really wanted was to go back to France and continue the work she'd been doing with Paul. But she didn't know if she'd be allowed to, and even if she was, she very much doubted it would be in Charente. And Charente was where her heart now lay.

Oh, Paul. Anne closed her eyes briefly, trying to shut out the image of her last sight of him, wounded and left behind, trapped by German soldiers. Trying not to think of what would happen to him. She simply couldn't bear it. And if he and Clarke did somehow manage to escape tonight, she knew Paul would go back to the resistance. He would fight to the last for the freedom of his country. That was the sort of man he was.

Her glance returned to Elise, who was quiet now. Rosie appeared to have been successful in stopping the bleeding from the gunshot wound in her shoulder. She wasn't out of the woods yet, though; she'd lost a lot of blood, and Anne had no way of knowing how serious was the damage to bone and muscle. But so far Elise had been very lucky in life. She had married into a wonderful family – apart from Guillaume's unpleasant sister, they were warm, loving and generous. She had two gorgeous healthy children – and most of all, she had Paul.

Anne thrust aside a moment's sharp envy and prayed that Elise's luck wouldn't desert her now.

'Where are your papers, *madame*?'

As Blanche's train had crossed the border into occupied territory, two German soldiers had boarded and made their way through the carriages checking the passengers' passports. She wasn't unduly concerned. As soon as her taxi had arrived at the chateau, she had ordered it to take her to the German HQ, and the moment she'd mentioned her great friend Colonel Schultz, she'd been allowed into the occupied zone. She had important information to impart to the colonel, she'd told the guard at the entrance to the HQ, and after a few checks had been made, she'd been shown into an office where Schultz himself sat behind a large oak desk.

'*Madame!*' he'd greeted her. 'If you have come to plead for your estate workers, I'm sorry but I cannot help you. They are already in the hands of the Gestapo.'

'Not them!' Blanche said contemptuously. 'They have only themselves to blame for their capture. But I imagine that sooner or later they will give you the names of those who are in charge of their so-called resistance cell, and I am here to warn you that if that hasn't yet happened, you may well be too late to arrest them. The man behind their treachery is planning to leave the country. Tonight.'

The colonel's eyes had narrowed. 'Who are we talking about? And how do you come by this information?'

Blanche's thin lips had compressed into a parody of a smile. 'The man who avoided meeting you when you dined with us at the chateau. My nephew, Paul Clermont, I'm ashamed to say. A flight out of the country has been arranged for tonight, for him and the rest of the family.'

'You are going with them?'

'Oh no. I am on my way to Bordeaux to stay with my son. He is heir to the estate. And with your permission, of course, he will be taking up residency in due course. But for the moment, I know he will be more than willing to offer you hospitality, should you so wish.' She looked around the rather shabby room. 'I'm sure you are accustomed to more comfort than this place affords you. And of course there is always the benefit of a cellar of the very best cognac . . .'

'Most kind, *madame*. And when are you intending to travel to Bordeaux?'

'Right away. But I wished to see you first.'

He inclined his head. 'Then I will ensure the border guards

there are informed and allow you swift passage. And again, my sincere thanks for your assistance.'

So it was that Blanche viewed the soldiers on the train with supreme confidence.

'I am a close friend of Colonel Schultz.'

'Ah. You. Come with me.' One of the guards took her roughly by the arm, jerking her to her feet and leading her to the door between the carriages and along the train.

'Where are you taking me?' she demanded belligerently.

'Orders,' he barked.

'Orders? Whose orders?'

The soldier shrugged and opened another door, and Blanche found herself in the guard's van, where she was confronted by a smiling Captain Klein.

'Ah, my dear *madame*. I regret that I must interrupt your visit to your son. Colonel Schultz has spoken of you to the Gestapo. I am to take you back to Charente so that you may answer their questions.'

'But I've already told him all I know!' Blanche protested.

'Yes, but they believe that with a little persuasion you will remember more . . .'

The door of the guard's van was opened, and taking her firmly by the arm, Captain Klein led her towards an armoured staff car.

The flight back to Somerset was largely uneventful. Somehow they had managed to avoid attack. Béatrice and Paulette had both fallen asleep, and Anne took the opportunity to slip out of her seat and sit down on the floor of the plane beside Rosie.

'Well, this is a surprise, isn't it?'

Rosie looked at her warily. Given the bad terms they'd parted on, she'd expected hostility from her former friend. But Anne's tone was warm.

'Not for me,' she said. 'Clarke told me everything before we flew out, and I gather he oversaw your training. How are you?'

Anne smiled ruefully. 'Worried about Paul.'

'Not Julian?' It was important to somehow banish the elephant from the room, Rosie felt.

'Not a bit. You?'

'Me neither. It's Clarke I'm worried about.'

'So we're agreed? Julian is a rat?'

'Definitely.'

Anne took her hand. 'Good. I'm glad you've seen the light too. We both deserve better.'

Tears pricked Rosie's eyes. 'Oh, Anne, I hated us falling out. I'm so sorry.'

'Me too. Come here.' Anne pulled Rosie towards her and the two girls hugged.

They were interrupted by the pilot's voice coming over the intercom.

'We're nearly there. Seat belts on and prepare for landing.'

'Let's meet when we can,' Rosie said urgently.

'It's a date.'

One last hug, and Anne returned to her seat to attend to her charges.

The pilot had radioed ahead for an ambulance to meet them, and as soon as they touched down, a stretcher party had boarded. Elise had been taken off, and Rosie had gone with her to the nearest hospital. A doctor would be called tomorrow to examine and treat Nancy, and if he thought it necessary, she too would be taken to hospital. But for now, to Anne's surprise, the rest of the party were shepherded into the Manor. *Back where I started!* she thought. They were given food, hot drinks and even brandy for those who wanted it. Anne put the children to bed in Clarke's room and stayed with them, while Guillaume and Nancy were made as comfortable as possible in the cramped common room. Tomorrow they would move to the temporary accommodation that had been booked for them in the village until something more permanent could be arranged. Now that they were safely in England, the strict secrecy in place for the rescue mission could be relaxed. But for the moment, a little discomfort in their sleeping arrangements was nothing but a minor inconvenience.

After she'd been thoroughly examined by a doctor at the local hospital, Elise had been given painkillers and a sedative. She would be seen later by a consultant and tomorrow would undergo emergency surgery to remove the bullet still embedded in her upper arm. An exhausted Rosie had been shown to an on-call rest room, and had collapsed, fully dressed, onto the narrow bed. But in spite of a glass of milk and a tablet the doctor had prescribed, sleep was eluding her as all that had happened played and replayed in front of her eyes like a visual version of a cracked record. Her concerns for Elise had been somewhat allayed – the doctor had said that he expected her to make a good recovery, though he warned that her shoulder might well trouble her for some months before it returned to normal. But Rosie had been so afraid of losing her on the flight home that a shadow of that fear refused to be dispelled completely.

Worse, she was desperately worried about Clarke. The thought of him still in France and involved in a firefight with goodness only knew how many Germans was unbearable. But how like him it was to have covered the rest of them while they boarded the plane. Were it not for him, there would undoubtedly have been more casualties, if not fatalities. His thoughts had been only for them, not sparing a single one for himself. And then to insist that the plane should leave without him the moment the last of them were aboard, presumably because he wouldn't leave Paul alone with the enemy, was valour of the highest order, and her heart swelled with pride that he could be so selfless. He truly had been ready to give up his life to save others.

And perhaps he already had done. The chances were that the Germans who had so nearly caught them would have radioed for backup. It was highly likely that a goodly number would have answered the call, all eager to be in on the action, and Clarke and Paul would be outnumbered. She had no idea how many shots Clarke could fire before having to reload, or if it was the sort of gun that could hit multiple targets, but to be honest, she doubted that. He wasn't an agent in the field, after all.

She was beginning to be convinced she would never see him again, and the thought was a black cloak of despair. She wanted him. She remembered his smile, his dark sense of humour, the wicked twinkle in his very blue eyes. How it had felt to be in his arms. That first kiss, which had stirred something deep inside her. She had wanted him for a very long time and refused to accept it. She remembered their wonderful lovemaking. How he'd asked her to marry him, and still she had convinced herself that for her he would always be second best. To that cad Julian! How could she have been so stupid? Hurt him so badly? All for a childhood obsession she had never been able to rid herself of. For a man she realised now she didn't even like, let alone love.

It was Clarke she loved. She knew that now. Now that it was too late, she'd finally accepted the truth, accepted her feelings for him. Now that she had almost certainly lost him.

Awash with despair and a heartbreak that was more real than anything she had ever felt for Julian, she turned her head into the pillow and wept.

Chapter Thirty-Two

Early the following morning, a local doctor had called to see Nancy. He must have been fully informed of her condition, as he had brought with him two bottles of pills to be taken three times daily, starting with a double dose. It might be a little while before they took effect, he'd warned, as she'd been without them for a considerable period.

Soon afterwards, they'd all been taken to the public house where Major Button had secured accommodation for them. They'd been shown into the lounge bar, where a log fire was blazing in the hearth. Nancy had been settled in a comfortable chair with a rug over her knees and a glass of warm milk placed on a low stool beside her, and the others were enjoying fresh coffee. The landlady had taken Béatrice and Paulette to the kitchen for lemonade and biscuits, and then into the garden where a swing and a see-saw had been installed for the amusement of patrons' children. She had guessed that the adults would have a great deal to talk about that really wasn't for young ears to hear.

When Anne saw them through the window, Béatrice laughing as she swung dangerously high and a dejected-looking Paulette sitting on one end of the see-saw trying in vain to get off the ground, she decided she'd join them. The doom and gloom about the situation back in France was depressing, and in any case, since she was now in charge of them, she felt she really should be doing her duty.

'Not so high, Béa!' she called, sitting on the opposite end of the see-saw to Paulette, and the little girl's frustration disappeared in an instant as she was hoisted up and down again.

Anne thought she heard a motor on the forecourt, and five minutes or so later the garden door opened and Dominic Button emerged.

'Morning, Françoise. You've got your hands full from the look of it.'

'A full-time job,' Anne agreed. 'Guillaume and Nancy are both in the lounge bar.'

'Yes, I've just seen them. Gwen Hibbert seems to be looking after you all very well. And *madame* is looking a little better already, I thought. But actually it's you I've come to see. Can we talk?'

Anne called to Béatrice. 'Béa, come and play with Paulette, please!'

Reluctantly the girl scuffed the ground to bring the swing to a halt. There was a table and chairs nearby, and Anne and Major Button sat down at it facing one another.

'I expect you are wondering what is going to happen to you now,' he began. 'I've spoken to the powers-that-be, and they're happy for you to remain with Paul's children until their mother is well enough to look after them.'

Anne nodded, relieved. 'Oh, that's good. Their grandparents really aren't up to coping with them all day, and they know me well. But I was wondering if I could take them to see their mother?'

'Not today. She's having an operation this morning, and she'll be groggy after the anaesthetic. But certainly someone can drive you there tomorrow, and hopefully it won't be long before she is discharged. When she's no longer in need of your help, you'll be expected to return to duty.'

Anne brightened. 'Really? I can go back to France?'

Major Button frowned. 'You can't go back to France, Miss Hastings. Your cover will have been well and truly blown,' he said baldly.

'But Paul is still there!' Anne argued. 'I know I couldn't go back to the chateau and I don't suppose he will be there either. But he has a network of Maquis all over Charente. He'll be in hiding somewhere . . . if he wasn't taken by the Germans.' She lowered her eyes, biting her lip, then looked up, defiant. 'I'm used to working with him. He'll need me more than ever.'

The Major sighed, shaking his head. 'It's not my decision, Miss Hastings. You'll have to plead your case with someone far more important than me. But I honestly don't think it will be agreed to. To go back to the same region would be far too dangerous, and as I understand it, it was your local accent that made you the ideal agent there. I've simply been instructed to tell you that you are to be given a WAAF posting, at least for now. I don't have any details at the moment, but I'm sure they will come through by the time Paul's wife is back on her feet.'

Anne's lips tightened imperceptibly. 'We'll see about that,' she said, deflated. 'If that's all, Major . . .'

'For now. I'm on my way to the hospital. As Rosie is no longer needed, I'm going to take her home, and then I'll report back to let you know how Elise is progressing.'

Soon afterwards, he drove off, leaving Anne dejected. She could see the sense in what he had said, and of course she'd need a completely new identity. But she was experienced in the field and surely that was what was needed? If she was willing to take the risk, she couldn't believe they'd turn her down.

'Françoise, can I go back on the swing now?' Béatrice came running towards her. 'Please!'

Anne sighed. 'Yes, go on then.'

With an effort she pushed her concerns to the back of her mind and returned to entertaining the children.

The town clock was striking eleven as Rosie opened the picket gate and walked up the path to Winnie's cottage. When the wind was in this direction, the sound carried clearly across the valley. Home! She was home!

She'd been loath to leave Elise, but the consultant who had attended last night was coming back today to remove the bullet that had lodged in her upper arm and repair any damage that it had caused. Since she was likely to be an inpatient for a few days at least, Major Button, who was standing in for Clarke at the Manor, had collected Rosie from the hospital and driven her to Hillsbridge. On the way he'd reassured her that a local GP had visited Nancy and prescribed the medicine she needed, which set her mind at rest. She'd been worried about the older woman too.

Now, as she opened the cottage door, the smell of baking bread greeted her. She hadn't eaten since the hot dog at the pub last night, but even the usually tempting aroma was making her feel sick. Anxiety for Clarke was a leaden weight that had settled in her gut.

'Rosie!' Winnie appeared in the kitchen doorway. 'Whatever are you doing home?'

Rosie managed a wan smile. 'Long story, Mum.'

'Well, don't just stand there! Come on in. Your brother's up – he's in there.' Winnie nodded in the direction of the front room. 'He'll be made up to see you.'

Rosie's heart sank. It was good, of course, that Don was well enough to come downstairs, but she didn't feel up to coping with anyone other than her mother.

Winnie bustled into the living room. 'Look who's here, son!'

Reluctantly Rosie followed her. 'How are you, Don? You're looking much better.'

Don's face lit up and he held out a hand to her. 'Rosie.'

She went to him and gave him a hug, shocked at how thin he still was.

'He's got a way to go, but he's getting there, aren't you, my love?' Winnie sounded delighted to have both her children together again.

'That's brilliant,' Rosie said. 'Well done, Don.'

'Kettle's on the boil,' Winnie said. 'I expect you could do with a cup of tea, Rosie. Me and Don have just had one.'

'Don't make it just for me,' Rosie said. 'I'm all right.'

'So have you got the day off?' Winnie asked her.

Rosie nodded. She couldn't tell the truth – that she'd been given the week off. Her mother was sure to ask why, and she couldn't explain in front of Don. In fact, she wasn't at all sure what she could say. Her mission would have been top secret.

'So what's been going on here?' she asked, changing the subject.

'Apart from me being able to get downstairs?' Don said with a wry smile. At least his sense of humour was returning, Rosie thought.

'Apart from that.' She returned his smile.

Winnie had settled herself on the sofa and Rosie sat down beside her.

'Well, something awful,' Winnie said. 'You know Philip Hastings is a Spitfire pilot? Oh, of course you do.'

A cold shiver ran up Rosie's spine. 'Oh, Mum, don't say he's been killed.'

Winnie shrugged helplessly. 'They're not saying so. Not yet. Officially he's missing. Like our Don was, and he came home, thank God. But a plane? If you get shot down, you don't stand much chance.'

'He could have bailed out somewhere,' Rosie suggested.

'Let's hope so. But if it was over England, surely he'd have turned up by now? Most of the Spitfires have been trying to see off the bombers that are over here pretty much every night. Lady Hastings thinks he might have come down in the sea. She's in a terrible way, of course.'

'Of course.' The horrible likelihood was reminding Rosie of Clarke, left behind in France surrounded by German soldiers.

'I think I will have that cup of tea after all,' she said, getting up. 'Stay there, Mum, I'll make it myself.'

Tears were pricking her eyes, and she didn't notice the concerned look from Winnie that followed her into the kitchen.

By some miracle, Clarke and Paul had managed to escape from the landing site. Clarke had taken out one of the Germans when they'd opened fire on the fugitives and Paul had got another while covering Clarke and Rosie as they'd carried Elise to the plane. As the aircraft had gathered speed and risen from the ground, the third German had begun firing wildly at it, so intent on his task he didn't notice the two men lying flat in the grass. He was a sitting duck, and Paul had had no problem bringing him down. As the plane gained height, both men had scrambled to their feet and headed back towards the woods.

But they weren't yet out of danger. Headlights and searchlights lit the dark sky around the field. Reinforcements were close. If one of the searchlights caught them, they were done for, and Clarke knew that Paul's injured leg would prevent him from covering the distance to the trees in time.

'Get down!' he yelled, throwing himself back onto the ground. Paul had followed suit, and wriggling like snakes they made for the woods as fast as they were able.

They had just reached cover when the lights had come to a stop, all concentrated in the clearing where Paul had left his car. There was no way they could use it to escape. But hopefully it would occupy the soldiers a little as they searched it, and the surrounding area.

'Back to the chateau!' Paul whispered hoarsely. 'We'll take Elise's car.'

The wood was dense here, the darkness complete but for the circles of light arcing round the clearing.

'But we can't . . .' Clarke was thinking that the clearing was the only way to the chateau. But Paul knew different.

'This way.' He started off through the trees, cursing as his injured leg caught in the undergrowth or on a fallen branch.

Clarke followed. It seemed to him that they were going in quite the wrong direction, but he realised he might simply be disorientated.

Quite suddenly the trees thinned and they emerged onto a road.

'That way.' Paul pointed the direction. 'At the crossroads turn right, then take the next left. It leads straight to the chateau, through the vineyards. I'll wait here – I'll only slow you down. But for God's sake, if you hear a vehicle, get into the ditch. It runs beside the road almost all the way.' He produced a set of keys from his pocket and handed them to Clarke. 'Lucky I brought these with me.'

'Right. I'll be as quick as I can.'

Clarke set off at a run down the road, following Paul's directions. Once he heard the roar of an engine behind him, and dived into the ditch, filthy with mud and fallen leaves, until the lights had passed him. He risked a look as to which way it was headed and saw it turn right. That must be the crossroads, and dammit, the car had gone the way he'd been told to. He just hoped that Paul had been out of sight when the vehicle had passed the place where he was waiting.

It wasn't far to the turning. Relieved, he took it and soon found himself in the vineyard. The moon had once more emerged from behind cloud, and following the path he saw the chateau ahead of him – and Elise's car parked on the forecourt.

As he exited the vineyard, he looked around warily in case any Germans had come here to search for the family, but the coast seemed to be clear. He sprinted to the little car, opened the door, then realised the driving seat was on the other side. This was France! He mustn't forget that he had to drive on the right rather than the left.

His first two attempts to start the car didn't work, and he prayed that the battery hadn't gone flat. But at the third try it coughed to life. He inched the choke back a little – he didn't want to flood the engine – then pulled away and headed back the way he had come, flattening a few vines along the path and putting his foot down on the last stretch of road. He didn't want to be on it any longer than was necessary and hoped Paul could direct him onto a route that wouldn't be used by any patrolling Germans.

As he approached the spot where he had left Paul, he slowed and flashed his lights twice to tell his friend it was him. To his relief, Paul appeared, limping his way round to the passenger door. 'Well done, *mon ami*.'

Clarke let out the clutch and pulled away. 'Where to?'

'How much fuel do we have?'

He glanced down at the dashboard. 'About half a tank.'

'That should be enough. If we're lucky.'

'Some distance then?'

'About a two-hour drive. Maybe more in this car. And we have to cut through occupied territory.'

'How the hell do we do that?'

'I know a way.' They had reached a junction. 'Turn left here,' Paul instructed. 'And if you feel too tired to drive, just shout and I'll take over.'

'With your leg? I don't think so.'

Clarke's common sense told him to drive slowly to conserve petrol, but neither did he want to hang about. It was imperative they reach their destination before daylight.

On and on they went, Paul directing Clarke along back roads with no visible markings, and through a gap in a barbed-wire fence that he assumed must be the demarcation line. 'Where are we headed?' Clarke asked.

'Le Massif. The mountains. There are hiding places there. Villages in the valleys. And many maquisards. I have connections with them.'

'Is there a doctor among them?' Clarke asked. 'Your leg should be attended to.'

'Don't worry about my leg. I will be *bien*.'

'Not if the bullet is still in there and the wound is infected. It could kill you,' Clarke said shortly.

'And the Germans will kill me if they catch me. You too. Keep going. We'll think about it later.'

Clarke checked the fuel gauge; the needle was hovering towards empty, but climbing as they were, perhaps it was giving an incorrect reading. He hoped so.

'There.' Paul pointed. Far beneath them Clarke could see a village tucked into a fold in the steep slope, and as they began to descend, the needle on the fuel gauge started to rise again. A quarter full. Perhaps an exaggeration, but enough to reach the village.

Just before the first street of little houses, Paul instructed Clarke to pull off the road and park behind what appeared to be a derelict barn. 'We'll stay here for what's left of the night,' he said. 'I'll find my friends in the morning. They won't betray us. The whole of this village is behind the resistance.'

'I hope so!' Clarke said ruefully.

'And then you must leave me. You should go back to England.'

'I'm going nowhere until I'm sure you're fit. And this country doesn't look very hospitable to aircraft.'

'You will take the car. There's a petrol pump in the village. You can refuel there.'

'And leave you here with a gammy leg and no transport? I'll fill up the tank tomorrow, but I'm not going anywhere. Come on.' Clarke got out, and between them they covered the car as best they could with whatever greenery they could find.

'Bed, I think,' Paul said. 'We'll talk some more about you leaving tomorrow. But for now . . .'

Clarke followed him to the barn, and was surprised to find straw palliasses and sleeping bags, along with mugs, a spirit stove, a kettle and other implements. Paul produced a bag containing coffee from the pocket of his overcoat. 'Fancy a cup?'

'We've no water,' Clarke pointed out, and to his amazement Paul held out a Thermos.

'*Voilà!*'

'Well I'm going to have a cigarette while the kettle's boiling,' Clarke said.

'And I'll join you, *mon ami.*'

Dead on their feet, but thankful to have reached shelter without incident, the two men sat down in the shelter of the barn and smoked their cigarettes – Paul his Gauloises and Clarke his Senior Service. And although neither mentioned it, both of them were hoping and praying that the plane carrying their loved ones had got safely back to Blighty.

Sir James had been to the George for a meeting with the officers of the Hillsbridge Home Guard. It wasn't his responsibility, that was down to the regular army, but he liked to be kept abreast of their training and exercises. It was a little after ten when he arrived home, and he went in search of Frances. He'd been reluctant to leave her alone – there had still been no news of Philip – but she had insisted he should go, she would be fine.

He found her in the library. The room was dimly lit with just one table lamp, and a persistent clacking sound was coming from the record player where the needle was repeatedly bumping against the centre of the record. Frances was slumped on the chaise longue, staring into space. A photograph album lay on her knees, open to some old pictures of the family when the children were young.

'Frances, my dear.' He lifted the needle from the record and went to sit beside her. 'What are you doing here in the dark?' he asked gently, and when there was no response, he took her hand. 'It's Philip, isn't it?'

Frances snapped the photograph album shut but still stared down at the embossed cover.

'Of course it is. Oh, James, I can't bear to lose him. And Anne . . . I don't know where she is. Why doesn't she let me know – something at least. Both my children. Gone.'

'Don't, my love,' James begged, unable to find the words to comfort his wife when he himself was tormented by the same fears.

'But it's true!' She lifted her face, wet with tears. Frances, who never cried. 'Don't you care?'

'Of course I do!' He spoke forcefully now. 'They're my children too, and I'd give the world to know they are both safe and sound. But dwelling on it does no good. We don't know for sure that either of them has come to harm. We have to be strong for them.'

'You might be able to. I can't. Philip is never coming back. I feel it in my bones. And Anne . . . It was me who encouraged Julian to propose marriage, me who asked you to announce their engagement. I thought that would keep her close. Instead I've driven her away. She despises me. And worse. Why did I think he would make her a suitable husband? Why did I trust him? He's evil, James.'

James stiffened, frowning. 'What do you mean by that?'

'I went to his surgery to talk to him about Anne. And what did I find? He had a young girl naked on the couch. And he . . . he was molesting her! In his consulting room! The man I wanted Anne to marry – no more than a common sex pest.'

James was horrified. 'You never mentioned this to me!'

'I couldn't. I couldn't bring myself to speak of it. I told him I would be reporting him to Medical Standards – that I'd see he was struck off. But I haven't done that either. With all that's going on, I just couldn't face it.'

'Oh, Frances . . .' James was lost for words. 'If he really is abusing his position, then he has to be stopped.'

'I know. She might not be the only one. But it's too much for me just now. Couldn't you . . .?'

'Of course I will.' Deeply shocked at the disintegration of his wife's normal personality, it was the only answer he could give. 'And we must find a different placement for Billy. He's an added problem that you could do without.'

'No!' Though her voice was thick with tears, Frances spoke sharply. 'Underneath it all, Billy's a good boy. I don't want him to go. He needs us. And I need him. It's Julian's proclivities I can't cope with.'

'Don't worry, Franny. I'll deal with it,' Sir James promised, putting an arm round her.

'Oh, thank you. Thank you so much.' She turned to him, burying her face in his shoulder, then raised it again as a sudden realisation struck her. 'Franny! It's been years since you called me that!'

She was right, of course. Once it had been his pet name for her, but it had been put aside when he had inherited the title. 'Franny' didn't seem to fit with 'her ladyship', or with the person she had become. He pulled her close, spoke softly into her ear.

'Too long, my darling. You'll always be Franny to me.'

She was crying again. Tears not only of gratitude, not only for her children, but for the young lovers they had once been. Their hopes. Their dreams. Some fulfilled, some lost in the mists of time. But through it all, they had had each other. Facing the triumphs and the losses together. Whatever the future held, they would weather the storm. Their love was strong enough to see them through. In that, at least, they were so very, very fortunate.

After a week of sleeping on a palliasse, Clarke was not only stiff and sore, he had developed a nasty cold. He was also restless and bored. He'd filled the car up with petrol and had driven Paul down to the village, where they bought meals to sustain them, followed by endless cups of coffee, the very strong brew served in tiny cups that the locals favoured. Sometimes they were joined by the village maquisards, but Clarke could understand hardly a word of the rapid French in which they conversed and had to rely on Paul translating for him when they were alone. It had apparently been agreed that any sabotage plans would be put on hold while they were in hiding here, in order to avoid anything that might draw attention to their location.

They had also driven out into the open countryside a couple of times so that Paul could use the radio belonging to one of the maquisards. The first time, he had tapped out a coded message asking if the plane had made it back to England and how Elise was; and on the second occasion, they were informed that it had and much to his relief Paul had received an answer to his question. Elise had undergone surgery, but was now stable and should be discharged from hospital soon.

His leg was healing well – it had been a flesh wound only – but the enforced inactivity was driving Clarke mad, and whereas before he'd objected, this time when Paul told him bluntly that it was time for him to go home, he heaved a sigh of relief. But he still felt responsible for his friend.

'Are you sure?' he asked.

'I'm fine now. I can drive, and I'm among friends. You're the biggest danger to me. I'm grateful for all you've done, but you'll inevitably draw attention to yourself and that will mean curtains for us both. The sooner we get something arranged, the better.'

'OK,' Clarke agreed. 'If you think that's best.'

'I do. And I'm not taking you with me when I go out into the country. We might be stopped by a patrol, and you'd stick out like a sore thumb.'

'We might get stopped by a patrol when I'm on my way to my transport,' Clarke pointed out.

Paul shrugged. 'That's a risk we'll have to take. But for today, you'll stay here. I'll look for a suitable landing site, and I'll ask that you be taken back to your base in Somerset.'

Clarke had a sudden thought. 'Could you include in the message not to share the information with anyone? I don't want to raise hopes when it's possible I'll never make it back.'

Paul nodded. 'Fair enough. I think I'll go right away. It might take them a day or two to get things organised. And you'd better stay out of sight while I'm gone.'

Clarke watched anxiously as Paul got the car going, but he certainly seemed to be managing the clutch, and would be using his good leg for the accelerator and – more importantly – the brake.

It was a cold, clear day and he leaned back against the wall of the barn and smoked a cigarette. He couldn't wait to get home. To have a proper job to do. And most of all, to see Rosie.

Guillaume and his family had received some very disturbing news. They'd wondered why Elise's release from hospital had been delayed, since the operation was deemed to have gone well. Now they were shocked when a doctor came to see them in their lodgings.

It seemed her wound had become infected. The doctor could offer no explanation other than 'these things happen sometimes'. But from his demeanour, it was clear that he was a worried man.

Anne in particular was beside herself with anxiety. If Elise died, the children might well be orphans, since they had had no news of whether Paul was alive or dead.

'If anything terrible happens to her, I'll be here to look after them,' she said with passion. 'At least they know and trust me. Surely I wouldn't be forced back into the WAAF in such a situation.'

Her mind was made up. If need be, she'd fight tooth and nail to be there for the children.

Rosie had a day off and had decided to go home. She guessed her mother had scarcely left the cottage since Don had come home – Fred Thomas was keeping her larder well stocked, shopping for any extras she needed, and she was just doing a few hours' work here and there at Bramley Court, where the strained atmosphere since Philip had gone missing was almost unbearable. Besides this, Rosie really didn't want to spend the day alone. It was almost two weeks now since she'd left Clarke in occupied France, and she'd heard nothing. When she was working, she could forget her desperate anxiety for a little while; a day of inactivity while her colleagues were frantically busy would give her far too much time to think.

She'd taken the bus home, only to find that Winnie had decided Don was fit enough to be left, for the morning anyway, and it was high time the big house had a good clean. She'd got him up and dressed, made him a flask of hot cocoa, leaving it and the biscuit tin within his reach, and gone to work.

He was sitting beside the fire leafing through the *Daily Mirror* when Rosie arrived. She made a cup of tea for them both and chatted for a bit, but she could see he was getting drowsy and decided to leave him in peace. She'd cook something for dinner – a vegetable stew, perhaps. That would be one less job for Winnie when she got home. But when she checked the larder, she saw a potato pie sitting on the shelf covered with a clean tea cloth. Knowing she was going to be at work today, Winnie must have made it either last night or early this morning. Something for afters, then? She went out to the garden shed to see if there were any apples stored there, and was just returning to the cottage when she heard a motor car approaching and stopping outside the gate.

Clarke! Oh, please let it be Clarke! But it wasn't. When she rounded the corner of the cottage, she saw that it was a big old Rover, covered in mud splashes, and Freda was getting out.

Rosie hurried down the path to meet her, and the two girls hugged a greeting as they always did.

'I can't believe I've caught you!' Freda said. 'I thought you'd be at work, and I was going to give your mum a message.'

'It's Mum who's not here,' Rosie said. 'I've got a day off and she's at work. Are you coming in?'

Freda shook her head. 'I can't stay. I'm on an errand for Ted, but I thought I'd call by while I was in Hillsbridge. I had a letter come by second post yesterday.'

Rosie cocked her head to one side. 'Who from?'

'Mrs Pruitt. You remember, she was our next-door neighbour in Bermondsey.'

Rosie had a bad feeling. Freda was looking very serious. And she didn't imagine Mrs Pruitt to be much of a letter writer if she could avoid it.

'What about?' she asked.

Freda swallowed. 'Granny's house. It's gone. Took a direct hit a couple of nights ago.'

'Oh my goodness!' Rosie was shocked, even though she knew she shouldn't be. 'That's awful!'

'Well.' Freda shrugged. 'At least we weren't in it.'

'Was it the only one? Was anybody killed?'

'I don't think so. They'd all been spending the nights in the Underground. But it was Granny's house and the one next door on the other side from Mrs Pruitt's that got the worst of it.'

'I'm so sorry, Freda,' Rosie said. 'Have you lost everything?'

'Pretty well. But not the things that really matter. I went up twice to bring home anything that was important to me. Did you leave anything behind?'

'No.' Rosie didn't even stop to think. The only thing that really mattered to her was that Clarke should be safe. 'But what are you going to do? You won't have a home to go back to when this damned war is over.'

'I'd already decided. I'm not going back,' Freda said. 'I love it on the farm, and they have promised to keep me on for as long as I like.'

'Oh! That's good.'

'I must be going, Rosie. This was just a flying visit. Ted needs the stuff I came into town for. I just wanted to let you know.'

She got back into the car, executed a neat three-point turn and waved as she drove off.

Well, at least it seemed Freda had landed on her feet, Rosie thought. She could only hope and pray she herself would be so lucky.

She went back into the house and tried to forget her worries by making a good old apple pie.

So engrossed was Rosie in her baking, she didn't hear another car on the lane outside, nor the rap of the knocker.

'Rosie! Somebody at the door!' Don called. She heard that, dusted down her hands on her apron and went to answer it. Then her mouth fell open in disbelief and for a moment she froze.

Clarke! She must be dreaming! It was Clarke, his very blue eyes twinkling, the dimple in his cheek made prominent by his smile.

'Well, say something, Miss Rosie Mitchell.'

Rosie shook her head wonderingly. 'Oh, Clarke! I thought you were dead!'

'Ah sure, you don't get away from me so easily.'

Right there on the doorstep, she threw her arms around him, burying her face in his uniform jacket, tears of joy streaming down into the rough wool. 'Oh, Clarke, tell me I'm not dreaming!'

'You're not dreaming, sweetheart. Aren't you going to ask me in?'

'Yes, but . . .'

Too late. He lifted her off her feet and carried her into the hall. He was kissing her soundly when a voice interrupted them.

'Rosie? Who is it?'

Clarke lifted his head to look at her. 'You've got another man here?'

'My brother. You remember . . .'

'Sure I was only teasing you.' He looked around the sitting room door. 'Pleased to meet you, Don. But would you mind if I borrowed your sister for a minute?'

Without waiting for a reply, he took Rosie by the hand and led her into the kitchen, where he kissed her again. And again. Then he took the carver chair and pulled her onto his lap. 'You're very elusive, Miss Rosie. I went to Bath to find you, only to be told you weren't there. And when I knocked at the door and no one answered . . .'

'Because I was busy! And thinking . . . no . . . trying *not* to think of you! I've been so worried, Clarke! How did you get away from the Germans? Where have you been all this time?'

'Make me a cup of tea and I'll tell you.'

'I can do better than that!' Rosie wriggled off his lap, went to the cold slab in the pantry and emerged with a bottle of beer in each hand. 'From our local brewery. Mum got them in for Fred. Oh, you need a glass . . .'

'Just a bottle opener will do,' Clarke said, and when she found one in the kitchen drawer and he had wrenched the metal cap from the bottle, he pulled her back into his lap again. 'This is the life! A bottle of beer in one hand and the prettiest girl in Hillsbridge in the other. Trouble is, I won't be able to stay long enough to drink two. I'm supposed to be on duty.'

'But I want to know everything!'

'Very well. Potted history lesson. Paul and I got away from

the Germans at the landing site and escaped in Elise's car. But Paul had been shot in the leg, so I had to drive. All the way to the mountains. A loyalist village where Paul has friends. We slept for a week in a tumbledown barn, and then I was picked up and brought back to England.'

Rosie frowned. 'You've been back for a whole week while I was worried to death!'

'I had a bummer of a cold – from sleeping on a damp palliasse is my guess – and I didn't want to give it to you.'

'You could have let me know somehow . . .'

'I wanted to surprise you. Besides, I didn't know what sort of reception I'd get. I'm sorry, sweetheart. Am I forgiven?'

'Course you are! I'm just so glad to see you!' She nuzzled her face in his neck. 'Clarke . . . you remember what you asked me before?'

'Big mistake,' he said ruefully.

'But does the offer still stand? Because if it does . . . then my answer is yes. I do love you, very much. I know that now. And I really do want to marry you.'

For a very long time, neither of them had any breath left for speaking.

When Clarke had left with a promise to see her again very soon, Rosie's heart was singing with joy.

Postscript

April 1946

The small granite obelisk stood in a corner of Bramley Court's vast lawn. An RAF insignia had been carved into it by a skilled stonemason, and its plinth bore the simple inscription: *Flight Lt Philip Charles John Hastings, who gave his life in the service of his country, September 1940.*

To its left, the members of the Hillsbridge Home Guard stood proudly to attention; to the right, the town band cornet player raised his instrument to his lips. As the Last Post sounded out to every corner of the garden, the people who were gathered there bowed their heads as one. Townsfolk who had come to pay their respects, employees and tenants, and those with close connections to the Hastings family. Directly in front of the obelisk and facing the crowd stood Sir James and Lady Hastings, their daughter, Anne, their adopted son, Billy, and the rector, his vestments billowing in the light wind, a prayer book open in his hands.

His voice rang out clear and strong, reaching even those at the back.

'Dearly beloved, we are gathered here today to honour our

dear departed brother Philip, who gave his life for us all, and to bless this memorial to his bravery and sacrifice, erected by his grieving parents. Will you now join me in the Lord's Prayer. Our Father . . .'

Tears filled Rosie's eyes as the murmur of voices rose over the spot where she stood in the front row, Clarke beside her. Her heart bled for the Hastings family, and especially for Anne. She herself had been so lucky. Not only had her brother come home safe, but so had Clarke. She reached for his hand, clasping it so tightly that the broad gold band on his finger pressed into her palm. She had placed it there last autumn when the war had finally ended, and the memory gave her strength now. The sun had shone its blessing on her that day, and she hoped with all her heart that Anne would be so blessed.

As the prayer ended, she glanced along the line at Paul Clermont, his hands on the shoulders of his daughters, who stood in front of him, awed by the ceremony. They had suffered a terrible bereavement too. Their mother, Elise, had succumbed to the infection caused by the gunshot wound. Anne had been given leave to care for them while Paul remained in France, not knowing if she would ever see him again, and she had brought them and their grandparents home to Bramley Court, where Sir James and Frances had welcomed them warmly.

By some miracle, Paul had avoided capture and continued his work with the resistance from his mountain hideout – thankfully in the home of one of the maquisards and not the damp barn where he and Clarke had spent that first week. Rosie was hopeful that when he took his children home to France, Anne would go with them. She'd certainly told Rosie that she had shed no tears for the now disgraced Julian Edgell, who had disappeared they knew not where. Her constant anxiety for Paul had made it obvious to Rosie that he had replaced Julian in her heart, and when he had arrived in Hillsbridge and she had seen them together, she was sure he felt the same way about her. Anne deserved some happiness, she thought.

Certainly Freda had been lucky. She and Ted, her farmer, had been married two years ago in the Methodist chapel in Hillsbridge, and Rosie had been her bridesmaid. Winnie had made dresses out of parachute silk, Freda's white and Rosie's dyed pale blue. They'd carried posies of wild flowers, picked that morning from the fields and hedgerows surrounding the farm, where they'd held a small reception following the ceremony. Freda and Ted weren't here today; with the advent of spring, they were far too busy, and in any case, with petrol still rationed, Ted liked to conserve it for emergencies.

As for her mother and Fred Thomas, Rosie was very pleased with the way things had turned out. They'd both kept their own homes, but Fred was a frequent visitor and they'd grown so close over the past years that they might as well have been married. Don had made a good recovery. He hadn't been discharged from the army, but was now doing clerical work at one of their bases on Salisbury Plain. He'd got engaged to his girl, so there would be another wedding to look forward to when he could get some leave.

Philip's name wouldn't be the only one added to the war memorial in the town square, of course. At least thirty young men from Hillsbridge had died in the service of their country – thankfully Jack Bendle was not one of them – but the town itself had survived almost unscathed. Yes, there had been incendiary bombs that had set fire to some houses, and a plane had come down on the cricket field at Downside, the Roman Catholic abbey and school just a few miles up the road. Luckily for the boys out there playing a game that day, the pilot was the only fatality.

Bristol hadn't been so fortunate. The docks and aircraft factories had been prime targets, and much of the city had been decimated. Bath, too, had been heavily bombed, the results of which Rosie had seen every day as she diverted her ambulance round craters in the roads. Lovely old churches of all denominations had been reduced to rubble, the Salvation Army citadel had been hit, and stained-glass windows in the abbey were shattered by blasts. A number of guests had died in the Regina Hotel, though the Assembly Rooms on the other side of the road had escaped unscathed. Two patients were lucky not to have been killed when the Royal National Hospital for Rheumatic Diseases suffered a direct hit. And houses were left with one wall only still standing, scraps of curtain hanging limp or billowing in the wind. Yes, Bath would take a great deal of rebuilding to regain its former glory.

After the reveille had sounded, the onlookers began to disperse. Lady Hastings and Anne laid red roses on the plinth, and Sir James straightened a framed photograph of his son that stood propped against the base of the obelisk. The two Clermont children ran to Anne, Paul following them, and they formed a close little group, reinforcing Rosie's belief that they would soon be a family.

Not wanting to intrude, she looked around for Winnie and Fred, and went to join them.

'Well, that was lovely. Sad, but lovely.' Winnie arm was tucked into Fred's.

'A fitting tribute to a hero,' Clarke said. 'I hope we'll continue to honour all those who have lost their lives in this damned war.' He was thinking especially of the agents he had trained and who had never returned.

'Well.' Winnie's gaze encompassed them both. 'I could do with a cup of tea. Let's go home.'

As the four of them made their way back to her cottage, the sun emerged and Rosie glanced behind her. It was shining directly onto the granite of the obelisk, making it shimmer softly.

It was, she thought, a fitting tribute, and it promised hope for the future for all of them.

Author's Note

As I'm sure you will have noticed by now *Rosie's Dilemma* is set in the early part of World War Two, rather than at the turn of the century. But I hope you will be pleased that it's still in the familiar setting of the Somerset coal mining town of Hillsbridge. I love my home town, with all its history and memories.

The war was already two years old by the time I put in an appearance, but I do have my own memories. Although I was, like the war, just two, I can clearly recall the day my sister was born. It was a cold and wet morning and I was kneeling up on the living-room window sill, drawing pictures with my finger in the steam on the window pane (I also remember the black out curtains), when the nurse came downstairs and asked if I would like to go up and see my new little sister.

I remember my gran's sister, Auntie Flo, who came to stay with us when the street in Bath where she lived with another sister, Auntie Edie, was badly bombed. I believe an air raid shelter was hit, with tragic loss of life, but my gran's two sisters had hidden under the kitchen table and were unharmed. With so many of their neighbouring houses nothing but rubble, Auntie Flo 'evacuated' to us and took over my bedroom. She was always regarded by the rest of the family as 'a bit simple' but I loved her because she would play with me and my dolls for hours on end, never tiring of the games.

Another clear memory is when a German fighter came down in a field not far from our house and my mother took me to see it. At least, I think it must have been a fighter as it wasn't very big. I wanted to see inside and my mother lifted me up onto the step to the cockpit. Whether the pilot was killed or captured I never knew, but since the plane was in pretty good shape, I believe he must have survived his emergency landing and become a prisoner of war. I also remember sitting on a rug on the front lawn and hearing heavy aircraft engines overhead. I even learned to tell from the sound whether it was a British or a German plane.

Before I was born, my mother had been an active member of the local WVS – the Women's Voluntary Service – and was one of the principal organisers of a dance in the Victoria Hall to raise the money to buy a Spitfire, just as my fictional characters do in *Rosie's Dilemma.* She had a scrolled picture of it that I loved to look at, but sadly the plane was shot down very soon after it went into service. I do still have her WVS badge in my child's jewellery box. I also still have a blue leather wallet with inlaid pictures that look Egyptian, and was sent to me by 'Uncle Ron', a friend of Mum's who was serving in the desert, and who wrote to me regularly on thin blue air mail paper and envelope.

I don't have any memories of celebrations when the war ended, but I do recall my sister and I playing with our gas masks. They weren't Mickey Mouse, just plain rubber, and I will never forget the rubbery smell when we took them out of their boxes and put them on. I used to sit in Mum's boat-shaped basket and pretend I was a sailor, until the sad day when I became too big to climb in under the handle. The plus side of this was that I was now big enough to be able to see out of the bedroom window without having to climb up . . .

I know I'm lucky to be able to remember so far back into my childhood days. Those memories are very precious to me – and I can call on them for just a flavour of what it was like for Rosie, Winnie, Freda, and the others you will have met in *Rosie's Dilemma*.

Acknowledgements

First mention must go to my lovely agent, Rebecca Ritchie. It's so lovely to have you back from maternity leave, and congratulations on the birth of your son Kip who will have been a year old at the beginning of this year. I really missed you! My thanks also to your colleagues at A.M. Heath, Florence Rees and Harmony Leung who looked after me in your absence.

As always everyone at Headline has been amazing, and my thanks go to the editorial team headed by Jennifer Doyle and ably assisted by Marion Donaldson, Imogen Taylor, Kashmini Shah and Zara Baig.

I have been incredibly blessed to have once again had truly helpful advice from a brilliant editor, Flora Rees and benefitted hugely from the eagle-eyed attention of my copy editor extraordinaire Jane Selley.

Thanks to my family and friends for their love and support, and last but far from least thanks to all my lovely readers. Without you this book would never have been written, and I hope you continue to enjoy reading it. Please keep in touch with me. I love to get messages even if I don't always reply immediately when I'm bogged down in writing the next Jennie Felton!

If you loved *Rosie's Dilemma*,
don't miss Jennie Felton's gripping novel

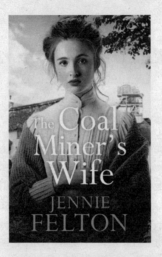

Somerset, 1911. Miner's wife Lorna Harrison sometimes wonders what became of her marriage. The affection has gone, and her husband Harry is surly and cold. But Lorna will always be grateful for the joy that their two daughters bring.

When a devastating accident occurs at the pit and Harry is unable to work, Lorna worries about how she will make ends meet. Worse, the pit owner wants them out of their house. And neighbours turn their backs, as rumours spread that Harry helped cause the mine collapse.

At her lowest ebb, Lorna is befriended by Bradley Robinson, the colliery safety officer, whose kindness is a beacon of light. But as shocking secrets are revealed, Lorna wonders if Bradley is only using her to learn the truth about the pit. As she struggles to keep her daughters safe, Lorna must decide if she can trust the man she is falling in love with . . .

HEADLINE

Have you met the Families of Fairley Terrace?

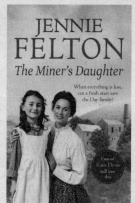

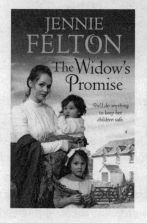

Jennie's compelling saga series
is available now from

Jennie Felton grew up in Somerset, and now lives in Bristol. She has written numerous short stories for magazines as well as a number of novels under a pseudonym. As well as the standalones *A Mother's Heartbreak*, *The Stolen Child*, and *The Smuggler's Girl*, she is also the author of the Families of Fairley Terrace Sagas series, about the lives and loves of the residents of a Somerset village in the late nineteenth century, which started with *All The Dark Secrets*.

Stay in touch with Jennie!

Visit her on Facebook at
www.facebook.com/JennieFeltonAuthor
for her latest news.

Or follow her on X **@Jennie_Felton**